D0393258

LaVyrle Spencer
Romance Writers of America
Golden Medallion Award Winner

"One of the finest romance writers around!"

—Romantic Times

"You will never forget the incredible beauty and sensitivity of LaVyrle's gifted pen."

—Affaire de Coeur

HUMMINGBIRD

"An enthralling book, with a love story as feisty and romantic as a Tracy/Hepburn movie."

—Lisa Gregory

"Bawdy, witty, touching, delightful."

—Francine Rivers

TWICE LOVED

"Highly emotional and moving . . . handled with great sensitivity."

—Romantic Times

"A beautiful love story . . . emotional . . . refreshing."

—Rocky Mountain News

continued . . .

SEPARATE BEDS

"A superb story capturing many human complexities and emotions, that transcend both age barriers and genres. 'Must' read for anyone who has lived and loved."

—***Los Angeles Times***

YEARS

"Splendid . . . Spencer describes the growth of Teddy and Linnea's love with sensitivity and refreshing candor and brings all the residents of Alamo to life in a way that makes the reader care about their satisfactions and heartaches."

—***Publishers Weekly***

THE GAMBLE

"Spencer again deals the reader a winning hand!"

—***Publishers Weekly***

"Novel of the Month . . . a grand new bestseller!"

—***Good Housekeeping***

"A brave and passionate epic."

—***Forecast***

"Told with honesty and humor."

—***Ralston Recorder (Nebraska)***

"Extraordinary . . . her most memorable characters to date!"

—***Romantic Times***

Now, LaVyrle Spencer presents her captivating new novel . . . a moving tribute to life and love . . .

VOWS

LaVyrle Spencer

Vows

J

JOVE BOOKS, NEW YORK

Also by LaVyrle Spencer from Jove

THE GAMBLE
A HEART SPEAKS
YEARS
SEPARATE BEDS
TWICE LOVED
HUMMINGBIRD

VOWS

A Jove Book / published by arrangement with
the author

PRINTING HISTORY
Jove edition / April 1988

For information address: The Berkley Publishing Group,
200 Madison Avenue, New York, New York 10016.

ISBN: 0-515-09477-3

Jove Books are published by The Berkley Publishing Group,
200 Madison Avenue, New York, New York 10016.

PRINTED IN THE UNITED STATES OF AMERICA

10 9 8 7 6 5 4 3 2 1

This book is dedicated to the many librarians who've helped me over the years, but especially to Nita Foster and Ardis Wiley of the Hennepin County Library System, who never fail to find what I need in the way of research materials. Also, thank you to Patty Myers of the Johnson County Library in Buffalo, Wyoming, and the staff at the Sheridan County Fulmer Public Library of Sheridan, Wyoming, for special help on this book.

Author's Note

The readers familiar with the Sheridan and Buffalo areas will find that I took liberties with the history of their towns. Actually, Sheridan's Main Street would not have been as built up as I've depicted, nor would the town have had Victorian homes as fine as the ones I've sketched; they were not built until around the turn of the century. In 1888 Munkers & Mathers didn't own their hardware store yet, and, of course, the Mint Saloon hadn't been built, either. But some landmarks call to be included, so forgive me for bending the calendar to suit my story.

L. S.

Chapter 1

Wyoming Territory
1888

TOM JEFFCOAT SHIFTED his rump on the hard wagon seat, blinked twice, and peered northward. From beneath the brim of a dusty brown Stetson, he squinted until the blurred outline of a town came into focus. A thrill shot through his belly—Sheridan, Wyoming, at last! And with any luck at all, a bath, a real bed, and a decent, hot supper, his first in eighteen days.

He clucked to the team and they picked up speed.

From several miles out the town appeared as no more than a mole on the jaw of the broad, fertile valley, but the setting proved as beautiful as promised in the ad. Basking in lush bluegrass, it nestled where the eastern face of the Big Horns met the wide Goose Creek Valley in which Big and Little Goose creeks merged. The paths of the streams were clearly marked by a meandering line of diamond willows and cottonwoods, the latter in seed now in early June, dropping their cottony tufts like a white flotilla onto the waters.

But the mountains themselves provided the grandeur; snow-capped, blue girded, they rose like knuckles on a tight fist, holding back the harsher Rockies to the west. Those mountains had become protective old friends, ever off Jeffcoat's left shoulder on his long journey up from Rock Springs. Already he loved them: the Big Horns, majestic giants clothed—up high—in the blue-black of Rocky Mountain cedars, fading at the foothills into every conceivable shade of green. Those foothills billowed like a giant ruffled skirt and in their velvet folds nestled his new home: Sheridan.

"West of worry," the ad had boasted, "with no heat, no dust, no wind, and where the nights are always cool."

Well, we'll see.

As he neared the town, individual buildings took shape, then a street—no, streets, by God!—a grid of them, laid out straight and wide and already named on wooden signs—Perkins, Whitney, Burkitt, Works, Loucks, and the widest artery, Main, by which he entered. Deeper in the heart of town the creeks themselves snaked together, breaking the streets into short, oblique avenues. Off on the side streets he saw houses, mostly of frame or peeled-log construction, with high pitched roofs to shed snow. Many of the plots were surrounded by lines of demarcation: picket fences, hitching posts, outbuildings at rear property lines, newly planted vegetable gardens, and hedgerows of flowers. Entering the business district, he slowed his horses to an easy walk, perusing his surroundings. There must have been fifty buildings, and boardwalks old enough to have become weathered but not warped, and a goodly number of established businesses: a hotel, butcher shop, barber shop, drug store, law office, several stores, a newspaper office; and the inevitable saloons that catered to the cowboys driving cattle up the Bozeman Trail, up which he himself had just come. There were the Star, the Mint, and one called the Silver Spur, beside which a corral held a half dozen wild elk. Several cowboys were using them for roping practice, and the sound of the men's laughter and the animals' bawling brought a smile to Jeffcoat's lips.

Farther along he passed other signs of progress; a building with its double doors thrown wide, revealing a side-stroke fire pump with its brass fittings gleaming; a house bearing a doctor's shingle—L. D. STEELE, PHYSICIAN; a school—settlers were bound to come faster with a school; and a harness and shoe shop, of which Jeffcoat took particular notice.

Eventually he came to a creek—bridgeless—swelled with spring runoff, where a lanky man in baggy pants and knee-high boots filled his water wagon with a bucket on the end of a long pole. Painted on the side of the tin drum was the advertisement: *Fresh Water Delivered Daily, 25¢ a barrel, 5 barrels for $1.00, Andrew Dehart's Sparkling Water Service.*

"H'lo, there!" Jeffcoat called, reining in.

The man paused and turned. "Hello!" He had a bushy beard and a great hook nose, which he blew—without benefit of a handkerchief—into the grass, leaning first left, then right.

"Which creek is this then, Big Goose or Little Goose?"

"Big Goose. Around here we just call it Goose. You new in town?"

"Yessir. Been here five minutes."

"Well, howdy! Andrew Dehart's the name." He nodded at the announcement on the side of his water wagon.

"Tom Jeffcoat's mine."

"You need water, I'm the man to see. You stayin'?"

"Yessir. That's the plan."

"Got lodging?"

"Not yet."

"Well you passed the only hotel, the Windsor, back that-a-way. And Ed Walcott runs the livery. Turn left on Grinnell." He pointed.

"Thank you, Mr. Dehart."

Dehart waved him off and turned back to his work, calling, "New blood's always welcome around here!"

The creek seemed to mark the end of the major business section. Beyond it lay mostly houses, so Jeffcoat reversed direction and headed back the way he'd come.

He found Grinnell without any problem and a huge unpainted barn of a building with a tent-shaped roof, gaping double doors, and a prominent white-and-black sign up high above the hay port: WALCOTT'S LIVERY, HORSES BOARDED & BEDDED, RIGS FOR RENT. He turned up Grinnell to have a look.

In a corral on the near side of the building a half dozen healthy-looking horses stood dozing in the two o'clock sun, their nose hairs touching the wall. On the far side was a deserted horseshoe pit overhung by a line of lopsided cotton-woods, which spilled a patch of shade onto the street over the far hitching rail. The barn itself was an immense, open-ended building constructed of vertical weatherbeaten boards and sliding double doors that stood open on both ends.

Choosing the shady hitching rail on the right over the sunny one on the left, Jeffcoat passed the open door, glimpsing inside the silhouette of a man framed clearly in the open-ended building, working over a horse's foot.

His competition.

He pulled up in the shade, wrapped the reins around the brake handle, pushed to his feet, and, with fists to ears, twisted at the waist. His hide felt stiff as whang-leather. Letting out a great gust of air, he vaulted over the side. At the great south door of the livery barn he paused, peering inside. It was like a railroad tunnel, dark and cool within, bright at both ends. At the far end the fellow still worked, facing the opposite door, couching the hoof of a huge liver chestnut stallion in his lap.

As Jeffcoat approached, he took stock of both the horse and the man. The stallion was snip nosed, broad chested, and tall. The man—upon closer perusal—turned out to be no man at all, but a skinny boy, no bigger than a good strip of trap bait, dressed in worn blue britches, a faded red shirt, black suspenders, an ankle-length leather apron, and a floppy brown wool cap with a button on its crown.

At Jeffcoat's approach, the chestnut nickered, dropped his forefoot, and belly-bumped the lad, knocking his cap askew.

"Blast you, Sergeant, you ring-boned hunk o' gleet! Hold still!" The boy cuffed the horse on the shoulder and centered his cap with a jerk. "You do that one more time and I'll leave you to take care of your miserable quarter crack by yourself!" He clapped a hand around the horse's off fore cannon, forced it into his lap, and resumed wielding the hoofpick.

Jeffcoat smiled; the animal outweighed the youth by a good thousand pounds. But young as he was the kid knew what he was doing. Quarter crack was nothing to fool around with.

"You in charge around here, young fellow?"

Emily Walcott dropped Sergeant's hoof and spun around indignantly. She let her eyes scan with deliberate distaste a swarthy young man who could use a shave and some sleeves on his shirt: someone had torn them off at the shoulder. She gave his bare arms, dusty britches, and whiskered face a singeing once-over before replying sardonically, "Yes, *ma'am*, I sure am."

Jeffcoat grabbed for his hat. "Oh . . . my mistake. I thought—"

"Never mind what you thought! I can do without hearing it again. And don't bother doffing your hat after *that*!"

She was thin as a whipsnake and about as shapely, seventeen or thereabouts, all blue eyes and indrawn lips and two cheeks flaring with indignation. Never having seen a woman in britches before, Jeffcoat stood nonplussed.

"I beg your pardon, ma'am."

"It's miss, and don't bother begging my pardon." She threw aside the hoofpick. "What can I do for you?"

"I've got a hungry team outside that needs putting up."

Sergeant chose that moment to stretch his neck, pluck off Miss Walcott's cap, and begin chewing it.

"Blast your hide, Sergeant, give me that!" She yanked it from his teeth, dried it on the seat of her pants, and examined it crossly while her black hair drooped in scraggles, half held to her skull by combs. "Now look what you've done, dammit. You put holes in it!"

Jeffcoat worked hard to hide a grin. "You ought to tie him off with two clip ropes instead of just one so he can't get by with that."

Emily eyed him maliciously while hooking the hat on her head, cramming her hair up inside it and cocking it toward her left ear so the short bill angled over her black, angry eyebrows. With the cap on, and covered to the collarbones by the dirty leather apron, she looked more like a boy than ever.

"Thank you, I'll remember that," she answered sarcastically, heading for the street, the apron thwapping her calves with each long step. "What do you want, stable 'em only? That'll be a buck a night, including hay. Dessert is extra. Two bits for an extra pail of oats. Curry 'em down'll be another two bits. Stable 'em outside in the corral you can save a dime." She reached the team and turned, but Jeffcoat hadn't followed. "Hey, mister," she bellowed, "I got work to do!" She hooked two dirty hands on her hips, fingers impatiently tapping the hard leather apron. "Where do you want 'em? Inside or out?" When no answer came she poked her head around the door, then bawled, "Hey, what do you think you're doing?" and steamed back inside with fists swinging at her sides like bell clappers.

"This is no quarter crack, it's a sand crack." He was

examining Sergeant's forefoot, for all the world as if he owned the place. "He'll need a three-quarter shoe or maybe even a copper plate to put pressure on the frog and wall if you want to keep him from going lame permanently. Or maybe a rivet might do."

"I'll see after my own horses, thank you," she returned acidly, untying Sergeant's single snap line and leading him into a stall. *Who the Sam Hill did he think he was, coming in here giving her advice? Some dirty cowpoke without so much as sleeves on his shirt, busting into somebody else's livery barn and spouting off like a geyser when she knew everything there was to know about the care of hooves. Everything!*

But Emily Walcott burned with indignation because she knew the stranger was right—she should have used two snap lines, but she'd been in too big a hurry.

She granted the stranger not so much as a flicking glance as she marched from the stall and left him behind. "We stable horses here. We feed 'em, and curry 'em, and water 'em, and outfit 'em, and rent out rigs. But we *don't* let tinhorn hostlers work out their apprenticeships on our stock!"

To Emily's chagrin, as she stormed past him, the man burst out laughing. She swung around with murder in her glare and the corners of her mouth looking as if they were attached to her shoes. "Mister, I don't have time to waste on you. Your horses, maybe, if you speak up fast. Now what'll it be, inside or out? Hay or oats?"

"Tinhorn hostler?" he managed, still chortling.

"All right, have it your way." Obstinately, she changed directions, heading toward an open hatch to the hayloft, passing him with a venomous expression on her face. "Sorry, we're all full up," she advised dryly. "You can try down at Rock Springs. It's a few miles that way." She thumbed southwest. Rock Springs was 350 miles, and it had just taken him eighteen days to cover them. Up the ladder she went, until her ascent was stopped by a hand grabbing her beat-up, stretched-out, horsey-smelling cowboy boot.

"Hey, wait a minute!"

The boot came off in Jeffcoat's hand.

Surprised as much as she, he stood gaping at her bare foot with its dirty ankle and flecks of hay pressed onto the skin, thinking this was the most bizarre introduction he'd ever had to one of the opposite sex. Where he came from, ladies wore gingham dresses with ten-gallon petticoats, and starched white aprons instead of leather ones, and leghorn hats instead of boys' knockabouts, and dainty buttoned shoes instead of dung-crusted cowboy boots. And stockings . . . wispy lisle stockings that no gentleman ever saw. But there he stood, staring at her bare foot.

"Oh, I . . . I beg your pardon, miss, I'm so sorry."

He watched her descend and turn stiffly, presenting a face as brilliant as an August sunset.

"Has anyone ever told you that you're a rude, infernal pain in the hindside?" She grabbed the boot, overturned an enamel bucket, and dropped onto it to pull the boot back on. Before she managed to do so, he snatched it from her hand and went down on one knee to do the honors.

"Allow me, miss. And to answer your question, yes, my mother and my grandmother and my fiancée and my teachers. All my life I've seemed to irritate women, but I could never understand why. You know, I've never done this before, have you?" He held the boot at the ready.

She felt her whole body flush, from her dirty bare toes clear up to her brother's cap. She grabbed the boot and yanked it on herself.

Watching, he grinned and answered belatedly, "Oats, please, and stable them inside and curry them, too. Do I pay in advance?"

"We're full up, I said!" Leaping to her feet, she fled him in a swirl of wrath and climbed to the loft. "Take your business elsewhere!"

He peered up after her, seeing nothing but rafters and dust motes.

"I'm sorry, ma'am. Really I am."

A pitchforkful of hay landed on his head. He doubled forward, blowing and snorting. "Hey, watch it!" Overhead her footsteps clunked as she dragged her boots across the floorboards. Another forkful of hay appeared and he backed off, calling, "Can I leave the horses or not?"

"No!"

"But this is the only livery barn in town!"

"We're full up, I said!"

"You are not!"

"We are, too!"

"If it's about your bare foot, I said I was sorry. Now come down here so I can give you some money."

"I said, we're full up! Now get out!"

From the other end of the barn, Edwin Walcott listened to the exchange with growing interest. He stood surveying the stranger with hay on his hat and shoulders, watched another load come raining down through the hatch, heard his daughter's obvious lie, and decided it was time to step in.

"What's going on here?"

Silence fell, broken only by a blacksmith's hammer from down the street.

Jeffcoat spun around to find a stocky man framed in the doorway standing with hands akimbo, his meaty arms and hairy chest showing beneath the uprolled sleeves and open collar of a faded red flannel shirt. His black britches were tucked into calf-high boots, and striped suspenders emphasized his muscular girth. He had tumbled black hair flecked with gray, a full black mustache, blue eyes, and a mouth reminiscent of the girl's.

"Something I can do for you, Mister—?"

Jeffcoat brushed off his shoulders and whacked his hat on his thigh. Stepping forward, he extended a hand. "Tom Jeffcoat's the name, and yessir, there is. I'd like to leave my horses for a few days if I could."

"Edwin Walcott's mine. Is there some reason why I shouldn't let you?"

"No, sir, none that I know of."

"What's this about you and my daughter's bare foot?"

"She was climbing up the ladder and I accidentally pulled her boot off, trying to stop her."

"Emily!" Walcott cocked his head toward the haymow. "Is that true?"

Beyond her father's range of vision, Emily buried the fork tines in the hay, wishing she could bury herself in it and stay till Tom Jeffcoat disappeared from the face of the earth.

"Emily?" her father repeated, more demandingly.

"Yes!" she delivered in an ornery bellow.

"He try anything else you want to tell me about?"

She kicked a lump of hay, sending it flying, but refused to answer.

"Emily?"

Mortified, she stared at the hay, her mouth cinched tighter than a seaman's knot, working her hands about the smooth pitchfork handle as if applying liniment to a horse's leg. At last she clomped to the hay hatch. Planting her feet wide and ramming the pitchfork tines into the pine floor, she met her father's upturned gaze.

"He came in here and started spouting off about the horses and how I should've cross-tied Sergeant, and taking the liberty of examining his hoof and offering advice on how to take care of it. He made me mad, that's all."

"So you turned his business away?"

Pride held her silent.

"I didn't mean any disrespect," Jeffcoat interrupted, placatingly. "But I'll admit, I was teasing her, and I made the mistake of thinking she was a boy when I walked in. It seemed to set her off, sir."

Turning away, Walcott bit his inner lip to keep from smiling. "Come into the office. We'll do business there. How many days will you be leaving your team here?"

Instead of following immediately, Jeffcoat stepped beneath the ladder and raised his eyes to the girl who glared down from above. "A week for sure, maybe more." He knew beyond a doubt that she'd like nothing better than to fire that pitchfork at his head. But she stood with both hands gripping its handle, staring him down with silent venom.

"Good afternoon, Miss Walcott," he offered quietly, and with a doffing of his hat, followed her father.

Walcott led him through a door into a lean-to attached to the east side of the barn, a small room with a bumpy concrete floor and four small-paned windows, two facing the street and two the empty lot. At sunrise the office would be bright but now in midafternoon it was cool and shadowed. It held a scarred desk with the rolltop missing, its pigeonholes overflowing with papers above a dusty top littered with bridle rings, snaffle bits, horseshoe nails, tack hammers, horse liniment, and a white dinner plate with a few green beans and a dried breadcrust stuck in a streak of hardening gravy. The desk chair was tilted on its casters and worn bare of varnish on its back and arms. Against the north wall slumped a metal daybed, its exposed springs covered with a homemade mattress made of stuffed burlap, topped by a multicolored rag rug where a taffy-colored cat slept. To the right of the door sat a small potbellied stove. The walls were hung with an assortment of oddities: beaver traps; stage schedules; patent-medicine trade cards; an advertisement for Buffalo Bill Cody's Wild West Show; a collection of oxbow keys; last summer's schedule for the Philadelphia Professional Baseball Club; and an ancient pendulum clock, ticking slow. The office smelled of onion gravy, aromatic liniment, grain, and hemp—the latter presumably exuding from a lineup of plump burlap bags propped against the wall to the left of the door.

"It's understandable why my daughter would be a little touchy over being criticized about the horses," Walcott commented, dropping onto the chair and rolling it toward his desk. It bumped over the rough floor like an unsprung wagon over frozen ruts. "She's been around 'em all her life and she's corresponding with a man from Cleveland, name of Barnum, who's teaching her veterinary medicine."

"Veterinary medicine—a girl?"

"There are a lot of animals out here. She's putting it to good use."

"You mean she's studying by mail?" Jeffcoat inquired with wonder.

"That's right," Walcott confirmed, reaching for a receipt book and a pen. "It comes pretty regular now, five times a week most weeks, by horseback. Here you go." Walcott swiveled around and handed Jeffcoat a receipt made out for two bays with white markings and a doublebox wagon, green with red trim. A careful man, Walcott, one who'd never be accused of horse theft, keeping records as he did.

"You mind my asking what you're doing in town, Mr. Jeffcoat?"

Pocketing the receipt, Jeffcoat answered, "Not at all. A man named J. D. Loucks placed an advertisement in the Springfield newspaper about this town and what it had to offer an enterprising young man. It sounded like a place I'd like to live, so I took the train to Rock Springs, outfitted there, and drove the rest of the way by wagon; and here I am."

"And here you are . . . to do what?"

"I intend to set up a business and make my home here as soon as I buy some land to do it on."

"Well"—the older man chuckled quietly—"J. D. Loucks'll be more than happy to sell you as many lots as you want, and this town can use more young people. What's your line of work?"

Jeffcoat hesitated a beat before replying, "I do some blacksmithing. Taught by my father in Springfield."

"Would that be Missouri or Illinois?"

"Missouri."

"Missouri, eh? Well then, he shod plenty that came through this territory on their way up the Oregon Trail, didn't he?"

"Yessir, he did."

"This town's already got one smithy, you know."

"So I see. I drove the streets before stopping here."

Edwin rose and led the way to the team still waiting outside. "But I'll tell you something that's no secret to anyone in Sheridan. Old Pinnick could do better work and more of it. Spends more time at the Mint Saloon than at his forge, and if he'd've shod Sergeant right in the first place we wouldn't be doctoring him now."

"Pinnick, huh?"

"That's the name of your competition: Walter Pinnick. Too lazy to put a sign out above his smithy that says so. Instead he just lets the sound of his hammer bring in the customers . . . when it's ringing." Outside in the sun Walcott paused to cock his head and listen, and—sure enough—the ringing of earlier was absent. "Old Pinnick must've got a touch of the *dry throat*," he ended with a sarcastic drawl, then moved on toward the team.

Jeffcoat cogitated momentarily before deciding it was best to be straightforward with this man.

"I want to be honest with you, sir. I've been around horses all my life, too, and I plan to do a little more than smithing. The truth is, I plan to open a livery stable."

Walcott paused with his hand on a bridle, and turned to look back at the younger man. The wind seemed to catch in his throat before he let it escape with a soft whistle.

"Well . . ." he said, letting his chin drop. For a moment he mulled, then chuckled and looked up. "You kind of took me by surprise there, young man."

"I think, from what I've seen and read, that there's business enough in this town for two of us. Lots of Texas cowboys either trailing herds through here, or starting their own small ranches in the vicinity, aren't there? And immigrants coming, too, now that the land has been thrown open for homesteading. A valley like this is bound to attract them. Hell, it's ninety-five miles wide, to say nothing of the sheep-ranching land in the hills up there. I think Loucks is right. This town is going to be the center of commerce, and soon."

Again Walcott chuckled wryly. "Well, let's hope so. So far it looks like the center of commerce around here is Buffalo, but we're growing." He turned toward the horses. "You plan to leave the wagon, too?"

"If I could."

"I'll pull it around back by the horseshoe pits. From the looks of this load you plan to get busy building right away."

"Soon as I buy that plot."

"You'll find Loucks's place up on Smith Street. Ask anybody, they'll point it out."

"Thank you, Mr. Walcott."

"Call me Edwin. It's a small town. We mostly go by first names."

Jeffcoat extended a hand, relieved that the man had taken the news so graciously.

"I appreciate your help, Edwin, and you can call me Tom."

"All right, Tom. I'm not sure whether to wish you good luck or not."

They laughed, parting; and Jeffcoat removed his carpetbag from his wagon, raised a hand in farewell, and advised, "The horses' names are Liza and Rex."

Watching Tom Jeffcoat move off, Edwin felt a brief stab of envy. Young—no more than twenty-five—and adventurous, far flying, with his whole life before him and choices still to be made in a territory where young people were granted the right to make those choices for themselves. It had been different when he was in his twenties. Then a man's future was often dictated—as his had been—by stern, dominating parents who planned his life with the best of intentions, but without consulting him. They'd planned it all, from how he would earn a livelihood right down to the woman he would marry, and he'd been a dutiful, obedient son. He'd become a hostler like his father, and had married one Miss Josephine Borley, to whom he was still respectfully wed. But there was another whom he'd never forgotten.

It had been twenty-two years but he thought of her still. Fannie. With her bright eyes and blustery spirit. Fannie, Josephine's cousin, as different from Josie as ash is from coals. Fannie, who instead of asking *why,* always asked *why not.* Fannie, who at age seventeen had fought for women's suffrage, ridden astride, and secretly smoked a cigar with him, then demanded, "Kiss me and tell me if I taste like smoke." Fannie, from whom he'd run soon after his marriage, because remaining near her would have proven dangerous. Fannie, who'd inherited her parents' wealth after their deaths and had used it to travel and experience things that most women would have found outlandish, even improper. Fannie, whose latest letter reported in her usual breezy fashion that she'd purchased a Monarch bicycle and had joined the Ladies' North Shore Bicycling Club, which was planning a four-day outing from Malden to Gloucester, Massachusetts, with overnight layovers at Pavilion and Essex House, briefer stops at Marblehead Neck and Nahant, and such attractions as a picnic lunch on the rocks at Pigeon Cove and visits to Rafe's Chasm and Norman's Woe.

Fannie, outrageous Fannie—what did she look like now? Was she happy? Did she love anyone? She'd filled her life with the uncommon, the progressive, the liberal, but never with a husband. Why? In twenty-two years, had there been anyone special? Her letters never included any mention of men beyond the most casual description of her social activities. But Edwin had never stopped wondering if there was one special man, and he never would.

It was because of his memories of Fannie, he knew, that he'd never resisted any of Emily's outrageous wishes. Emily was so much like the Fannie he remembered that he loved her unconditionally and had always secretly hoped she might turn out like Fannie—part rebel, part sprite, but all woman. When his daughter began tagging along to the livery stable, asking to help with the horses, Edwin had laughingly allowed it. When she narrowed a pair of his pants and began wearing them around the barn, he made no comment. When she read in the newspaper of Dr. Barnum's correspondence course on veterinary medicine and asked permission to apply, he had obligingly paid for it.

Because his own life had been indubitably dulled by parents who'd forced their will on him, he had, as a young father, vowed he'd never do the same to his children.

And now Emily was eighteen, and quite, quite like the Fannie of old—single-minded, wearing britches, taking up masculine interests, an upstart in the eyes of many.

Returning to her after the departure of Tom Jeffcoat, Edwin found Emily much mollified. She was waiting in the corridor between the box stalls with two feed boxes already filled and four snap lines in her hand as he led Jeffcoat's horses inside and stopped before her.

"Oh, Papa, I'm sorry." She walked against him and hugged his chest with the ease of one accustomed to doing so often. With reins in both hands, Edwin could only drop his cheek affectionately against her scratchy wool cap.

"No harm done. We got his business anyway."

She stepped back and looked into her father's face, finding the forgiving grin she'd expected.

"He did make me angry though, calling me *young fellow.* Do I look like a young fellow to you?"

"Mmm . . ." With a half smile on his face he assessed her cap, apron, and boots. "Now that you mention it . . ."

She tried to hold back a smile, but it won in the end. "Honestly, Papa, sometimes I don't know why I love you so." She gave him an affectionate mock punch, then sobered. "How's Mother?"

"Resting. There's no need for you to hurry back. Help me take care of the horses first." He understood that she preferred the work at the livery barn to the nursing and housework at home and tried not to burden her unfairly with domestic tasks that seemed never ending as the ailing Josephine grew less and less able to cope with them. He sensed his daughter's unconscious relief as she eagerly took a pair of reins, looked up into the mare's brown eyes, and asked, "What's her name?"

"Liza."

"And his?"

"Rex."

"Come on, Liza, let's get you undressed and rubbed down."

They worked together amiably, securing the horses in the center of the corridor, removing their harnesses, cleaning their coats with dandy brushes, raising the fecund scent of horse sweat. While she stroked Liza's warm, damp hide, Emily inquired, "How long will these two be staying?"

"A week . . . maybe more."

"While he does what?" She refused to speak Jeffcoat's name, though she'd clearly overheard it.

"Buys himself a lot and puts up a building."

Emily's hand stopped moving. "A building?"

"He's a blacksmith. He's here to set up a business."

"A blacksmith!"

"That's right, so try to get along with him if you can. We'll probably be using his services in the future if he turns out to be even a quarter as sober as Pinnick."

She started brushing again, with more elbow grease than necessary. Edwin glanced at his daughter's face to find it darkened with a scowl as she wielded the dandy brush, then tossed it aside in favor of a curry comb. Guessing her reaction to the rest of his news, Edwin added carefully, "That's not all."

Emily's head snapped up and their gazes met.

"What else?"

"He plans to do his smithing in his own livery barn."

Her mouth dropped open. "He what!"

"You heard me right."

"Oh, Papa . . ." Her dropping note held true sympathy. With all he had to worry about, must there be more? Mama ill and everybody trying to do double shifts at home and here. And now this! She'd like to take J. D. Loucks *and* his advertisement *and* Mister Tom Jeffcoat and drop them off the edge of a butte!

"At least he was honest about it," Edwin observed.

"What else could he be when he's going to build something as big as a livery barn?"

"It's a free country, and for all we know he might be right. There might be enough business here for two."

"Where does he plan to build?" she asked belligerently.

"Your guess is as good as mine."

But they both knew J. D. Loucks could sell him whatever lot he wanted. The town was his. He'd bought it seven years ago, staked it out on a forty-acre plot, drawn up a plat on a piece of brown wrapping paper from his store, prepared a petition for incorporation, and was granted such a year later by the Wyoming Territorial Assembly. He got himself chosen as mayor, named the town after his Civil War commander, General Philip H. Sheridan, and went to work enticing young blood to settle there.

It was a rancher's town. Loucks had made it so, recognizing the value of the valley's rich grassland and anticipating a prosperous future brought by the drovers herding cattle up the Bozeman Corridor from the depleted grasslands of Texas. The town had everything: vast tracts of sub-bituminous coal within a few miles, meandering Goose Creeks tracing irregular dark green lines across it, the second-lowest average wind velocity in the United States, and thousands of adjacent acres of Indian lands thrown open to the public domain now that the Indian Wars were over.

The tempting ads Loucks had placed in eastern newspapers bore speedy results. Naturally, the lots along Main Street had sold first; already Main was filled with businesses, from the Windsor Hotel at the south end to the creek at the north. It was the side streets such as Grinnell on which lots were still available.

"Well, he'd better stay away from here!" Emily Walcott seethed, turning Jeffcoat's horse into a stall. "I don't want to be bumping into him any more than I have to."

As it turned out, she bumped into him less than an hour later. She was heading home to check on her mother as Jeffcoat and J. D. Loucks came rolling down the street in Loucks's fine Peerless buggy, obviously on a tour of the town. She came up short in the middle of the boardwalk as Loucks, with his flowing white beard, drove past behind his matched grays. Emily glared, tight-lipped, at the man beside him. He must have gone to the hotel and mucked off. The whiskers were gone, and his frock coat had sleeves, and his string tie looked proper enough against a clean white shirtfront. But his grin made her fists ball.

Jeffcoat touched his hat brim and nodded while Emily felt the color soar to her cheeks. His eyes remained fixed on her until the carriage drew abreast and passed. Only then did she resume her angry stride, wishing she had fired the pitchfork at him when she'd had the chance.

Chapter 2

THE HOME OF Emily Walcott was unlike the other homes she knew. It was always messy; meals were never ready on time; sometimes they ran out of clean laundry; and the lamp chimneys were in constant need of polishing. It hadn't always been that way. When Mother was healthy, back when they lived in Philadelphia, their house had been cheery and well maintained. Suppers were ready on time, laundry hung on the line every Monday morning and was ironed on Tuesday. Wednesday meant mending, Thursday odd jobs, Friday bread baking, and Saturday cleaning.

Then Mother had started ailing and all that had changed. At the beginning they hadn't thought much of her fatigue. In fact, they'd all laughed and teased her the first time they'd come home to find her napping when dinner should have been on the table. Her illness had advanced insidiously, and months passed while none of them attributed her weight loss to anything out of the ordinary. She'd always, since bearing her two children, been plump. As the pounds disappeared and she took on a trimmer, younger shape, Papa had looked pleased and sometimes teased her and made her blush. But then the coughing started and his teasing changed to concern.

"You must see a doctor, Josephine," he'd insisted.

"It's nothing, Edwin, really," Mother had countered. "Just old age creeping up on me."

But that had been only two years ago, when she was thirty-eight. Thirty-eight, yet she had begun withering away before their eyes. Her cough grew harsh and frequent and left her increasingly weaker while her family stood by feeling helpless.

Then Papa had read the article about the successful Philadelphia hatter, John B. Stetson. Stetson had been a young man when the doctors told him he had lung trouble and gave him but a few months to live. Deciding there was only one way to prove their prognosis wrong, young Stetson had made up his mind that he must get away from the crowded, smoke-clogged city and out into the open; he'd struck out for the Far West, which at that time meant Missouri. Yet he'd continued even farther, all the way to Pike's Peak, tramping much of the way on foot, sleeping in the open, taking the weather as it came. In spite of the hardships of the trail and of the year he spent as a placer-miner in the high Rockies, his health made a remarkable improvement. He'd returned to Philadelphia with a mere hundred dollars in diggings, but with the most robust health he'd ever enjoyed. Strapping and strong, John B. Stetson had credited the West with giving him back his health.

With the hundred dollars he'd built a hatting empire. And with his eternal gratitude for the restoration of his good health, he'd schooled and cared for others, becoming a stickler for fresh air and sunshine, flooding his factories with both. He'd been too busy to go to a doctor, so when the need arose, his physician came to him in his own office. Stetson next began bringing into his office any of his employees needing treatment. This idea, like all of his ideas, was enlarged upon. When his own physician's services were outgrown, specialists in various lines were called in. A day came when Stetson realized that if he wanted to escape the parade of doctors and employees now marching through his office, he must make other arrangements.

So he'd built a hospital, magnanimously refusing to confine

its relief to his employees only, but making its benefits free to all.

It was there that Edwin Walcott took his wife after reading the article, hoping to find a possible cure for her consumption. The fates had smiled upon them both that day, for while waiting in an anteroom, they had met the great John B. himself. It was impossible to meet and discourse with the man and go away unencouraged. Hale and fit, he made a convincing case for clean living, and credited his cure to that single year of fresh air, pure water, and sunshine.

"Go west!" he'd advised Josephine Walcott. "Go west where the climate is salubrious, where mountain streams are pure as crystal, and the high altitudes purify and strengthen your lungs by making them work harder. Build your house facing south and east, give it plenty of windows, and open them daily. Nightly, too."

And so they had come. They'd built their house facing not only south and east, but west, too, and had given it all the windows John B. Stetson recommended. They had added a wraparound porch where Josephine could take the air and sunshine in long drafts, and from which she could watch the sun rise over the Powder River pampas and set behind the majestic Big Horns.

But what had cured John B. Stetson had failed to cure Josephine Walcott. In the eighteen months they'd been here she had only grown weaker. Her body, once portly and Rubenesque, had dissipated to a mere ninety-five pounds. Her cough had become so constant it no longer awakened her children at night. And recently, bloodstained handkerchiefs had begun appearing in the dirty laundry.

It was the laundry that concerned Emily as she returned home that June afternoon.

Climbing the wide porch steps, she glanced over her left shoulder at the sun, wondering if there was time enough for things to dry before dusk.

She entered the parlor and paused despondently, glancing around. Dust. Everywhere dust. And bric-a-brac enough to dizzy a person. Papa had prospered as a Philadelphia liveryman and in spite of Mother's debilitated condition she wanted everyone in Sheridan to know of his success. Being a modern Victorian matron, she displayed the proof in her parlor, as had her friends in Philadelphia, adapting to the modern decorating principle that *more was better.*

Though the room had been designed by Papa to give an impression of space, Mother had done everything to fill it, insisting not only on bringing her piano but on placing it in the popular way with its back to the room instead of to the wall, thereby enabling her to "dress" it. Festooned with a drapery of swagged multicolored China silk edged with gimp and cord-ball fringe, the huge upright formed the nucleus of the monstrosity Mother called a parlor. Against the piano was shoved a backless divan; upon it was displayed an assortment of fans and framed photographs; beside it a jardiniere of peacock feathers. She had insisted on leaving behind not one item of her life's collection of litter, and had stuffed the room with an eye-boggling clutter of umbrellas, plaster busts, wicker rockers, cushions, coat racks, china cabinets, scarves, piecrust tables, clocks, and gimcracks. The floor was covered with fillings, then Oriental rugs, and then the easychairs hidden by embroidered cushions and Turkish tidies. The lovely bay window, which Papa had installed to let in plenty of light, was nearly obscured by hanging ferns and tassled draperies.

Perusing it all, Emily sighed. Often she wished Papa would insist on clearing it out and leaving only a wicker chaise and a table or two, but she knew her mother's illness prevailed upon him to let her have her way.

For Mother was dying.

They all knew it but nobody said so. If she wanted her fringed piano cover and gimcracks around her while she did, who in this family would deny her?

Emily collapsed onto the ugly rolled divan, dropped her crossed arms and head onto her knees, and gave in to the depression that hung over this house.

Oh, Mother, please get well. We need you. Papa needs you. He's so lonely and lost, even though he tries to hide it. He's probably worried sick right now about what will happen with another livery stable starting up right under his nose. He'd never let on to me, but he would to you if you were strong.

And Frankie—he's only twelve and he needs so much mothering yet. Who'll give it to him if you die? Me, when I still need mothering myself? I need it at this very moment. I wish I could run to you and talk about my fears for Papa, and my hopes of becoming a veterinarian, which I want more than anything I can ever remember, and about Charles and my uncertainties regarding him. I need to know if what I feel is strong enough or if there should be more. Because he's warned me—he's going to ask me again, soon; and what should I say this time?

With her face buried in her arms, Emily thought of Charles. Plain, good, hard-working Charles who had been her playmate since childhood, who'd been so devastated by the news of her leaving Philadelphia that he'd made the monumental decision to come along with her family to the Wyoming Territory and make his start in the world.

Charles, whom she was so grateful to have at first, living in a new place where there were few other young people her age. Charles, who was becoming insistent about setting a date for their wedding when she wanted instead to learn veterinary medicine first. Charles, to whom she felt betrothed even before she was.

She sighed, pushed herself up, and went to the kitchen. By virtue of necessity, it was the only room in the house devoid of extraneous decor. It had the best range money could buy, and a real granite sink with an indoor pump. A washroom was located at the back with a coal oil heater, a washing machine with metal gears and an easy-to-manipulate hand agitator, and real wooden wringers with a convenient hand crank.

Emily took a look at it and turned away in disgust, wishing she could be at the livery barn cleaning stalls.

Instead, she went upstairs to check on her mother.

The house was rich by Sheridan standards, not only because Papa doted on his ailing wife, but also because Charles Bliss was a carpenter and had brought along his talent and his blueprints—a great relief to Mother, who'd been so afraid she'd have to live in a peeled-log hut with mice and insects. Instead, she'd been built an elegant frame house of two full stories with large airy rooms, long windows, and an impressive entry hall with an open stairway and spooled railings.

Mounting that stairway, Emily turned at the top and paused in the doorway of her parents' bedroom—a spacious room with a second doorway giving onto a small railed roof facing south. Papa had insisted that Charles include the veranda so Mother could step out and enjoy fresh air and sunshine whenever she felt the need. But Mother hardly used the veranda anymore. Its door stood open now, throwing sunshine across the varnished floor of the room where she lay upon the immense sleigh-design bed in which Emily and Frankie had been born. Upon that bed, Mother looked frailer than ever.

She had been handsome once, her hair thick and glossy, a rich bay color. She had worn it with as much pomp as she'd worn her bustles, the rich dark skeins twisted up tightly into an impressive figure-eight knot that thrust out in back even as her generous bust had thrust forward in front. Now her hair was lustreless, lying in a limp braid, and her bust nearly nonexistent. She wore a faded silk bed jacket instead of the crisp sateens and malines she once had donned. Her skin had taken on an alarming number of wrinkles and had become flaccid on her frame.

While Emily studied her sleeping mother, Josephine coughed, covering her mouth with the ever-present hanky, a function that had become as involuntary as the cough itself.

Emily's sad eyes moved to the cot against the side window where her father had taken to sleeping in recent months so as not to disturb his wife—reasoning over which Emily often wondered, since it was most certainly Mother's coughing that disturbed Papa.

She stood for a moment, wondering things a proper Victorian young lady ought not wonder, things about mothers and fathers and shared beds and when—if ever—that sharing ceased to matter. She had never seen Papa touch Mother in any but the most decorous manner. Even when he came into this room, if she—Emily—were there, and Mother was having a bad day, he never kissed her, but only touched her forehead or her hand briefly. Yet he loved her unquestionably. Emily knew he did. After all, she and Frankie were living proof, weren't they? And Papa was so sad since Mother's illness had worsened. Once, in the middle of the night, Emily had discovered him sitting on the front porch with tears running down his face reflecting the moonlight. She had crept back inside without his ever suspecting that she'd discovered his secret grief.

If a man loved a woman, did he display it in the respectful way Papa displayed it to Mother, or by touching her as Charles had recently begun touching Emily? How had Mother reacted the first time Papa had touched her so? And had he done it before they were married? Emily had difficulty imagining her mother allowing such intimacies even when she'd been healthy, for there was an air of propriety about Josephine Walcott that seemed to shun such possibilities.

How disrespectful to be thinking such thoughts in the doorway of her parents' bedroom when her mother lay ill and dying, and her father faced not only that sad truth but a business crisis as well.

"Emily?"

"Oh, Mother, I'm sorry. Did I wake you?" Emily moved to the bedside, taking her mother's frail hand. Josephine smiled, closed her eyes, and rolled her head weakly. They all knew she rarely slept soundly anymore but existed in a state of quasi-sleep as tiring as a day of manual labor might be for a healthy person. She opened her eyes and tapped the bedding at her hip. More and more often lately she used motions to convey her messages, saving every possible breath.

"No," Emily replied. "I'm dirty. I've been helping Papa in the barn. And besides, I have some things to do downstairs. Can I get you anything?"

Josephine answered with a desultory wag of her head.

"If I can, just ring the bell." A small brass handbell had rolled down along the ridge of bedding below Josephine's knee, and Emily retrieved it and put it near her palm.

"Thank—" A spasm of coughing interrupted and Emily escaped the room, feeling guilty for having brought it on and for preferring even washing clothes to watching her mother suffer.

It took the better part of an hour to heat the water, and a lot of knuckle-work to remove the bloodstains. Emily was still at it when Frankie came home with two black-spotted trout gill-strung on a forked stick.

"Look what I got, Emily!"

He was the prettiest boy Emily had ever seen—she'd often said Frankie got the looks in their family—with long-lashed blue eyes, twin dimples, a beautiful mouth, and a head of dark hair that was going to make plenty of female fingers itch to touch it within a very few years. Once he'd lost the last of his baby teeth, he'd grown a set of the most remarkably large and perfect ones. They never failed to startle Emily, for though they were the only part of him that had attained their mature size, they brought with them the promise of complete maturity in the very near future. His limbs were stretching already, and if the length of his toes was any indication, Frankie would soon gain the height of their mother, who topped Papa by a good two inches.

Emily felt bad for Frankie. He was still only twelve, but with Mother so sick, the last of his boyhood was being robbed of the happy abandon he deserved. It wasn't fair; but then this trial wasn't fair to any of them, least of all Mother, was it? They had to pitch in and handle the housework the best they could, like it or not. So Emily steeled herself against the appeal she knew was forthcoming as she admired Frankie's catch.

"Mmm . . . nice fish. Who's going to clean them?"

"Me and Earl. Where's Papa?"

"Still at the livery."

"I gotta go show him!"

"Wait a minute!"

"But Earl's waiting!" Frankie halted impatiently, his face skewing as he realized his mistake in stopping by the kitchen.

"You promised to be home by three to help me."

"I didn't have any watch."

"You can see the sun, can't you?"

"I couldn't." His eyes widened to best advantage. "Honestly, I couldn't, Emily! We were down by the big cottonwoods in the empty lot behind Stroth's place and I couldn't see the sun behind the trees!"

She pitied the poor girl who tried to tie this one down. Dressed in a straw hat, wearing neither shirt nor shoes beneath his overalls, with his wide eyes shining and his lips open in feigned innocence, Frankie presented a charming picture, one Emily had difficulty resisting. Still, she tried.

"Here." She released the agitator lever on the washing machine. "Your turn. My arm is ready to fall off."

"But I want to take my fish uptown and show Papa. And besides, Earl's waiting, and soon as we show Papa we're gonna come straight back here and clean these so you can fry them for supper. Please, Emily . . . *pleeeease?"*

She let him go because when she was twelve she had not had to wash clothes at four o'clock on a warm summer afternoon. Without his help, the washing took longer than she'd planned, and she was just finishing up when Papa came home for supper. True to his word, Frankie had cleaned the trout, and tonight he and Papa took over the cooking while Emily put the washroom in order and stacked the wet laundry to wait till morning.

Papa's cooking left room for improvement. The potatoes were mushy; the trout was a little too brown; the coffee boiled over; and the biscuits stuck to the pan. But worst of all, Mother was absent from the table. Edwin took a tray up to her but returned to catch Emily's eye across the room and give a sad shake of his head. The empty chair cast a pall over the meal, as usual, but Emily tried to brighten it.

"From now on, I'll do the cooking and you can clean up the washroom," she chided.

"We'll do as we've been doing," Edwin returned. "We'll get along just fine."

But when his eyes met those of his daughter she caught a momentary hint of despair such as she'd witnessed in his private midnight session on the porch. As quickly as it appeared, Edwin hid it and lurched to his feet, reaching for dishes to carry to the sink.

"We'd better clean up. Charles said he'd be stopping by later tonight."

Charles stopped by most nights. He had a house of his own, but it was undeniably lonely for him living in it by himself. It was natural for him to want to be with the Walcotts, having known them all his life, and having come to Wyoming at the same time as they. Since their relocation in Sheridan he had come to be a dear friend to Edwin in spite of the difference in their ages. And Mama had always shown a distinct affection for him, having known him since he was a boy. Charles, she often reiterated, came from a staunch religious upbringing, knew the value of hard work, and would someday make a dedicated husband for Emily. As for Frankie—well, Frankie absolutely idolized Charles.

Charles arrived in time to help wipe dishes. Whenever he arrived lately, it seemed there was something he could help with, and he always did so gladly. Emily had grown tired of hearing her father say, "That Charles, he sure knows what work is." Of course Charles knew what work was—didn't they all?

After dishes Frankie talked Charles into a game of dominoes. They all retired to the parlor where the two set up their pieces while Emily watched and Edwin smoked a last pipe before going upstairs to read to his wife.

"I suppose you met the new man in town," Charles said to nobody in particular.

"We've got his horses at the livery," Edwin responded.

"What new man?" Frankie inquired.

"His name is Jeffcoat. Tom Jeffcoat," Charles answered, placing a five on a five.

"So you've met him, too?" Edwin inquired.

"Yes. Loucks sent him over, told him I was a carpenter."

"He wants to hire you, of course," Edwin ventured.

Charles glanced up. His eyes met Edwin's, and Emily witnessed the ambivalence in his glance.

"Yes, he does."

"Well, if his money is green, you'd better say yes."

"Do you know what he's building, Edwin?"

"A livery stable, he tells me."

"He *told* you?"

"As Emily pointed out, it'd be hard to hide a livery stable once it starts going up."

"Emily met him, too?" Charles's eyes veered to her as she leaned over Frankie's shoulder, studying his domino selection.

"I'm sorry to say I did," she replied coolly, without once raising her eyes to Charles's.

"Oh?"

She picked up one of Frankie's dominoes and played it while answering. "First he called me 'young fellow,' then tried to give me advice about how to take care of Sergeant's cracked hoof. I didn't appreciate either one."

Edwin chuckled, holding the pipestem at the corner of his mouth. "I can vouch for that. She was whetting the edge of her tongue on him when I walked in and saved a week's worth of business she had just sent packing."

"Papa!" Emily spouted irritably. "You don't have to tell everything!"

"Emily did that?" Frankie put in, losing interest in the game, grinning with wonder at his sister.

"Now, Emily, we have no secrets from Charles."

Which, in Emily's opinion, was one of the reasons she couldn't generate any romantic gust for him. It felt as if she'd already lived with him for the last two years, he was here so much. She gave up playing Frankie's dominoes and plopped down on the divan.

"I hope you spit in his eye, Charles!" she said pugnaciously.

"Now, Emily, be sensible. How could Charles do that?" her father chided.

"*I* did it, didn't I?" she challenged.

To Emily's surprise Charles said, "As a matter of fact, I rather liked him."

"Liked him!" Emily exclaimed. "Charles, how could you!"

"Emily, you seem to forget Charles has a business to run!" Edwin's tone grew sharper, then mellowed as he turned to Charles. "Whatever she says, you know I wouldn't hold it against you if you worked for Jeffcoat."

"He wants to see my blueprint collection, too. After the livery barn he intends to put up a house."

"So he said. And it could mean a tidy profit for you, Charles."

"Maybe so, but I don't like working for your competition."

Edwin took a puff on his pipe, found it dead, fished a horseshoe nail from his shirt pocket, and began scraping out the dottle into an ashtray. "Charles, I'm not your father," he began after a thoughtful silence, "but I think I know what he'd say if he were here to advise you at this moment. He'd say this is one of those occasions where you have to be a businessman first and a friend second. As for me, I'll respect you as much for making a prudent business decision as I will for being loyal, so tell Jeffcoat yes. It's what you came here for, isn't it? Because you thought the town would prosper, and you, too, along with it? Well, you can't do that by turning down paying customers."

Charles turned his gray eyes to Frankie. "Frankie, what do you say?"

"I don't care if Papa doesn't care."

"Emily?" He lifted his eyes to her and she had difficulty separating her distaste for Jeffcoat from the realization that Papa was probably right. Was she the only one in the place aggravated by the entire situation? Well, she hadn't their magnanimity, and she wouldn't pretend she did! With a flash of annoyance, she shot from her chair toward the front door. "Oh, I don't care!" she called back. "Do what you want!" A moment later the front screen door slammed.

Emily's peevishness put an end to the games in the parlor. Charles rose and said, "I'll go out and talk to her."

Edwin said, "Frankie, make sure you bury those fish guts before you go to bed." He went up to spend the remainder of the evening with his wife.

The porch wrapped around three sides of the house. Charles

found Emily on the west arm, sitting on a wicker settee, facing the Big Horns and the paling peach sky.

She heard Charles's footsteps approach but continued leaning her head against the wall as he perched on the edge of the settee beside her, making the wicker snap. He joined his hands loosely between his knees and studied them.

"You're upset with me," he said quietly.

"I'm upset with life, Charles, not with you."

"With me too, I can tell."

She relented and rolled her head his way, studying him. She had grown up in an era when most men wore facial hair, yet she would never grow accustomed to it on Charles. His sandy brown mustache and beard were thick and neatly sculptured, yet she missed the clean, strong lines it hid. He had a fine jaw and a good chin, too attractive to hide beneath all that nap. The beard and mustache made him look older than he really was. Why would a man of twenty-one want to look like one approaching thirty? She stifled the critical thoughts and studied his eyes—intelligent gray eyes watching her now with the hurt carefully concealed.

"No," she assured him more softly, "not with you. With all the work, and the worry about Mother, and now this new man coming to town and competing with Papa. It's all very upsetting." She turned her gaze back to the Big Horns and sighed before going on. "And sometimes I miss Philadelphia so badly I think I'll simply die."

"I know. Sometimes I do, too."

They watched the sky take on a blue tint and eventually Charles inquired, "What do you miss most?"

"Oh . . ." She missed so many things—at that moment she could not choose one. "The skating parties and the round of visiting on New Year's Day and the summertime picnics. All the things we used to do with our friends. Here all we do is work and sleep, then work again and sleep again. There's no . . . no gaiety, no social life."

Charles remained silent. Finally, he said, "I miss it a lot, too."

"What do *you* miss most?"

"My family."

"Oh, Charles . . ." She felt tactless for having asked when she knew how lonely she herself would feel if she were suddenly two thousand miles away from Papa and Mother and

Frankie. "But we're here for you anytime you need us," she added, because it was true. Because she could not imagine her home without Charles there most evenings and Sundays. Too late she saw the appeal in his eye and knew he would reach for her hand. When he did, she felt no more excitement than she had when she was six and he was nine and he had squired her down a Philadelphia street with their mothers behind them pushing perambulators.

"I have an idea," Charles said, suddenly brightening. "You're missing the picnics in Philadelphia, so why don't we plan one?"

"Just the two of us?"

"Why not?"

"Oh, Charles . . ." She retrieved her hand and dropped her head against the wall. "I barely have time to do the washing and ironing and fix suppers and take my turn with Mother."

"There's Sunday."

"The cooking doesn't stop for Sundays."

"Surely you can find a couple of hours. How about this Sunday? I'll bring the food. And we'll take your father's little black shay for two and drive up into the foothills and drink sarsaparilla and stretch out in the sun like a couple of lazy lizards." In his earnestness he captured both of her hands. "What do you say, Emily?"

To get away for even an afternoon sounded so wonderful that she couldn't resist. "Oh, all right. But I won't be able to leave until the others are fed."

Elated, Charles kissed her hands—two grazing touches meant to keep the mood gay. But when his head lifted, he gripped her fingers more tightly and the expression in his eyes intensified.

Oh no, don't spoil it, Charles, she thought.

"Emily," he appealed softly while lifting one of her hands again to his lips. The sky had darkened to midnight blue and nobody was around to see what happened in the shadow of the deep porch as he took her arms and drew her close, dropping his mouth over hers. She acquiesced, but at the touch of his warm lips and prickly mustache she thought, Why must I have known you all my life? Why can you not be some mysterious stranger who galloped into town and gave me a second look that rocked me off my feet? Why is the scent of wood shavings on your skin and of tonic on your hair too familiar to be exciting? Why must I love you in the same way I love Frankie?

When the kiss ended her heart was plunking along as restfully as if she'd just awakened and stretched from a long nap.

"Charles, I must go in now," she said.

"No, not yet," he whispered, holding her arms.

She dropped her chin so he wouldn't kiss her again. "Yes . . . please, Charles."

"Why do you always pull away?"

"Because it isn't proper."

He drew an unsteady breath and released her. "Very well . . . but I'll plan on Sunday then."

He walked her to the door and she felt his reluctance to leave, to return to his empty house. It brought to Emily a nagging sense of guilt for being unable to conjure up the feelings he wanted of her, for being unable to fill the void left by his family, even for finding disfavor with his mustache and beard when other women, she was sure, found them most appealing.

She knew when he paused and turned to her that he wanted to kiss her again, but she slipped inside before he could.

"Good night, Charles," she said through the screen door.

"Good night, Emily." He stood studying her, banking his disappointment. "I'll win you over yet, you know."

As she watched him cross the porch she had the deflating feeling he was right.

Upstairs, Edwin was reading to Josephine from *Forty Liars and Other Lies* by Edgar Wilson Nye, but he knew her mind was far from Nye's humorous depictions of the West.

". . . leading a string of paint ponies along an arroyo where—"

"Edwin?" she interrupted, staring at the ceiling.

He lowered the book and studied her anxiously. "Yes, dear?"

"What are we going to do?" she whispered.

"Do?" He set the book aside and left his cot to sit on the edge of the big bed.

"Yes. What are we going to do from now until I die?"

"Oh, Josie, don't—"

She gestured to silence him. "We both know it, Edwin, and we must make plans."

"We don't know it." He took her pale, frail fingers and squeezed them. "Look at what happened to Stetson."

"I've been here well over a year already and by now I know I won't be as lucky as Stet—" She broke into a spasm of coughing that bent her and made her quiver like a divining rod. He bolstered her back and leaned close. "Don't talk anymore, Josie. Save your breath . . . please."

The racking cough continued for a full two minutes before she fell back, exhausted. He brushed the hair away from her sweating brow and studied her gaunt face, his own weighted with despair at being unable to help her in any way.

"Rest, Josie."

"No," she mouthed, grasping his hand to keep him near. "Listen to me, Edwin." She struggled to control her breathing, taking deep drafts of air, building her reserve for the words ahead. "I'm not going to get downstairs again and we both know it. I scarcely have the strength to feed myself—how will I ever handle house chores ag—again?" Another cough interrupted momentarily, then she went through the struggle again, recouping her strength before finally continuing: "It isn't fair to expect the children to do my part and care for me, too."

"They don't mind, and neither do I. We're getting along just f—"

She squeezed his hand weakly. Her sunken eyes rested on his, begging for his indulgence. "Emily is eighteen. We've put too great a load on her. She'd rather . . ." Josephine stopped again for breath. "She'd rather work at the livery stable with you and she needs more time to study if she's to complete the course from Dr. Barnum. Is it fair of us to expect her to be housekeeper and nurse, too?"

He had no answer. He sat stroking her blue-white hand, staring at it while regret filled his throat.

"I believe," Josephine added, "that Charles has asked her to marry him and she turned him down because of me."

He couldn't deny it; he was certain that what his wife said was true, though Emily had never admitted it to either of them.

"She's a good girl, Edwin, devoted to us. She'll help you in the livery stable and me in this house until Charles grows tired of waiting and asks someone else."

"That will never happen."

"Perhaps not. But suppose she wanted to say yes right

now—don't you see that she should be caring for her own house . . . her own children, instead of Frankie and you and me?"

Despondent, Edwin had no answer.

"Edwin, look at me."

He did, his face long with sorrow.

"I am going to die, Edwin," she whispered, "but it may take . . . some time yet. And it will not be easy . . . on any of you, least of all Emily. She should have . . . the right to say yes to Charles, don't you see? And Frankie still needs a woman's strong hand, and this house should be cared for . . . and meals cooked properly, and you . . . should not have to take turns hanging laundry and frying fish . . . so I have written to Fannie and asked her to come."

A bolt of fire seemed to shoot through Edwin's vitals. "Fannie?" He blinked and his spine straightened. "You mean your cousin, Fannie?"

"Do we know any other?"

He sprang from the side of the bed to face the veranda door and hide his heating face. "But she has a life of her own."

"She has no life at all; surely you can read between the lines of her letters."

"On the contrary, Fannie has so many interests and . . . and friends, she . . . why, she . . ." Edwin stammered to a halt, feeling his blood continue to rush at the mere mention of the woman's name.

Behind him Josephine said softly, "I need her, Edwin. This family needs her."

He spun and retorted, "No, I won't have Fannie!"

For a moment Josephine stared at him while he felt foolish and transparent, by turns. All these years he'd hidden the truth from her and he would not risk her learning it now when she had so much else to suffer. He forcibly calmed himself and softened his voice. "I won't have Fannie put in the position of having to say yes, just because you're family. And you know she would do just that, in a minute."

"I'm afraid it's too late, Edwin . . . she's already agreed."

Shock drained the blood from his face. His fingertips felt cold and his chest tight.

"Her letter arrived today." Josephine extended a folded

piece of stationery. He stared at it as if it were alive. After a long silence he reluctantly moved toward it.

Josephine watched the color return to his face as he read Fannie's reply. She saw him carefully attempt to mask his feelings, but his ears and cheeks turned brilliant red and his Adam's apple bobbed. Watching, she hid the regret begotten by years of marriage to a man who had never loved her. *Edwin, my gallant and noble husband, you will never know how hard I tried to make you happy. Perhaps at last I've found a way.*

When he'd finished reading, he folded the letter and returned it to her, unable to hide the reproof in his eyes and voice. "You should have consulted me first, Josephine." He only called her Josephine when he was inordinately upset. The rest of the time it was Josie.

"Yes, I know."

"Why didn't you?"

"For exactly the reason you're displaying."

He slipped his hands into his rear pockets, afraid she would see them trembling. "She's a city woman. It's not fair to ask her to come out here to the middle of nowhere. The children and I can handle it. Or perhaps I could hire someone."

"Who?"

They both knew women were scarce out here in cowboy country. Those of eligible age remained single very briefly before taking on their own husband and house. He would find no one in Sheridan willing to hire on as nurse and housekeeper.

"Edwin, come . . . sit by me."

Reluctantly he did, studying the floor morosely. She touched his knee—a rare intimacy—and took his hand. "Grant me this . . . please. Set the children free of the burdens I've brought them . . . and yourself, too. When Fannie comes, make her feel welcome. I think she needs us as badly as we need her."

"Fannie has never needed anyone."

"Hasn't she?"

Edwin felt a tangle of emotions: fear as great as any he'd ever known, matched by unbounded exhilaration at the thought of seeing Fannie again; pique with Josie for putting him in this ungodly position; relief that she had at last found an answer to their domestic turmoil; a sense of encroaching duplicity, for surely he would practice it from the very moment Fannie

Cooper set foot in this house; resolution that, no matter what, he would never desecrate his marriage vows.

"Where do you intend to put her?"

"In with Emily."

Edwin sat silent for a long time, still adjusting to the shock, trying to imagine himself lying in this room on his cot night after night with Fannie across the hall. There was nothing he could do; she was already en route, even as he sat with his stomach quaking and his leg muscles tense. She would arrive by stagecoach within the week and he would pick her up at the hotel and pretend he had not kept her memory glowing in his heart for twenty-two years.

"Of course I'll be cordial to her, you know that. It's just—"

Their eyes locked and exchanged a silent acknowledgment. Fannie's coming represented so much more than the arrival of help. It represented the first in a series of final steps. Always until now they had lived with the delusion that one day soon Josephine would awaken and feel revived enough to take up her duties again. That life would return to normal. Upon Fannie's arrival they would lay that idea to rest with the same darkening finality as the knowledge that this woman—this wife and mother—would herself be laid to rest in the foreseeable future.

Edwin felt his throat tighten and his eyes sting. He doubled forward, covering Josie's frail torso with his sturdy one, slipping his hands between her and the stacked pillows. He rested his cheek upon her temple but dared not press his weight upon her. She felt like a stranger, bony and wasted. Odd how he could experience such deep sorrow at the difference in her emaciated body when he'd taken so little pleasure in it while it was plump and healthy. Perhaps it was that, too, which he mourned.

Dear Josie, I promise my fidelity till the end—that much I can give you.

She held him and pinched her eyes closed against the pain of losing him to Fannie, wondering why she had never been able to welcome his embrace this effortlessly during her hale years.

Dearest Edwin, she'll give you the kind of love I was never able to give—I'm sure of it.

Chapter 3

EMILY WAS IN the tack room at the livery stable the following day when Tarsy Fields came flying in like a kite with a broken string. "Emily, have you *seen him yet!* He's absolutely *gorgeous*!" Tarsy was given to flamboyant gestures, exaggeration, and general excess of enthusiasm over anything she liked.

"Seen who?"

"Why, Mr. Jeffcoat, of course! Tom Jeffcoat—don't tell me you haven't *heard* of him!"

"Oh, him." Emily made a distasteful face and turned away, continuing her preparation of a linseed-meal poultice for Sergeant's foot.

"Did he bring his horse in here?"

"We're the only livery in town, aren't we?"

"So you *did* see him! And probably met him, too. Oh, Emily, you're *soooo* lucky. I only passed him on the boardwalk as he was coming out of the hotel, and I didn't get a chance to talk to him or meet him, but I went inside and found out his name from Mr. Helstrom. Tom Jeffcoat—what a name! Isn't he absolutely *dazzling*?" Tarsy clasped her hands, straightened her arms, and gazed at the rafters in a surfeit of ecstasy.

Dazzling? Tom Jeffcoat? The man with no sleeves and no manners? The know-it-all bounder who was setting out to ruin her father's business?

"I hadn't noticed," Emily replied sourly, spreading the thick yellow paste on a white rag.

"Hadn't noticed!" Tarsy shrieked, throwing herself against the workbench at Emily's elbow, bending at the waist to gush in Emily's face. "Hadn't noticed those . . . those bulging arms! And that face! And those eyes! Emily, my *grandmother* would have noticed, and she's got cataracts. Mercy sakes, those lashes . . . those limpid pools . . . those drooping lids . . . why, when he looked at me I went absolutely limp." Tarsy affected a swoon, falling forward across the workbench like a dying ballerina, overturning a bottle of carbolic acid with an outflung hand.

"Tarsy, would you mind going limp somewhere else?" Emily righted the bottle. "And how could you notice all that when you only passed him on the street?"

"A girl's *got* to notice things like that if she doesn't want to live her life as an old maid. Honestly, Emily, don't tell me you didn't notice how good-looking he is."

Emily picked up the poultice and headed for the main part of the barn with Tarsy at her heels, still rhapsodizing.

"I'll bet he's got fifty eyelashes for every one of Jerome's. And when he smiles he gets a dimple in his left cheek. And his lips—oh, Emily." Tarsy appeared about to be laid low by another near-collapse, then popped out of it to demand, "Tell me everything you know about him. Everything! Which horse is his? What's he doing here? Where did he come from? Is he staying?" Tarsy folded her hands along her chest, squeezed her eyelids closed, and lifted her face. "Oh, please, God, let him stay!"

Entering Sergeant's stall, Emily said, "You're wasting your time, Tarsy. He's engaged."

"Engaged!" Tarsy wailed. "Are you you sure?"

Squatting to strap the poultice to Sergeant's foot, Emily added, "He mentioned a fiancée."

"Oh, horse puckey!" the blonde pouted, stamping her foot. "Now I *will* end up an old maid!"

Though Tarsy was Emily's best friend, there were times when Emily thought the girl hadn't a brain in her head. She was an inveterate flirt, constantly vocalizing her fear of being an old maid when there was about as little chance of that happening as of Sergeant strapping this poultice on himself. But Tarsy was fond of agonizing over the possibility, sitting on Emily's porch swing or in her bedroom, or coming here to the livery stable and flinging her body about as if in near-despair, waxing melodramatic about how lonely life would be at fifty when she was a childless, gray-haired spinster living alone sewing gloves. It wasn't Tarsy's fault she was born needing constant compliments in order to be happy. Or that she'd been endowed with a bent toward melodrama. Emily found both traits amusing and irritating, by turns, especially in light of Tarsy's ability to charm men. For Tarsy, too, had fifty eyelashes for every one of Jerome Berryman's, and poor Jerome was smitten with each one of hers, as were several other local swains. She had reams of bouncing blond hair, a beautiful heart-shaped face highlighted by her abundently fringed brown eyes, tiny bones, and a nearly nonexistent waist that drew second glances like a field of blooming buckwheat draws honeybees.

But, as always, she wanted one more bee.

"Emily, tell me about him anyway, *pleeze*."

"I don't know much except that he's staying and I'm not too happy about it. He's already seen Loucks about buying property and he intends to build a livery stable and go into competition with Papa."

Tarsy came out of her self-absorption long enough to cover her lips in dismay. "Oh, dear."

"Yes. Oh, dear."

"Whatever is your papa going to do?"

"What can we do? It's a free country, he says."

"You mean he isn't upset?"

"*I'm* the one who's upset!" Emily finished doctoring Sergeant, stood, and wiped her hands agitatedly. "Papa's got enough to worry about with Mama getting worse. And now this." She related what had transpired the previous day, ending, "So if you hear where he intends to put up his livery stable, I'd appreciate your letting us know."

But before the day was out Emily learned for herself. She was in the office studying, sitting Indian-fashion on the cot with her shoulders curled against the wall, one hand on the sleeping cat and a book in her lap, when Jeffcoat himself appeared in the doorway.

She glanced up and her eyes iced over.

"Oh, it's you."

"Good afternoon, Miss Walcott." He surveyed her unladylike pose while she defiantly refused to alter it on his behalf. A grin unbalanced his mouth as he tipped his hat, and she cursed Tarsy for being right: he did have a dimple in his left cheek and his eyelashes were devilishly thick and long, and he had a disarmingly attractive mouth. And dressed in the same shirt with the missing sleeves, his bulging biceps were as conspicuous as the spine of the Big Horns. But she sensed a cockiness in his unconventional attire, a flaunting of masculinity to which a gentleman would not stoop: his tall black boots led to high-waisted black britches with bright red suspenders that looked quite superfluous on pants that tight. But above all he flaunted those muscular arms, framed by the threads of blue chambray where the sleeve had been chewed off at the armhole. Oh, and didn't he know how to pose the whole collection to best advantage, standing with feet wide-spread, hands hooked at his waist, as if to say, take a look, lady.

"What do you want?" she demanded rudely.

"My horses. I'll need them for a few hours."

Emily flopped her book facedown, sending the cat bounding away. She bounced off the cot and strode for the door at full steam, refusing to excuse herself as she forced Jeffcoat to jump back or be flattened. He jumped. Then whistled as if singed and ambled farther into the empty office to glance amusedly at the cover of her book. *The Science of Veterinary Medicine* by R. C. Barnum. The amusement left his face, replaced by interest as he turned the volume over, cocked his head, and perused the header on the open page: "Diseases of the Generative Organs of Both the Horse and Mare." His eyes wandered across the cot, across the rag rug, which still held a depression from her rump, to a sheaf of papers that had been at her knee. With a single finger he pivoted them and saw what appeared to be a prepared quiz. He read: *What is the most common cause of barrenness in mares and what is its treatment?*

Beneath it she had filled in the answer: *An acid secretion of the genital organs or a retention of the afterbirth. The most common treatment is with yeast as follows: Mix 2 heaping tsp. of yeast into a pint of boiled water, keep warm for 5 or 6 hours. Flush affected parts first with warm water, then inject with yeast. Animal should be mated from 2–6 hours after treatment.*

His eyebrows rose. So the little smart-mouth knew her stuff!

A hand reached around and snatched the papers from under his nose. "This is a private office!"

He neither flinched nor blustered but turned loosely to watch her bury the papers beneath a ledger on the littered desk. She was dressed once again in britches and the wool cap, but this time the leather apron was absent and he saw that he'd been mistaken; she did have breasts after all, plum sized and minimized by a perfectly atrocious open-collared boy's shirt the color of horse dung. He made sure his survey of her breasts was completed before she whipped around to confront him with her fists akimbo.

"You're a nosy, rude man, Mr. Jeffcoat!"

"And your parents could have taught you a few manners, Miss Walcott."

"I don't appreciate people sticking their noses into my personal business, and you've done it twice now! I'll thank you not to do it again!"

For a moment he considered making some comment on her mode of dress, compliment her on how the hue of the shirt did wonders for her complexion, just to nettle her. Actually, she looked quite fetching with her feet spraddled, her fists bunched, and her blue eyes bright and angry. It was a curiosity to find a woman so feisty and outspoken in an age when the ideal female was purported to be one of dulcet voice and retiring comportment. She possessed neither, and it fascinated him. But in the end Jeffcoat decided he might need the use of her veterinary medicine book sometime, so he decided to soothe the waters.

"I'm sorry, Miss Walcott."

"If you want your horses, follow me. I don't see any reason why I should get them both out while you dally in here reading other people's mail." She strode for the door, calling back, "What do you want them hitched to, your own wagon?"

"Are all the women in this town as friendly as you?" he called, following.

"I said what do you want them hitched to?"

"Nothing. Just harness 'em and I'll drive 'em out."

She returned, hands on hips, to advise him with an air of long-suffering, "I don't *just harness* them, you help me."

"So what am I paying you for?"

"You want your horses or not, Jeffcoat?"

Taking a lead rope, she tossed him another, pushed aside a pole barrier to a stall, and nodded toward an adjacent one. "Liza's in there. Get her."

Bossy young thing, he thought, grabbing the rope on the fly. But before he could say so she disappeared and he dropped the pole from Liza's stall and stepped inside. "Hiya, girl." He gave Liza a critical look-over, rubbing her withers and shoulders. She'd been brushed down as ordered; her hide was smooth and flat. Miss Britches might have the tongue of an adder but she knew how to put away a horse.

"Liza looks good," he offered, backing the horse into the corridor where Emily was already waiting with Rex. "I can tell you spent plenty of time brushing her."

For his efforts he received a scowl that said clearly, only an idiot abuses good horseflesh. With the snap lines secured, she turned away haughtily, leading the way to the rear of the barn where carriages and wagons were stored. Inside a separate tack room the equipage hung on wooden pegs. They took his gear down together—she sullen, he amused—and carried it to the main aisle where they began in silence to harness Rex and Liza. When the job was done, she headed for the office, offering not a word of farewell.

"I'll have them back tonight," he called, "but you can charge me for the full day."

"You can bet your shabby shirt I will!" she returned without a backward glance, and disappeared into her lair.

He glanced down at his bare arms, grinned, and thought, all right, so we're even, young fellow.

Inside the office, sitting cross-legged again with the book on her lap, Emily found her concentration shattered. Her stomach was jumping and her tongue ached from being pressed so tensely to the roof of her mouth. Damn his insufferable hide! When she tried to read, his criticism seemed to superimpose itself upon the words in the book. Infernal, distasteful man! She heard him cluck to the team, heard their hooves clop across the hard dirt floor and move up the street. When the sound disappeared she sat with her head against the wall and her eyes closed, agitated as no man had managed to make her before. Where was he taking the horses without the wagon? And how dare he criticize her papa, whom he didn't even know! His own manners left plenty to be desired!

Twenty minutes later she'd managed to refocus her attentions on her studies when a screech distracted her. She cocked her head and listened—it sounded like metal on stones. *Metal on stones?* Suspicion dawned and she tore outside, halted at the wide double doors, and gaped at the jarring sight of Jeffcoat leveling a lot not a hundred feet down the street on the opposite side. He had rented Loucks's steel grader, a monstrous affair painted parsley green that kept the town's streets bladed during summer and plowed in winter, and made Loucks some fairly decent rental money with each lot he sold. The implement had a long-nosed frame upon which the metal blade was tilted by a pair of upright wheels and attached cables. Jeffcoat stood between the wheels on a railed metal platform driving his team like some misplaced Roman gladiator.

Emily was marching toward him the moment her outrage blossomed.

"Just what do you think you're doing, Jeffcoat!" she bellowed, approaching him as the rig moved away from her, rolling dirt to one side.

He glanced over his shoulder and smiled, but kept the team moving. "Leveling my land, Miss Walcott!"

"In a pig's eye!" She stomped along off his right flank while he rode three feet above her.

"No, in J. D. Loucks's grader!"

It was a toss-up who screeched louder, the rocks or Emily. "How dare you pick this spot right on top of my father's!"

"It was for sale."

"So were twenty others on the outskirts of town where we wouldn't have to look at you!"

"This's prime land. Close to the business section. It's a much better buy than the ones out there."

He reached the far edge of his site and brought the team about, heading back toward Emily.

"What'd you pay for it?" she shouted.

"Now who's sticking their nose into other people's business, Miss Walcott?" While he spoke he concentrated on adjusting the two huge metal wheels. His muscles stood out in ridges as the cables groaned and the blade tilted to the proper angle. When he drove past Emily the blade sent a furl of soil cascading across her ankles.

She jumped over it and roared, "How much!"

"Three dollars and fifty cents for the first lot and fifty cents each for the other three."

"Other three! You mean you bought four?"

"Two for my business. Two for my home. Good price." He grinned down at her while she stalked along beside him, shouting above the screech of steel on stone.

"I'll buy them all from you for double what you paid."

"Oh, I'd have to get more than double. After all, this one's already been improved."

"Jeffcoat, stop that blasted team this minute so I can talk to you!"

"Whoa!" The team halted and into the sudden silence he said, "Yes, Miss Walcott," flipped the reins around a flywheel, and bounced down beside her. "At your service, Miss Walcott."

His choice of words, drawled through his insufferable grin, made her agonizingly aware that she was dressed in her brother's gnawed-up cap and britches. She scowled menacingly. "This town is only big enough for one livery stable and you know it!"

"I'm sorry, Miss Walcott, but I disagree. It's spreading faster than gossip." He wiped his brow on a forearm, tugged off a pair of dirty leather gloves, and flapped them toward the north end of Main Street. "Just look at the building going on. Yesterday when I rode through I counted four houses and two businesses under construction, and by my count the town's got two harnessmakers. If there's business enough for two harnessmakers, there's business enough for two stables. And a school already up, and I hear tell the next thing's going to be a church. That sounds like a town with a future to me. I'm sorry if I have to run your father a little competition, but I'm not out to ruin him, I assure you."

"And what about Charles? You've already talked to Charles!"

"Charles?"

"Charles Bliss. You intend to hire him to help you put up your buildings!"

"You have some objection to that, too?"

She objected to everything this man had precipitated in the last twenty-four hours. She objected to his brazenness. To his choice of lots. To his grin and his sweaty smell and his tight trousers, and his cocky good looks, and his stupid unnecessary suspenders and the way he set Tarsy in a dither, and the fact that he tore the sleeves off his shirts, and the more distressing fact that both she and her father would have to look at his damned livery stable out the office window of their own for the rest of their lives!

She decided to tell him so.

"I object, Mr. Jeffcoat, to everything you do and are!" She thrust her nose so close to his that she could see herself reflected in his black pupils. "And particularly to your putting Charles into a position where he must choose loyalties. He's been a friend of our family since we were both knee high."

For the first time she saw the spark of anger in Jeffcoat's cobalt blue eyes. His jaw took on the same tense bulge as his biceps, and his voice had a hard edge. "I've traveled over a thousand miles, left my family and everyone I hold dear, ridden into this backwoods cow town with honorable intentions, honest money, and a strong back. I've bought land and hired a carpenter and I plan to take up my trade in peaceable fashion and become a permanent, law-abiding citizen of Sheridan. So, what do they send me as a welcoming committee but a sassy-mouthed young whelp who needs to have her mouth washed out with soap and be shown what a petticoat is! Understand this, Miss Britches . . ." Nose to nose, he backed her up as he spoke. "I'm getting mighty damned tired of you raising objections to my every move! I'm not only tired of your orneriness, I'm in a hurry to get my place raised, and I don't intend to take any more sass from an impertinent young tomboy like you. Now, I'll thank you, Miss Walcott, to get off my property!"

He pulled on his gloves and swung away, leaving her red-faced and speechless. With a deft leap he mounted the railed platform of the grader, took the reins, and shouted, "Hey, giddap, there!"

And with that their enmity was sealed.

The following day was Sunday. Church services were held in Coffeen Hall, the only building in town with enough adult-sized chairs to accommodate the worshipers from mixed denominations who congregated and were led in prayer by Reverend Vasseler, who'd recently arrived from New York to organize an Episcopal congregation. His voice was mellifluous, his message inspired; thus he'd already attracted an impressive number of families to his fold. The hall was crowded when Reverend Vasseler began the service by leading the gathering with the hymn, "All Praise, All Glory Now We Sing." Standing between Charles and her father, Emily sang in a doubtful soprano. Halfway through the song she felt eyes probing and turned to find Tom Jeffcoat in an aisle seat at the rear, singing and watching her. She snapped her mouth shut and stared at him for a full ten seconds.

"*. . . worship now our heav'nly king . . .*"

He sang without benefit of a hymnal, belting out the notes robustly, startling her. She had been prepared to see him as the Devil incarnate, but finding him singing hymns at her own church service cast him in quite the opposite light. She snapped her attention to the front and vowed not to give him so much as another glance.

The hymn ended and they sat. Reverend Vasseler gave a short sermon on the Good Samaritan, then announced that J. D. Loucks had donated a lot on East Loucks Street for the building of a real church. Smiles and murmurs accompanied a general scanning of the room as members of the congregation picked out Loucks and beamed approval. The minister appealed to all the men to do their fair share. He outlined a building plan by which the structure would be up and roofed by midsummer, and totally completed by autumn. Joseph Zollinski had volunteered to organize the volunteer building crew, and Charles Bliss to oversee the work, and all the men present were to see either one of them after the service to volunteer at least a day of their time.

When the service ended Charles stayed to organize volunteers while Emily left the hall on her father's arm. Halfway to the door, Emily was caught by Tarsy, who grabbed her arm and whispered breathlessly, "He's here!"

"I know."

"Introduce us."

"I will not!"

"Oh, Emily . . . pleeeeze!"

"If you want to meet him go introduce yourself, but don't expect me to. Not after yesterday!"

"But, Emily, he's absolutely the most luscious creature I've—"

"Well, good morning, Tarsy," Edwin interrupted.

"Oh, good morning, Mr. Walcott. I was just saying to Emily that the neighborly thing to do is to welcome newcomers to the town, wouldn't you say?"

Edwin smiled. "I would."

"So would you mind introducing me to Mr. Jeffcoat?"

Edwin was familiar with Tarsy's flighty ways and thought little of her suggestion. He was too congenial a person to snub anybody—even his competitor. Outside in the sunlight of the fair June morning Edwin guided Tarsy to Jeffcoat while Emily hung back, pretending disinterest in the entire episode, excusing herself by saying she'd wait near the door for Charles.

But she kept one eye on the introductions.

"Mr. Jeffcoat, hold up there!" called Edwin.

Jeffcoat turned in mid-stride and smiled congenially. "Ah, good morning, Edwin."

"You look like a man in a hurry."

"I've got a building to put up. I'm afraid I can't waste a day like this, whether it's the Lord's day or not." He cocked his head at the faultless blue sky.

Edwin did likewise. "Can't say I blame you. It is a fine day."

"Yessir, it is."

"I'd like you to meet my daughter's friend, Miss Tarsy Fields."

Jeffcoat transferred his attention to the pretty blonde. "Miss Fields."

"Mr. Jeffcoat." She bobbed and flashed her most dazzling smile. "I'm positively delighted to meet you."

Jeffcoat had been around enough women to recognize eager interest when it stood pent up before him. She was curvier, prettier, and more polite than Emily Walcott, who stood by the door, feigning indifference. He extended his hand and, when Miss Fields's was in it, gave her face the lingering attention such beauty deserved, and her fingers enough pressure to suggest reciprocal interest.

"I must confess," Tarsy admitted, "I asked Mr. Walcott to introduce us."

Jeffcoat laughed and held her hand longer than strictly polite. "I'm glad you did. I believe we passed each other in front of the hotel yesterday, didn't we? You were wearing a peach-colored dress."

Tarsy's pleasure doubled. She touched her collarbone and opened her lips in the beguiling way she often practiced in the mirror.

Jeffcoat smiled down into her stunning brown eyes with stunners of his own and refrained from allowing them to pass lower. But he was fully aware of her flattering rose frock and how it endowed each of her estimable assets.

"And you, I believe, were wearing a shirt without sleeves."

He laughed with a flash of straight, white teeth. "I find it's cooler that way."

In the silence that followed, while they allowed their eyes to tarry and tally, Jeffcoat recognized her for exactly what she was: a flirt looking for a husband. Well, he was willing to oblige with the flirting. But when it came to matrimony, he was admittedly aisle-shy, and with good reason.

"I hear you're a liveryman, Mr. Jeffcoat," Tarsy ventured.

"Yes, I am." His gaze drifted to Walcott, still at Tarsy's elbow, and on to Emily. He caught her watching, but immediately she snapped her attention away.

"And a blacksmith," Edwin added.

"My goodness, a blacksmith, too. How enterprising of you. But you must promise not to interfere with Mr. Walcott's business." Tarsy took Edwin's arm and smiled up at him, wrinkling her nose attractively. "After all, he was here first." Again she shifted her smile to the younger man. "My father is the local barber, so I'm sure you'll meet him soon. Until you do, I thought it only neighborly to extend a welcome on behalf of our family, and let you know that if there's anything we can do to help you get settled, we'd be delighted."

"That's most gracious of you."

"You must stop by the barbershop and introduce yourself. Papa knows everything about this town. Anything you need to know, just ask him."

"I'll do that."

"Well, I'm sure we'll meet again soon." She extended her gloved hand.

"I hope so," he said charmingly, accepting it with another lingering squeeze.

She sent him a parting smile warm enough to sprout daisies in the dead of winter and he responded with a flirtatious grin while speaking to Edwin.

"Thank you for stopping me, Edwin. You've definitely made it a memorable morning."

As they parted, Jeffcoat again found Emily Walcott watching. Perversely, he gave her a nod and tipped his hat. She offered not so much as a blink, but stared at him as if he were made of window glass. She was wearing a dress this morning, but nothing so pretty or colorful as Tarsy Fields's; a hat, too—a flat little specimen nearly as unattractive as the boy's wool cap had been. She had hair as black as his own, but it was hitched up into some sort of utilitarian twist that said very clearly she hadn't time for female fussing. She was long-waisted, slim, and, as always, sour-faced.

To Jeffcoat's surprise, she suddenly smiled. Not at him but at Charles Bliss, who stepped out of Coffeen Hall and took her hand—not her elbow, her hand—winning a full-fledged smile that Jeffcoat would have sworn her incapable of giving. Even a stranger could see it was unpracticed, unaffected. No batting lashes, no syrupy posturing such as Tarsy Fields put on. Jeffcoat observed the interchange with interest.

"We can go now," he heard Bliss say, turning Emily in his direction. "I'm sorry it took so long."

"I didn't mind waiting, and anyway, Papa was busy visiting. Oh, I'm so glad it's sunny, Charles, aren't you?"

"I ordered it for you," he said, and they laughed as they headed for the street.

"Good morning, Tom," Charles greeted, in passing.

"Hello, Charles. Miss Walcott."

She nodded silently and her eyes turned glacial. They moved past and Charles called back, raising a hand, "See you tomorrow morning, bright and early."

"Yessir, bright and early," replied Jeffcoat. He overheard Charles ask Emily, "What time should I pick you up?"

And her reply, "Give me an hour and a half so I can . . ."

Their voices faded and Jeffcoat heard no more. Looking after them as they moved away with their heads close together, he thought wryly, well, well, so the tomboy has a beau.

The tomboy had more than a beau. Charles Bliss was a devoted servant who would have done anything for her. He had first fallen in love with her when they were ten and thirteen years old but had waited to declare it until she was sixteen and had brought him the news that her family was moving to Wyoming.

"If you're going, I'm going," Charles had declared unequivocally.

"But, Charles—"

"Because I'm going to marry you when you're old enough."

"M—marry me?"

"Of course. Didn't you know that?"

Maybe she always had, for she'd stared at him, then laughed, and they'd hugged for the first time and she'd told him how very, very happy she was that he was coming. And she had remained happy, until earlier this year when she'd turned eighteen and he'd proposed seriously for the first time. He'd asked her twice since, and she was becoming guilt-ridden from refusing so often. Yet Charles had become a habit that was hard to break.

When he came at noon to pick her up for their picnic she found herself more than anxious to get away with him. He gave a sharp, shrill whistle of announcement as he jogged across the front yard, and slammed inside without knocking. "Hey, Emily, you ready? Oh, hello, everybody!"

Edwin and Frankie were both in the kitchen. Frankie ducked a mock punch, then collared Charles from behind. Charles bent forward with the boy on his back, and spun around twice before dumping his burden off.

"Where you two going?" Frankie wanted to know, hanging on to Charles's arms.

"That'd be telling."

"Can I go?"

"Nope, not this time." Charles made a fist and pressed it dead center on Frankie's forehead, fending him off affectionately. "We're taking the shay for two."

"Aww, gee . . . come on, Charles."

"Nope. This time it's just Emily and me."

Edwin inquired, "Is everything all right at the stable?"

"Yup. I left the back door open. Nobody's around." Charles rambled in and out of their livery stable as he did in and out of their house, and, naturally, any time he had need of a rig there was no thought of charging him. "How's Mrs. Walcott doing today?"

"A little tired, I'm afraid, and somewhat forlorn. She misses going to church with us."

"Tell her Emily and I will bring her some wildflowers if we find any. Are you ready, Emily?"

Emily removed an apron and hung it behind the pantry door. "Are you sure there's nothing I can bring?"

"It's supposed to be your day off. Just turn your cuffs down and follow me. I've got everything in the rig."

It was a perfect day for an outing—clear, warm, and windless. The Big Horns appeared as multiple tiers of blue rising to greet the sky along a clear, undulating horizon line. They headed southwest into the foothills, toward Red Grade Springs, following Little Goose Creek until they left the valley to begin climbing. Ahead, the jagged top of Black Tooth Mountain appeared and disappeared as they paralleled draws and rounded the bases of rolling green hills. They startled a herd of white-rumped antelopes and watched them spring away across a green rise. They disturbed a jackrabbit who bounded off on oversized feet to disappear into a clump of sage. They reached the vast forests where the pinery crews had cleared great open tracts and cut skidding roads. The smell was spicy, the road quiet with its bed of needles. At Hurlburn Creek they forded, rounded a curve, and broke into the open above an uplands meadow where the creek looped around nearly upon itself. In the center of the loop, Charles brought the team to a halt.

The sylvan spot, so perfect, so peaceful, brought Emily immediately to her feet. She stood in the buggy, shaded her eyes, and gazed about in rapture.

"Oh, Charles, however did you find it?"

"I was up here last week buying lumber."

"Oh, it's beautiful."

"It's called Curlew Hill."

"Curlew Hill," she repeated, then fell silent to appreciate the scene before her.

The creek rushed out of the mountains, purling over rocks that shone like silver coins, smoothed by years of liquid motion. The water made a tight horseshoe bend enclosing a field of thick bluegrass that gave way to tufts of feathery sheep fescue nearer the water. In certain places the creek was outlined by balsam poplars, their new olive-yellow leaves filling the air with a sweet resinous scent. Huddling beneath them were thickets of wild gooseberry and hawthorn blooming in clusters of pink. In the distance a dense patch of golden banner spread across the meadow in a mass of yellow, following summer up to the tree line.

"Oh, look." Emily pointed. "Yellow peas." She called the wildflowers by their common name. "After we've eaten we must walk out and pick some. They're Mother's favorites."

Charles dropped off the wagon into grass a foot high, and Emily followed. From the storage box beneath the seat he drew a hamper and blanket, which, when spread, remained aloft on the sturdy green stems of grass. On hands and knees they flattened it, laughing, then settled cross-legged in their warm nest. Charles opened the hamper, displaying each item with a flourish. "Smoked sausage! Cheese! Rye bread! Pickled beets! Tinned peaches! And iced tea!" He set the fruit jar down and admitted, "It's not fried chicken and apple pie, but we bachelors eat pretty simple."

"It's a feast when you don't have to cook it."

They ate the plain food while a tattler called in tinkling notes from its hidden spot at the stream's edge, and overhead a sparrow hawk hunted, drifting on an updraft, cocking his head at them. Nearby an electric-blue bottlefly buzzed. The sun was beatific, captured in their bowl like warm yellow tea in a cup.

Their stomachs filled, Emily and Charles grew heavy with thought.

"Charles?"

There were things Emily needed to talk about, painful things that somehow seemed approachable out here where the sun and grass and flowers and birdsong made the formidable seem less dire.

"Hmm?"

For moments she was silent, toying with two breadcrumbs caught in a fold of her skirt. She lifted her eyes to the distant yellow flowers and told him quietly, "My mother is going to die."

Charles changed his mind about the bite of bread he'd been about to take and laid it aside. "I guessed as much."

"Nobody's ever said it in so many words, but we all know. She's already begun coughing blood."

He reached across the picnic hamper and took her hand. "I'm sorry, Emily."

"It . . . it felt good to say it at last." To no one but Charles would she have been able. With no one but Charles would she have allowed her tears to show.

"Yes, I know."

"Poor Papa." She turned her hand over and twined her

fingers with Charles's because he understood her devastation as no one else. Again she lifted her eyes to his. "I think it's hardest on Papa. I've seen him crying on the porch at night when he thinks everybody else is asleep."

"Oh, Emily." Charles squeezed her hand tighter.

Suddenly she forced a bright expression. "But guess what?"

"What?"

"We're going to have a houseguest."

"Who?" Charles released her hand and laid his plate in the hamper.

"Mother's cousin Fannie, whom she hasn't seen since the year she and Papa got married. She was due in today. Papa is probably picking her up at the stage depot right now."

"Fannie of the outrageous letters?"

Emily laughed. "The same. I'm curious to meet her. She's always seemed so worldly, so . . . so unfettered by convention. Papa says she certainly is—he knows her, too, of course, since they all grew up in Massachusetts. After all these years of outlandish letters I'm not sure what to expect. But she's coming to take care of Mother."

"Good. That'll take the pressure off you."

"Charles, can I tell you something?"

"Anything."

She pleated and repleated the fabric of her skirt as if reluctant to divulge her thought. "Sometimes I feel guilty because I tried very hard to take over Mother's chores, but I . . . well, I don't care much for cooking and cleaning. I'd much rather be with the horses." She abandoned the pleating and turned sharply away from Charles, displeased with herself. "Oh, that sounds so self-indulgent, and I don't want to be that way. Really, I don't."

"Emily." He took her shoulders and pivoted her around to face him. "You'll like housework better when the house is your own."

She stared into his familiar eyes and answered frankly, "I doubt it, Charles."

Disappointment touched his face, then he swallowed and asked in a pained voice, "Why do you fight it so? How many more times will I have to ask?"

"Oh, Charles . . ." She shrugged free of his touch and placed her plate in the hamper.

"No, don't avoid the issue again." He set the hamper aside

and moved closer to her, face to face, hip to hip. "I want to marry you, Emily."

"You want to marry a woman who's just admitted she hates housework?" She forced a chuckle, unable to meet his gaze. "What kind of wife would I make?"

"You're the only one I've ever wanted." He took her by both arms. "The only one," he repeated softly.

At his words her eyes lifted. "I know, Charles, but with Mother ill I don't think—"

"You've just said Fannie is coming to take care of her, so why must we wait? Emily, I love you so . . ." His caresses became more insistent. "I rattle around in that great big house of mine wishing you were in it with me. I built it for you, don't you know that?"

She did know, and it added to her sense of obligation.

"I want you in it . . . and our children," he pleaded in a low, throaty voice, transferring his hands to her shoulders, rubbing his thumbs over her collarbones.

"Our children?" she repeated, feeling a shaft of panic at the thought. Taking care of a stableful of horses she could handle, but she felt totally unprepared for motherhood. Another thought came and a blush warmed her chest and rose to her cheeks. She tried to imagine herself begetting children with Charles but could not. He was too much like a brother for it to be seemly.

"I want children, Emily, don't you?"

"Right now I want a certificate of veterinarian medicine much more than I want children."

"All right—a year, two years. How long will it take you to get it? We'll wait to get married until you've finished your course. But in the meantime, we'll announce that we're betrothed. Please say yes, Emily." As he lowered his face toward hers he repeated in a whisper, "Please . . ." Their mouths touched as he drew her close, raised one knee, and lay her in the crook of his lap. She felt her breast flatten against his chest, and his arms slip to her back. His hands spread upon it and began moving. His elbow brushed the side of her breast and sent a spear of reaction to its tip. Goose bumps shivered up her nape, which he circled with his fingers. She rested a palm on his breast and felt his heart ramming against it, and wondered—if she waited long enough, would the same thing happen to her own?

Then Charles did the most unexpected thing. He opened his lips and touched her with his tongue, holding absolutely still everywhere else, waiting for her reaction. The warm wet contact sent a jolt of fire to her extremities. He rode his tongue along the seam of her lips, wetting them as if to dissolve some invisible stitches holding them sealed. She forgot about the prickliness of his mustache as he touched her teeth, drew wider circles, inscribing upon her a message that seemed shocking. Yet her virgin body hearkened to it. Curiously, timidly, her tongue reached out to touch him, too. She felt the difference in him immediately. He shuddered, and expelled a great gust of breath against her cheek, and held her hard against him while their tongues tasted each other for the first time and increased their ardor in a great, grand rush.

This, then, was the forbidden, the reason for all the veiled warnings, a thing only husbands and wives were supposed to do. His head began moving, his mouth opened wider, and his hands caressed her waist, her spine. She allowed it, partook, because it was the first time and she had not expected such an immediate response. Phrases from the Bible crossed her mind—sins of the flesh, lust—now she understood. His hand began moving toward her breast and she quickly drew back.

"No, Charles . . . stop."

His eyes glittered, his cheeks blazed; a lock of hair had fallen on his forehead.

"I love you, Emily," he uttered through strident breaths.

"But this is forbidden. We must not do it till we're married."

Surprise wiped his face clean of passion and replaced it with elation. "Then you'll do it? Oh, Emily, you really mean it?" He embraced her fiercely, rocked and hugged her till the breath whooshed from her lungs. "You've made me the happiest man on earth!" He was ecstatic. "And I'll make you the happiest woman."

So she had agreed. Or had she? Perhaps it had been an intentional slip of the tongue, a way to agree without having to agree. Whatever her intention, wrapped in Charles's arms Emily knew there was no reneging. How could she say to this glad man, No, Charles, I didn't mean it that way? And must she not love him to have allowed such a kiss, and to have experienced such a forbidden thrill? And wasn't it almost predestined that she marry him? And to whom else in the world could she talk as she could to Charles? And with whom could she trust her tears? If that wasn't love, what was?

But rocking in his arms she opened her eyes to a blue sky and a hawk still circling and felt again a ricochet of panic. *What am I doing, hawk?* She squeezed her eyes closed and willed away her apprehension. *Oh, don't be silly, who else would you ever marry but Charles?*

He kissed her once more, jubilant, then cupped her face and looked into her eyes with adoration so palpable she felt small for her misgivings.

"I love you so much, Emily, so very, very much."

What else could she say? "I love you too, Charles." And it was true, she told herself, *it was!*

He placed a light, reverent kiss on her lips, then rested his fingertips on her jaws and looked into her eyes. "I've dreamed of this day for years. I've been dead certain for so long. I even told your father when I was thirteen that I wanted to marry you some day; did he ever tell you that?"

"No." She laughed, but it felt forced.

"Well, I did." He, too, chuckled at the memory, then his face took on a satisfied expression. "Your mother and father are going to be so pleased."

That much she knew indubitably and it was a great reassurance. "Yes, they will."

"Let's go home and tell them."

"All right."

They packed up their picnic gear and made a quick trip across the meadow for golden banner before heading home. Charles chattered all the way, already making plans. Emily held the flowers and replied to his exuberant questions. But long before they reached town she realized she'd been squeezing the flower stems so tightly they'd wilted and stained her palm green.

Chapter 4

FANNIE COOPER WAS due to arrive on the 3:00 P.M. stage from Buffalo, thirty miles to the south. Emily had promised to be back by three but at ten minutes before the hour she hadn't returned. Frankie was gone fishing and Edwin tried his best to appear unruffled as he fetched a clean bed jacket for Josie and helped her rebraid her hair.

"You'd better go, Edwin," Josie said.

He pulled his watch from his vest pocket, needlessly flipped open the cover—he already knew the exact time—and agreed, "Yes, I'd better. When those children get back here they're going to get a good talking-to."

"Now, Edwin, you know Fannie isn't one to s . . . stand on formalities. She would rather have them off enjoying themselves than pay . . . paying duty calls on their o . . . old-maid cousin."

He pocketed the watch, patted Josie's shoulder, and asked, "You're sure you'll be all right?"

"Yes. Just help me into b . . . bed, then you must hur . . . hurry."

It had been months since he'd seen Josie this excited about anything. It robbed her of breath. Leaning over her, Edwin smiled as he lifted the coverlets to her hips. "If the stage is on time I should have her back here in twenty minutes. Now you rest so you'll have plenty of strength to visit with her."

She nodded, settling back on the pillows stiffly as if to keep her hair undisturbed. He smiled into her eyes and squeezed her hand before turning to leave.

"Edwin?" She spoke anxiously.

"Yes, dear?"

When he turned, she was reaching out a hand. He put his in it and received a squeeze. "I'm so happy Fan . . . nie is coming."

He bent and touched his lips to her fingers. "So am I."

Once free of the room he paused at the top of the steps, took a deep breath, and, with eyes closed, pressed both palms against his diaphragm. *So am I*. Did he mean it? Yes. Lord help him, yes. He took the steps at a jog, like a twenty-year-old.

Downstairs he sidetracked into the dining room, where the mahogany sideboard contained the only mirror on the main floor. It was built in at rib height, separating the upper glass from the lower dresser. He ducked down to check his appearance in the beveled glass. His cheeks were flushed, his eyes too bright, his breath fast and shallow. Damn, had Josie noticed? This was insanity, trying to fool her. Why, Fannie wasn't even here yet and his hands were shaking as if with chills. Abruptly he made two tight fists, but it helped little, so he pressed their butts against the sharp dresser edge and locked his elbows, feeling his heart sledge until it seemed it would rattle the dishes above his head.

His intentions had been good: to have the children with him when he went to collect Fannie, to avoid at all costs their being alone. But it hadn't worked out that way. *Emily, I was relying on you! Where the devil are you? You promised you'd be back by now!*

Only his thumping heart answered.

He checked his reflection once more, happy it was Sunday, and that he'd been able to leave on his worsted suit after church and hadn't had to worry about how it would look if he changed clothes in the middle of a work day. He reworked his black four-in-hand tie, tugged at his lapels, and ran a hand over the graying hair at his temples. Will she be gray, too? Will I look old to her? Are her hands shaking like mine and her heart pounding as she rides toward me? When our eyes meet for the first time will we see breathlessness and blushes in each other, or will we be lucky and see nothing?

What do you think, Edwin, when your hands are already sweating and your heart is galloping like the leader of a stampede?

He dried his palms on his jacket tails, then spread them wide, studying their backs and their palms. Great, wide, callused hams that had been a young man's hands—soft and narrow and unmarked—when they'd first held Fannie. Hands with three chipped nails, ingrained dirt, and scars meted out by years of hard work; two crooked fingers on the left upon which a horse had stepped; a scar on the back of the right from a run-in with barbed wire; and the ever-present rim of black beneath his nails that he was unable to clear, no matter how hard he scrubbed. He hurried to the kitchen, pumped a basinful of water, and scrubbed them again, but to no avail. All he had done was make himself late for the stage.

Grabbing his black bowler off the hat-tree in the parlor he took the porch steps at a trot. Within half a block he was winded and had to slow down lest he arrive at the stage depot panting.

The Rock Creek Stage—better known as the jerky—pulled in at the hotel at the same time as Edwin. It stopped amid a billow of dust, the clatter of sixteen hooves, and the roaring of Jake McGiver, an ex-bullwhacker who'd miraculously made it through the Indian Wars and last year's blizzards with neither arrow wound nor frostbite. "Whoa, you sons-o'-bitches," Jack bawled, hauling back on the reins, "before I make saddlebags out o' your mangy, flea-bit hides! Whoa, I said!"

And before the dust had settled, Fannie was peering up at McGiver from an open window, laughing, holding onto her mile-high hat. "Such language, Mr. McGiver! And such driving! Are you sure my bicycle is still on board?"

"Indeed it is, ma'am. Safe and sound!"

McGiver clambered onto the roof to begin untying both the bicycle and the baggage while Fannie opened the door.

Edwin hurried forward and was waiting when she bent to negotiate the small opening.

"Hello, Fannie."

She looked up and her mirthful face sobered. He thought he saw her breath catch, but immediately she brought back the wide smile and stepped down. "Edwin. My dear Edwin, you're really here."

He took her gloved hand and helped her down to find himself heartily hugged in the middle of Main Street. "How good it is to see you," she said at his ear, quickly backing away and studying him while continuing to squeeze both his hands. "My, you look wonderful. I worried that you might have gotten fat or bald, but you look superb."

So did she. Smiling, as he always pictured her, her hair faded from its earlier vibrant red to a soft peach color but still with its unruly natural curl that looked as if it were put in with tongs. It was—he knew—part of her own natural sizzle. Her hazel eyes had crow's-feet at the corners but more merriment and sparkle than a gypsy dance. She had retained the tiny waist of her teen years but her breast was fuller. The spare cut of her copper-colored traveling suit pointed out the fact, and Edwin felt a swell of pride that neither had she gotten fat nor lost her teeth or her inimitable spirit.

"I've wondered about you, too, but you're just as I remember you. Ahh, Fannie, what has it been? Twenty years?"

"Twenty-two." He knew as well as she but had intentionally miscalculated for the benefit of those looking on. When he would have pulled free she held him anchored with a two-handed grip, as if she had no notion it was as improper as the hug had been. "Imagine that, Edwin, we're middle-aged."

He chuckled and released himself under the pretext of having to close the stage door. "Middle-aged and riding bicycles, are we?"

"Bicycle—oh, my goodness, that's right!" She swung around and looked up, shading her eyes with one hand. "Be careful with that, Mr. McGiver! It's probably the only one for three hundred miles around."

McGiver's head appeared above their heads. "Here it comes, all in one piece!"

She reached up as if to take it herself, asking no help from Edwin.

He suddenly jumped. "Here, let me!"

"I've lived without a man's help for forty years. I'm perfectly capable."

"I'm sure you are, Fannie"—he had to move her bodily aside—"but I'll help just the same."

The contraption was passed into his hands and dropped to the ground with a thud. "Good Lord, Fannie, you can't mean to say you actually ride this thing. Why, it's heavier than a cannon!"

"Of course I ride it. And you will, too, as soon as I can teach you. You'll love it, Edwin. Keeps the legs firm and the blood healthy, and it's great for the lungs. There's nothing like it. I wonder if we could get Josie on it. Might do her wonders. Did I tell you about the trip to Gloucester?"

"Yes, in your last letter." Edwin found himself smiling already. She hadn't changed at all. Unpredictable and unconventional, and spirited as no other woman he'd ever known. He had grown so accustomed to Josie's weakness that Fannie's robust independence was startling. While he stood examining the bicycle she reached up as if to take the luggage Mr. McGiver was handing down.

Again Edwin had to interrupt. "*I'll* help Mr. McGiver with your luggage. You hold the bicycle!"

"All right, if you insist. But don't get bossy with me, Edwin, or we shan't get along at all. I'm not used to taking orders from men, you know."

As he reached up for the first dusty bag, he glanced over his shoulder to find her smirking like a leprechaun. The first bag was followed by a second, third, fourth and fifth. When her luggage sat in a circle at their feet he pushed back his bowler and, with his hands on his hips, scanned the collection of grips and trunks. "Good Lord, Fannie, all this?"

She arched one of her strawberry-blond eyebrows. "Why, of course, all that. A woman can't traipse out into the middle of no-man's-land with nothing more than the clothes on her back. Who knows *when* I'll get to a proper toggery again. And even if I did, I doubt that out here I could even *find* a pair of knickerbockers."

"Knickerbockers?"

"Kneepants. For riding the bicycle. Whatever would I do with all these bustles and petticoats in those wheels? Why, they'd get tangled in the spokes and I'd break every bone in my body. And I value my bones very highly, Edwin." She held out one arm and assessed it fondly. "They're still very serviceable bones. How are your bones, Edwin?"

He laughed and replied, "I can see Emily is going to love you. Let's get these off the street."

"Emily—I can't wait to meet her." While he transferred her baggage to the boardwalk, Fannie chattered. "What's she like? Is she dark like you? Did she get Josephine's seriousness? I hope not. Josie was always too serious for her own good. I told her so from the time we were ten years old. There's so much in life about which we *must* be serious that I simply cannot abide being so when it's not necessary, don't you agree, Edwin? Tell me about Emily."

"I can't do Emily justice with words. You'll just have to meet her. I'm sorry she's not here. Both of the children assured me they would be, but Frankie is gone fishing and must have lost track of time, which he does quite frequently, and Emily went off on a picnic with Charles. They're not back yet."

"Charles Bliss?"

"Yes."

"Ah, the young man in her life. I feel as if I've met them both, I've heard so much about them in Josephine's letters. Do you think they'll be married, Edwin?"

"I don't know. If so, they haven't told us yet."

"Do you like him as much as Josie claims you do?"

"The whole family likes him. You will, too."

"I'll reserve my opinions till I've met him, if you please. I'm not a woman whose judgments can be dictated."

"Of course," Edwin replied with a crooked smirk. Her quicksilver spunkiness was only one of the attributes to which his parents had objected years ago. Thank heaven she hadn't lost it. She could scold and praise in the same breath, inquire and preach, sympathize and rejoice without breaking rhythm. Life with her would have been a ride on an eccentric wheel instead of a walk on a treadmill.

"I'm afraid I wasn't expecting you to have so much baggage. If you'll wait here I'll go over to the livery and get a wagon for it. It'll only take me—"

"I wouldn't dream of waiting here. I'll come along. You can give me a tour of your place."

He threw a cautious glance along the street, but it was Sunday, people were at home resting. The only ones about seemed to be the stage driver and a pair of cowboys lounging on the hotel step. He reminded himself Fannie was a relative. It was only his own apprehensions leading him to believe people would peek through their lace curtains and raise eyebrows.

"All right. It's only three blocks. Can you make it in those?" He gestured toward her shoes, which sported two-inch heels shaped like rope cleats.

She pulled up her skirt, revealing that her shoe tops were made of golden-brown silk vesting, which shimmered in the sun. "Of course I can make it. What a silly question, Edwin. Which way?" Her skirts fell and she captured his arm, striding in a strong, long step that made her skirts sound like flapping sails. He was struck anew by her vitality and lack of guile. Obviously, she was a woman to whom conventionalities came second to naturalness. Everything she did seemed natural, from her strong, loud laugh to her almost masculine stride to her unaffected hold on his arm. She seemed unaware that the side of her breast brushed his sleeve as they moved along Main Street toward Grinnell.

"How was your trip?"

"Ach! Ghastly!" she shot back, and while she amused him with tales of jarred bones and Jake McGiver's ribald language Edwin nearly managed to forget about the proximity of her breast.

They rounded the corner and approached the livery barn. The town seemed as sleepy as the horses who stood on three feet to the west of the building. Edwin rolled back the broad front doors, which hung on a steel track. He opened them to their limits so that anyone passing could freely look inside and see that the only thing happening was an innocent tour of the facilities.

Inside all was quiet, different on Sunday when little commerce was about. A slice of sun fell across the dirt floor, but inside it was cool, shadowed, redolent of horses and hay. Fannie walked ahead, straight up the aisle between the stalls, looking left and right while Edwin stayed in the sun shaft and watched her. When she reached the far end she took it upon herself to roll open one of the north doors three feet and look out back. He watched her silhouette, stark black against the bright rectangle as she leaned over and poked her head out, looking up at the doorsill, then turned. She bracketed her mouth with both hands. When she called, her voice sounded distant and resonant through the giant barn.

"Edwiiiiiiiiiiiin!"—as if she were atop an Alp.

He smiled, cupped his mouth, and returned, "Fannieeeeeee?"

"You have a great place heeeeere!"

"Thank youuuuuuuu!"

"Where did you get all these buggieeeees?"

"In Rockforrrrrrrrd."

"Where's thaaaaaaat?"

"West of Cheyeeeeeeene."

"Are you riiiiiiiich?"

Edwin dropped his hands and burst out laughing. *Fannie, darling Fannie, I will play hell resisting you.* He slowly walked the length of the barn and stopped before her, studying her for a long moment before answering quietly, "I've done all right. I've built Josie a fine house with two stories and plenty of windows."

Fannie sobered. "How is she, Edwin? How is she, really?"

For the first time their eyes met with all pretense stripped away and he saw that she cared deeply, still, not only about him but about her cousin.

"She's dying, Fannie."

Fannie moved to him so swiftly he had no chance to evade her. "Oh, Edwin, I'm so sorry." She captured his two hands, folded them between her own, and rested her lips against the tips of his longest fingers. For moments she stood just so, absorbing the truth. Drawing back, she gazed into his eyes with a determination so palpable he could not look away. "I promise you I'll do everything in my power to make it easier on both of you. As long as it takes . . . whatever it takes . . . do you understand?"

He could not answer, for his heart seemed to have expanded and filled his throat, where it clamored at her touch. She was near enough that he could smell the dust in her clothing, the scent of her hair, of her skin; could feel her breath upon their aligned hands while a sunprick of light touched her somber hazel eyes.

"Because I have never stopped loving either one of you," she added, and stepped back so abruptly he was left with his hands folded in midair. "Now show me your stable quickly so I can go see my cousin."

He did so in a tangle of emotions, her words shimmering along his nerve endings. Whatever it takes . . . do you understand? He feared that he did understand, but in the next instant her mercurial mood change made him wonder if he was right. As he showed her the office, which he had neatened for her arrival, and the stalls, which he'd cleaned, and the stock, which he'd curried, she was as breezy as she'd been while calling messages across the barn; as if her quieter, startling words had never been spoken. When the brief tour ended she stood motionless, watching him hitch a horse to a wagon. She did not try to disguise her keen study of him under any pretense of studying the interior of the barn but stood arrow straight with her hands pressed down along her skirts. Not so much as a muscle moved, save those with which she breathed. He moved about, completing his chore, avoiding her glance, feeling as he thought a piece of fruit must feel as it ripens on a tree—warm inside, pressing out, out against its own skin, expanding. She might have been the sun, ripening him.

It was her way. She was an observer, a listener, an imbiber. When they were young she had hauled him by the hand into her mother's side yard one night and said, "Shh! Edwin, listen! I believe I can hear the apples growing." And after a moment: "They grow by starlight, instead of by sunlight, you know."

"Fannie, don't be silly," he'd said.

"I'm not silly. It's true. I'll show you tomorrow."

The next day she had cut an apple in half cross-wise and shown him the star inside, formed by the seeds. "See? Starlight," she'd chided, and made a believer of him.

Perhaps now she was cataloging the changes in him. Whatever her thoughts, he grew uneasy while her eyes followed him as he moved around Gunpowder, a pure black gelding, whom he was hitching to the buckboard.

"Do your children know?"

Neither of them had spoken for so long he'd lost the train of conversation. For one startled moment he thought she meant about them—did his children know about himself and Fannie, twenty-two years ago?

"The children?" He stood with the gelding between them, his hands on the animal's broad, curved back.

"Yes, do they know she's dying?"

He released his breath with superb control so she could not guess his thoughts. "I believe Emily has guessed. Frankie's too young to dwell on it much."

"I want one thing understood. There'll be no talk of death as long as I'm in your house. She's alive, and as long as she is we must do her the honor of enhancing that life in whatever ways possible."

Their eyes met over the horse's back, carrying another unspoken vow of honor. Nothing had changed for either of them, but this was as close as they must come to saying it. Still, they plucked from the afternoon this one ripe moment to look truly into each other's eyes, to accept the creases added to their skin by the years, the paleness of her hair, the brush of silver in his; and to pledge silently never to allow their naked feelings to show like this again.

"You have my word, Fannie," he said quietly.

The sound of an approaching wagon interrupted as Emily and Charles pulled into the open doorway.

Emily spoke before Charles drew the rig to a halt. "Oh, she's here!" Emily bounced down and went straight to Fannie. "Hello, Fannie, I'm Emily."

"Well, of course you are. I'd have picked you out in a crowd of strangers." The mercurial Fannie was capable of shifting moods as the situation demanded and chattered gaily, "Edwin, she's the spitting image of you with those blue eyes and black hair. But the mouth I think is Josie's." Holding Emily's hands, she added, "My goodness, child, you're lovely. You got the best of both parents, I'd say."

Emily had never considered herself lovely, by anybody's yardstick. The compliment went straight to her heart and brought a moment of self-consciousness as she searched for a graceful response.

"Unfortunately, I didn't get Mother's domestic skills, so the entire family is overjoyed to see you here."

They all laughed and Emily turned to her father. "I'm sorry we're late, Papa. We went a little farther than I expected."

"No harm done."

"Fannie, you haven't met Charles." He had drawn up beside them and stepped from the rig. "Charles, this is Mother's cousin, Fannie Cooper. This is Charles Bliss."

"Charles . . . quite as I pictured you." She took stock of his neatly trimmed beard and gray eyes.

"How do you do, Miss Cooper."

"Now that's the *last* time I want to be called 'Miss Cooper.' I'm Fannie. Just Fannie." They, too, exchanged handclasps. "You realize, of course, that I know at what age you learned to walk on stilts and what kind of a student you were and what an excellent carpenter you are."

Charles laughed, readily charmed. "From Mrs. Walcott's letters, of course."

"Of course. And speaking of which, I've written one of my own telling her when to expect me and I'm not there, am I?"

Edwin spoke up. "Fannie and I were just leaving to collect her baggage and go on up to the house. Will you be coming along?"

"As soon as we put Pinky up and check Sergeant's foot. How is it, Papa?"

His startled expression turned momentarily sheepish. "I haven't looked. I was . . . well, I was giving Fannie a tour."

"I'll do it. You two go on and we'll be right along."

When Edwin tried to help Fannie clamber onto the buckboard, she brushed his hand aside and declared, "I'm limber as a willow switch, Edwin. Just help yourself up."

Emily watched them leave with an admiring glow in her eyes. "Isn't she wonderful, Charles?"

"She is. I don't know what I expected but in spite of her letters I pictured her more like your mother."

"She's as different from Mother as snow is from rain."

It was true. Edwin felt it even more sharply than his daughter. When Fannie saw his house from the outside she tipped her head back to glimpse the roof peak where a web of wheel-shaped gingerbread trim highlighted the fish-scale siding. "Why, Edwin, it's beautiful. Charles built this?"

"Charles and I. With a little fetching and carrying from Frankie and a surprising amount of help from Emily."

"Absolutely beautiful. I never knew you were so talented." It was more than Josie had ever said, for she'd taken the house as her due, and any appreciation she might have felt was eclipsed by her relief in not having to live in a dreary hovel.

"I built the wraparound porch so Josie could sit outside and face the sun at any time of day. And upstairs, there . . ." He pointed to the white-railed balcony contrasted against the black shingles. "A small veranda off our bedroom so she could step outside anytime she wanted."

Fannie, who had never owned a house of her own, thought, lucky, lucky Josie.

Edwin took Fannie in past the front parlor. Though her eyes scanned the clutter, she made no comment.

"Josie is upstairs." He motioned her ahead of him and watched her bustle bounce and her long copper skirttail glide ahead of his boots as he followed with two grips. "The first door on your left," he directed.

Inside, Josephine waited with excited eyes, her hands extended. "Fannie . . . dear Fannie. You're here at last."

"Joey."

Fannie rushed to the bed and they hugged.

"That awful name. I haven't . . . heard it for twenty years." Josephine lost her breath on a flurry of choked laughter.

"How your parents hated it when I called you that."

They parted and took stock of one another. Josephine said, "You look elegant."

Fannie retorted, "Dusty and battered from that jerky ride, more likely, but I enjoyed Mr. McGiver immensely. And you look thin. Edwin said you've been having a bad time of it." She laid a hand on her cousin's cheek. "Well, I'm going to pamper you silly, just watch and see. Up to a point. I've actually learned how to cook—imagine that. But I can*not* make pudding without scorching it, so don't expect any. I'm fair at meat and vegetables, however, and devilishly good with shellfish, but wherever will we get shellfish out here in the mountains? Then there's bread . . . hmm . . ." Fanny gave her attention to tugging off her gloves. "I fear my bread is rather glutinous, but edible. Just barely. I'm always in too much of a rush to let it rise properly. You wouldn't happen to have a bakery in this town, would you?"

"I'm afraid not."

"Well, no worry. I can make biscuits light as swansdown. I know that's hard to believe after the way my mother threw her hands up in despair when she was trying to teach me my way around a kitchen." Fannie bounced off the bed and toured the bedroom, glancing at the dark, handsome furniture, batting not a lash at the spare cot. "Light as swansdown, I swear. Shall I bake you some for supper?"

"That would be wonderful."

"And when I put them before you, you'd better eat!" Fannie pointed at her cousin's nose. "Because I've brought along my bicycle and I fully intend to get you strong enough to ride on it."

"Your bicycle! But, Fannie, I can't ri . . . ride a bicycle."

"Why ever not?"

"Because . . ." Josephine spread her hands. "I'm a . . . a consumptive."

"Well, if *that* isn't the frailest excuse I've ever heard, I don't know what is! All that means is that you've got weak lungs. You want to make them strong, you get on that set of wheels and make them work harder. Have you ever seen a blacksmith with puny arms? I should say not. So what can be so different about lungs? It'll be the best thing for you, to get out in the fresh mountain air and rebuild your strength."

Looking on, Edwin thought there hadn't been so much merry chatter in this bedroom since it had been built. Fannie's gaiety was infectious; already Josie's face wore a dim hint of pink, her eyes were happy, her lips smiling. Perhaps he tended to mollycoddle her and in doing so, encouraged her to feel worse.

The young people arrived; they'd picked up Frankie somewhere along the way and from below came his voice as he led the trio up the steps. "Hey, everybody, there's a bicycle downstairs!"

He burst into the bedroom, followed by Emily and Charles.

"It's mine," Fannie announced.

Edwin stopped his son's headlong charge into the room. "Frankie, I want you to meet your cousin Fannie. Fannie, this is our son Frank, who smells a little fishy right now, if my nose doesn't deceive me."

Fannie extended her hand nonetheless. "I'm pleased to meet you, Master Frank. How long would you guess your legs are?" She leaned back to take a visual measure. "They'd have to be—oh, say, a good twenty-four inches for you to ride the bicycle with any ease at all."

"Ride it? Me? Honest?"

"Honest." Fannie held up a palm as if taking an oath and charmed yet another member of the Walcott family.

Emily could not take her eyes off Fannie. She was a dazzling creature, the same age as Mother, yet years younger in action, temperament, and interest. Her voice was animated, her movements energetic. She had a contumacious look about her—that kinky apricot hair, perhaps, frizzing about her face like lantern-lit steam around a newborn colt—that made her seem untrammeled by the gravity that made most women dull and uninteresting. Her eyes constantly shone with interest and her hands never remained still when she talked. She was worldly: she rode bicycles and had traveled alone clear from Massachusetts, and had boated under sail to a place called Nantucket where she gigged for clams; and she had attended the opera, had seen Emma Abbott and Brignoli starring in *The Bohemian Girl,* and had had her fortune told by a palm reader named Cassandra. The list went on and on—tales from her letters that Emily had been absorbing ever since she was old enough to read. How incredible to think such a worldling was here, and would stay, would sleep in Emily's own bed where they could talk in the dark after the lanterns were extinguished. Already the house seemed transformed by her presence. Gaiety came with her, a carnival atmosphere that had been so badly needed. Mother, too, had fallen under Fannie's spell. She had forgotten her illness for the moment; it was plain on her face. And Papa stood back with his arms crossed, smiling, relieved at last of a portion of his worries. For bringing all this to the Walcott family within an hour of her arrival, Emily loved Fannie already.

Just then Papa boosted himself away from the chiffonier and said, "Speaking of bicycles, I'd best get Fannie's in the shed and bring her trunks up, too. Charles, perhaps you could give me a hand."

"Just a minute, sir . . ." Charles stopped Edwin with a hand on his arm.

"Sir?" Edwin's eyebrows elevated and amusement quirked his mouth. "Charles, since when do you call me *sir*?"

"It seemed appropriate today. I thought as long as we're all together, and Mrs. Walcott is feeling so well, and Fanny's just arrived and the mood is festive, I might as well add to it." He took Emily's hand and drew her against his side. "I want you all to know that I've asked Emily to be my wife and she's accepted . . . at last."

Myriad reactions broke through Emily: a sinking sense of finality now that the announcement was made, contraposed by gladness at the pleased look on her mother's and father's faces, and amusement at Frankie's reaction.

"Yippee! It's about time." Everyone in the room laughed and exchanged hugs. Josephine wiped a tear from her eye, and Papa clapped Charles on the arm and pumped his hand and gave him a solid thump on the back. Fannie kissed Charles's cheek and in the middle of it all someone knocked on the door downstairs.

"Emileee?" It was Tarsy, calling to be heard above the happy voices. "Can I come in?"

Emily went to the top of the stairs and shouted, "Come in, Tarsy, we're up here!"

Tarsy appeared below, excited, as usual. "Is she here?"

"Yes."

"I couldn't wait to meet her!" She started up the steps. "Are all those bags outside hers?"

"Every one. And she's exactly like her letters."

Another devotee fell under Fannie's spell the moment introductions were performed. "But, of course," said Fannie, "Emily's friend, the barber's daughter, the girl with the prettiest hair in town. I've already been told to expect to see a lot of you around here." She laid a touch on Tarsy's golden curls, and gave the proper amount of attention before turning the focus back toward the recent announcement. "But you haven't heard Emily and Charles's news, have you?"

"What?" Tarsy turned to her friend with a blank, receptive expression.

"Charles has asked me to marry him and I've accepted."

Tarsy reacted as she did to all excitement: giddily. She threw herself on Emily with nearly enough force to break bones, and went into raptures of *oohs* and gushes of felicitations; and overtook Charles next, kissing his cheek and exclaiming she knew they'd be *sooooo* happy and she was positively *green* with envy (which wasn't true, Emily knew); then threw her attention back to Fannie with amusing abruptness.

"Tell me all about your ride on the stagecoach."

Fannie told, and Tarsy stayed for supper, which turned out to be a picnic on Josephine's bed, at Fannie's insistence. She declared Joey was simply not to be left at the height of this celebration while the others went downstairs. They would bring the festivities to her.

So Papa and Fannie and Frankie sat on the big bed while Emily, Charles, and Tarsy took Papa's cot and balanced their plates on their knees. They all supped on creamed peas over Fannie's swansdown biscuits and Frankie's latest catch, fried to the texture of a bootheel, for which Fannie laughingly refused to apologize: "The biscuits are perfection itself. The rest I'll get better at in time." And afterward Emily announced they'd all draw straws to see who'd help with dishes. Frankie lost and his mouth grew sulky. Fannie scolded, "Better get used to it, lad, because I intend to draw straws every night and you'll have to expect to draw the short one occasionally. Now let's get going and leave your father and mother a little time to themselves."

Charles said he had an early day tomorrow and bid them good night, kissing Emily briefly on the mouth when she saw him out to the porch. But she was too impatient to linger long with Charles. Fannie was in the kitchen, and where Fannie was, Emily wanted to be.

The girls let Frankie off the hook and said they'd do dishes tonight because Tarsy was nowhere near ready to go home and leave Fannie's magical presence. Though Fannie had good intentions of doing a share of the cleanup work she somehow never got her hands wet. They were occupied instead gesturing and illustrating as she told enchanting tales of attending Tony Pastor's Vaudeville Emporium, where the dancers twirled umbrellas and sang "While Strolling through the Park One Day." She sang the song in a clear-pitched voice and performed a dance around the kitchen table, twirling the stove poker as if it were an umbrella, filling the girls' heads with vivid pictures.

Fannie seemed to recall that she was here to do dishes, wiped one, then forgot to wipe another as she launched into the intriguing account of her recently acquired passion for archery. She illustrated by stepping on one corner of the dish towel, stretching the diagonal corner high, and drawing back on it as if seating an arrow and taking aim. When the arrow hit its mark on the kitchen stovepipe she snapped the towel around her neck as if it were a fur collar and declared she had, to date, participated in three tournaments, the last of which won her a loving cup and a kiss on the hand from an Austrian prince. And as soon as she got back East, where more and more sidewalks were being laid, she intended to buy herself a pair of the astonishing things called roller skates and give them a try.

Fannie seemed amazed when she realized the dishes were all put away.

"Gracious, I didn't do a one!"

"We don't care," Tarsy said. "Tell us more."

They trailed upstairs where the stories continued as Fannie began unpacking a trunk, winning a series of near-swoons from Tarsy as she pulled out dress after dress, more glamorous than anything Sheridan had ever seen.

"The last time I wore this one, I swore I never would again." Fannie held up a dress with lace rosettes running diagonally from breast to hip. "We were playing parlor games and it gave me away."

"Parlor games?" Tarsy's eyes danced with interest.

"They're the rage back East."

"What kind?"

"Oh, many different kinds. There's whist and dominoes and hangman. And of course, the men-and-women kind."

"Men-and-women kind?"

Fanny laughed enchantingly and collapsed on the side of the bed with the dress heedlessly smashed onto her lap. "I'm afraid I shouldn't have brought them up. They can be quite naughty at times."

Tarsy bent forward, insisting, "Tell us!"

Fannie seemed to consider, then folded the dress with the rosettes and crossed her hands on it. "Very well, but it wouldn't be a good idea if your parents found out about them, particularly Joey. She never approved of levity, and most certainly not this sort!"

Agog, Tarsy wiggled closer. "We won't tell, will we, Emily? What kind of games?"

"Well, there's Poor Pussy and Musical Potatoes, for laughs, and Alice, Where Art Thou, in which the suspense gets hair-splitting. And then when the night gets older and everyone is feeling . . . well, freer, shall we say, there's the Blind Postman, and French Blind Man's Buff. That's the one we were playing the night this dress gave me away."

Fannie gave a provocative sideward glance and a mincing grin. Tarsy fell forward in a melodramatic show of impatience. "But what were you *doing*?"

"Well, you see, one player is blinded—he has a scarf tied over his eyes, naturally—*but* . . ." Fannie paused effectively. "His hands are tied behind his back."

Tarsy gasped and waved her hands beside her cheeks as if she'd just taken a bite of something too hot. Emily barely kept her eyes from rolling.

Fannie went on: "The others position themselves around the room and the blind man is only permitted to walk backwards. The others tease and buff him by pulling at his clothes or tickling his face with a feather. When he finally succeeds in seizing someone, the blind man has to guess who it is. If he guesses right, the prisoner must pay a forfeit."

"What's a forfeit?"

"Oh, forfeits are the most fun."

"But what *are* they?"

"Whatever the blind man decides. Sometimes the prisoner must become the blind man, sometimes if everyone's in a silly mood he must imitate an animal, and sometimes . . . if it's one of the opposite sex, she must pay a kiss."

Emily found herself startled by the very idea. Kissing was an intimate thing; she could not imagine doing it in a parlor with a roomful of people looking on. But Tarsy flung herself backwards and groaned ecstatically, fantasizing. She gazed at the ceiling, one foot dangling over the edge of the mattress. "I'd give anything to go to a party like that. We *never* have parties. It's dull as liver around here."

"We could have one—not that kind, of course. It wouldn't be proper. But it certainly seems that Emily's betrothal deserves a formal announcement. We could invite all your young friends, and certainly Edwin and Joey will want to ring out the news to *their* friends and business acquaintances. Why don't we plan one?"

Tarsy sprang up and grabbed Emily, nearly toppling her off the bed. "Of course, Emily! It's the perfect idea. I'll help. I'll come over and . . . and . . . well, anything at all. Say yes, Em . . . pleeeeease!"

"We could have it next Saturday night," Fannie suggested. "That would give you a full week to get the word out."

"Well . . . it . . . I . . ." The idea became suddenly exciting to Emily. She imagined how Papa would enjoy having people in the house again, and how proper it would be for both him and Charles to invite those with whom they did business. And Tarsy was right, this town was dull as liver, hadn't she just said as much to Charles? But suddenly Emily's expression became a warning signal and she pointed straight at Tarsy. "No kissing games though, do you understand?"

"Oh, perfectly," Tarsy agreed breezily. "Right, Fannie?"

"Oh, none!" Fannie seconded.

The two of them had only met today and Emily had heard every word they'd said to one another. Yet she couldn't shake the uneasy feeling that they were wordlessly conspiring.

Chapter 5

ON MONDAY MORNING, Tom Jeffcoat awakened in his room at the Windsor Hotel and lay staring at the ceiling, thinking of Julia. Julia March, with her heart-shaped face and almond eyes, her caramel-blond hair and dainty hands. Julia March, who'd worn his betrothal brooch for more than half a year. Julia March, who had thrown him over for another.

His eyes slammed shut.

When would the memory stop stinging?

Not today. Certainly not today when it was only 5:30 A.M. and she was on his mind already.

It's done with. Get that through your head!

Throwing the covers back, he leapt from bed and skinned on his britches, letting the suspenders dangle at his sides. Snatching the white porcelain pitcher from the washstand, he stepped barefoot into the hall and helped himself to a generous slough of hot water from a covered tin container waiting on a trivet.

Hell, the Windsor wasn't so bad. It was clean, the food was decent, and the water hot when promised. Besides, he wouldn't be here long. He fully intended to have his own house up before the snow flew.

But what about then? Would it be any less lonely? Would he miss his family any less? Would he miss Julia any less?

Julia's practically on her way up the aisle. Put her from your mind.

But it was impossible. Being alone so much gave him plenty of time for thinking, and Julia filled his thoughts day and night. Even now as he washed from the waist up he studied himself in the mirror, wondering what it was that she'd found preferable about Hanson. The blond hair? The brown eyes? The beard? The money? Well, he wasn't blond, his eyes were blue, he didn't like beards, and he sure as hell wasn't rich. He was so *un*rich he'd had to borrow money from his grandmother to come here. But he'd pay her back and make something of himself in this town. He'd show Julia! He might even become rich as a lord, and when he was, he wouldn't share a penny of his money with any woman alive. Women! Who needed the mercenary, fickle bitches?

He poured hot water into his shaving mug, worked up a lather, and lifted the brush toward his face. But he paused uncertainly, running four fingertips over his scratchy jaw, wondering if he should let the beard grow. Was it true? Did women really like them? Why, even that mouthy Walcott tomboy preferred a man with a beard. But he'd tried one before and found it hot, dangerous around the forge, and prickly when the hair grew in a tight curve and got long enough to poke him in the underside of his chin. Resolutely he lathered and scraped his face clean, then observed his bare-chested reflection with a critical eye. *Too dark. Too much hair on the chest. The wrong color eyes. Eyelashes too short. The dent in the left cheek ridiculously lopsided without a matching one on the right.*

Suddenly he threw down the towel and released a disdainful snort.

Jeffcoat, what the hell are you doing? You never gave a damn before about how you measured up to other men.

But the fact remained: being spurned by a woman undermined a man's self-regard.

In the hotel dining room he ate an immense breakfast of steak and eggs, then headed toward Grinnell Street to get his wagon, dreading the idea of running into Emily Walcott in his present state of mind. If that damned little snot was there she'd better button her lip this time or he'd wrap that leather apron over her head and slip a horseshoe around her neck.

She wasn't. Edwin was. A likable man, Edwin Walcott, affable even at seven A.M.

"I hear you're meeting Charles this morning and going up to the Pinery after lumber."

"That's right."

Edwin smiled smugly. "Well, you'll be spending the day in the company of a happy man."

He offered no more, but minutes later when Jeffcoat pulled up before Charles's house, Bliss jogged out with a smile on his face. "Good morning!" he called.

"Morning," Tom replied.

"A wonderful morning!" exclaimed his companion.

It was, in fact, drearier than a Quaker wardrobe.

"You look happy."

"I am!" Charles bounded aboard.

"Any special reason?"

As the wagon began rolling Charles slapped both knees, then gripped them firmly. "The fact is, I'm getting married."

"Married!"

"Oh, not for a year or more, but she's finally said yes."

"Who?"

"Emily Walcott."

"Em—" Jeffcoat's eyes bugged out and his head jutted forward. "Emily Walcott!"

"That's right."

"You mean the Emily Walcott with the britches and the leather apron?"

"That's right."

Jeffcoat rolled his eyes and muttered, "Jesus."

"What does that mean . . . Jesus?"

"Well, I mean . . . she's . . ." Tom gestured vaguely.

"She's what?"

"She's a shrew!"

"A shrew . . ." Surprisingly, Charles laughed. "She's a little spunky, but she's no shrew. She's bright and she cares about people, she's a hard worker—"

"And she wears suspenders."

"Is that all you can think of, is what a girl wears?"

"You mean it doesn't matter to you?"

"Not at all."

Tom found that magnanimous. "You know, I like you, Bliss, but I still feel like I ought to offer condolences instead of congratulations."

Amiably, Charles replied, "And I'm damned if I know why I don't knock you off that wagon seat."

"I'm sorry, but that girl and I get along like a pair of cats in a sack."

The two assessed each other, realizing they'd been wholly honest in a way that friends—even friends of long standing—can rarely be. It felt good.

Suddenly they both laughed, then Tom angled his new friend a half grin and challenged, "All right, tell me about her. Try to change my mind."

Charles did so gladly. "In spite of what you think of her, Emily's a wonderful girl. Our families were friends back in Philadelphia, so I've known her all my life. I decided when I was thirteen that I wanted to marry her. Matter of fact, I told Edwin so then, but he wisely advised me to put off asking her for a while." They both chuckled. "I asked her the first time about a year ago, and it took four proposals to get her to say yes."

"Four!" Jeffcoat raised one eyebrow. "Maybe you should have stopped while you were ahead."

"And maybe I'll knock you off that wagon seat yet." Charles playfully tried to do so. He punched Tom soundly on the arm, rocking him sideways.

"Well, *four*! My God, man, I'd have gone where I was welcome long before that."

Charles turned serious again. "Emily had things she wanted to do first. She's taking a correspondence course in veterinary medicine but she ought to finish that sometime next summer."

"I know. Edwin told me. And I made the mistake of peeking at her papers the first time I walked into the livery office. As usual, she lit into me. If I remember right, *that time* she called me rude and nosy." His inflection made it clear the altercation was only one of many.

Charles had no sympathy. "Good for her. You probably deserved it."

They laughed again, then fell into companionable silence.

Odd, Jeffcoat thought, how you could meet some people and

feel an instant aversion, meet others and feel like an empty spot inside you is about to be filled. That's how Bliss made him feel.

"Listen"—Charles interrupted Tom's thoughts—"I know Emily wasn't exactly cordial to you when you came into town, but—"

"Cordial? She ordered me out. She came over to my lot and stomped along beside the grader and called me names."

"I'm sorry, Tom, but she's got a lot on her mind. She's really devoted to her father, and she spends nearly as much time in the livery stable as he does. It's natural that she'd be defensive about it. But it isn't just the livery stable. Things around her house are pretty grim right now. You see, her mother is dying of consumption."

A faint thread of remorse spiraled through Jeffcoat. Consumption was incurable, and not pretty to watch, especially near the end. For the first time, Jeffcoat softened toward the tomboy. "I'm sorry," he said. "I didn't know."

"Of course you didn't. It's getting bad now. I have a feeling Mrs. Walcott is failing fast. It was another reason I wanted Emily to finally say yes to me. Because I think her mother will die a little more peacefully knowing Emily will be safely married to me."

"The Walcotts were happy about the news then?"

"Oh, yes, and Fannie, too. I haven't told you about Fannie." He explained about Mrs. Walcott's cousin having arrived from Massachusetts to help out the family. "Fannie is remarkable," he ended. "Wait till you meet her."

"I probably won't. Not as long as she lives in your fiancée's house."

"Oh, yes you will. Somehow we'll all be friends. I know we will."

They rode in thoughtful silence for some time before Tom inquired, "How old are you?"

"Twenty-one."

"Twenty-one!" Tom straightened and studied Bliss's profile. "Is that all?" He looked older; undoubtedly it was the beard. And he certainly acted older. "You know, in some ways I envy you. Only twenty-one and already you know what you want out of life. I mean, you left your family and came out here to settle. You have your trade, and a home, and you've picked out a woman." Tom ruminated momentarily, studying the tip of a mountain ridge shrouded in haze. "I'm twenty-six and mostly I know what I *don't* want."

"For instance?"

Tom dropped a sideward glance at Bliss. "Well, a woman for starters."

"Every man wants a woman."

"Maybe I should say a wife, then."

"You don't *want* to get married?" Charles sounded astonished.

A cynical expression settled on Tom's face as he spoke. "A year ago I became engaged to a woman, a woman I'd known for years. Next Saturday she's going to marry another man. You'll pardon me if I don't think too highly of the fairer sex right now."

Charles looked appropriately sympathetic and breathed, "Damn, that's tough."

In a hard voice Jeffcoat observed, "Women are fickle."

"Not all of them."

"You're besotted right now; naturally you'd say that."

"Well, Emily isn't."

"I thought the same about Julia." Jeffcoat gave a rueful chuckle, staring straight ahead. "I thought I had her signed, sealed, and delivered until she walked into the blacksmith shop one afternoon and announced that she was breaking our engagement to marry a banker named Jonas Hanson, a man fifteen years older than her."

"A banker?"

"You guessed it. Inherited money . . . lots of inherited money."

Charles digested the news, eyeing Tom covertly while Tom stared pensively at the horses' rumps. For a while neither of them spoke, then Tom sighed heavily and leaned back. "Well, I guess it was better that I found out beforehand."

"That's why you came here then? To get away from Julia?"

Tom glanced at Charles and forced a lazy grin. "I wasn't sure I wouldn't break into her bedroom one night and toss old moneybags onto the floor and jump into bed in his place."

Bliss laughed and scratched his bearded cheek, admitting, "To tell you the truth, I've spent some time lately thinking about bedrooms myself."

Surprised, Jeffcoat peered askance at his new friend. How could a man get spoony over a girl who dressed like a blacksmith, smelled like horses, and wanted to be a veterinarian? Curiosity prompted his next question.

"Does *she*?"

Bliss glanced at him calmly. "Does she what?"

"Think about bedrooms?"

"Unfortunately, no. Did your Julia?"

"Sometimes I think she was tempted but I never got beyond her corset stays."

"Emily doesn't wear a corset."

"I'm not surprised. Course, she wouldn't need one with that stiff leather apron."

They laughed together yet again, then rode for some minutes in silence. At length Tom commented, "If this isn't the damnedest conversation. I had friends back in Springfield I couldn't talk this easy with, friends I'd known for years."

"I know what you mean. I never talked about things like this with anyone. As a matter of fact, I'm not sure a gentleman should."

"Maybe not, but here we are, and I don't know about you, but I've always considered myself a gentleman."

"Me, too," Charles agreed.

They rode in silence for several minutes before Charles added dubiously, "But do you feel a little guilty for talking behind the girls' backs?"

"I probably would if I were still engaged to Julia. Do you?"

Charles studied the clouds and said, "Well, let's put it this way . . . I wouldn't want Emily to find out what I said. But on the other hand, it feels good to know other men go through the same thing when they're engaged."

"Don't worry. She'll never find out from me. If you want to know the truth, that woman of yours scares me a little. She's a regular hellcat and I don't want to tangle with her any more than I have to. But one thing's for sure—life should never be dull with a woman like that."

When they reached the Pinery, Charles introduced Tom as "my new friend, Tom Jeffcoat," and indeed it became true. Throughout the remainder of that day, and those that followed, while the two men worked side by side, the spontaneity between them began to grow into a strong bond of friendship.

Right from the first, Charles did all he could to smooth the way for Jeffcoat in the new town, amid new people. At the

Pinery he joshed the owner, Andrew Stubbs, and his son, Mick, into giving Tom a more than fair price on his lumber. In town he took him personally into J. D. Loucks's store and introduced him to the locals while Tom bought nails. Together they began constructing the framework of Tom's livery barn, and when the skeleton walls and roof joists lay stretched out on the earth, Charles took a walk down Main Street and came back with nine hearty townsmen to help raise them. He brought Will Haberkorn, the local butcher, and his son, Patrick, both still wearing their stained white aprons. With the Haberkorns came Sherman Fields, Tarsy's father, a congenial and dapper man with center-parted hair and a waxed handlebar mustache. There were Pervis Berryman and his son, Jerome, who bought and sold hides, and made boots and trunks. Charles also brought the stocky Polish cabinetmaker, Joseph Zollinski, whom Tom recognized from church. J. D. Loucks came with the hotel owner, Helstrom, who said to his tenant, "You support me, I support you." And Edwin Walcott, in a true show of welcome, walked over from across the street. Charles introduced Tom to those he hadn't already met and arranged a fast, sincere welcome in the form of the wall-raising.

Loucks had brought new rope from his store, and within minutes after the group convened, muscles strained in the June sun. By the end of the day the skeleton of the building stood silhouetted against the evening sky.

"I don't know how to thank you," Tom told Charles when everyone else had gone and they were left together, gazing up at the sharp angles of the roof.

"Friends don't need thanks," Charles replied simply.

But Tom clapped his friend's shoulder just the same. "This friend does."

As they began picking up their tools Charles said, "Fannie insists on throwing an engagement party for Emily and me this Saturday night. It might be just what you need to forget about that wedding back East. Will you come?"

Tom considered declining, in deference to Miss Walcott. But nights got long and lonely, and he was anxious to socialize with the young people he'd met, many of whom would be his future customers. More importantly, it was Charles's party, too, and Charles was his friend. He *wanted* to go, whether it was to the tomboy's house, or not.

He put a wry twist on his lips and inquired, "Will Tarsy Fields be there?"

Charles shot him a man-to-man grin. "Oh, Tarsy, is it?"

Tom turned his attention to closing a nail keg for the night. "Sometimes a man gets a message from a girl the minute they meet. I think I got one from Tarsy."

"She's easy on the eye."

"I thought so."

"And entertaining."

"She seems to be."

"And empty-headed as that nail keg is going to be when we're done building this barn."

Jeffcoat laughed freely, slapped Bliss on the shoulder, and declared robustly, "Damn, but I like you, Bliss!"

"Enough to come on Saturday night?"

"Of course," Tom agreed, hoping he and Emily Walcott could remain civil to one another.

The following day Tom and Charles began enclosing the roof and sides of the livery barn, but the next day they gave to the church, which was in a similar stage of development. It was that, more than anything, which earned Tom Jeffcoat the full approval of the town's matrons. With a building of his own only half-done, they gossiped on the boardwalks, that young man gave his full day to help erect the new church. Now, *there* was an example for their young boys to follow!

One young boy took to following everything that was going on at the new lot on Grinnell Street. Frankie Walcott showed up the first morning, drawn by his idol Charles, only to find before day's end that he had *two* idols. They put him to work, and he worked willingly, carrying, measuring, even hammering. When they went to church to offer their day's labor, Frankie went along. When Frankie went along, so did his fat friend Earl Rausch. Earl had an unmanageable sweet tooth and spent much of his time filching doughnuts and cookies sent along with the workers by their wives. But Earl's idol was Frankie, and what Frankie did, Earl did. He brought the men drinks in the dipper and ran errands and straightened bent nails. When the town matrons learned that Frankie and Earl had volunteered their time to help at the church, they signed up their own sons to do likewise.

* * *

Frankie Walcott was having the time of his life. Things had never been so lively around Sheridan. All day long he could be with Charles and the new guy, Tom. He liked Tom. Tom grinned a lot, and teased, and his livery barn was *really* going to be something.

At suppertime he chattered constantly about the building going up on Grinnell Street.

"Tom brought windows clear from Rock Springs—twenty-four of 'em! And he's gonna put in a floor made of real bricks! He already ordered 'em down in Buffalo!"

Emily refused to glance up or to acknowledge Frankie's exuberance.

"But guess what else he brought? This . . . this thing. This turntable, and he's gonna put it in the middle of the floor so it'll turn the wagons around and head 'em back out the door just as easy as *I* can turn around. He brought it clear from Springfield on the train and from Rock Springs to here on his wagon. Tom says back East all the roundhouses have turntables and he says they use 'em to turn the trains around."

"Why, that's the silliest thing I ever heard of!" spouted Emily, unable to hold her tongue any longer. "Back East where it's crowded they need turntables. Out here in the wide open spaces it's nothing but a waste."

"Well, I don't think so. I think he's smart to think of it, and Tom says as soon as it's in Earl and me can ride on it."

Emily jumped to her feet. "Tom says! Tom says!" She reached for two empty serving bowls and plucked them off the table. "Honestly, Frank, I get so tired of you talking about that man. Surely there are other things happening around this town besides that infernal building of his!"

Fannie's speculative gaze followed Emily as the younger woman whisked to the granite sink, clunked down the bowls, and began agitatedly pumping water. Fannie calmly rested her spoon in her sauce dish and remarked, "He sounds enterprising."

"He's rude and outspoken!" Emily exclaimed, pumping harder.

"He is not!" Frankie retorted. "He's just as nice as Charles, and Charles likes him, too. Ask him if he don't!"

"I'll ask nothing about him!" shot back Emily, glaring over her shoulder at her brother. "Not when he's competing with Papa!"

Fannie chose the moment to inform her niece, "Charles has invited him to your party tomorrow night."

Emily spun around so fast water sprayed from her fingertips. "He what!"

"He invited Mr. Jeffcoat to your betrothal party tomorrow night. And Mr. Jeffcoat accepted."

"Why didn't you tell me!"

Fannie ate a spoonful of applesauce and replied negligently, "Oh, I thought I did."

"I won't have him here!"

"Now, Emily—" put in Edwin.

"I won't, Papa! Not when he's down there at this very minute, building a . . . a *livery stable*!"

"But Charles has invited him, and it's Charles's party, too. The two of them seem to have become quite good friends already."

Emily appealed to her cousin. "Do something, Fannie."

"Very well." Fannie arose calmly, carrying her dirty dishes to the sink. "I'll ride my bicycle down there tomorrow and tell him he's not invited to the party after all. I'll explain that there simply isn't room in the parlor for the number who've accepted so we'll have to cut it down. I'm sure he'll understand. Charles will, too. Shall we draw straws now to see who helps with dishes?"

"Fannie, wait."

Fannie paused in mid-motion, lifting innocent eyes to her young cousin. "Is there something else you want me to tell him?"

Emily wilted onto a chair and sat sulkily, her hands dangling between her knees.

"Let him come," she grumbled bad-naturedly.

Fannie stepped before Emily and straightened several strands of her black hair, stretching them back from her forehead as if measuring out embroidery skeins. When she spoke her voice held a quiet note of reasonableness. "He plans to live here for a good long time. You'll be—shall we say—contemporaries. The two of you will be thrown together on both social and business occasions many times in the years to come. You're very young, dearling. Young and stubborn. You haven't learned yet that life necessitates many compromises. But believe me, you'll feel better if you make up your mind to greet him civilly and make him feel welcome. If your father can, and Charles can, you can, too. Now what do you say?"

Emily lifted indignant eyes. "He called me a tomboy."

Fannie cupped the younger woman's chin in her palm. "Ah, so that's the reason for this stubborn lip. Well, we shall just have to show him that you're not, won't we?"

Emily stared at Fannie, her chin still stubborn. "I don't want to show him anything."

"Not even that a tomboy can magically be transformed into a lady?"

Fannie could see she had fired Emily's interest. Before losing it, she swung on Frankie. "And you, young man . . ." She leveled him with a warning stare. "Not one word about this conversation to anyone, do you hear?"

Everyone in the room knew Frankie wanted to run down to Grinnell Street and spout what he'd heard. But nobody crossed Fannie.

"Yes, ma'am," Frankie mumbled, disappointed.

Fannie's curiosity had been understandably piqued. What was he like, this man who raised Emily's ire so? Fannie had watched her young cousin all week long, and every time Tom Jeffcoat's name was mentioned she grew irascible. But her cheeks also got pink and she refused to meet anybody's eyes. Such a reaction for a man she hated?

On Saturday morning when the breakfast oatmeal had been set to simmer, Fannie wheeled her bicycle from the backyard shed and took a ride. It was early—6:30. Behind, she left a sleeping house, but from somewhere across town came the sound of hammering. Sheridan was small and Edwin lived a mere five blocks from Main Street and only six from his livery stable on Grinnell. As she turned down Grinnell the sun roosted on the brim of the eastern plain like a flaming orange. Against it loomed the outline of the new livery building, with its roof already enclosed. She passed Edwin's place on her left. One of his horses whickered a soft greeting. Her bicycle wheels grated softly on the sandy street while the breeze unfurled strands of her loosely upswept hair and ruffled the folds of her scratchy woolen knickers against her legs. Somewhere in the distance a rooster crowed, and the sound of Jeffcoat's hammer cracked like an oxwhip as it reverberated off the valley walls.

She was happy as she'd never been in her life. She was living in Edwin's house, sharing his life, growing acquainted with his children, passing his stable and greeting his horses. She was cooking his meals and pouring his morning coffee and rolling the used napkin that had brushed his lips, and washing and ironing the clothes that had touched his skin. If there was the slightest chance that Emily was planning to do these things for a man named Bliss when she ought to be doing them for one named Jeffcoat, Fannie was making it her business to find out before it was too late.

She pulled up beside the livery barn, sat astraddle the bicycle, shaded her eyes, and peered at the figure high above, nailing shingles in place.

"Mr. Jeffcoat?"

The hammering ceased and he turned to look over his shoulder. "Well . . . good morning!"

She liked how he said it, with a half turn and a nudge of his hat, setting it farther back on his head. The roof was steep; he had a rope tied about his waist, threaded over the ridgepole to the opposite side. He balanced, hunkered, with his boot caught on a temporary rung he'd nailed to the sharp slant below him.

"I'm Fannie Cooper!"

"I thought so. Wait a minute." He descended the roof like a mountain climber, kicking into thin air, falling in breathtaking sweeps, slipping down the rope until he reached the ladder leaning against the building. Down it he came, agilely, while she watched and admired his grace and form and his outlandish mode of dress—the britches too tight, the suspenders red, and the shirt devoid of sleeves. Before he reached her he'd pulled off a leather glove and extended a hand.

"Hello, Fannie, I'm Tom Jeffcoat."

"I know."

"You're Emily Walcott's cousin."

"Yes, after a fashion. Second cousin, to be exact. And you're Edwin's competition."

He smiled. "I didn't mean to be."

She liked his answer. She liked his dimple. She liked him. Fannie Cooper was not a typical Victorian woman who postured and pretended indifference to men. When she met one of whom she approved she felt justified in manifesting that approval in whatever way struck her fancy. Sometimes by flirting, sometimes by complimenting, often by parrying words as she did now.

"Yet you seem to be an early bird . . . out after the worm perhaps?"

Again he laughed—a masculine motion—tipping back from the waist and releasing his enjoyment to the morning sky. "Shouldn't you be making comfits and straining fruit juices for tonight?"

"I'm not serving comfits, I'm serving finger sandwiches. And for a betrothal party it's entirely proper to serve spiked punch so don't get cheeky with me, Mr. Jeffcoat."

"I didn't mean to get cheeky." Drawing the glove back on he made a shallow, flirtatious bow. "I apologize."

She perused him. She perused the great roof, half-shingled. "The barn is coming along nicely. You've ordered bricks for the floor."

"Yes."

"And you've brought twenty-four windows."

"My goodness, word spreads."

"Frankie spreads it quite effectively."

"Ah, Frankie. I like that boy."

"Your livery barn is going to be quite something. Emily is jealous."

His face gave no clue to his feelings. It contained an easy smile that changed not in the least as he divulged, "Emily wishes I were on a windjammer with a broken mainmast, rounding Cape Horn. I try not to aggravate her."

"You've also brought a turntable for the carriages, I hear."

"Yes."

"Why?"

"A curiosity, nothing more. A whim. As a boy, I liked the train yards—the turntables in particular. An engineer once gave me a ride on one. I've wanted to own one ever since."

"Are you an impetuous man, then, Mr. Jeffcoat?"

"I don't know. I never thought about it one way or the other. Are you an impetuous woman, Miss Cooper?"

"Most assuredly."

"I thought so by your bicycle and your . . ." He leaned back from the waist and scanned her legs. "What are they called?"

"Knickerbockers. Do you like them? Don't answer that! They're convenient in any case, and there are women who wear what suits them whether the men like it or not."

"So I've learned since I got to Sheridan."

She gave a smile with an abrupt start and finish, then mercurially shifted subjects. "Do you dance, Mr. Jeffcoat?"

"As little as possible."

She laughed and advised, "Well, get ready. There will be dancing tonight, among other distractions. We're all happy you're coming. Now, I must get back for breakfast. Observe my technique in getting this contraption rolling, and don't take it lightly. Starting and stopping are the hardest parts. It took me three weeks to learn how to start without falling on my face and I'm rather proud of it." She gave the bicycle a push and hopped on with perfect balance. Pedaling away, she called without turning back, "I'm pleased to meet you, Mr. Jeffcoat."

"And I you, Miss Cooper."

"Then call me Fannie!"

"Then call me Tom!" He smiled, watching her roll up the street.

It was a hectic day but Fannie had things under control. She spoke with Josephine about the parlor and its overcrowded condition and suggested that they place the piano against the wall and clear out some of the clutter to give the young people space for dancing. Josephine agreed. But she would have agreed to anything; she was happier than she'd been in months, for she, too, had been put to work and it felt so refreshing to be useful again. She sat on a chair in the sun on the upper veranda, polishing silver.

Downstairs, dust flew. Tarsy had come to help, as promised. She made sandwich filling while Frankie polished the stair rungs, carried the ferns into the yard, and beat the rugs. Emily packed away bric-a-brac and Fannie found places to hide the heavy furniture draperies, scarves, Turkish tidies, peacock feathers, and plaster busts. They washed the windows and lamp chimneys and pushed the piano's sounding board against the wall where it belonged. They mopped the floor, left it bare, and relegated the offensive pieces of furniture to the porch, returning to the room only enough chairs and tables to give it balance and grace. An excess of chairs, claimed Fanny, only encouraged guests to sit on their duffs instead of dancing and making merry. The fewer chairs, the better!

Frankie washed the piano keys, Tarsy polished the punch bowl, Emily hung the clean lace curtains (leaving the heavy, tassled draperies folded away), and Fannie selectively chose small items to be scattered sparsely about the room.

When it was finished the four of them stood staring at it in its fresh, bright state, and Fannie clapped once, declaring, "This calls for a celebration. A musical celebration!" Abruptly she plunked onto the claw-foot piano stool, swiveled to face the keys, and performed a rousing rendition of "The Blue-Tailed Fly."

The piano notes drifted upstairs, through Josephine's bedroom and out the open door to the veranda where Josie smiled and stopped polishing. She dropped her head against the back of the chair and closed her eyes, unconsciously tapping a half-polished spoon against her knee in rhythm with the music.

When she opened her eyes, Edwin was coming home along the street below. It was halfway between dinner and supper, and she felt a stir of gladness to see him arriving at the uncustomary time. She waved and he waved back, flashing a smile up to her. She watched him cross the yard and disappear onto the porch below while the music continued, and Fannie's voice came along with it.

". . . *the devil take the blue-tail fly. Jimmy crack corn and I don't care* . . ."

Downstairs, Edwin stepped into his front parlor to find it transformed. Sunlight cascaded through white lace curtains, lighting the polished floor to the color of deep tea. The furniture had been thinned, and uncovered, and was complemented by only a few figurines and knicknacks and a single feathery fern beside the bay window. The piano, with its back against the wall and its top swept clean of all but an oil lamp and their family pictures, rang out while Tarsy clapped and his children laughingly danced an untutored, reckless polka.

Fannie sat at the piano, pounding the ivory keys and singing gustily. Her head was covered with a white dish towel, knotted top-center where sprigs of peachy-colored frizz stuck out. Her apron and skirts were hiked up to her knees, showing black high-topped shoes, which thumped the foot pedals powerfully enough to set the oil lamp rocking. She saw Edwin's entry reflected in the polished wood of the piano front, and turned a glimpse over her shoulders, continuing to sing and play full force.

"*That horse he run, he jump, he pitch, he throw my master in de ditch* . . ."

When she reached the chorus, the children chimed in, and Edwin stood laughing.

"Sing, Edwin!" Fannie ordered, interrupting herself only for that second before jumping back into the song.

He added his inexpert tenor, and the five of them together made enough racket to shake the soot out of the kitchen stovepipe. Still dancing, Emily tripped over Frankie's feet. They giggled, caught their balance, then continued thumping their way around the room with as much grace as a pair of lumberjacks.

During the final chorus, Fannie raised her face to the ceiling and bellowed, *"Are you singing, Joey?"*

In that instant Edwin felt a burst of renewed love for Fannie.

He made it upstairs—two at a time—before the final chorus died and found Josie, indeed, singing softly to herself on the veranda in the sun, with a smile on her face.

Sensing him behind her, she stopped and smiled self-consciously over her shoulder.

"Edwin, you're home early."

"I left a note on the door at the livery. I thought they might need my help downstairs, but it doesn't look like it." He stepped onto the veranda and went down on one knee beside her chair, squeezing her hand, which still held the polishing rag and spoon. "Oh, Josie, it's so wonderful to hear you singing."

"I feel so much better, Edwin." Her smile reiterated her words. "I think I can go downstairs tonight . . . for a while anyway, and greet Emily's guests."

"That's wonderful, Josie . . ." He squeezed her hand again. "Just wonderful." Looking into her eyes he recalled their own betrothal party. How he had despaired, and how he'd hidden it. But their life hadn't been so bad after all. They'd had twenty good healthy years before she'd grown ill, and from those years had come two beautiful children, and a lovely house, and a deep respect for one another. And if their relationship had not been as intimate or demonstrative as he'd hoped, perhaps it was partly his fault. He should have admired her more, complimented, wooed, touched. Because he hadn't, he did so now.

"You look very lovely sitting here in the sun." He took the spoon from her hand and fitted his palm to hers, entwining their fingers. "I'm so glad I came home early."

She blushed and dropped her eyes. But her glance lifted in

surprise when he turned his head and kissed her palm. With her free hand she tenderly touched his bearded cheek.

"Dear Edwin," she said fondly.

Downstairs the piano stopped and laughing voices drifted off to the kitchen. For a while, both Edwin and Josephine were happier than they had been in years.

Chapter 6

WITH TWO HOURS to spare before the guests began arriving, the house was in perfect order. The finger sandwiches were sliced, the cakes frosted, and the brandy punch mixed. Tarsy had gone home to change clothes; Josephine, her hair freshly washed, was resting; in the kitchen, Edwin was combing Frankie's hair and giving him strict orders about allowing Earl no more than two sandwiches before getting him out of the house and over to Earl's, where the boys would spend the night.

Upstairs in the west bedroom Fannie was having a grand time creating a mess, strewing dresses from her trunks like a rainbow across Emily's bed and rocker.

"Green?" She whisked a silky frock against Emily's front. It was pale as seafoam and trimmed with bugle beads. Emily scarcely got a glimpse of it before it was gone. "No, no, it does nothing for your coloring." Fannie tossed it onto the pile, while Emily's eyes followed it longingly.

Next Fannie plucked up a splash of yellow. "Ah . . . saffron. Saffron will set off your hair." She plastered the dress to Emily, gripped her shoulders, and whirled her to face the mirror.

Emily found the yellow even more inviting than the green. "Oh, it's beautiful."

"It's good . . . still . . . mmm . . ." Fannie lay a finger beside her mouth and studied Emily thoughtfully. "No, I think not. Not tonight. We'll save it for another time." The becoming yellow dress went flying while Emily disappointedly watched it hit the bed and slide to the floor in a puddle of material. "Tonight it's got to be the absolute perfect frock . . . mmm . . ." Fanny tapped her lips, perused the jumble on the bed, and abruptly spun toward the closet. "I've got it!" She fell to her knees and dragged out another trunk, thumped the lid back, and scavenged through it like a dog disinterring a bone.

"Pink!" Kneeling, Fannie held it high—a dress as true hued as a wild rose. "The perfect color for you." She stood and whacked it against her knees, then whisked the rustly creation against Emily's front. "Would you look at how that girl can wear pink! I never could. I don't know why I bought this thing. It makes me look like a giant freckle. But you, with your black hair and dark complexion . . ." Even wrinkled, the dress was stunning, with a dropped neckline bordered by embroidered tea roses, wondrous bouffant elbow-length sleeves and a matching pouff at the spine. When it shifted, it spoke—a sibilant whisper telling of Eastern soirees where such frocks were customary. The dress was more beautiful than anything Emily had ever owned, but as she gazed wistfully at her reflection she was forced to admit, "I'd feel conspicuous in something this eye-catching."

"Nonsense!" Fannie retorted.

"I've never had a dress this pretty. Besides, Mother says a lady should wear subdued colors."

"And I always told her, Joey, you're old before your time." Conspiratorially, Fannie added, "Let your mother choose all the subdued colors she wants for herself, but this is your party. You may wear whatever you choose. Now what do you think?"

Emily gazed at the strawberry-pink confection, trying to imagine herself wearing it downstairs in the parlor as the guests arrived. She could well imagine Tarsy wearing such a dress—

Tarsy with her blond curls, pouting mouth, pretty face, and undeniably voluptuous figure. But herself? Her hair might be dark, but it had not been curled since she was old enough to say no to sleeping in rags. And her face? It was too long and dark-skinned, and her eyebrows were as straight and unattractive as heel marks on a floor. Her eyes and nose, she guessed, were passable, but her mouth was less than ordinary, and her teeth overlapped on top, which had always made her self-conscious when she smiled. No, her face and body were much better suited to britches and suspenders than to rose-colored frocks with bouffant sleeves.

"I think it's a little too feminine for me."

Fannie caught Emily's eye in the mirror. "You wanted to make Mr. Jeffcoat eat his words, didn't you?"

"Him! I don't give a rip what Mr. Jeffcoat thinks."

Fannie whisked the dress into the air and brushed at the wrinkles with her hand. "I don't believe you. I think you would love to appear downstairs in this creation and knock his eyeballs out. Now, what do you say?"

Emily reconsidered. If it worked, it would be better than spitting in Tom Jeffcoat's eye, and she had never been one to resist a challenge.

"All right. I'll do it . . . if you're sure you don't mind."

"Heavens, don't be silly! I'll never wear it again."

"But it's all wrinkles. How will we—"

"Leave that to me." Fannie flipped the dress over her shoulder and went off to shout over the banister, "Edwin, I'll need some fuel . . . kerosene, preferably! Coal oil if that's all you have." A moment later she stuck her head back into Emily's bedroom. "Brush your hair, light the lantern, and heat the curling tongs. I'll be right back." Again she disappeared, trailing a call. "Edwiiiiin?"

Within minutes she returned with Edwin in tow. From the depths of a trunk she produced a hunk of steel she introduced as a steamer. She held it while Edwin filled it with coal oil and water, and when it was lit and hissing, she put him to work steaming his daughter's dress while Fannie herself took over the curling tongs and arranged Emily's hair.

Submitting to her cousin, Emily watched her transformation while Papa, happy and humming, exclaimed as the wrinkles fell out of the pink satin; Mother came from across the hall dressed in a fine midnight blue serge dress, with her hair neatly coiled, and sat on the rocking chair to watch. Clamping a tress of hair in the hot tongs, Fannie described the newest hairdos from the East—crimps or waves, which would Emily prefer?

Emily chose crimps, and when the hairdo was done, piled atop her head like a dark puffy nest, she stared at herself disbelievingly, with her heart jumping in excitement. Standing behind Emily, inspecting her handiwork in the mirror, Fannie yelled, "Frankie, where are you?"

Frankie appeared in the doorway behind them. "What?"

"Go downstairs and pick a sprig of impatiens and bring them here—and don't ask me what they are. Those tiny pink flowers beside the front door!"

When he returned, and when the delicate blossoms were nestled in the misty-looking curls above Emily's left ear, Frankie stood back with big eyes and open lips, exclaiming in astonishment, "Wowwww, Emily, do you ever look pretty!"

At eight P.M. she stood before the dining room mirror *feeling* pretty, yes—but conspicuous. She dipped down to peer at her reflection and glimpsed her flushed cheeks. Goodness! It was a little breathtaking to see one's self in pink and crimps for the first time. She touched her chest—so much of it was bare—and stared.

She had never spared time for feminizing herself; she'd had no reason. Most girls primped and preened to attract the attentions of men, but she'd had Charles's attention forever. Staring at her reflection, she felt a sting of guilt, for it was not only Charles she wanted to impress tonight, but Tom Jeffcoat—that jackal who'd called her a tomboy. What pleasure she'd take in making him eat his words. All the while Fannie had been fussing over her Emily had gloated, imagining it.

But now, peering in the dining room mirror with her stomach trembling, she feared she'd be the one who felt awkward, instead of him. Fannie had powdered her face and chest with a light dusting of flour, and had tinted her cheeks by wetting swatches of red crepe paper, then rubbing them lightly on her skin. "Lick your lips," Fannie had ordered. "Now clamp them hard over the paper." Again . . . magic! But it was very uncertain magic, for a mere touch of the tongue removed it. Staring at her pink lips, Emily scolded herself silently: So help me, if you lick them before Jeffcoat arrives, you deserve every name he's called you!

"Emily?"

Emily jumped and spun around.

"Oh, Charles, I didn't hear you come in."

He stared as if he'd never seen her before. His cheeks became pink and his mouth dropped open, but not a word came out.

Emily laughed nervously. "Well, gracious, Charles, you act as if you don't recognize me."

"Emily?" Astonished and pleased, he let out the single word while moving slowly toward her, as if permission might possibly be required. "What have you done to yourself?"

She glanced down and plucked at her voluminous skirts, making them rustle like dry leaves. "Fannie did it."

He took her hands and held her at arm's length, turning them both in a half-circle. "Aren't I the lucky one? The prettiest girl in town."

"Oh, Charles, I'm not either, so stop your fibbing."

"That dress . . . and your hair . . . I never saw your hair so pretty before."

She felt herself blushing profusely.

Holding her hands, Charles let his eyes drift down over her floured chest and her corseted waist. She grew even more uneasy under his obviously delighted regard. "Oh, Emily, you look beautiful," he said softly, dipping his head as if to kiss her.

She feinted neatly aside. "Fannie colored my lips with crepe paper, but it comes off easily. I wouldn't want you looking marked." Though Charles politely straightened, he continued holding her hands and studying her with ardent eyes the way other men often studied Tarsy. Again Emily felt a pang of guilt. After all, it was fifteen minutes before their engagement party, and her fiancé wanted nothing more than an innocent stolen kiss. Yet she put him off, more concerned about keeping her lip coloring intact so she could make an impression on Tom Jeffcoat. She assuaged her guilt by telling herself that when she was married to Charles she would kiss him any time he wanted, and would make up for all the times she'd coyly withdrawn.

The guests began arriving, and Charles and Emily went to join the family in the parlor, where Mama had insisted upon having a receiving line. Edwin had carried and seated Josephine in the bay window, where he stood between her and

Fannie, introducing the latter to each new arrival, and announcing Tom and Emily's engagement with great alacrity. The house filled fast with businessmen and their wives, neighbors, fellow church members, owners of outlying ranches, Reverend Vasseler, Earl Rausch and his parents, Mr. and Mrs. Loucks. There were young people, too, all acquaintances of Emily's and Charles's—Jerome Berryman, Patrick Haberkorn, Mick Stubbs; and girls who'd come with their parents—Ardis Corbeil, Mary Ess, Lybee Ryker, Tilda Awk.

When Tarsy arrived she left her parents at the door and rushed directly to Emily. "Oh, Emily, you look stunning, is he here yet?"

"Thank you and no, he's not."

"Does my hair look all right? Do you think I should have worn my lavender dress? I didn't think my mother and father would *ever* get ready! I almost wore a hole in the rug, waiting for them. Poke me if you see him come in when I'm not looking. Fannie says there's going to be dancing later on. Oh, I hope he'll ask me!"

Emily found herself aggravated by Tarsy's gushing over the wonders of the mighty Jeffcoat, and further annoyed by the realization that she herself was unable to stop her own fixation with the front door. By 8:30 he still had not walked through it. Her lips felt stiff from smiling without rubbing them together. Though she was thirsty and tense, and though Charles had brought her a cup of punch, she would not touch the cup to her lips. Her ribs itched from the corset Fannie had forced her into, but she was afraid to scratch for fear he'd walk in and catch her at it.

That swine was thirty minutes late!

So help me, Jeffcoat, if you don't come after all this I'll make you suffer just like I'm suffering!

He arrived at 8:45.

Emily had intended to have Charles at her side, and a line of guests moving past them. She'd intended to give Tom Jeffcoat the full two seconds' worth of attention he deserved before scattering her courtesy to the others waiting in line. She'd intended to show him how little he mattered, so little that she need not even be caustic with him any longer.

But as it turned out, by 8:45 the receiving line had already broken up, Charles was in the dining room with his back to her, the guests were mingling, and she stood in the middle of the room alone. Tom Jeffcoat's eyes found her immediately.

For several uncomfortable seconds they took measure of one another, then he began moving across the room toward her. She felt an unwelcome panic and the absurd pounding of her heart—hard enough, she feared, to shake the flour off her chest. *Please, God, don't let it fall off!*

She watched him approach, feeling trapped and frantic, tricked by some unkind fortune who'd painted him more attractive than she wanted him to be, who'd given him a preference for clean-shavenness and blessed him with beautiful black hair, startlingly handsome blue eyes, a full, attractive mouth, and an easy saunter. She damned Tarsy for pointing it all out, and Charles for abandoning her when she needed him, and her own stupid heart, which refused to stop knocking in her chest. She noted, as if distanced from herself, that his suit was faintly wrinkled, his boots by contrast shiny and new, and that Tarsy had appeared in the dining room archway and was staring at him like a drooling basset hound. But his eyes remained riveted upon Emily as he crossed the room.

By the time he reached her, she felt as if she were choking. He stopped before her, so tall she had to raise her chin to meet his eyes.

"Good evening, Miss Walcott," he said in a painfully polite voice.

"Good evening, Mr. Jeffcoat."

He let his eyes whisk down and up once, without lingering anywhere, but when they returned to hers he wore a faint grin, which she longed to slap from his face.

"Thank you for inviting me." But they both knew she hadn't invited him; Charles had. "I understand congratulations are in order. Charles told me about your engagement."

"Yes," she replied, glancing away from his eyes, which, though holding a surface politeness, seemed to be laughing at her. "We've known each other forever. It was only a matter of time before we named a date."

"So Charles tells me. A year from now, is it?"

"Give or take a month or two." She was, after all, no good at guile; her responses came out brusque and cool.

"A pleasant time of year for a wedding," he observed conversationally, proving himself much better than she at observing the amenities. Her tongue seemed to be bonded to the top of her mouth as she stared at anything in the room but Tom Jeffcoat. After several beats of silence, he added, "Charles is . . . ecstatic."

His pause injected the remark with dubious undertones, and she felt herself coloring. "Help yourself to punch and sandwiches anytime you want, Mr. Jeffcoat. I'd best talk to some of the other guests." But when she moved he caught her lightly by an arm.

"Are you forgetting? I haven't met your mother yet."

He hadn't said a word about her appearance. *Not one word!* And damn him for making her lose her composure. She dropped her glance to the hand that sent an unwarranted sizzle up her arm, then pierced him with a haughty look. "You're wrinkling my sleeve, Mr. Jeffcoat."

"I apologize." He dropped her elbow immediately, and ordered, "Introduce me to your mother, Miss Walcott."

"Certainly." She spun to find that her mother had been watching them all the while, and for a heartbeat she froze. When Jeffcoat touched her politely on the back she shot forward. "Mother, this is Charles's friend, Tom Jeffcoat. You remember, Papa was talking about him during supper the other night?"

"Mr. Jeffcoat . . ." Queenlike, Josephine presented her frail hand. "Edwin's competitor."

He bowed over it graciously. "Fellow businessman, I hope. If I didn't think there was enough business in Sheridan for both of us I'd have settled someplace else."

"Let us hope you're right. Of course, any friend of Charles's and Emily's is welcome in our home."

"Thank you, Mrs. Walcott. It's a beautiful house." He glanced around. "I can't wait to have my own."

"Charles and Edwin built it, of course."

"Charles will be building mine, too, as soon as the barn is done."

"What's this we hear about a turntable in your barn?"

He laughed. "Oh, Charles has been talking?"

"Mostly Frankie."

"Ah, Frankie, our young apprentice . . ." He chuckled fondly. "The turntable is a whim, Mrs. Walcott, nothing more than a whim."

Fannie sailed up on the tail end of the comment. "What's a whim? Hello, Tom."

He turned and let his hands be captured. "Hello, Fannie."

"You two have met?" inquired Emily, surprised.

"Yes, this morning." Fannie slipped her arm through Tom's as if they were old friends while he smiled down at her upraised face.

"She was out for a bicycle ride and stopped by my place to introduce herself."

"I'm so glad you've come. Have you talked to Charles yet?"

"No, I was just heading over."

"Oh, and here's Tarsy. Tarsy, you've met Tom already, haven't you?" Tarsy's hand shot out fast enough to create a draft. He bowed over it gallantly.

"Miss Fields, how nice to see you again. You're looking lovely tonight."

"Why don't you take him over and see that he gets a cup of punch?" Fannie suggested to the blonde.

Tarsy appropriated Tom's arm and gave him a 150-candle-power smile while leading him away, chiding, "Shame on you for being late. I was about to give up hope."

Emily steamed, watching them move off toward Charles. *Miss Fields, you're looking lovely tonight!* Wasn't he just *oozing* charm?

She watched all night while men and women alike succumbed to it. He moved among the houseful of guests with singular effortlessness, comfortable meeting strangers, quick to pick up conversational threads, to win slaps on the back from the men and charming smiles from the ladies.

Reverend Vasseler shook his hand heartily and thanked him for getting the young boys to help at the church. The young boys themselves followed him, avid-eyed, and asked when his turntable would be ready. The mothers with unmarried daughters invited him to dinner. The ranchers with stock for sale invited him to look over their horseflesh. Fannie made plans to teach him how to ride her bicycle. Charles spent more time with him than with his bride-to-be. And Tarsy clung to his arm like a barnacle.

Meanwhile, Emily had one of the most miserable evenings of her life.

When the punch bowl was half-empty and the first wave of socializing past, Fannie called upon Edwin to make a betrothal toast. He filled Josephine's glass and his own, handed drinks to

Charles and Emily, and stood in the bay window with his arm around his daughter.

"Before the evening gets away from us," he addressed his guests, "Emily's mother and I want you all to know how happy we are over the announcement of Emily's engagement. We've known Charles here since . . ." He turned to glance affectionately at his future son-in-law. "How long has it been, Charles?" He turned back to his guests. "Well, since he was wiping his nose on his shirtsleeve, anyway." Everyone laughed.

"For those of you who may not know it, his parents were our dear friends back in Philadelphia, friends we still miss, and we wish they could be here with us tonight." He cleared his throat and went on. "Well, for years Charles and Emily have been running in and out of our house together. I think we've fed him as many meals as we've fed our own two. I seem to recall back around the time they were waist-high or so she stole his pet frog and left it in a cricket box until it was flat and hard as a silver dollar, and Charles—if memory serves—beat her up and gave her a black eye."

After another ripple of mirth Edwin continued: "But they worked it all out and, believe it or not, Charles came to me when he was just about eye level to my chin and announced very seriously . . ." Edwin paused to study the contents of his wineglass. "'Mr. Walcott.'" He lifted his face like an orator. "'I want you to know that I'm going to marry Emily as soon as we're old enough.' I remember trying hard not to laugh." Edwin turned toward Charles with a rubicund glow on his cheeks. "Good heavens, Charles, do you realize your voice hadn't decided yet at that point whether it wanted to be bass or soprano?" After more laughter Edwin grew serious.

"Well, it was good news then and it's good news now. Sometimes it's hard to believe our little Emily is all grown up. But Emily, honey . . ." He squeezed her shoulders and gazed adoringly into her face. "A year from now when we make a toast to the bride and groom, you know you'll have your mother's and my blessings. We already think of Charles as our son." Edwin raised his glass, inviting his guests to follow suit. "To Charles and Emily . . . and their future happiness."

"Hear, hear!"

"To Charles and Emily!"

Salutations filled the room. Edwin kissed Emily's right

temple and Charles kissed her left. Josephine reached up from her chair and took Emily's hand. As she leaned down to kiss her mother's cheek Emily felt small for having been so sulky all night long and promised herself she would throw herself into the spirit of the party for the remainder of the evening. As she straightened she saw Tom Jeffcoat studying her. He raised his glass in a silent salute and emptied it, watching her over the rim of his glass.

The brandy in her stomach felt as if it had been touched by a match. Confused, she turned her attention to Charles.

"I'm warm, Charles. Could we step outside for a few minutes?"

But out on the porch she discovered that Charles had imbibed enough brandy to make him distinctly amorous. He took her around the corner of the porch, flattened her against the wall, and removed all traces of Fanny's handiwork from her lips, then tried to do the same with the flour on her chest. But she caught his hand and ordered, "No, Charles. Anyone could come out."

He caught her head in both hands, kissing her insistently, passionately, and she realized her mistake in coming outside with him, dressed in Fannie's dress, when he'd been drinking. In the end, she had to snap at him, "Charles, I said no!"

For a moment he glared at her, frustrated, looking as if he wanted to either shake her or drag her off the porch, away from the window lights, and make their engagement official with far more than a paltry kiss. She watched him gather composure until finally he stepped back and drew a shaky breath. "You're right. You go back in and I'll follow in a minute."

When she reentered the parlor her cheeks were flushed and she had lost the impatiens from her hair. Father was carrying Mother upstairs, Fannie was playing the piano, and Tom Jeffcoat was watching the doorway with rapt absorption.

Their eyes met and she felt again a flash of attraction for him, felt as if he could divine everything that had transpired on the porch. Were her lips puffy? Did the path of Charles's hand show? Did she look as kissed clean and defloured as she felt?

Well, it was no business of Tom Jeffcoat's what she did with her fiancé. She lifted her chin and turned away.

Though she avoided him for the remainder of the evening, she knew where he was each moment, whom he talked with, how many times he laughed with Tarsy, and how many times with Charles. She knew, too, exactly how many times he studied Charles's new fiancée in her borrowed pink dress when he thought she wasn't aware.

Shortly before midnight Fannie sat down at the piano and struck into the mellifluent strains of Strauss's *Blue Danube* and called everyone to dance. The married couples did, but the young people held back, the males declaring they didn't know how, the females wishing the men would learn. Fannie leapt from the piano stool and scolded, "Nonsense! Anyone can dance. We'll have a lesson!" She made everyone form a circle, experienced dancers interspersed with novices, and taught them the steps of the waltz, singing all the while, *Da da da da dum . . . Dum-dum! Dum-dum!* Guiding the unbroken ring of feet first forward, then back, first left, then right, she made everyone vocalize the familiar Viennese waltz. *Da da da da dum . . . Dum-dum! Dum-dum!* And while they sang and waltzed she chose a partner and drew him into the center—Patrick Haberkorn, who blushed and moved clumsily, but gave in to Fannie good-naturedly.

"Just keep singing," she instructed in Patrick's ear, "and forget about your feet except to pretend they're leading mine instead of following them." When Patrick was moving reasonably smoothly she danced him to Tilda Awk and negotiated the transition of partners. One after another she took the young men and showed them how fun dancing could be. When she had trained the feet of Tom Jeffcoat she turned him over to Tarsy Fields. When she'd done the same for Charles, she paired him off with Emily. And when all were matched and only Edwin remained, she opened her arms to him and became his partner, hiding the fact that her heart swelled at being in his arms at last, and that her laugh was only a facade for the intense love she felt. Edwin obliged, sweeping her around the parlor as together they sang *Da da da da dum . . . dum-dum!*

Less than a minute they danced before Fannie reluctantly left him and slid back onto the piano stool and called out, "Change partners!"

Shuffling and confusion ensued, and when it settled Emily found herself in her father's arms. He was smiling and smart-stepping as he led her.

"Are you having a good time, honey?"

"Yes, Papa. Are you?"

"The best."

"I didn't know you could dance."

"I haven't done it in years. Your mother never cared to."

"Do you think we're keeping her awake?"

"Of course. But she told me she would enjoy listening."

"I think she had a good time tonight."

"I know she did."

"She seemed stronger, and her cheeks were actually pink."

"It's Fannie. Fannie is a miracle worker."

"I know. I'm so happy she's here."

"So am I."

"Change partners!"

"Oops!" Papa said. "Here you go."

Emily whirled around and found herself with Pervis Berryman, short and broad as a washtub, but a surprisingly agile dancer. He congratulated her on her engagement and said the party was just what this town needed and wasn't it good to see the young people dancing this way?

"Change partners!"

Pervis turned her over to Tarsy's father, whose hair was parted down the middle and slicked flat with pomade. He smelled like his barber shop—slightly soapy, slightly perfumed—and his waxed mustache twitched when he talked. He, too, congratulated her on her engagement, told her she was getting a hell of a good man, and told her that Tarsy was so excited about the party tonight she'd asked permission to have one of her own next Saturday.

"Change partners!"

Emily twirled around and found herself in the arms of Tom Jeffcoat.

"Hiya, tomboy," he said, grinning.

"You insufferable wretch," she returned pleasantly.

"Ha-ha-ha!" He laughed at the ceiling.

"I'll get even with you yet."

"For what? I've been on my best behavior tonight, haven't I?"

"I don't think you know what good behavior is."

"Now, Emily, don't start fights. I promised Charles I'd do my best to get along with you."

"You and I will never get along, and you know it perfectly well. You also know that if it weren't for Charles you wouldn't be in this house right now."

"Do you practice being mouthy or does it just come naturally?"

"Do you practice insulting women or does it just come naturally?"

"Hostesses are supposed to be polite to their guests."

"I am. To *my* guests."

"You know, Charles and I get along remarkably well. I have a feeling he and I are destined to be friends. If you're going to marry him, don't you think we should try to grin and bear each other—for his sake?"

"You already grin more than I can bear."

"But we'll be bumping into each other at occasions like this for . . . well, who knows how long?"

It was essentially what Fannie had said, but he need not know that.

Jeffcoat went on. "Take for instance next Saturday night. Tarsy is planning another party and we'll probably end up dancing together again."

"I hope not. You're a terrible dancer."

"Tarsy doesn't think so."

"Get off my toes, Mr. Jeffcoat. Tarsy Fields has never danced before in her life. How would she know?"

"You've never danced before either, so how would you know?"

"Look . . ." She pulled back and flattened her skirt with one hand. "You've undoubtedly scuffed the toe of Fannie's shoe."

He glanced down briefly, then resumed dancing. "Fannie? So that's where you got the clothes."

"Not that you noticed."

"Did you want me to?"

"You're the one who called *me* a tomboy!"

"After you called me shabby. I dress the way I do because it's the most sensible when I work."

"So do I."

Their eyes met and each gave the other a begrudging point.

"So what do you say, should we call a truce? For Charles's sake?"

She shrugged and glanced aside indifferently.

"He tells me you're going to be a veterinarian."

"Yes, I am."

"Those were some of your papers I saw at the livery stable that day?"

"I was studying."

"You think you're strong enough?"

"Strong enough?" She tossed him a puzzled glance.

"To treat farm animals. It can take a surprising amount of strength."

"Sometimes a smaller hand and a thinner arm can be an advantage. Have you ever pulled a calf?"

"No, only foals."

"Then you know."

Yes, he did. And he understood her reasoning.

"So you know a lot about animals."

"I suppose I do."

He glanced around. "Out of all the ranchers here, who would you say raises the best horseflesh?"

She was surprised that he'd ask her opinion but his face was serious as he scanned the guests. She, too, took their measure. "It's hard to say. Wyoming's climate produces some of the finest horses in America. We have one hundred and fifty different grasses in this state and each one is better than the next for grazing. The cold winters, the clear water, and the pure air give our horses stamina and good lungs. The army buys most of their horses here."

"I know that. But who would you buy from?"

Before she could answer, Fannie called, "Change partners!"

They stopped dancing abruptly and withdrew from each other to stand uncertainly, realizing they'd embarked upon their first civil exchange and that it hadn't hurt one bit.

"I'll think about it," she said.

"Fine. And think about who I ought to buy hay from, too. I'll need advice if I'm going to make it here."

Again she felt stunned that he'd seek it from her. But he was offering an olive branch for Charles's sake, and the least she could do was accept it.

"Hay's not so touchy. Anybody."

He nodded as if accepting her word.

A new partner waited, but as Emily turned to him, Jeffcoat grabbed her arm and twirled her back to face him. Grinning into her eyes, he said in an undertone, "Thanks for the dance, tomboy."

He stood too near, his lopsided smile six inches from her

eyebrow, and she could smell the faint scent of his flesh, warm from dancing, and see clearly the grain of his skin on his clean-shaven chin, the single dimple in his left cheek, the edges of his teeth, the humor in his eyes. She felt something stir between them and wondered in a brief flash how it would feel to be flattened against the porch wall and kissed clean by him instead of Charles.

The insanity lasted a mere second before she pulled free and quipped, "You'd better brush up for next week. My toes are wrecked."

For the remainder of the night they politely avoided each other, while Fannie taught everyone to dance the varsovienne—a cross between the polka and the mazurka. Emily stuck to Charles and Tom to Tarsy. Before the evening broke up Tarsy spread the word that her party would be at the same time next week at her house and all the young people were invited. When it was time to wish their guests good night, Emily and Charles stood at the door side by side, accepting parting wishes. Charles got a handshake from Tom while Emily got a hug from Tarsy, who whispered into her ear, "He's walking me home! I'll tell you about it tomorrow!"

When Charles was gone, Emily helped Fannie and Papa clean up the house and wondered if Tom Jeffcoat was pushing Tarsy against her porch wall and if Tarsy was enjoying it.

Silly question! Tarsy probably had *him* pushed against the porch wall!

She wondered about kissing and why some girls enjoyed it and others didn't. She thought about herself earlier tonight with Charles, and how she'd felt almost reviled by his groping. She was engaged to him now, and if Tarsy were any authority, it was supposed to be enjoyable, even desirable.

Maybe there was something wrong with her.

She went upstairs five minutes before Fannie and sat in the lamplight worrying about it. Should a girl prefer working in a stable to kissing her intended? Surely not. Yet it was true—sometimes when Charles kissed her, when she gave in to him out of a sense of sheer obligation, she thought of other things—the horses, pitching hay, riding across an open field with her hair blowing like the mane of the animal beneath her.

Dejectedly Emily removed the pink dress and hung it up, took down her hair and brushed it, thoughtfully studying her reflection in her mirror. She touched her lips, then closed her eyes and skimmed her fingertips over her own chest, pretending it was Charles. When he was her husband he would touch her not only here, but in other places, in other ways. Her eyes flew open and met their mirrored images, chagrined. She'd seen horses mating and it was a graceless, embarrassing thing. However could she do that with Charles?

Worrying, she donned her nightdress and slipped into bed, listening to the murmur of Papa and Fannie as they came up the stairs and said good night in the hall. Then Fannie came in and closed the door, unhooked her dress, untied her corset, and brushed her hair, humming.

Oh, to be like Fannie. To whisk through life worrying about nothing, single and happy to be, pursuing whatever flight of fancy beckoned. Fannie would have the answers, Emily was certain.

When the wick was lowered and the bedsprings quiet, Emily stared at the black ceiling with a lump in her throat.

"Fannie?" she whispered at last.

"Hm?" Fannie murmured over her shoulder.

"Thank you for the party."

"You're welcome, dearling. Did you have a good time?"

"Yes . . . and no."

"No?" Fannie rolled over and touched Emily's shoulder. "What's wrong, Emily?"

Emily took a full minute summoning her courage before enquiring, "Fannie, can I ask you something?"

"Of course."

"It's something personal."

"It usually is when girls whisper in the dark."

"It's about kissing."

"Ah, kissing."

"I'd ask Mother, but she's . . . well, you know Mother."

"Yes, I do. I wouldn't ask her either, if she were my mother."

"Have you ever kissed a man?"

Fannie laughed softly, rolled to her back, and snuggled more deeply into her pillow. "I love kissing men. I've kissed several."

"Do they all kiss the same?"

"Not at all. A kiss, dearling, is like a snowflake—no two are alike. There are brief ones, long ones, timid ones, bold ones, teasing ones and serious ones, dry ones and wet ones—"

"Wet ones, yes. Those are the ones. They're . . . I . . . Charles . . . what I mean to say is . . ."

"They're heavenly, aren't they?" mused Fannie.

"Are they?" Emily returned doubtfully.

"You mean you don't think so?"

"Well, sometimes. But other times I feel like . . . well, like it's not allowed. Like I'm doing something wrong."

"You don't get heady or impatient?"

"Once I did . . . rather. It was the day Charles proposed. But I've known him so long sometimes he seems more like a brother to me, and who wants to kiss their brother?"

All grew quiet while the two lay in private thought.

Finally Emily spoke. "Fannie?"

"Hm?"

"Have you ever been in love?"

Silence again until, across the hall, Josephine coughed and another occupant of the house rolled over in his bed.

"Deeply."

"How does it feel?"

"It hurts." The pillowslip rustled as Emily turned her head sharply to study Fannie in the dark. But before she could ask any more questions, Fannie ordered gently, "Go to sleep now, dearling, it's late."

Chapter 7

THE FOLLOWING DAY was Sunday, and Tarsy was waiting to pounce on Emily outside Coffeen Hall even before church services began. She grabbed Emily's arm and pulled her aside without so much as a greeting.

"Emily, wait till I tell you! You won't believe it! But there isn't time now. Tell Charles you're walking home with me and I'll tell you everything then!"

As it turned out, Tarsy was walked home by Tom Jeffcoat, but she found Emily later that afternoon at the livery stable.

"Em, are you here?" she called.

"I'm up here!" Emily answered from the hay loft.

Tarsy crossed to the foot of the ladder and peered up. "What are you doing up there?"

Emily's head appeared overhead. "Studying. Come on up."

"I can't climb that ladder in my dress."

"Sure you can. I'm wearing mine. Just hike it up around your waist."

"But, Emily—"

"It's nice up here. This is one of my favorite places, especially on Sunday when nobody's around. Come on."

Tarsy hitched up her skirts and made the climb. The immense arrow-shaped grain door was open, letting a swash of sunlight set the hay alight. Swallows flew in and out, nesting in the rafters, and beyond the open door lay a panoramic view of the town, the southerly opening into the valley and the blue Big Horns to the southwest. Tarsy noticed none of it. She collapsed and fell back supine, stretching and closing her eyes.

"Oh, I'm so tired," she breathed.

Emily sat nearby, watching a battalion of dust motes lift, smelling the scent of stirred hay. "It was a late night," she said.

"But I had such a good time. Thank you, Emily." Tarsy opened her eyes to the swallows and the rafters, stretched out a tress of her hair, and murmured dreamily, "I think I'm in love."

Emily threw the girl a jaundiced glance. "With Tom Jeffcoat?"

"Mmm . . . who else?"

"That was fast."

"He's wonnnderful." Tarsy gave a self-satisfied smile and wound the lock of hair around a finger to her scalp. "He walked me home last night and we sat on the porch steps talking until nearly three o'clock. He told me everything about himself . . . everything!" Tarsy's exhaustion seemed to vanish in a blink and she popped up with bright-eyed exuberance. "He's twenty-six years old and he lived in Springfield, Missouri, all his life with his mother, father, one brother, and three sisters who still live there. He borrowed the money to come here and set himself up in business from his grandma. But he says he plans to pay her back within five years and he knows he can do it because he's sure the town will grow and he's not afraid of hard work. But listen to this!" Sitting cross-legged, Tarsy leaned forward avidly. "A year ago he got engaged to a woman named Julia March, but after nine months she threw him over for a rich banker named James or Jones or something like that, and yesterday, back in Springfield, it was her wedding day. Imagine that! All the while he was dancing and putting on a happy front at your party, he was really hiding a broken heart because it was his ex-fiancée's wedding night.

He seemed so sad when he was telling me about it, and then he put his arms around me and held me and rested his chin on the top of my head and pretty soon he kissed me."

What was it like? The question popped into Emily's mind before she could block it out, and Tarsy answered it unwittingly.

"Oh, Emileeeee . . ." She sighed and fell backwards in the hay as if bedazed. "It was heavenly. It was like sliding down a rainbow. It was like angels dancing on my lips. It was—"

"You've only known him a week."

Tarsy's eyes opened. "What difference does that make? I'm smitten. And he's so much more grown up than Jerome. When Jerome kisses me nothing happens. And Jerome's lips are hard. Tom's are soft. And he opened them, and I thought I'd absolutely *die* of ecstasy."

Emily felt a flash of irritation. It had never been like that for her with Charles. Sliding down a rainbow? How absurd. And how imprudent of Tarsy to reveal such private details to anyone. What the girl did with Jeffcoat should have been held in strictest confidence. It made Emily uncomfortable, listening, as if she'd hidden and watched the episode undetected.

After that day in the hayloft, every time Emily saw Tom Jeffcoat she remembered Tarsy's rapturous account and, picturing it, speculated about what *his* reaction had been. By choice she would have avoided him, but he walked past several times a day on his way to and from his own livery stable. Often as not, Charles was with him, since the two ate many of their meals together at the hotel and worked daily, side by side, on Jeffcoat's building. Sometimes Charles would drop in at Walcott's Livery just to say hello or to let Emily know if he'd be coming to the house in the evening, and Jeffcoat would stand in the background, never intruding, but always making her wholly aware of his presence. While she and Charles talked he'd lean against a beam chewing a piece of hay with his hat pushed back and one thumb in the waist of his indecently tight pants. As the two left Jeffcoat would nod politely and speak for the first time: "Good day, Miss Walcott," to which she'd reply flatly without glancing at him. Why he should irritate her so keenly, she didn't understand, yet he did. His very presence in her father's stable made her want to plant a boot in his backside and send him flying!

She avoided his livery stable assiduously, even when Charles was there working. Sometimes she would stand at the great open grain door of her own and listen to their hammers, watching the building near completion and wish a bolt of lightning would flash down out of heaven and level the place.

And sometimes she'd stand there and wonder if his lips were really soft.

On the Friday afternoon following her party she was alone in the office, memorizing ointment recipes with her feet propped on the desk and her back to the door, when a voice spoke behind her.

"Hiya, tomboy."

She catapulted from the chair as if propelled by black powder. Her book clapped to the floor as she spun. There, lounging in the doorway, grinning crookedly, stood the rat, Jeffcoat.

"A little jumpy, aren't you?"

"What are *you* doing here?" she glowered.

"Is that any way to greet a friend?" He peeled himself from the doorframe, swiped up the book, and handed it to her. "Here. You dropped something."

His lips—damn them!—did look like something angels might dance on. She grabbed the book rudely and slammed it on the desk. "What do you want?"

"Can we talk?"

"About what?"

Without answering, he sauntered toward the cot where the caramel cat slept in its customary place, scooped it up, and stood with his back to Emily, nose to nose with the creature while it hung from his thumbs. "You've got some kind of life, critter. Every time I come in here you're curled up sleeping. What's your name, huh?"

"Taffy," Emily replied indignantly. "Is that what you came to find out, the name of my cat?"

Jeffcoat threw a half grin over his shoulder, then returned his attention to the cat. "Taffy," he repeated, scratching it beneath the chin. In his own good time, he dropped to the cot, still cradling the feline and making it purr. "I need to buy stock for my livery stable," he announced, with his eyes still on the cat. "Will you help me?"

"Me!" Surprise set Emily back on her chair. "Why me?"

At last Jeffcoat looked at her. "Because Charles says you know horses better than most men do."

"Doesn't it strike you as a little presumptuous, Mr. Jeffcoat—"

"Tom."

"—to ask me to help you set up your business when I don't want it here in the first place?"

"Maybe. But you've lived here longer than I have, you know the ranchers—who's honest, who's not, who's got the best horses, where they live. I'd appreciate your help."

She drew in a breath and held it, preparing a tirade. Instead the lungful came out with an unexpected chug of laughter. "You know, you amaze me."

"What's so amazing?"

"Your temerity."

He blew on the cat's face and suggested, "We could go this afternoon maybe. Or Monday." The cat sneezed and shook its head. Jeffcoat chuckled, then shifted his regard to Emily. "I need to pin down a good dozen horses, and find a rancher who'll contract to sell me hay. By the end of next week I'll have the turntable in place, but I haven't got horses *or* wagons yet. What do you say, will you help?"

For a moment she was tempted. He would, after all, open his doors for business and there was no way she could stop him. Also, his friendship with Charles seemed cemented; it would be hard on Charles if she, as his wife, continued discouraging it.

But while she was considering, her eyes dropped to Jeffcoat's lips and out of nowhere came Tarsy's description of kissing him.

"Sorry, Jeffcoat." She leapt to her feet and headed for the door. "You'll have to find somebody else. I'm busy."

Naturally, Charles heard that she'd refused to help his friend, and that evening he chided gently, "You know, you could be a little nicer to him. It's tough on him being alone out here."

"I dislike him. Why should I help him?"

"Because it's the neighborly thing to do."

"He claims he's been around horses all his life. Let him find his own."

The following morning Emily was cleaning stalls when she heard a wagon approach and tie up outside. Footsteps hurried toward her father's office and a moment later she heard two men talking. Momentarily, Edwin came out to find her.

"Emily?"

"I'm back here, Papa."

He stopped at the stall opening followed by a shorter man with a worried face. "Well, little doctor." Edwin smiled indulgently at his daughter. "You wanted a chance to practice, this is it. You know August, don't you?"

"Hello, Mr. Jagush."

August Jagush was a stocky Pole, fresh from the Old Country. His face was round, ruddy and mustaschioed, and his hands as wide as soup plates. He wore a red plaid shirt buttoned to the throat, and on his head a flat-billed wool cap brought from Poland. Jagush removed the cap and bowed servilely.

"*Ja,* hullo, miss," he said with a heavy accent.

Edwin acted as spokesman. "August has a brood sow who's ready to farrow but she's been trying for over sixteen hours and nothing's happened. He's afraid the pigs will die and maybe the sow, too, if something doesn't happen soon. Will you go out there and have a look?"

"Of course." Emily was already hurrying across the stable. The baby pigs—she knew—could survive in the birth canal a maximum of another two hours, and it might take her most of that to reach Jagush's place. "I'll need to saddle a horse and get my bag."

"I'll saddle Sagebrush for you," Edwin offered.

Jagush said, "The missus she sends a list, so I go to Loucks's first before I head back."

"Have you got some beer out at your place?" Emily asked, shouting from the office.

"Beer? *ja,* what *Polak* don't have beer?"

"Good. I'll need some."

If she waited for Jagush, precious minutes would be wasted. The animal was doubtless in pain and Emily found herself unwilling to prolong its suffering any longer than necessary. "If it's all right with you, Mr. Jagush, I won't wait for you. I know where you live."

"*Ja,* you hurry, miss," he agreed.

Jagush lived—it occurred to Emily—on the road out to the Lucky L ranch. Tom Jeffcoat wanted to buy horses. And Charles was haranguing her to help him. And Cal Liberty had a reputation for raising healthy hearty American saddlehorses and for being too proud of his stock to sell any inferior animals. Emily made a snap decision.

"Papa?" she called.

"What?"

"Saddle Gunpowder, too. I'm taking Jeffcoat along with me."

Her stomach danced with excitement. At last, a real call. Few ranchers had asked for her help. They instinctively doubted her ability since she was a woman, and since she hadn't fully earned her certificate from Barnum yet. Even when she did, it would not be the equivalent of a degree from a college of veterinary medicine. Those colleges were all back East or she'd be attending one right now. But she cared about animals and had what Papa had always called a natural instinct for helping them. It would take time before the bigger ranchers would trust her. In the meantime, she'd help the smaller farmers like Jagush whenever possible, and wait for her reputation to grow.

In the office she opened a black leather satchel and took stock of her instruments: pincers, twitch, probang, and hopples; forceps in two sizes; balling iron and a balling gun; a pair of curved scissors, hand clippers, a clinch cutter; funnel and rubber tubing; a blacksmith's hoof knife; and an assortment of ordinary tools—a steel chisel, a pair of pliers, and a claw hammer. Yes, everything was there. And the bottles and vials too, neatly lining the sides of the case, each buckled into place by a leather band.

Satisfied, she snapped the bag closed, wrapped it in a black rubber apron, and went to tie it behind her saddle and mount up.

"Wish me luck, Papa," she called, taking Gunpowder's reins from Edwin.

"Bring 'em in alive, honey!" he called as she touched heel to Sage's flanks and took off at a canter through the double-wide door.

Thirty seconds later she reined in at the great north door of Jeffcoat's livery stable leading the spare black gelding.

"Jeffcoat?" she shouted. Inside, the syncopated beats of two hammers stopped. "Jeffcoat, you in there?" She peered into the depths of the building, which she'd never come near before. It was bigger than her father's and promised to be much more serviceable, with its brick floor, loft *steps* instead of a ladder, half-doors on the stalls, and the capstan for the turntable already in place. The windows were seated, the sliding door hung, pushed wide now to light both ends of the building. The stalls along the left were nearly complete, and from one, halfway down, Jeffcoat emerged. Even in silhouette she could tell it was he instead of Charles by the outline of his cowboy hat and the length of his legs.

"That you, tomboy?" he called.

"It's me. You wanna look at horseflesh or not?"

"Hey, Charles!" Tom threw down a hammer. "Can you work without me for a couple hours? Somebody's here who says she'll take me out shopping for horses."

Charles appeared behind Tom and walked with him the length of the building. "Emily, this is a surprise." He stopped beside Sagebrush, pulling off his work gloves, smiling up at her. "Why don't you come in and see the building? It's really shaping up."

"Sorry, I don't have time. I'm on my way out to August Jagush's to look at one of his brood sows that's having trouble farrowing."

"You're taking Tom out *there?*" Charles asked, surprised.

"No, out to the Lucky L after I'm done—it's close by and I figure Cal Liberty will treat him fairly. If you're coming, Jeffcoat, hurry up."

"You sure you don't mind, Charles?" Jeffcoat paused to ask.

"Not at all. Get going."

As Jeffcoat took the reins from Emily and mounted up, Charles squeezed her calf and said quietly, "Thanks, Emily. He's been worried about getting those horses."

"I'll see you tonight," she replied, giving Sagebrush both heels. Tom's stirrups needed lengthening, but Emily took off at a trot leaving him leaning sideways in the saddle.

"Hey, wait a minute."

"You can catch up!" she called without slowing.

While Charles volunteered to adjust the stirrups Tom glanced after his friend's fiancée and inquired, "Is she always this ornery?"

"She'll get used to you. Give her time."

"She's got the temperament of a wounded buffalo. Hell, I don't even know this horse's name."

"Gunpowder."

"Gunpowder, huh?" And to the horse: "Well, you'd better have some in you because we've got some catching-up to do." When the stirrups were adjusted Tom said, "Thanks, Charles. I'll see you here when I get back if it's early enough. Otherwise, at Tarsy's."

He took off at a canter, scowling at the rider ahead. She rode prettier than most women walked, with a natural roll and balance, her back straight, the reins in one hand, the other resting on a thigh. She wore her brother's cap again but she sat her saddle so perfectly it didn't even bounce. As Jeffcoat came up on her left flank he noted the sleek fit of the trousers over her thigh, her intent stare at the horizon, her taut lips. There was no warmth in her today at all, only spunk and determination. Yet she fascinated him.

"Hey, slow up there. You'll get that horse lathered."

"He can take it. Can you?"

"All right, sister, they're your horses."

They rode in silence for nearly an hour and a half. He let her control their pace, slowing to a walk when she slowed, cantering when she cantered. She spoke only once, when they were turning into the driveway at their destination. "This is no country to raise pigs in but Jagush is Polish and the Polish eat pork. He'd have been better off to bring lambs out here when he homesteaded."

A short pudgy woman in a *babushka* came from an outbuilding the moment they arrived. Her face was round as a pumpkin and contorted with worry. "She is down here!" Mrs. Jagush called, gesturing toward the crude log barn. "Hurry."

Dismounting, Emily told Jeffcoat, "You can wait here if you want. It'll smell a lot fresher."

"You might need some help."

"Suit yourself. Just don't get sick on me." Turning sideways in the saddle, she slid to the ground, landed lightly, and let Tom tie both horses to a fence post while she retrieved her pack from behind the saddle. They walked to the barn together, met by Mrs. Jagush, whose creased face spoke of long hours of anxiety.

"Tank you for comink. My Tina she is not so good."

No, her Tina wasn't. The sow lay on her side, shaking violently from fever. It appeared she had gathered straw and arranged a nest, sensing her time was at hand. But she'd been lying in it, probably thrashing, for the better part of a day and at some point her water broke and soiled the bed, which was flattened now into a dish shape. Emily donned her rubber apron, and, disregarding the condition of the pen, dropped to her knees and touched the sow's belly, which was bright red instead of its usual pale pink. Her ears, too, were scarlet: a sure sign of trouble. "Not feeling so good, huh, Tina?" She spoke quietly, then informed Mrs. Jagush, "I'll need to wash my hands. And your husband said you have beer in the house. Could you bring me about a quart?"

"*Ja.*"

"And lard, a half cup should do."

When Mrs. Jagush went away, Jeffcoat inquired, "Beer?"

"It's not for me, it's for Tina. Pigs love beer and it calms them. Hand me that pitchfork, so I can get her up."

Jeffcoat obliged, then watched while she slipped the tines beneath the pig and gently rocked them against the floor. Pricked, but unhurt, the sow grunted to her feet.

"Pigs are very malleable. They get up and down naturally all through the birthing anyway, so nudging her up won't hurt her a bit. Good gal," Emily praised, rubbing the sow's back when she was on her feet.

She spoke to the pig with more warmth than she offered most people, Jeffcoat observed. But her concern for the animal had loosened her tongue and she explained to him, "Pigs give birth on two sides, did you know that? First they lay down and bear half the litter on one side, then they get up and clean them before flopping over onto the other side and do the same thing again. Nobody has an explanation why."

Mrs. Jagush returned with the supplies—a white basin, lard, and the beer in a wrinkled tin kettle. When the latter was placed before Tina, she reacted like a true sow, slurped the kettle dry, then fell to her side with a snort.

Emily washed her hands first with plain soap and water, then in a carbolic acid solution, and when they were dry, systematically went on to carbolize the lard and lubricate her right hand.

Jeffcoat watched with growing admiration. Having been around animals his whole life he'd heard plenty of stories of carelessness, and knew that more animals died from infection caused by unsanitary hands than of the natural complications of birthing.

Emily greased her skin well past the wrist, then met his eyes for the first time since entering the barn.

"If you want to help you can hold her head." Without words he took up his station at Tina's head.

"All right, Tina." Emily kept her voice low and soothing while dropping to her knees. "Let's see if we can give you some help."

Jeffcoat observed with added deference as she grasped the pig's tail, made a dart of her fingertips, and forced them into the animal. There could be no more repugnant job in all of animal husbandry, yet she performed it with single-minded purpose. The sow's muscles were tight and not easily breached; had they been otherwise, the baby pigs would undoubtedly have been born already and suckling. Emily set her jaw, stiffened her wrist, and performed the task with an alacrity most men would have found difficult to muster. Her hand disappeared to the wrist, then farther. Her eyes were fixed, her concentration centered deep within the animal. Groping blindly, she bit her lower lip, then whispered, "There you are." When she withdrew the first baby pig the stench hit like a fetid explosion, rolling Tom's stomach with such suddenness he found himself swallowing back his gorge. Emily whipped her face sharply aside, sucked in a quick breath against her shoulder, then turned back to check the piglet.

"It's dead," she reported, "Take it away or she'll try to eat it." Mrs. Jagush hurried over with a shovel and took the fetus away. Emily buried her face against her shoulder to momentarily muffle the stench while she refilled her lungs.

Coming up, she said, "Hang on. Here we go again."

She pulled out five of them and the miasma seemed to grow worse with each one. Tom found his nose flattened against his shoulder more often then not, and he wondered why anybody, much less a woman, would *choose* an occupation like this. After the sixth dead pig was pulled, he said, "Why don't you take a break and grab some fresh air?"

"When I've got them all," she answered stoically, taking no more relief than a quick breath against her own sleeve. In time it, too, grew soiled, dampened by her sweat, fouled in spots by animal offal and excretions. The stench became noxious as the straw grew wet and rank, but she knelt in it without complaint. Toward the end she gagged, but staunchly forced herself to finish the job.

The last few fetuses were carried away by August, who'd arrived from town in time to watch them being delivered dead.

Finally Emily told Tom, "That was the last one. Come on, now we can take a break."

They hurried outside into the clean air and sunshine, fell against the barn wall and sucked in great gulps of breath, closed their eyes and let their heads drop back in relief.

When he could speak again, Tom whispered, "Jesus."

"The worst is over. Thanks for helping."

For minutes they shared the gift of clean air while the Jagushes buried the nine baby pigs. At length, Tom rolled his head to study Emily's profile, her nose raised to the sun, her mouth open, drawing in the freshness.

"Do you do this often?"

She rolled her face toward him and produced a weary, self-satisfied grin. "First time with pigs."

His respect for her grew immensely. There were compliments he might have offered. They crossed his mind in ribbons of praising words. But in the end he simply grinned and said softly, "Y' did good, tomboy."

To his surprise, she replied, "Thanks, blacksmith, you didn't do so bad yourself. Now what do you say we wash our hands before we finish up?"

"There's more?" he asked, dismayed.

"More."

He boosted himself away from the wall. "Lead the way, Doc."

They washed at the well in the yard, and when they'd finished, returned to the barn, where Emily mixed up a solution of tincture of aconite and fed it to Tina to reduce her fever, then prepared a carbolic acid wash to clean out the sow's womb. From her bag Emily produced a rubber hose with a funnel attached to one end.

"Would you mind holding this?" she asked Tom, handing him the funnel.

He found he minded less and less, for watching her was not only an education, it was becoming enjoyable. She had dropped all her veneer of iciness and had become a strong, resolute person who, captivated by her work, had forgotten her antagonism toward Tom Jeffcoat. He could not help admiring again her tolerance and nervelessness as she inserted the hose into Tina, ordered, "Lift the funnel higher," and poured the wash into it. They stood close in the smelly barn, listening to the liquid gurgle as gravity took it down slowly. What they'd been through bound them with a curious, earthy intimacy. Repugnant, at times, yes, but fascinating, as birth always is. They had time now to think back over the past hour and the changes it had wrought in their respect for one another. She filled the funnel again and while they stood waiting for it to empty, their eyes met. Tom flashed a smile—an uncertain, disquieted smile. And Emily returned it. Not the tired grin she'd given without thought as they'd leaned back exhaustedly against the barn wall. This was a genuine, willing smile. Though she dropped her glance the moment she realized what she'd done, the exchange toppled a barrier. Realizing it, too, Tom thought, be careful, Jeffcoat, this tomboy could grow on you.

When the job was done and the instruments washed, he followed her outside where she stood in the late afternoon sun, instructing Mr. and Mrs. Jagush.

"Don't breed her every time she comes into heat. If you do she'll be weak and so will her babies. Give her a rest between times and start feeding her extract of black haw, no more than one ounce each day, mixed with her water. You can get it at the drug store and it'll help prevent abortions. Any questions?"

"*Ja,*" replied August, "how much do this cost me?"

She smiled and tied her pack onto her saddle. "Would one baby pig be too much? If the next brood lives, I'll take one at weaning time and raise him in the corral at the livery stable."

"One baby pig you will get, young missy, and I tank you for comink to help Tina. The missus, she was plenty upset this mornink, wasn't you, missus?"

Mrs. Jagush nodded and smiled, clasping her hands in gratitude. "God bless you, missy. You're a good girl."

Emily and Tom mounted up and waved to the two standing shoulder to shoulder in the driveway.

The road beyond the Jagush place angled northwest and as they took it the sun already shone on their left shoulders. Tom pulled out a pocket watch and snapped it open. "It's already four o'clock and Tarsy's party starts at seven. Maybe you'd rather put off introducing me to Liberty until another time."

"Tarsy's party is going to be silly anyway. I'd rather go to Liberty's than play parlor games."

"Oh, we're going to play parlor games, are we?"

"Fannie put ideas into her head. Musical chairs and charades and who knows what else."

"Seems to me you could stand a little merrymaking after an afternoon like you just put in."

She tossed him a sidelong glance laced with the hint of a smile. "Given a choice between looking at horses and playing parlor games, I'll take the horses every time."

Though he secretly agreed, Tom felt obliged to remind her, "Charles is looking forward to it."

"I know. So I'll go, but he'll find his way to Tarsy's himself if I'm a little late. Come on, let's ride."

With a touch of her heels she sent Sagebrush into an easy canter and Tom followed suit on Gunpowder. Cantering just off her left flank, he studied what he could see of her profile: her stubborn jaw; the full lower lip—jutting slightly as she concentrated on the road ahead; her black eyelashes and the cap angled over her left ear; the single hand holding the reins; her breasts, firm and unbouncing as her spine curved into each rise and fall of the broad back beneath her. His eyes lingered upon her breasts longer than was prudent, and with some shock he realized what he'd been thinking.

Whoa, there, Jeffcoat, just by God, whoa!

He glanced away and concentrated on the scenery instead.

They were in true ranching country where the uncertain horizon changed with each curve in the road. It was a landscape of gulch and rolling hill, sun-baked plateau and cloud-freshened valley. The hillsides were splotched with clusters of chartreuse aspens and darker strings of cottonwoods where busy streams brattled down from the great top country above timberline. Up there, snow still clung, startlingly white against the purple peaks. At lower altitudes additional seams of white appeared: gypsum interbedded with red chugwater rock giving the impression of smears of snow. Aromatic sage thrived everywhere in clumps of downy silver-green, trimmed with yellow blooms that spread their turpentinelike scent through the summer air. In the distance, sheep corrals tumbled like spilled matchsticks down the faces of green hills. So much green—bluegrass, wheatgrass and redtop, all lush and verdant.

In the distance they saw a sheepherder's wagon, tucked beneath a greasewood tree, and a tiny dark dot—a herder watching them from a nearby hillside, where he sat surrounded by his dun-colored herd and two black moving spots—his dogs.

To Tom's surprise, Emily reined in, stood in the stirrups, waved, and bugled, "Halloooo!" They sat still, listening to her call echo and reecho across the valley. The herder stood as the sound reached him. He cupped his mouth. Seconds later his greeting came back: the distinctive Basque yell, "Ye-ye-ye-ye-ye!", undulating across the valley like a shrill coyote yip.

"Who is he?" Tom inquired.

"I don't know. Just a Basque. They live year round in those little wagons with their herds. In the spring they take the sheep up the mountain, and in the fall they bring them back down. The most they ever own is their wagon, a rifle, and a couple of sheep dogs. I've always thought they must have such terribly lonely lives."

As they rode on, Tom puzzled over Emily Walcott. Was it her real self he was seeing today, at last? If so, he was beginning to like it. Animals and Basques warmed a response in her. He wondered what else did.

Once again he forced his thoughts into safer paths. Scanning the hills, he commented, "I hadn't expected so much green."

"Enjoy it while it lasts. By mid-July it'll all be yellow."

"When will winter start?"

She cocked her head and glanced at a distant white-topped peak. "The old-timers have a saying—that in Wyoming winter never ends, that when summer's coming down the mountain it meets winter going back up."

"What? No autumn?"

"Oh we have autumn, all right. Autumn's my favorite. Wait till you see these cottonwood in late September. Papa calls them 'the Midas gift' because they look like hoards of gold coins."

They topped a rise just then and below lay the Lucky L Ranch, spread out across an irregular-shaped valley on Horseshoe Mountain. The Little Tongue River ran through it and its perimeter was clearly defined by the black wall of pine and spruce, which gave it a protected look. Before they'd traveled half the length of the driveway, Jeffcoat realized the Lucky L was more than lucky, it was prosperous. The buildings were painted, the fences in repair, and the stock they passed looked impressively healthy. The house and outbuildings had a planned look, laid out in pleasing geometric relationship to one another. The barns, granaries, and bunkhouse were painted white with black trim, but the house was built of native sandstone. It had two stories, with thick roofbeams extended beneath the eaves, a deep, full-width front porch, and a great fieldstone chimney. Elms surrounded the house on three sides and the outbuildings flanked it, right and left.

Before the house a line of hitching posts waited, each topped by a steed's head of black iron, gripping a brass ring in its teeth.

"Looks like Liberty does all right for himself," Jeffcoat observed, dismounting.

"He sells horses to the army. The army not only pays top dollar, they create a constant demand. If the army thinks Lucky L horses are good enough, I do, too."

Emily led the way to the house, whose door was answered by a short, round woman in a white mobcap and apron. "Mr. Liberty is down behind C Barn." She pointed. "It's that one over there."

The first thing Jeffcoat noticed about Cal Liberty was not his impressive barrel-chested stature, or his expensive, freshly brushed Stetson trimmed with a leather band studded with turquoise set in silver, but the way he treated Emily Walcott—as if she were a ghost he could see through. Liberty immediately shook hands with Tom but ignored the hand that Emily offered. Upon learning that Tom was there to buy horses the rancher invited him over to the next barn, where his foreman was working, but he suggested Emily go to the house to have coffee with his wife.

Emily bristled and opened her mouth to retort, but Jeffcoat cut her off. "Miss Walcott is here to help me choose the horses."

"Oh." Liberty spared her a brief, derogatory glance. "Well, I guess she can come along then."

As they followed Liberty, Tom felt Emily sizzle with indignation. He squeezed her elbow and dropped her a pointed glance that ordered, Shut up, tomboy, just this once? To his relief, she only puckered her mouth and glared at the back of Liberty's head. Tom did likewise, thinking, You pompous ass, you should have seen her an hour ago pulling dead pigs.

They found Liberty's foreman, a seasoned cowboy with skin like beef jerky and hands as hard as saddle leather. His eyes were pale as jade, his legs bowed like a wishbone, and when he smiled the plug of tobacco in his cheek gave him the appearance of a pocket gopher.

"This's Trout Wills," Liberty announced. "Trout, meet Tom Jeffcoat."

Tom shook Trout's hand.

"Jeffcoat wants to look at—"

"And this is Miss Emily Walcott," interrupted Tom.

Trout tipped his hat. "Miss Walcott, how-do."

Liberty picked up where he'd left off, turning a shoulder to cut Emily out. "Jeffcoat wants to look at some horses. See what you can fix him up with."

Though Trout followed orders, Liberty stayed close by, watching. After the rancher's cool dismissal of Emily, Tom took perverse pleasure in allowing her every opportunity to display her knowledge of horseflesh. By some unspoken agreement they'd decided to take Liberty down a notch.

When the cavvy of horses milled before them, Tom asked, loud and clear, "What do you think, Emily?"

They both ignored Liberty, who lounged at a nearby fence. Tom watched as Emily singled out a two-year-old mare, won its confidence, and began a minute inspection. Tom stood back, impressed himself as she went through an entire half dozen animals with educated thoroughness. On each one she checked to make sure the skin was soft and supple, the hairs of the coat lying flat and sleek, the eyes bright, the bearing alert. She checked the membranes of the nostrils to be sure they were a pale salmon pink, felt each crest for possible soreness, each tendon for bursal enlargements, pulled back lips to inspect molars and tushes, picked up feet to examine the condition of the frogs, and even checked pulse rates beneath jaws.

While she was checking that of a healthy-looking sorrel, Tom stood close and inquired in an undertone, "What should it be?"

"From thirty-six to forty. He's right in there."

When one of the horses lifted its tail and dropped a few yellow nuggets, instead of jumping back as most women would, Emily nudged the droppings with her boot and commented, "Good . . . not too soft, not too hard, just the way they're supposed to be." When another urinated she watched the proceedings, unfazed, and approved of the urine's color and the lack of strong odor.

"As a lot, they're healthy," she told Tom, adding, "but I was more concerned with their internal health. Anybody who's been around horses as long as you have knows what makes a sound one and which ones are light of bone. You can look them over yourself for conformation."

She stood back and took her turn at studying him as he went through the herd, sizing them up for conformation. She watched each move he made, recognizing what he was searching for: ample width between the eyes; eyes with little white showing; long, arched necks; well-developed shoulders; broad knees tapering front to back; flat shinbones and fetlocks angling at forty-five degrees. He disqualified one for its bell-shaped feet, winning a glance of approval from Emily, then singled out another for its thick cannon bones. Bridle-leading it, he checked its leg and foot action, and led it back to Emily.

"This one's a beauty."

She gave the big buckskin a hand-check and a perusal, then called to Liberty, "What's his name?"

"Buck." It was the first word he'd spoken directly to Emily.

She turned Jeffcoat aside and advised in an undertone, "You're right, he's beautiful, but let Liberty's foreman tack and ride him first. Just because he's beautiful doesn't mean he's manageable. And with a name like Buck . . . well, it might be because of his color, but there's no sense taking chances. If anyone gets flattened against the fence or thrown, better the foreman than you."

Jeffcoat smiled and bowed to her wisdom.

Buck turned out to be a real gentleman. He stood docilely while Trout tacked him, then performed with absolute manners while being ridden. When Jeffcoat himself mounted and took Buck through his paces, Emily watched, once more impressed. He wisely walked Buck first instead of sending him into an immediate canter, as a greenhorn might have. He patiently circled, bent, halted, walked on, assessing the horse's reaction to the bit and the strange rider.

When he nudged Buck into a trot Emily watched him master the awkward juggling gait with unusual grace. At trot most women looked like corn being popped, most men like eager children reaching into a candy jar. Jeffcoat rode it rising, perfectly balanced, his hands steady, his loins relaxed, body inclined slightly forward, not just tipped from the hips. Emily's father had taught her to ride, had pointed out how few people could perform the trot gracefully, and that fewer still rode it on the correct diagonal.

Jeffcoat did it all effortlessly.

Equally as effortlessly he kicked Buck into a canter, changed rein to make certain the stallion performed correctly on either lead, and finally set him into a gallop. When Jeffcoat wheeled and stretched out, galloping back to her, he made an impressive sight, with leathers properly shortened, his weight out of the saddle carried on the insides of his thighs and knees, lifting on the balls of his feet.

Damn you, Jeffcoat, you look like you might have been born in that saddle, and the sight of you there does things to my insides.

When he reined in, his touch was light; already he'd learned that much about Buck. He dropped to the ground before the dust had settled, smiled, and told Emily, "This one'll be mine."

She couldn't resist teasing, "Don't you know, Mr. Jeffcoat, that a wise horseman never lets his heart be captured by the first animal he tests?"

"Unless it's the right one," he returned, smiling back.

She relented by patting Buck on his broad forehead. "He's a good choice."

Tom told Liberty, "This one's sold. I'll need four others for riding."

"Three should do," interrupted Emily, quietly.

"Three?"

"You'll find that around here you'll be renting out rigs mostly, to land agents taking immigrant families out to pick out their eighty acres for preemption. You'll need a few who are saddle-broke, sure, but most of your stock should be wagon-trained."

Again Jeffcoat bowed to her judgment, and the selection went on until his four saddlehorses were chosen and the deal made. The horses for the rigs would have to wait until another day, as it was getting late and they'd have to head back or get caught by dark.

"Pleasure doing business with you, Mr. Liberty. I'll be back sometime next week." Tom extended a hand. When Liberty had shaken it he found another waiting.

"You've got basically good sound stock," Emily approved, holding her hand poised where it could not be avoided.

"Thank you. What did you say your name is again?"

"Emily Walcott. I'm Edwin Walcott's daughter and I'm studying to be a veterinarian. That black pointed bay you call

Gambler has what appears to be a touch of thoroughpin on his rear off hock that might be worth watching. My guess is he probably had a small sprain that you might not even have known about. It's no cause for worry, but if I were you I'd treat it with equal parts of spirits of camphor and tincture of iodine, and if it should ever grow to where pressure on one side makes it bulge on the opposite side, it should be drained and trussed. In that case, I'll be happy to come out and do it for you. You can find me at my father's livery stable most days. Good-bye, Mr. Liberty."

She and Jeffcoat mounted up and trotted their horses down the driveway feeling smug and amused. When they got beyond earshot, he released a whoop of laughter.

"Did you see the expression on his face!"

She laughed too. "I know I was showing off, but I couldn't resist."

"He deserved it, the pompous ass."

"I should be used to it. I'm a woman, and women, after all, are better at blacking stoves and punching down bread dough, aren't they?"

"I doubt that Liberty thinks so anymore."

She cast her companion an appreciative sidelong glance. "Thanks, Jeffcoat. It was fun."

"Yes, it was. The whole afternoon."

They rode on for some time in companionable silence, adjusting to it with some lingering astonishment after their turbulent beginning. It was a beautiful time of day, nearly sundown, conducive to amity. Behind them a flaming orange ball rested half-submerged below the tip of the mountain. Before them their mounted shadows stretched into distorted caricatures that slipped across the roadside grasses. They flushed a great flock of crows who flapped their way upmountain. At a narrow creek they startled a heron who winged his way to some distant rookery. They passed a spot where blossoming fireweed spread a great sheet of color, its bright pink flowers turned gilt by the flaming sun behind them. And farther along they turned in passing to study a picket-pin gopher sitting motionless atop his mound, as straight as his own shadow. From a roadside fence a meadowlark trilled and overhead the goshawks came out, calling their haunting flight song.

And the peace of evening settled within the two riders.

They listened to the squeak of shifting saddles, the three-time waltz rhythm of cantering hooves, the steady rush and pull of the horses' breath. They felt the east cool their fronts and the west warm their backs and realized they were enjoying each other's presence far more than advisable . . . riding . . . riding . . . a mere horse's width apart . . . eyes correctly ahead . . . digesting the mellowing turn their relationship had taken in a single day. Something indefinable had happened. Well, perhap not indefinable—inadmissible, rather—something startling and compelling and very much forbidden. They rode on, each of them battling the urge to turn and study, to confirm with an exchange of glances that the other was feeling it, too—this newfound confederacy, this inadvisable, insidious fascination. To feel it was one thing; to allow it to show was another.

They rode on, downhill all the way, toward a party they would both be attending, and a dance they might conceivably end up sharing, and an attraction that should never have begun, schooling themselves to remain outwardly aloof while both of them thought of Charles Bliss—his friend, and her intended.

Chapter 8

THEY WERE BOTH late to Tarsy's party. By the time Tom walked through the door, the hostess was in a state of near-panic, thinking he wasn't coming.

"Where have you *been*?" Tarsy flew across the room and grabbed his arm hard enough to cause black-and-blue marks.

"At the Lucky L Ranch, buying horses."

"I know *that*. Charles told me. But you're so late."

"We just got back half an hour ago." He scanned the room but Emily hadn't arrived yet.

"We've been waiting for you so we could start the games."

Tarsy commandeered Tom across a parlor filled with many of the same faces he'd met last week, but this time the older generation hadn't been invited. The group appeared to be all young and single. In the adjoining dining room they'd gathered around the table where they talked and laughed and drank punch. Charles was there but when Tom tried to veer over and talk to him Tarsy dragged him away. "Oh, you and that

Charles! You see him every day at work, isn't that enough?" She raised her voice and beckoned everyone into the parlor. "Come on, everybody, we can start the games now! Everybody in here!" Tarsy began arranging chairs in a circle.

Tom slipped away to get himself a cup of punch and met Charles in the dining room archway.

"How did it go?" Charles inquired.

"I got a good start—four riding horses."

"And you actually made it back with no mortal wounds?" Grinning, Charles pretended to inspect Tom for damage, front and back. "No broken bones?"

"She was the epitome of politeness. We got along remarkably well."

"I'll know by one glance at her face when she walks through that door."

"Sorry I made her late. Mmm . . . who spiked the punch?"

"Probably Tarsy herself, the little wildcat."

Tom glanced around the two rooms. "No parents around, either?"

"No. I think Tarsy has designs on you and having parents around would be against her better interests. They're out for the evening, playing whist. I think we're being summoned . . . for the second time."

They went to join the others. While Tarsy began explaining the game, Emily arrived—a transformed Emily. Tom took one look at her and felt an involuntary force field build within himself. She'd spent less than an hour converting from tomboy to woman, but the transition was complete. Her hair was twisted high onto her head like an egg in a nest, with loose wisps rimming her face. She wore an astonishing dress of mauve, the rich hue of a spring hyacinth. It was as proper, feminine, and concealing as anything Queen Victoria herself might wear, with its high, banded neck, tucked, tight top, form-fitting long sleeves, and a hip ruffle dropping in a bouncing cascade over her rump. Ivory lace trimmed the garment in such a way that it drew a man's eye to strategic places. Over it she'd thrown a large, fringed shawl, caught carelessly over one shoulder and the opposite elbow. Where was the girl who'd pulled dead pigs all afternoon? And assessed horseflesh? And ridden several hours on horseback?

She was gone, and in her place a woman whose appearance momentarily knocked the breath from Tom Jeffcoat.

He watched her eyes seek and find Charles and telegraph him a private hello, watched his best friend cross the parlor to touch her shoulders and take her shawl while he himself felt the sting of jealousy. Charles rested a hand just above her rear flounce and said something that made her release a short huff of laughter. She replied and they both glanced Tom's way. The amusement fell from her face as if she'd run up against a barbed-wire fence. Immediately she glanced away and Tom raised his punch cup to his lips, realizing Charles observed.

Tarsy called across the parlor. "Oh, Emily, you're here at last. Hurry and take a chair so we can start the game."

Emily and Charles sat across from Tom while he attempted to forget they were there.

He shifted his attention to Tarsy. Tarsy was giddy with excitement, announcing a game called Squeak, Piggy, Squeak. She had placed the chairs in a circle facing inward and when everyone was seated, stood in the center, ordering, "Everyone has to pick a number between one and a hundred to see who's first."

"To do what?" someone asked.

"You'll see. Now pick."

The winning number was chosen by Ardis Corbeil, a tall, freckled redhead who blushed as she reluctantly got to her feet in the center of the circle.

"What do I have to do?"

"You'll see. Now turn around." Tarsy produced a folded scarf.

"You're not going to blindfold me, are you?"

"Well, of course I'm going to blindfold you. Then I'll spin you around a few times and give you a cushion, and the cushion is the only thing you can touch anybody with. The first person you touch, you have to sit on his lap and say 'Squeak, piggy, squeak.' Then he has to squeak and you have to guess who he is."

"That's all?"

"That's all."

Snickers began around the room while Ardis allowed herself to be blindfolded and spun around. Tarsy spun her until the poor girl could scarcely tell up from down.

Muted laughter and whispers tittered through the room.

"Shh! No talking or she'll know where you are! Are you dizzy yet, Ardis?"

Poor Ardis was more than dizzy; she reeled and groped and nearly toppled over when released. Tarsy steadied her. "Now, here's your cushion, and remember, no hands! You get three squeaks to guess whose lap you're on, and if you guess right, it's that person's turn to be blindfolded, otherwise you have to pay a forfeit. All right now?"

From beneath the blindfold came Ardis's uncertain nod.

The room quieted of all but smothered snickers. Tipped forward at the waist, Ardis shuffled and stumbled three steps, leading with the cushion.

TT-tt.

"Shh!" Tarsy slipped into a chair and the room grew silent.

Ardis scuffed forward with the cushion extended in both hands, sliding her soles cautiously across the floor. The cushion bumped Mick Stubbs in the face. He drew back and compressed his lips to keep from laughing outright. Ardis patted the cushion up his head, down his shoulder to his chest, and finally to his knees.

Some of the girls blushed and clapped their hands over their mouths.

Tom glanced at Emily and found her watching him. They sat like islands of stillness in the jollity around them while everyone else's attention was riveted on the game. How long? A second? Five seconds? Long enough for Tom Jeffcoat to realize that what he'd sensed happening between them this afternoon had not been a figment of his imagination. She was feeling it, too, and was doing her best to submerge it. He had been in love once before and recognized the warning signs. Fascination. Watchfulness. The urge to touch.

Beside her, Charles laughed, and she glanced aside with forced nonchalance. Tom, too, returned his attention to the game in progress.

Ardis was perched on Mick's knees and his face was red with suppressed laughter.

"Squeak, piggy, squeak," Ardis ordered.

Mick tried, but his squeak sounded more like a snort.

Everybody snickered.

"Shh!"

"Squeak, piggy, squeak!"

This time Mick managed a high-pitched vocal rendition that

brought laughter erupting all around. Ardis still failed to identify him.

"Squeak, piggy, squeak!"

Mick's third try was a masterpiece—high, shrill, porcine. Unfortunately for Mick, at its end the entire roomful of people was hooting so loud that he lost control himself, giving away his identity.

"It's Mick Stubbs!" Ardis shrieked, yanking off her blindfold. "I knew it! Now you have to wear this thing!"

Mick Stubbs weighed a good 215 pounds. He had a bushy brown beard, and arms as thick as most men's thighs. He made a hilarious sight being blindfolded, twirled, and groping his way onto the lap of Martin Emerson, another bearded guest. It was impossible not to get caught up in the hilarity of the evening as the game proceeded. Everybody loved it. Martin Emerson groped his way to Tarsy, and Tarsy groped her way to Tilda Awk, and Tilda Awk groped her way to Tom Jeffcoat, and Tom groped his way to Patrick Haberkorn; and along the way Tom found himself laughing as hard as the others. He knew the moment Emily, too, began enjoying herself. He saw her resistance to the game melt when the humor grew infectious. He saw her first smile, heard her first laughter, admired her face wreathed in gayness, a facet of her he'd observed too few times. Emily, smiling, was a sight to behold. But always, beside her was Charles. Charles, to whom she was betrothed.

After "Squeak, Piggy, Squeak," everybody voted to pause and refresh their punch cups.

Tarsy monopolized Tom during the break, and he turned his attentions to her gladly, relieved to have them diverted from Emily Walcott. Tarsy was a pretty girl, amusing, and very lively. He made up his mind the best thing he could do for himself was to enjoy her and forget about this afternoon, and the becoming arrangement of Emily Walcott's hair, and how pretty she looked in the mauve dress, and the glances they'd exchanged across a crowded room.

"Tom, come here! I have to talk to you!" Excited, Tarsy tugged him aside and lowered her voice secretively. "Will you do something with me?"

"Maybe." He grinned down flirtatiously into her brown eyes, sipping his drink. "Depends on what it is."

"Will you be first with me on the next game?"

"Depends on what it is."

"It's Poor Pussy."

His grin idled on her eager face. He knew the game. It was filled with innuendo and a certain amount of touching, and he sensed in an instant her underlying reason for introducing it. "And who's the poor pussy, you or me?"

"I am. All you have to do is sit on a chair and try to stay sober while I do my best to make you laugh."

He took another sip of brandy punch, enjoying her avid brown eyes and thinking, what better way to show everyone—Charles included—that Tarsy was the one who sparked his interest?

"All right."

Tarsy giggled and hauled him by an arm into the parlor to resume the fun. "Come on, everybody, we're going to play a new game. Poor Pussy!"

Tarsy's guests returned eagerly, their party mood enhanced by the brandy and the success of the first game. When everyone was seated, once more in a circle, Tarsy explained, "The object of Poor Pussy is for two people to try not to laugh. I'm going to be a cat, and I'll choose anyone I want to play to. The only word I can say is 'meow,' and whoever I say it to is only allowed to say, 'poor pussy.' Three times is all we can speak. If either one of us laughs we have to pay a forfeit of the other one's choice, all right?"

Tarsy's guests murmured approval and settled into their chairs for more amusement.

"Of course," Tarsy added, "all of you can talk all you want—you can prod and tease and offer any suggestions that come to mind. Here we go."

Poor Pussy was so ridiculously simple, it succeeded for its sheer absurdity. Tarsy dropped to her hands and knees and affected a kittenish pout that began everyone laughing immediately. She arched her back and sidled up to several knees before finally adopting a supplicating posture at Tom Jeffcoat's feet. She batted her eyelashes up at him and gave a pitiful *"Meoooow."* The observers chuckled as Tom sat cross-armed and consoled, "Poor pussy."

From Tom's left, Patrick Haberkorn nudged his elbow and teased, "You can do better than that, Jeffcoat. Stroke her fur a little!"

Unable to speak, lest he end up being the one owing a

forfeit, Tom looked her over as if with piqued interest, tilting his head to one side.

Tarsy tried again with a doleful, feline, "*Meeeeeeowwwwww.*" She made a winning cat, preening herself against Tom's knee and putting on an appealing pout.

"Poor pussy looks like she's starved for attention," Haberkorn improvised.

Tom reached down and petted Tarsy's head, then scratched her beneath the chin, running his fingertips down her throat. "Poooooor pussy," he sympathized. He was in no danger of laughing, but the dimple in his cheek deepened and his mouth took on a half grin as he teased her overtly.

The others got into the spirit of the game and strengthened their efforts to get either of the pair to laugh.

"Who let that mangy cat in here!"

"Hey, pussy, where's your sandbox?"

Tarsy was in the midst of meowing and rubbing her ear against Tom's pant leg when Charles called, "Anybody got a mouse to feed her?" and Tarsy collapsed in merriment, followed by everyone else in the room. Tarsy knelt on the floor, head hanging, too overcome with mirth to get to her feet, having too much fun to try. Tom caught her arm and drew them both to their feet, enjoying himself immensely. "All right everybody, you heard Tarsy. She has to pay me a forfeit."

Yes, yes, a forfeit. Everyone in the room recognized a budding romance when they saw one.

In the center of the circle Tom kept Tarsy's elbow while perusing her with mock lasciviousness. "What'll it be, puss?" he asked, to everyone's amusement.

Two suggestions were thrown at Tom simultaneously.

"Make her spend the night on the back-porch step."

"Make her take a bath—cat-style!"

Tom knew perfectly well what Tarsy was hoping for. His eyes dropped to her lips—pretty lips, full and pink and slightly parted. A kiss would certainly seal within the minds of everyone here which way the wind blew for Tom Jeffcoat. But this was Tarsy's party: if she wanted to start risqué forfeits, she'd have to instigate them herself.

"Bring her a saucer of milk," he ordered, still holding her arm while her flush grew becoming.

Somebody brought a saucer of milk and set it on the floor. Tarsy promised in an undertone, "I'll get even with you, Tom Jeffcoat. You can't escape me forever." With a flourish of skirts, she gamely dropped onto hands and knees to pay her forfeit.

She made a provocative sight, kneeling bustle-up, lapping milk from the edge of the saucer, as provocative a sight as she'd made rubbing her breast against his knee. Watching her, Tom laughed with the rest, but when she'd been in the ignominious position for a mere fifteen seconds he relented and hauled her to her feet. "Poor pussy is excused," he said for all to hear. Then privately to Tarsy, ". . . for the time being."

Not a soul in the room doubted that there was a genuine spark of interest between the two.

Emily Walcott watched the entire farce with a queer tightness in her chest and a strange, forbidden heaviness in her stomach. It had been highly suggestive. Sometimes she'd tried not to laugh, but had been unable. Sometimes she'd felt embarrassed, but could not drag her eyes away.

What would her parents say? Mother, in particular.

She and every girl in the room had been raised upon rigid, Victorian mores. Blatant flirtatiousness was strictly forbidden and physical contact with the opposite sex was limited to a brief touch of hands in greeting or holding an escort's elbow when walking. Yet these games encouraged a good deal of tactile and vocal innuendo.

She wondered if the other girls felt as she did, drawn and repelled at once, flushed and uncomfortable. Was it the subtle naughtiness of the games themselves or was it Tom Jeffcoat? Watching Tarsy rub against his trouser legs Emily had felt an insidious stirring inside. When he'd petted Tarsy's hair and run his fingers down her throat Emily had experienced a startling rush of excitement. And something more. Prurience, she was sure, which made these games indecent. Yet she'd been unable to turn away. Not even when Tom had gazed into Tarsy's eyes and employed his flirtatious grin had she turned away. She'd stared, galvanized by a bewildering jolt of jealousy while everyone in the room expected him to demand a kiss as a forfeit. Then he'd called for the saucer of milk and she'd released her breath carefully, hoping Charles wasn't watching her.

Whatever had Tarsy started here?

Tarsy knew precisely what she had started, and she'd done it consciously. At the end of the evening she asked Tom Jeffcoat to stay after the others had gone, to help her push the furniture back into place.

It was a convenient ruse, Tom knew, but he was a red-blooded American male with a little brandy coursing through his veins, and Tarsy was a tempting young lady whose admiration wasn't exactly unwelcome. Furthermore, Miss Emily Walcott was off limits and he'd been too aware of her all night long.

When the punch bowl was carried to the kitchen, the chairs put back in place, and all but one lamp wick lowered, he decided to take advantage of Miss Tarsy Fields's thinly veiled invitation. She had walked him slowly to the door and was reaching for his jacket, which hung on the newel post.

"Come here," he ordered quietly, catching her around the waist and swinging her against him. "Now I'll take the rest of my forfeit."

She forgot about his jacket as he tipped his head and kissed her, chastely at first, then with growing intimacy. He invited her to open her lips and she did. He brushed his tongue across hers and she responded. He ran his hands up her back and she did likewise up his.

He found, to his enjoyment, that it stirred him. Lifting his head slowly he let her read it in his eyes. "I think you've been planning that all night," he told her.

"And you haven't?"

He laughed and ran the backs of his fingers along her jaw. His lips softened into a speculative crook as he continued caressing her jaw, letting his gaze rove from her eyes to her mouth and back again. "I wonder what it is you want from me."

"To have fun. Innocent fun. That's all."

"That's all?"

She took another kiss, in lieu of anything more she might want. She had lush lips and knew instinctively how to use them to best advantage. When she pulled away Tom's lips were wet and he found himself pleasantly aroused.

"You're looking for a husband, aren't you?" he inquired pleasantly.

"Am I?"

"I think so. But I'm not him, Tarsy. I might enjoy kissing you and being your partner for parlor games, and letting you rub against my pant leg, but I'm not in the market for a wife. You'd best know that from the start."

"How honorable of you to forewarn me, Mr. Jeffcoat."

"And how tempting you are, Miss Fields."

"Then is there anything wrong with"—she shrugged—"enjoying each other a little?"

He kissed her once more, lingeringly, resting a hand at the side of her breast, delving deep with his tongue. Their mouths parted reluctantly.

"Mmm . . . you do that so well," she murmured.

"So do you. Have you had much practice?"

"Some. Have you?"

"Some. Shall we have another go at it?"

"Mmm . . . please."

The next "go" was wetter, more promiscuous. When his hand strayed to her breast she drew back discreetly—a woman who knew how to leave a man with something to anticipate. "Perhaps we'd better say good night now."

He found himself mildly amused but scarcely heartbroken. She was a pleasant diversion, nothing more, and as long as they both understood it, he was willing to dive as deep or shallow as she'd allow.

"All right." Unhurriedly he reached for his jacket. "Thank you for a truly amusing party. I think everyone agreed it was an unqualified success."

"It was, wasn't it?"

"I think you've really started something with these parlor games. The men loved them."

"So did the girls, though they don't think they should admit it. Even Emily, who's as prudish as they come, and Ardis, who's decided to have the next party. Will you be there next week?"

"Of course. I wouldn't miss it."

"Even if it's you who has to pay the forfeit?"

"Forfeits can be fun."

They laughed and she smoothed his lapel. On her porch they shared one last, lingering good-night kiss, but in the middle of it he found himself wondering if Charles was doing the same thing with Emily right now, and if so, how obliging she was.

He caught only glimpses of her that week. He chose his carriage horses without her aid, and signed a hay contract with a rancher named Claude McKenzie, who said he'd be cutting his crop by mid-July. He talked with the local harnessmaker,

Jason Ess, about the harnesses he'd need. Ess told him Munkers & Mathers Hardware down in Buffalo handled new Bain wagons, and he made the thirty-mile trip to place an order.

Emily, Charles said, had been called out twice that week: to diagnose and treat a cow whose paunch was bound up by a hairball, and to extract a decayed tooth from a horse. In both cases she'd been paid in hard cash and was elated to have earned her first money as a veterinarian.

Frankie came by and said his sister had been trying to ride Fannie's bicycle and had fallen and knocked the wind from herself and gotten so angry she climbed back on, fell a second time, and scraped a patch of skin off her hand and another from her forehead.

"You should've heard her cuss!" Frankie exclaimed. "I never knew girls could cuss like that!"

Tom smiled and thought about her for the remainder of the day.

On Saturday night she showed up at Ardis Corbeil's house sporting a pair of strawberry-red scabs, one just below her hairline and another on her nose. Tom was near the door when the two of them walked in. He offered Charles a congenial hello, but glanced down at Emily and made the mistake of chuckling.

"What are you laughing at!" she snapped, scowling at him.

"Your battle scars."

"Well, at least I tried riding it! If you think it's so easy, you try!"

"I told Fannie I'd love to."

Charles put in, "The subject of the bicycle is a touchy one right now."

Smiling, Tom tipped a shallow bow of apology. "I'm sorry I brought it up, Miss Walcott."

"I'll *bet* you are!" She turned and stalked away.

"Mercy, she really doesn't take teasing well, does she?"

"Especially from you, I'm afraid."

The crowd played a new game that night called "Guessing Blind Man" and what Tom had feared, happened: when it was his turn, he was blindfolded, surrounded by a ring of seated players, and ended up on the lap of Emily Walcott. Something told him immediately it was she. The reaction of the others, perhaps. To his left he heard a soft "Oh-oh!", then "Shh!"

Everyone in the room knew that from the moment Tom Jeffcoat had come to town Emily Walcott had considered him her archenemy. She would as soon bury him as look at him. Yes, she'd helped him buy horses, but she'd done it begrudgingly, at Charles's request. Even tonight, at the door, she'd snapped at Jeffcoat the moment she'd stepped into the house.

Now here he sat, blindfolded, on her lap, surrounded by titters.

The rules of the game were simple: he had a free pair of hands and three tries to guess who she was.

The tittering stopped. The silence grew pregnant and Tom imagined Charles looking on. The games were getting more and more daring. There was no cushion in use this time, and if his hand groped in the wrong place, no telling what it might touch. Emily sat stone still, scarcely breathing. Someone snickered. Someone else whispered. Beneath him he felt the contact with her slim knees but he let them bear his full weight—anything to make this look as if he were continuing to nettle her for his own amusement. Behind his blindfold he pictured her cheeks, burning with embarrassment, her breath indrawn, her shoulders stiff.

He reached . . . and found her right hand gripping the edge of the chair seat. For a moment they engaged in a silent tug-of-war, but he won and lifted the hand by its wrist, much smaller than the circle of his fingers.

The game gave him license to do what he might never get a chance to do again and he'd do it, by god, with Charles watching, and satisfy his curiosity. Those looking on would see only what they'd been seeing all along—a teasing man having his fun with a woman who could scarcely tolerate him.

Still holding her wrist, her explored with his free hand each long, thin finger, each nail clipped veterinarian-short; callouses (surprising) at the base of her palm, then the palm itself, working it over mortar-and-pestle fashion. Sure enough: a scab—undoubtedly caused by her fall from the bicycle. He felt an acute forbidden thrill.

"Ah, tough hands. Could it be Charles Bliss?"

Everyone roared while Tom concealed his own disturbing reaction beneath a veneer of teasing. He lifted his right hand and found her cheek. She stiffened and drew back sharply. His hand pursued, examining everything but the two scabs he knew were there—one silky eyebrow; one eye, forcing it to close; a soft temple where a pulse drummed crazily; a velvety earlobe.

He leaned close and sniffed: lemon verbena . . . a surprise.

"Mmm . . . you don't smell like Charles."

More laughter as he examined her gauzy hair and the curls outlining her face.

"Charles, if it's you, you've done something new with your hair."

Laughter intensified as he touched Emily's cheek—hot, hot, afire with self-consciousness—and finally her mouth, which opened, emitting a faint gasp. She jerked back so sharply he imagined her head bowed over the back of the chair. When he'd discomfited her to the degree that he was certain everyone in the room knew he was doing it intentionally, he touched her scabbed nose and forehead.

"Is it you, tomboy?" he asked, loud and clear, then bellowed, "Emily Walcott!" leaping from her lap and ripping the blindfold from his eyes.

She had ripened like an August tomato and was staring at her skirt as if trying to suppress tears of mortification.

Tom swung toward Charles. "No offense intended, Charles."

"Of course not, it's all in fun," Charles replied.

Emily's expression turned mutinous and Tom knew he must do something to alleviate the tension. So, there before all her friends he bent swiftly and dropped a kiss on her cheek. "You're a good sport, Walcott," he declared.

She shot up from her chair and skewered him with a feral glare, planted her hands on her hips and came at him with slow, insidious intent while their ring of friends laughed at their antics. Tom retreated behind Charles's chair, extending his palms as if to stave her off. "Charles, help me! Tell your woman to back off!"

Charles joined the parody, pretending to subdue Emily, who strained toward Jeffcoat, warning, "Next time, hostler, I'll dump you on the floor!"

Though Emily had drawn upon feigned vitriol to escape having her incipient feelings for Tom detected, the incident had been unnerving. Not nearly so unnerving as one that happened later in the evening, however.

It was bound to happen sooner or later: Tarsy insisted on

playing French Postman. The rules of the game needed no explanation for Emily to guess that its outcome would be kissing. She herself escaped being sent a "letter," but before the game was over, Tarsy sent one to Tom, and when it was delivered, Emily watched with derelict fascination as the two of them stood in the middle of the room and kissed as she had never observed anyone kissing before, with Tom's hands running freely over Tarsy's back, and their mouths open—wide! For a good half minute! A lump formed in Emily's throat as she watched. Hot tentacles of unwanted jealousy and undeniable prurience painted blotches on her neck. Even before the game ended she vowed she would never attend one of these parties again.

To Tom, kissing Tarsy had been nothing but a false show, a convenient opportunity to further divert memories from how he'd made free with Emily Walcott.

For that was the encounter that had rocked him.

Just a game to some, but to him it had been the first feel of her skin, the first scent of her hair, and a telltale gasp that she'd been unable to control when he'd touched her lips. Whatever outward appearance Emily Walcott maintained, she was far from indifferent to him, and the knowledge put a tension around his chest that refused to go away.

During the days that followed, while he worked beside Charles, Tom pretended casual disinterest or amusement whenever her name was mentioned. But at bedtime he fell onto his pillow to stare at the ceiling and ponder his dilemma: he was falling in love with Emily Walcott.

He dreamed up an excuse to avoid the next party, spending instead a miserable night at the Mint Saloon, listening to veiled slurs from his competitor, Walter Pinnick, who sat with a group of his drunken henchmen and blubbered about his failing business. Next he went to the Silver Spur where he played a few hands of poker with a handful of weatherbeaten ranch hands. But they were a poor substitute for the company of his friends who were gathered across town.

The following week he and Charles completed work on his livery barn and Charles suggested, "You should have a party in the loft before McKenzie delivers the hay."

"Me?"

"Why not you? It's the perfect place. Plenty of room."

Tom shook his head. "No, I don't think so."

"A dance, maybe, and invite the local merchants and their wives—a grand opening, if you will. It wouldn't be bad for business, you know."

Upon further consideration, the idea took on merit. A dance. What trouble could he get into at a dance, especially with the older generation around? Hell, he wouldn't even have to dance with Emily Walcott, and Charles was right—it would be a wonderful goodwill gesture from the newest businessman in town. He'd need a band and refreshments, a few lanterns, little more.

He found a fiddler who sometimes played at the Mint, and the fiddler knew a harmonica player, and the harmonica player knew a guitar player, and in no time at all, Tom had his band. They said they'd play for free beer, so on a Saturday night in mid-July the whole town turned out to christen Jeffcoat's Livery Stable.

Josephine insisted that Edwin take Fannie. "She's been in the house too much. She needs to get out and so do you."

"But—"

"Edwin, I won't take no for an answer, and you know how she loves dancing."

"I can't take her to a—"

"You can and you shall," Josephine stated with quiet authority.

He did.

They walked uptown together: Charles and Emily, Edwin and Fannie, through a molten summer sunset, through a windless violet evening, the older couple without touching, except for Fannie's skirts brushing Edwin's ankle like an intimate whisper. He felt young again, released, strolling along beside the woman who was vital and healthy and whose desirability had in no way diminished over the years. If anything, it had grown. He allowed this admission to surface while keeping his gaze locked on his daughter's back. If things had turned out differently Emily might have been theirs—his and Fannie's.

"Oh, Edwin," Fannie declared, when they were halfway to their destination, "I'm so incredibly happy."

Who but Fannie would be happy with this impossible situation?

"You always are."

Their gazes met and hers held a question: Shall I feel guilty because Josephine has shared you with me for the evening, or shall I make the most of it?

They made the most of it. They danced the waltz and the varsovienne, the Turkish trot and the reel. Their hands learned the feel of one another—his as it lay on her waist, hers as it rested on his shoulder. They accepted these touches as a gift.

They grew warm and drank beer to cool off. They laughed. They talked. They conversed and danced with others, distancing themselves to covertly admire one another from room's width. They learned that they could be happy with this and no more.

Tom hadn't intended to ask Emily to dance. He'd brought Tarsy, and Tarsy was enough to wear out any man on the dance floor. He danced with others, too, from his new circle of friends—Ardis and Tilda, Mary Ess, Lybee Ryker; the list had grown. And with many of their mothers, and, of course, with Fannie, who was sought as a partner by every man in the place, regardless of his age.

Fannie brought it about, what Tom had been determined to avoid. She was waltzing with him, chattering about Frankie's capacity for molasses cookies, when Edwin danced past with his daughter.

"Oh, Edwin, could I talk to you?" Fannie heralded, swinging out of Tom's arms. "I wonder if one of us shouldn't go home and check on Joey."

While they carried on a brief conversation Emily and Tom stood by, trying not to look at each other. At length, Fannie touched their arms and said, "Excuse me, Tom, you don't mind finishing this one with Emily, do you?"

And so it happened. Tom and Emily were left facing each other on a crowded dance floor. She wouldn't look at him. He couldn't help himself from looking at her. He saw the telltale hint of pink creeping up her cheeks and decided it was best to keep the mood convivial.

"I guess we're stuck with each other." He grinned and opened his arms. "I can bear it if you can."

They moved toward each other gingerly and began waltzing, maintaining a careful distance but bound by unmerciful memories of the last evening they'd spent together.

His fingertips learning the textures of her face.

His hands and tongue on Tarsy.

"I wasn't sure you'd come," he said, meeting the eyes of Charles, who watched from the edge of the floor.

"Papa and Fannie and Charles wouldn't have missed it."

"So you got roped into it."

"You might say that."

"You're still angry about that silly game." He turned his back to Charles and glanced down at her compressed lips as she stared over his shoulder. "I'm sorry if it embarrassed you." His glance slipped lower, to her chest, tinted by a charming if unladylike vee of sunburned skin shaped like the neck opening of her brother's shirt. There, again, he detected a blush behind a peppering of freckles.

"Could we talk about something else, please?"

"Certainly. Any subject you like."

"You have a fine barn," she offered dutifully.

"I picked out the rest of my horses last week. I can get them any time."

With the subject of horses she was comfortable; she risked meeting his eyes. "From Liberty?"

"Yes. One mare is in foal." She relaxed further as Tom continued with her favorite subject. "And I went down to Buffalo and ordered carriages and wagons from Munkers and Mathers. I'll get them as soon as my hay is delivered."

"Bains?"

"Yup."

"They're good, sturdy wagons. Good axles. They'll last you. What brand of carriages?"

"Studebakers."

"Studebakers . . . good."

"I thought I'd need the best, what with these damned washboard roads out here—where there are roads. I ordered my hay from McKenzie, too. As soon as it comes I'll be open for business."

They danced on in a more comfortable silence after the impersonal talk, still careful not to stray too close.

"So what have you been doing?" he inquired, implying casual disinterest when actually he was avid to know everything that had affected her life since they'd seen each other.

"Not much."

"Charles tells me you removed a hairball and a rotten tooth. Got paid for it, too."

"I removed the tooth, not the hairball. That I took care of with epsom salts and a little raw linseed oil. Distasteful but effective."

"But you *did* get paid."

He watched her face for signs of satisfaction and found them as she answered, "Yes."

"I guess that makes you a real doc now, huh?"

"Not really. Not until spring."

Silence again while they moved to the music, still separated by a body's width, searching for a new distraction. At length she remarked, "Charles says you've picked out blueprints for your house."

"I have."

"Two stories and an L-shaped porch."

"It seems to be the going thing. Tarsy says everybody's got a porch these days."

Their gazes collided and they danced in a web of confused feelings.

You're building it for her?

The tension between them became palpable.

Hoping to remind them both of their obligations, Emily commented, "Charles will do a good job for you. He does everything well."

"Yes," Tom replied, "I imagine he does."

Somewhere a harmonica wailed and a fiddle scraped, but neither of them heard. Their feet continued shuffling while they grew lost in one another's eyes.

Stop looking at me like that.

You stop looking at me like that.

This was impossible, dangerous.

The tension built until Emily felt a sharp pain between her shoulder blades and she lost her will to keep the conversation impersonal. "You didn't come to the party last week," she lamented in a breathy voice.

"No, I . . . I worked on the barn." It was an obvious lie.

"After dark?"

"I used a lantern."

"Oh."

At that moment someone bumped Emily, throwing her against Tom. Her breasts hit his chest and his arms tightened for the briefest moment. But it took no longer for their hearts to race out of control. She jumped back and began prattling to cover her discomposure. "I never did care much for dancing, I mean some girls were born to ride horses and some were born to dance but I don't think many of them were born to do both but just put me on a saddle and watch—"

"Emily!" Tom caught her hand and squeezed it mercilessly. "Enough! Charles is watching."

Her inane chatter stopped mid-word.

They stood before one another feeling helpless beneath the grip of a growing attraction neither of them had sought or wanted. When she had regained some semblance of poise he said sensibly, "Thank you for the dance," then turned her by an arm and delivered her back to Charles.

Chapter 9

LATER THAT NIGHT, Emily lay beside a sleeping Fannie, recreating Tom Jeffcoat in thought—gestures and expressions that became disconcertingly attractive in the deep of night. His blue, teasing eyes. His disarming sense of humor. His lips, crooking up to make light of something that felt heavy and treacherous within her. She wrapped herself in both arms and coiled into a ball facing away from Fanny.

I scarcely know him. But it didn't matter.

He's Papa's competition. But noble about it.

He's Tarsy beau. It carried little weight.

He's Charles' friend.

Ah, that one stopped her every time.

What kind of woman would drive a wedge between friends?

Stay away from me, Tom Jeffcoat. Just stay away!

He did. Religiously. For two full weeks while his livery stable opened up for business. And while the framework of his house went up. And while word came back to Emily that he was seeing Tarsy with growing regularity. And while Emily thought, good, be with Tarsy—it's best that way. And while Jerome Berryman hosted a party which Tom again avoided. And while Charles grew more randy and began pressuring Emily to advance the date of their wedding. And while full summer stole over the valley and parched it to a sere yellow, bringing daytime temperatures in the high eighties. The heat made work in a livery barn less enjoyable than at any other time of year. Flies abounded, skin itched from the slightest contact with chaff, and the horses tended to get collar galls from sweating beneath their harnesses.

One morning Edwin took Sergeant across the street to have him shod and in the late afternoon asked Emily to go get him.

Her head snapped up and her heart leapt to her throat. She blurted out the first excuse that came to mind. "I'm busy."

"Busy? Doing what, scratching that cat?"

"Well, I . . . I was studying." His impatient glance fell to her hip where a book rested, facedown.

It was a beastly hot day and her father was fractious, not only from the heat. Mother was worse again, someone had returned a landau with a rip in the seat, and he'd had a set-to with Frankie over cleaning the corral. When Emily balked at collecting Sergeant, Edwin displayed a rare fit of temper.

"All right!" He threw down a bucket with a clang. "I'll go get the damn horse myself!"

He stomped out of the office and Emily shot after him, calling, "Papa, wait!"

He brought himself up short, heaved a deep sigh, and turned to her, the picture of forced patience. "It's been a long day, Emily."

"I know. I'm sorry. Of course I'll go get Sergeant."

"Thanks, honey." He kissed her forehead and left her standing in the great south doorway with doubts amassing as she pondered Jeffcoat's place of business a half block away. In all the time it was going up, and since it had been open for business, she had never been in it alone with him, and now she knew why. She stepped outside and hesitated, telling her pulse to calm, concentrating on the newly painted sign above his door: JEFFCOAT'S LIVERY STABLE—HORSES BOARDED & SHOD, RIGS FOR RENT. A new pair of hitching rails stood out front, their posts of freshly peeled pine shining white in the sun. The line of windows along the west side of his building reflected the blue sky, and in one the afternoon sun formed a blinding golden blaze. In a corral on the near side of the building his new string of horses stood dozing with their tails twitching desultorily at flies.

So, go get Sergeant. Two minutes and you can be in and out.

She drew a deep breath, blew it out slowly, and headed down the street, unconsciously stepping to the rhythmic beat of a hammer on steel.

At his open door she stopped. The sound came from inside: *pang-pang-pang*. Sergeant stood at the opposite end of the building, cross-tied near the smithy door. She walked toward the stallion, skirting the wooden turntable in the center of the wide corridor without removing her eyes from the far doorway.

Pang-pang-pang! It rang through the building, shimmered off the beams overhead and skimmed along the brick floor, as if repeating the rhythm of her heart.

Pang-pang-pang!

She approached Sergeant silently and gave him an affectionate if distracted scratch, whispering, "Hi, boy, how y' doin'?" The hammering stopped. She waited for Jeffcoat to appear, but when he didn't she stepped to the smithy door and peered inside.

The room was hot as hell itself, and very dark, but for the ruddy glow from the forge, which was set in the opposite wall: a waist-high fireplace of brick, with an arched top and deep, deep hearth, ringed with tools—hammers, tongs, chisels, and punches—hung neatly on the surrounding brick skirt. To the right stood a crude wooden table scattered with more tools, to the left a slake trough, and in the center of the room a scarred steel anvil, mounted on a pyramid of thick wooden slabs. Above the forge hung a double-chambered bellows with its tube feeding the fire. Working the bellows, with his back to the door, stood Jeffcoat.

The man she'd been avoiding.

His left hand pumped rhythmically, sending up a steady hiss and a soft thump from the accordion-pleated leather; his right held a long bar of iron, black at one end, glowing at the other, nearly as red as the coals themselves. He worked bare-handed, bare-armed, wearing the familiar blue shirt, shorn of sleeves, and over it a soot-smudged leather apron.

He stood foursquare to the forge, his silhouette framed dead-center in the glowing arch, limned by the scarlet radiance of the coals, which brightened as the current of forced air hit them. A roar lifted up the chimney. The sound buffeted Emily's ears, and as the fireglow intensified it seemed to expand Jeffcoat's periphery. Sparks flew from the coals and landed at his feet, unheeded. The acrid odor of smoke mingled with that of heated iron—a singeing, bitter perfume.

Seeing him at his labor for the first time, her perception of him again changed. He became permanent; he was here to stay. Tens and tens of times in her life she would step to this door and find him standing just so, working. Would the sight make her breath catch every time?

She watched him move—each motion enlarged by his hovering vermilion halo. He flipped the iron bar over—it chimed like a brass bell against the brick hearth—and watched it heat. When it glowed a yellowish-white he reached out for a chisel, cut it, and picked it up with a pair of heavy tongs.

He turned to the anvil.

And found her watching from the doorway.

They stood as still as shadows, remaining motionless for so long that the perfect yellow-whiteness of the hot iron began to fade to ochre. He came to his senses first and said, "Well, hello."

"I came to get Sergeant," she announced uneasily.

"He's not quite ready." Jeffcoat lifted the hot iron in explanation. "One more shoe."

"Oh."

Silence again while the bar cooled even more.

"You can wait if you want. It shouldn't take long."

"Do you mind?"

"Not at all."

He turned back to the forge to reheat the bar and she moved farther inside, across a crunching layer of cinders that covered the floor, stopping with the tool table between herself and Jeffcoat. She studied his profile keenly, somehow feeling safe doing so in the darkness of the room. He wore a red bandana tied around his brow. Above it, his hair fell onto his forehead in damp tangles; below it, sweat painted gleaming tracks down his temples. Radiant red light lit the hair on his arms, and that which showed above the bib of his apron. She studied him until it became necessary to invent a distraction. Lifting her eyes to the dark thick-beamed ceiling and shadowed walls, she scanned them as a hunter might the sky.

"Did you run out of windows?" she inquired.

He glanced at her and grinned, then returned his attention to the forge. "Did you come to give me a hard time again?"

"No. I'm curious, that's all."

He turned the bar over and made more music. "You know as well as I do why blacksmiths work in the dark. It helps them gauge how hot the metal is." He brandished the bar, which was brightening to white again. "Color, you see?"

"Oh." And after a moment's silence: "Shouldn't you wear gloves?"

"I caught a cinder down one one time, so now I work without them."

Glancing down, she scuffed a boot against the cinders. "Your floor could use sweeping."

"You *did* come to pester me."

"No. I only came to get Sergeant, honest. Papa sent me."

He considered her askance for a long stretch, then shifted his gaze to his work and decided to enlighten her further. "The cinders keep the floor cool in the summer and warm in the winter."

"This is cool?" She spread her hands in the torpid air.

"As cool as it gets. You can wait outside if you want."

But she waited where she was, watching another bead of sweat trail down Tom Jeffcoat's jaw. He shrugged and caught it with a shoulder. His face held absolutely no shadow, and his eyes looked like two red coals themselves, so intense was the heat from the forge. Yet he pumped the bellows regularly and stood in the blast of heat as if it were little more than a warm chinook wind drifting over the Big Horns.

Time and again she glanced away, but her eyes had a will of their own. She didn't want to find him handsome, but there was no arguing the fact. Or masculine, but he was. Or any of the thousand indefinable things that drew her to him, but she was drawn just the same, against her will.

"It's ready now," he informed her.

The iron bar glowed once more the near-white hue of a full moon. He picked it up with tongs and swung about, selecting a hammer and setting to work at the anvil, battering the metal with singing, ringing blows.

She loved the sound—to the farmer it meant shares being mended; to the wheelwright, rims being formed; but to her it meant horses being cared for. It filled the room, it filled her head—smith's music in the steady repeating note she'd been hearing in the distance all her life.

Pang-pang-pang!

She watched him make it; a maestro in his own right, this man who raised her pulsebeat each time she saw him.

His muscles stood out as he wielded the hammer, changing the shape of the iron, wrapping it beat by beat around the pointed end of the anvil. The music paused. With the tongs he lifted the horseshoe, assessed it, returned it to the anvil and began again the measured staccato strikes. Each blow resounded in the pit of her stomach and fragmented to her extremities.

"I'm using a three-quarter shoe," he shouted above the ringing. "And a copper plate, too, on that off fore. It should keep that sand crack from coming back."

She was reminded of the first day she'd first seen him and how angry he'd made her. If only she could recapture some of that anger now. Instead, she watched his skin gleam in the fireglow and thought how warm it must be. She watched sweat bead in the corner of his eye and thought how salty it must be. She watched his chest flex and thought how hard it must be.

She distracted herself by picking up the conversation. "We took him back to Pinnick and said to reshoe him, but he only did a remove instead of a replace."

"He's a queer little man, that Pinnick. Came in here drunk one day and stood staring at me and weaving on his feet. When I asked if I could help him he muttered something I couldn't hear and stumbled back out again."

"Think nothing of it. He's always drunk, which will work in your favor, I'm sure. You'll get plenty of shoeing business."

He headed for the door, taking the hot shoe along. "Come on. I'll show you what I've done."

In the corridor a blessedly cool draft sailed door-to-door. Surrounded by the mingled scents of new wood, and hot iron and horse, Emily crouched beside Jeffcoat, catching, too, a faint whiff of his sweat as he lifted Sergeant's off forefoot to his lap. Sizing the shoe, he pointed out, "I've put the copper plate on the side, and the longer shoe will give added protection to the wall. This hoof will be like new by the next shoeing. Maybe even before then—in four weeks, I'd say."

"Good," she replied, studying his dirty arm only inches from her own.

The shoe was slightly wide. He took it back inside while she waited in the cool corridor, watching as he gave it several deft raps, then returned to lift Sergeant's hoof again. This time the shoe fit as if it had been cast in a sand mold. He took it back into the shop and she watched from the doorway as he picked up a punch and drove holes in the horseshoe on the flat end of the anvil.

Lifting the shoe, whistling softly through his teeth, he checked the holes against the light of the coals. "There, that should do."

Stepping to his left, he plunged the hot shoe into the slake trough. It sizzled and steamed while he glanced back over his shoulder.

"Grab a handful of clenches from that table, will you?" He gestured with his head.

"Oh . . . oh, sure."

She picked up the nails while he found a square-headed hammer and together they returned to Sergeant. She stood, looking down on his head while he assumed the pose as familiar to her as any a man could assume, thinking how different it looked when he did it. She studied the curve of his spine, the wet blue streak down the center of his shirt, the taut britches belling out infinitesimally at the waist.

He swung on the balls of his feet and caught her staring.

"Nails," he requested, holding out a palm.

"Oh, here!" She dropped four into his hand but he held them without moving. Their eyes locked and fascination multiplied until the air between them seemed to burn like that above his forge.

Abruptly he swung back to work. "So how was the party last week?"

"All right, I guess." She had changed her mind and gone in hopes of seeing him there.

"Charles enjoyed it."

She had gotten caught and had to kiss Charles during French Postman.

"It was silly. I don't like playing those games."

"He does." Tom centered a nail and rapped it in while she stood beside him blushing, unable to think up a reply.

"Did everybody come?" he inquired.

"Everybody but you and Tarsy."

He finished the last nail and straightened, letting the hoof clack to the floor. "Oh, she and I were painting the sign that night." He gestured toward the door with the hammer.

"Ah. Yes. It looks nice."

Their eyes met and parted discreetly. "Well . . . I'd better clip those clenches." He got the proper tool and spent several minutes nipping the ends of the protruding nails from all four hooves while Emily glanced around his barn at the fresh-milled lumber and cobwebless windows, reminding herself that he and Charles had done all this, and while doing it, had become friends.

Tom finished the nails and asked, "Want to lead him toward me and I'll see how the new shoes look?"

He squatted near the smithy door while she led Sergeant away, then back to him, feeling his eyes on her own feet as much as on the horse's. When she approached, he stretched to his feet and scratched Sergeant's nose. "Feels good, huh, Sergeant?" To Emily he added, "I should see him at trot and gallop to make sure they're perfectly flat."

"Pinnick's never in his life taken the time to check things like that."

"That's the way I was taught."

"By your father?"

"Yes."

"He was a farrier?" She glanced into Jeffcoat's clear blue eyes.

"Both my father and my grandfather were." While he spoke he removed his red headband and swabbed his face and neck, then stuck it in a hind pocket. "The bellows and the anvil were his, my grandfather's. My grandmother insisted that I take them when I came out here. For luck, she said." They both raised their eyes to the horseshoe above the smithy door.

"Don't you know you're supposed to hang it heels up so the good luck will get caught inside?"

"Not if you're a blacksmith." He looked down at her. "We're the only ones allowed to hang it heels down, so the luck will run out on our anvil."

Their eyes caught and held. The shoeing was done. She could ride Sergeant out the door any time, and they both knew it. So they dreamed up conversation to keep her here.

"You're superstitious," she observed.

"No more than the next man. But horseshoes are my business. People expect to see them up there."

She glanced up at the horseshoe again and he watched the curve of her throat come into view. He dropped his eyes to the line of her breasts flattened at the tips where her red suspenders crossed them, her thumbs hooked into their brass clasps at the waist of Frankie's britches. He found her as attractive in boy's wear as he did in a mauve gown. He'd never met a more unpretentious woman, nor one who shared as many of the same interests as he. Suddenly he wanted her to see all of his realm, to understand his joy in it, because only another livery owner could appreciate what all this meant.

"Emily, the night of my party you wouldn't look at a damn thing in here except the loft. I'd like you to see the rest. Would you like a little tour?"

She knew it would be wisest to get out of here with all due haste, but she couldn't resist the appeal in his voice.

"All right." In deference to Charles, she added, "But I can't stay long. Fannie will have supper ready soon."

"It'll only take five minutes. Wait a minute." He ducked into the shop and leaned over the slake trough, swabbing off his face and arms with the wet bandana. From the doorway she watched the masculine procedure with a growing lump in her stomach.

"Sorry," he offered sheepishly, straightening and turning to find her watching. "Sometimes I smell worse than my horses." He draped the wet bandana over the warm bricks, dried his palms on the rear of his britches, and said, "Well, we might as well begin in here. Come in." He waited until she stood at his elbow. "The bellows were made in Germany in 1798. They'll last all of my lifetime and longer. The anvil is the one my father learned on, from his father, then taught me on. The one I'll probably teach my sons on." He gave it an affectionate slap and rubbed his hand over the scarred iron. "I know every mark on it. When I left Missouri my mother sent me off with four loaves of her homemade bread for the road. Don't get me wrong—I loved it, but eventually I ate them up. This, though . . ." He gazed down at the anvil, his hand lingering upon it with great affection. ". . . the marks from their hammers will never disappear. When I get to missing them it helps to remember that."

It was an odd, passionless moment in which to recognize that she had fallen in love with him, but it happened to Emily in that instant while she met Tom Jeffcoat's eyes, while he let her see the soul inside the body, and admitted how he longed for his family and how he valued his birthright. It struck her with the force of a blow—*Pang-pang!*—I love him.

She turned away, afraid he'd read it in her eyes. The heat of the room pressed hard upon her flesh, joining the heat from within, an awesome heat spawned by the sudden, jolting admission.

"The slake trough I made myself," Tom continued, "and the base for the anvil—out of railroad ties—and the tool bench. The bricks came from the brickyards in Buffalo." He gestured her ahead of him through the doorway. They walked the length of the barn separated by a full six feet of space while Emily applied herself to the view of box stalls, windows, tack room, and office, when all she wanted was to look at him, at the face of the love she'd only now discovered.

They stopped at the foot of the loft stairs while his monologue continued. "I sleep up there now. No sense paying for a hotel room if I don't have to. It's plenty warm this time of year, and Charles says the house will be finished well before cold weather sets in."

She glanced up the steps, caught the sweet scent of new hay, and pictured herself climbing these stairs some night. Denying the possibility, she turned away.

"You haven't shown me your turntable."

"My turntable. Ah . . ." He laughed and raised one eyebrow. "My folly?"

"Is it?"

They sauntered back to the center of the barn. "The children don't think so. They come in and beg for rides on it."

Stopping on opposite sides of the wooden circle, Tom nudged it with a foot while Emily watched it turn. It scarcely made a sound, rolling on ball bearings.

"So smooth," she commented.

"Folly or not, it comes in damned handy when I want to turn a wagon around. Want to try it?"

Her chin lifted and she gazed at him with a feeling of imminent disaster thrumming through her veins. Ignoring it, she answered, "Why not?"

He halted the turntable and she stepped on. He set it in motion with the toe of a boot and she lifted her face, watching the ceiling beams spin slowly, distracted by the knowledge that he watched her as she circled. The faint tremble of the ball bearings shimmied up her legs to her stomach. She came around and passed him—once, twice—with her face to the rafters. But on the third pass she gave up and dropped her eyes to his as she came around the last half circle.

She reached him and his boot hit the turntable, stopping it.

They stood transfixed, with their pulses drumming crazily, fighting the compulsions that had had them on edge ever since he'd seen her standing silently in the smithy door, watching him. At his hips his fists opened once, then closed. Her lips dropped open but no sound came out. They stood together in a whorl of uncertainty, two people unspeakably tempted.

"Emily . . ." he said in a constricted voice.

"I have to go!" She tried to shoot past him but he reached and caught her forearm.

"You haven't seen the horses." It was not why he'd detained her and they both knew it.

"I have to go."

"No . . . wait." His hand burned on her arm, a poor substitute for the touches they wanted to share.

"Let me go," she pleaded in a whisper, raising her eyes to him at last.

He swallowed once thickly and asked in a tight voice, "What are we going to do?"

"Nothing," she replied flatly, jerking her arm free.

"You're angry."

"I'm not angry!" But she was, not at him, at the hopelessness of this situation.

"Well, what do you expect me to do?" he reasoned. "Charles is my friend. He's out there right now, building my house while I stand here thinking about—"

"Don't you think I know that!" Her eyes blazed into his.

"I've intentionally stayed away from the parties," he argued as if in self-defense.

"I know."

"And I've been seeing a lot of Tarsy, but she's—"

"Don't say it. Just . . . please, Tom, don't say any more. She's my friend, too."

They gazed at each other helplessly, each of them breathing as if they'd just sprinted over a finish line. Finally he stepped back and said, "You're right. You'd better go."

But now that he'd released her, she couldn't. She had taken no more than two steps away from him before she stopped in the middle of the corridor and dropped her forehead into her hands. She neither cried nor spoke, but her dejected pose spoke more clearly than tears or words.

He stood behind her, clinging to control by a thin thread. When he could stand it no longer he spun away and stood back to back with her, picturing her behind him.

It was Emily who broke the silence. "I don't suppose you'll be coming to Tilda's party tomorrow night."

"No, I don't think I'd better."

"No, it's . . . I . . ." She stammered to a halt and admitted, "I don't want to go, either."

"Go," he ordered sensibly, "with Charles."

"Yes, I must." They thought of Charles again, still back to back, staring at opposite walls.

"I'm getting a lot of pressure from Tarsy to go. I've invited her to dinner instead at the hotel."

"Oh."

He felt as if his chest were being crushed, and finally, in desperation, he turned around to study her slumped shoulders, her wool cap, the nape of her neck, the suspenders pressing her tan shirt against her shoulders. How the hell had this happened? He loved her. She was Charles's woman and he loved her.

"This is terrible . . . this is dishonorable," he whispered.

"I know."

When another minute had passed without producing any solutions, Tom repeated, "You'd better go."

Without another word she grasped Sergeant's bridle, swung onto his back, and slapped the reins, shouting, "Heeaww!" By the time she hit the double doorway she was galloping hell-bent for redemption, on an escape route from Tom Jeffcoat and the unpardonable turmoil he had caused in her life.

In the weeks that followed she learned there was no escaping. The turmoil was with her day and night. Days, while she worked within a thirty-second walk of Tom Jeffcoat. Nights, while he infiltrated her dreams.

Such crazy, improbable dreams.

In one he was riding Fannie's bicycle and fell, knocking the wind out of himself. She stood beside him laughing. Then suddenly he was bleeding and she fell to her knees in the middle of Main Street and began tearing bandages from her mother's favorite linen tablecloth. She awakened, thrashing, working at the bedsheets as if to rip them in strips.

In another dream—the one Emily had with the most disturbing frequency—she was dressed in a strange mixture of clothing: Frankie's cap and Mama's bed jacket and Fannie's knickerbockers. She walked down a strange street, barefooted. At the bottom of a hill the roadbed turned into a fetid quagmire of pig dung, and as she slogged through it, Tom stood on the tip of the new church roof with his arms crossed over his chest, laughing at her. She became incensed and tried to fly up to the steeple and tell him so, but she was mired deep and her arms refused to lift her.

In another, they were playing French Postman and he kissed her, which was absurd, because though she continued attending the local parties at Charles's insistence, Tom continued staying away, often as not with Tarsy.

Yet the dream persisted. One night, lying restless and troubled beside Fannie, Emily decided to confide in her.

"Fannie? Are you asleep?"

"No."

Across the hall Mama coughed, then the house became silent while Emily formulated questions and worked up the courage to voice them.

"Fannie, what would you think of an engaged woman who dreams of somebody besides her fiancé?"

"Another man, you mean?"

"Yes."

Fannie sat up. "Gracious, this is serious."

"No, it's not. It's just . . . just dumb dreams. But I have them so often, and they bother me."

"Tell me about them."

Emily did, omitting Tom's name, while Fannie settled herself against the headboard as if for a lengthy talk. She described the two nightmares, and asked, "What do you think they mean?"

"Goodness, I have no idea."

Emily gathered her courage and admitted, "There's another one."

"Mmm . . ."

"I dream that we're playing French Postman and he's kissing me."

Fannie said simply, "Oh, my."

"And I like it."

"Oh my oh my."

Emily sat up and punched the blanket in self-disgust. "I feel so guilty, Fannie!"

"Why feel guilty? Unless, of course, there's a reason."

"You mean have I actually kissed him? No, of course not! He's never even touched me. As a matter of fact there have been times when I'm not even sure he likes me." After pondering silently for a minute Emily asked, "Fannie, why do you suppose I never dream of Charles?"

"Probably because you see him so much that you don't have to."

"Probably."

After a moment of thoughtful silence Fannie asked, "This man you dream about—are you attracted to him?"

"Fannie, I'm engaged to Charles!"

"That's not what I asked."

"I can't . . . he . . . when we . . ." Emily stammered to a halt.

"You are."

Emily's silence was as good as an admission.

"So what *has* happened between you and your dream man?"

"He's not my dream man."

"All right, this man who doesn't like you sometimes. What happened?"

"Nothing. We've looked at each other, that's all."

"Looked? All this guilt over a few innocent looks?"

"And we played your damned game once—Guessing Blind Man. He was wearing the blindfold and he sat on my lap and he . . . he touched my face . . . and my hair . . . it was awful. I wanted to die on the spot."

"Why?"

"Because Charles was right there watching!"

"What did Charles say?"

"Nothing. He thinks those games are purely innocent."

"Oh, Emily . . ." With a sigh Fannie folded Emily in her arms and held her close, drawing the girl's head to her shoulder and petting her hair. "You're so like your mother."

"Well . . . isn't that good?"

"To a point, yes. But you must try to laugh more, to take life as it comes. What harm is there in a kissing game?"

"It's embarrassing."

Fannie's response, rather than soothing Emily, only added fuel to her misgivings. "Then I fear, you poor misguided dear, that you simply haven't kissed the right one."

In late August Tom received a letter from Julia:

> Dear Thomas,
>
> I have been very troubled by what I did to you. It seems the only way to appease my conscience is to write to you and apologize. On my wedding morning I cried. I awakened and looked out my window at the streets where you and I walked so many times, and thought of you so far away, and I remembered the look on your face the day I told you of my plans to marry. I'm so sorry if I hurt you, Tom. I did not mean to. My abrupt termination of our engagement was unpardonable of me, I know. But, Tom, I am so happy with Jonas, and I wanted you to know. I made the right choice, for me, for both of us. Because I am so happy, I wish for you the same kind of happiness. It is my dearest hope that you will find it with a woman who will cherish you as you deserve. When you find her, please don't be pessimistic because of my ill treatment of you. I should not like to believe myself responsible for any cynicism you might harbor toward women. Connubial life is rich and rewarding. I wish it for you, too, perhaps the more so since Jonas and I have learned that we are expecting our first child next March. I hope this finds you content and flourishing in your new environs. I think of you often and with the deepest affection.
>
> Julia.

He read the letter on the boardwalk outside Loucks's store. When he'd finished it he found himself amazed at how little sentiment it engendered for Julia. There was a time when the sight of her handwriting alone would have made his heart leap. It came as somewhat of a shock to realize that she no longer had the power to hurt him.

But her letter made him homesick. The mention of the street

where they'd walked brought back other vivid images of his hometown and family. He was sick of eating in a hotel, of sleeping in a loft, of working fourteen hours a day, first in the livery stable, then on his house. Sometimes, weary from hours of plastering, when he'd walk back to the livery barn for the night, he'd stare at the early lanternlight in the homes he passed and feel utterly dismal.

So he began spending more time with Tarsy.

Had there been any other girl in Sheridan who interested him, he would have wooed her. But other than Emily Walcott, Tarsy was the only one, and it was natural that the longer they saw one another, the freer they became with each other. In time they found themselves treading a dangerous line between discretion and disaster.

Frustrated by the fact as much as Tom, Tarsy finally had to talk to somebody about it and sought out Emily. She came to the Walcott home after supper on a dreary, misty evening in late September. Charles and Edwin were playing a game of backgammon. Frankie answered the door and took Tarsy back to the kitchen where Emily was helping Fannie with the dishes.

"Emily, can I talk to you?"

"Tarsy—" One look told Emily something was amiss. She laid down her dish towel immediately. "What's wrong?"

"Could we go upstairs to your room?"

Unsuspectingly, Emily obliged.

Upstairs in the lamplight Tarsy removed her wool coat and poked around Emily's room as if reluctant to reveal what was troubling her, now that she had Emily's ear. At the dresser she picked up a brush and absently ran a thumb over the bristles. Discarding it, she chose a comb and ran it once down the back of her hair, which was caught in a black bow and cascaded to her shoulders.

Emily studied her, waiting patiently for whatever it was Tarsy had come here to say. She was slim and pretty, dressed in a white blouse and red plaid skirt, easily the prettiest girl in Sheridan. It often crossed Emily's mind that it was no wonder Tom found himself attracted to Tarsy. They'd been seeing a lot of each other lately, Emily knew, and the effect upon Tarsy had been noticeable.

She had changed over the summer. The giddy, giggly girl was gone, replaced by a level-headed young woman who no longer flung herself across beds or flopped into haystacks, gushing.

Ironically, the change had endeared Tarsy to Emily much more than ever before.

Emily went to her now and turned her around by the arms. "Tarsy, what is it?"

Tarsy raised distressed brown eyes. "It's Tom," she admitted quietly. She spoke his name differently than in the past, with respect now.

"Oh." Emily's hands slid from Tarsy's sleeves.

Tarsy caught one before it could slip away. "I know you don't like him, Emily, but I . . . I don't have anyone else I'd trust with this. I think I love him, Em."

There it was: the confidence. Another load for Emily to carry. Had Tarsy only pretended to swoon as she had a few months ago, it wouldn't have been so tragic. But she was absolutely earnest.

"You love him?"

"Oh, I know, I've said it before. I've mooned around like a star-struck little girl and I've flung myself down in the hayloft and drooled and acted like a perfect ninny over him. But it's different now. It's the real thing." Tarsy pressed a fist beneath her left breast and spoke with alarming sincerity. "It's here, in the deepest part of me, and it's so big I can scarcely carry it around anymore. But I'm afraid to tell him because if he found out, he'd stop seeing me." Tarsy dropped to the edge of Emily's bed and sat disconsolately, staring at the floor. Her hands lay calmly in her lap instead of flapping about melodramatically as they once had.

"You see," she continued, "he told me quite a while ago that he suspected I was looking for a husband. But he made it clear that he was not in the market for marriage. I knew that all along, even when I began to let him kiss me. At first that was all we did, but then we kept on seeing each other and now . . . well, it's only natural that—" Tarsy rose abruptly and walked to the window where she stood staring out at a misty rain. "Oh, Emily, you must think I'm terrible."

"Tarsy, have you and Tom . . ." Emily couldn't think of a discreet way to ask the question. Terrified, she waited for an answer.

Tarsy followed a raindrop with one finger and said levelly, "No, not yet." She turned, fully composed, and returned to sit at Emily's side. "But I'm so tempted, Em. We've come so close."

The girls' eyes met, and in Tarsy's was honesty and culpability such as Emily had never expected to see there. To Emily's chagrin, her friend's eyes flooded with tears and she covered her face with her hands. "It's a sin. I know it's a sin. And it's dangerous, but what do you do when you love someone so much that it no longer seems wrong?"

"I don't know," Emily replied simply, abashed at the turn in the conversation.

"But you're engaged, Emily; you and Charles are together as much as Tom and I are. What do you do when you start feeling that way?"

Was it insight or naïveté that prompted Tarsy to believe love smote everyone in the same way, that it struck mindless passion into a woman simply because she had agreed to marry a man? To Emily's great and growing dismay, Charles had never incited those feelings in her. Indeed, she had come closer to them with Tom Jeffcoat than with her own fiancé.

Which only added to the irony of the situation.

"I don't know what to say, Tarsy."

"There's more. Something even worse," Tarsy admitted. "Sometimes I think about letting it happen and trapping him."

"Don't say that!" Emily exclaimed, horrified. "That's foolish!"

"But it's true. If I got pregnant with his baby he'd have to marry me and sometimes I almost believe the disgrace would be worth it."

"Oh, Tarsy, no." Emily gave in to her own aching heart and held Tarsy with an affection she'd never felt before. How many times had she called this girl a silly twit, and scoffed at her flightiness? Now it was gone and Emily wanted it back, wanted their girlhood back because womanhood was too hurtful and dismaying. "Promise me you'll never do that. Promise. It could ruin your lives forever, and it would be so unfair to him."

Tarsy hid her face against Emily's shoulder and cried. "Oh, Emily, what am I going to do? He loves somebody else."

Panic struck Emily. Panic and guilt. Her face turned red as she held Tarsy tightly, lest she lift her eyes and see.

But Tarsy went on. "It's that woman he was engaged to. He still loves her."

"Well, maybe he does. It's only been a few months since she broke their engagement. It takes time to get over a thing like that. He'll come to see that you're . . . well, that you've grown up, that you're ready for marriage." In an effort to cheer her further, Emily added, "And you're just about the prettiest thing this dumpy little town has ever seen. Why, he'd be a real fool not to see that."

She lifted Tarsy's trembling chin. At first Tarsy resisted being cajoled, but finally gave a sheepish snuffle of laughter. "Oh, *I'm* the fool." She dashed tears from her face with the back of her hand. "I know I am. Just a . . . a silly fool, saying I'd do a thing like that. I never would, you know that, Em, don't you?"

"Of course, I do. Here." Emily found a handkerchief in her bureau drawer and handed it to Tarsy, waiting while she mopped her face and blew her nose. When she had, Tarsy absently wrapped the edge of the hanky over her thumbs and sat staring at it.

"But, Emily . . ." she said plaintively, lifting sad eyes, "I do love him."

Emily dropped to her knees before Tarsy and covered the girl's hands. "I know."

The new, adult Tarsy tried bravely to control the tears that were dangerously close to brimming over again. "Oh, Emily, why does it have to hurt so bad?"

Neither of them knew the answer, nor did they suspect that the hurt would intensify in the weeks that followed.

Chapter 10

THERE WERE TIMES when Fannie asked herself why she'd come. Watching someone die was not easy. In recent days the consolation of being near Edwin could not compensate for the pain of dealing with Joey. Poor, failing Joey. She could not lie, nor could she sit, for to recline meant to cough and to sit erect took strength she didn't possess. So she spent her days and nights angled against the pillows, hacking away what little strength she'd garnered from her fitful naps.

Caring for her took a staunchness Fannie had not anticipated. The bedroom stank now, for the coughing had grown so violent it brought on simultaneous incontinence, and no matter how often Fannie changed the sheets, the smell of stale urine persisted. Blood, too, Fannie discovered, had a sickening smell, not only when freshly spilled but when soaking in a tub of lye water.

Fannie's hands burned: every day was washday now, and though Emily helped often, the bulk of the chore fell to Fannie.

She disregarded her own minor irritation, which seemed petty compared to the raw bedsores on Joey's elbows. Joey had become a living skeleton, shrunken to a mere ninety pounds, so gaunt there were times Fannie was forced to stifle a gasp when entering the room. Her cousin's hair was nearly too thin to braid, showing pink skull between the limp skeins. The skin over her cheekbones looked like dry corn husks and bruised at the lightest touch. Any physical contact caused her pain; she'd even had to remove her wedding ring from her knobby finger because it felt, she said, like an iron shackle. Wherever she was touched by helping hands, those hands left blue bruises.

She coughed again and Fannie slipped a hand behind the pillows, holding Josephine straighter. The blood came—brilliant carmine against the clean white cotton rags they substituted for handkerchiefs, which were too small to be adequate anymore. They rode it out together, and when the spasm ended, Josephine sank back depleted. Fannie gently released her, touching her hair—the only thing touchable without causing more pain.

"There, Joey, rest now . . ." Trying to compose soothing words had become as great a drain upon Fannie as witnessing Josephine's pain. *Dear God, either take her or produce a miracle.*

"I've got some things to hang on the line. Will you be all right?" Josephine lifted a finger, too weak to nod. "I won't be gone long," whispered Fannie.

She hung the last sheet and returned to the kitchen to hear the coughing resume overhead. Closing her eyes, she dropped her forehead against the cool, varnished doorsill.

That's how Emily found her.

"Fannie?"

Fannie straightened with a snap. "Oh, Emily." Under the guise of picking up the laundry basket she swiped away her telltale tears. "I didn't hear you come in."

"Mother is worse?"

"She's had a bad afternoon. A lot of coughing, and her bedsores are so terrible. Is there anything in your medicine bag that might help her? The poor thing is suffering so."

"I'll see what I can come up with. What about you? You don't look so perky yourself."

"Oh, bosh. Me?" Fannie manufactured an air of blitheness.

"Why, you know me . . . I'm like a cat, always land right side up."

But Emily had seen the glint of tears and the dejection. She had seen, in recent days, how tired and care-worn Fannie looked. She crossed the room and took the laundry basket from Fannie's hands. "You need to get away from here for a couple of hours. Leave this, and whatever isn't finished. Comb your hair and put on your knickerbockers and take a ride on your bicycle. Don't come back until you smell supper cooking, and that's an order."

Fannie closed her eyes, composed her emotions, pressed a hand against her diaphragm, and blew out a steadying puff of air. "Thank you, dearling. I'll do exactly that, and gratefully."

She took fifteen minutes to strip off her dress and wash away the stench of sickness, which seemed to pervade her own skin and clothing lately. In a starched white shirtwaist, a trim nutmeg-colored jacket, and matching knickerbockers, with her peachy hair twisted like a cinnamon bun atop her head, she took her bicycle from the shed.

Sweet heavens, it was good to be outside! She lifted her face to the sky and sucked deep. October, and the heavens as blue as a trout's side, the air like tonic, and all around the cottonwoods turning to a king's ransom—gold against blue. Striking out, she reveled in her freedom and wiped concerns from her mind. In the distance the hills rose like the sides of a golden teacup, but along Little Goose Creek the grassy banks still wore Irish green ruddled by splashes of sumac, the earliest foliage to blush. How good to be strong, healthy, robust, out in the open, nosing the wind. Fannie balanced on her bicycle seat and pedaled harder, feeling the breeze catch her hair and drag it like thick, rough fingers. Up the hill southwest of town, down a long grade where rocks made her grip the handlebars tightly to keep from keeling over—pedaling, pedaling, pushing her limits, feeling her tensile muscles tauten and heat, and loving every minute of it, simply because she was firm and hale and able to exert herself to such limits. She stopped at a creek whose name she did not know, and watched it ripple, catch the sky, and toss it back in sequin flashes. She abandoned her bicycle and lay in the grass, pressing her shoulder blades to the earth and imbibing its permanence, letting the sun bake her face. She opened her bodice and let it bathe her chest. She listened to a red-winged blackbird churr in a clump of sedge across the water and knelt to answer, scaring it away. She drank from the stream, rebuttoned her shirtwaist, and returned to town.

Straight down Grinnell Street to Walcott's Livery Stable.

She rode right in, down the aisle dividing the building, and stopped beside a wheelbarrow full of fresh straw outside a stall Edwin was lining. He turned in surprise as she dropped the bicycle on its side.

"Edwin, don't ask any questions, please. I simply need this today." She walked into the stall and straight into his arms.

"Fannie?" Taken by surprise, he stood becalmed, a pitchfork dangling from one fist.

She clasped his trunk and turned her face against his chest. "Dear heavens, you smell good."

"Fannie, what is it?"

"Would you hold me, Edwin? Very hard, and very still for only two or three minutes? That should be enough."

The pitchfork handle thumped against the wooden divider and Edwin's arms tightened around her shoulders.

Edwin had had no time to fortify himself. One moment he'd been forking hay, the next she had stepped against him, fragrant and supple, smelling of crushed grass and fresh air and the herbs she packed among her woolens. From her skull lifted the faint scent of warmth, as if she'd ridden hard. He rested his nose against her sunrise-colored hair and breathed deeply, spread his hands across her back and memorized its contours.

"Mmmmm . . . yes," she murmured, nuzzling his shirt, catching the unadulterated scent of man, sweat, and horse, sweetened by the newly strewn hay that filled the stall. "Edwin, I apologize. I simply needed this."

"It's all right, Fannie . . . shhh."

They pressed close, rubbing each other's backs—healthy resilient flesh, thought Edwin, such as he had not held in years.

"You feel so good," she whispered.

"You do, too."

"Hard and strong and good."

Edwin's heartbeat seemed to fill his throat. Incredible—he was touching her at last, holding her—the thing he had imagined doing ever since she came, for years before she came. How typical of Fannie to surprise him this way when he least expected it, to walk against him and surround him as if this were her natural place.

"Why today?" he asked, disbelievingly.

"Because I wasn't sure I could go on without it."

"You too, Fannie?"

She nodded, bumping his chin. "You smell of life and vitality."

"I smell worse than that, I've been cleaning stalls."

"Don't! Don't pull away! I'm not through yet."

He closed his eyes and smiled against her hair, feeling it catch in his beard, steeping himself in her unexpected nearness, pulling in deep drafts of her herbal scent. He leaned back to watch her eyes while his hands skimmed her sides, caught her waist—like notches in a fiddle, that waist, dainty and curved. He girded her ribs, rode his thumbs in the depression just below them, wanting to touch her breasts but refraining, because these simple acknowledgments were heaven in themselves. How long had it been since he'd caressed a woman this way? He'd lost track of the years. It might have been as long ago as the last time he'd held Fannie. Josie had always resisted open petting. Whatever sexual—even affectionate—contact they'd shared had happened in the dark of night, discreetly, according to her code of mores. He drew Fannie close once again. Ah, how good, how natural it felt to lay hands on a woman in broad daylight, to drop his face to her hair and draw her hips flush to his. He spread his hands and ran them up till his thumbs touched her armpits, fingers splaying behind, as if she were a nut he might crack open and savor. She shuddered palpably and made an enraptured sound against his throat. When he pushed back to see her face a strand of her pale melon-colored hair caught on his shirt button, tethering them together. Their gazes met, filled with love so certain, so ingrained, it could no longer be denied.

"Forgive me, Fannie, but I must," Edwin uttered softly, and claimed her lips and breasts at once, urging her near with his huge, work-stained hands wrapped around those soft mounds, lowering his head to taste her waiting mouth. They were not children as they'd been when he'd first touched and kissed her. What they did, they did with full acknowledgment of its import and significance. They kissed as two who had paid long and hard for the right, tongue upon tongue, mouths open and pliant, while he reshaped her breasts from below and stroked their tips with his thumbs. He backed her against the rough board wall, sending the pitchfork clattering to the floor as he leaned against her, fully aroused and unwilling to hide it. She was all he remembered, sensuous and passionate and inventive with her mouth. She drew upon his tongue and lips, tasting him shallow and deep with deft swirls of her agile tongue, then with eager lips. The kiss didn't end, it pacified, scattered to other areas—necks, shoulders, throats, ears.

"Fannie, I never forgot . . . never." His words were longing whispers.

"Neither did I."

"We should have been together all these years."

"In my heart we were."

"Oh Fannie, Fannie, my dear, sweet Fan—" Her mouth severed the word, anxious and open beneath his. They kissed with the urgency of time lost—wet, agitated kisses punctuated by wordless sounds and the ardent pressure of their bodies, as if by holding hard enough they might wipe out the long lapse they'd suffered.

When they paused, panting, he told her, "I'd forgotten how it feels. Do you know how long it's been since I've done anything like this?"

"Shh . . . nothing about her, not ever. This is dishonorable enough."

He gripped her head, held it as a priest holds a chalice, and drank her—Fannie of the bright hair and insatiable spirit and crushed-grass scent. He cherished her—Fannie of the memories and warmth and dew-kissed days of youth. How had he sustained through all these years without her? Why had he ever tried?

He lifted his head and delved into her eyes. "The dishonor was mine in giving you up. What a fool I was."

"You did what you thought you must do."

His thumbs stroked her cheeks. "I love you, Fannie. I've always loved you."

"And I love you, Edwin. I never stopped either."

"You knew it when I married Josie, didn't you? You knew I loved you."

"Of course I did, just as you knew what I felt."

"Why didn't you try to stop me?"

"Would it have done any good?"

"I don't know." His eyes were pained, his voice regretful. "I don't know."

"Your parents exerted very strong wills. So did hers."

"Isn't it strange then, that when I told them Josie and I were leaving Massachusetts they put up no argument? Almost as if they recognized our leaving as a penance they had to pay for manipulating our lives. I knew it was the only way my marriage would survive—I couldn't live near you and not have you. I'd have broken my vows within the year, I'm sure. My precious Fannie . . ." He took her in his arms again—a tender repossession. "I love you so much. Will you come up to the loft with me and let me make love to you?"

"No, Edwin." In typical Fannie fashion, she remained content in his arms, even while refusing.

"Haven't we wasted enough of our lives?" Holding her head, he showered her face with kisses, leaving her skin damp. "When we were seventeen we should have damned the consequences and become lovers like we wanted to. Those consequences couldn't have been any worse than the ones we paid. Please, Fannie . . . let's not prolong the mistake."

She caught his hands and hauled them down, folded them between her own beneath her chin. Her eyelids closed and trembled while emotions tumbled through her aroused body.

"Enough, Edwin. We must stop. You're a married man."

"Married to the wrong woman."

"But married just the same. And I would never do that to Joey. I love her, too."

"Then why did you come here?" he demanded in near-anger.

She would not be harassed by his understandable frustration. Calmly she flattened his hand upon her thrusting heart. "Feel what you've done to me. My blood is coursing. Inside I'm quivering, and I feel very much alive, with a reason to go on. I took this much of you because I felt Joey would have approved. For now it's enough." She refolded his hands between her own, kissed the tips of his longest fingers, and sought his eyes. "I am restored and so are you. But we would suffer within ourselves if we betrayed Joey. You know that as well as I, Edwin. Now I must go back to the house."

He searched her eyes, feeling his momentary irritation fade. "Fannie, when will we—"

"Silence," she ordered softly, covering his lips with a finger. She brushed the width of his mouth lovingly, letting her eyes follow the path of her fingertip. "We are human, Edwin. What we feel for one another cannot always be held in abeyance. Sometimes, when we are bleak and in need, we may find ourselves seeking one another, as I sought you today. But we will not speak of eventualities, nor will we consign ourselves to deceitful *tête-à-têtes*. It would only compound our guilt." Her voice lowered to whisper, "Now I must go. Please let me."

She backed away, reaching out, sliding her hands down his wrists, knuckles, and finally from his fingertips.

"I think of you in bed at night, though," she whispered as she slipped away.

"Fannie . . ."

She turned to her bicycle and mounted while she still possessed a thimbleful of honor.

During those days while Josephine suffered her final decline, Tom Jeffcoat worked hard to complete the interior of his house. On a night in mid-autumn, after fifteen hours of nonstop work, he dropped his plastering hawk and trowel, braced his spine with two fists, and bowed backwards. Above his head hung a hissing coal-oil lantern that sent shadows arching across his half-plastered kitchen wall. He'd wanted to get the room done tonight—usually he worked till ten o'clock—but his back ached and the shakedown at the stable sounded irresistible.

He scanned the room, its windows set, its floor covered with canvas drop cloths, wondering what woman might reign over it some day. A disconcerting picture of Emily Walcott appeared, standing where the range would be. Ha. Emily Walcott probably didn't know which end of a spoon to stir with. Hadn't Charles confided that she wasn't very good around the kitchen? In spite of the fact, her image remained while Tom stared, glassy-eyed with fatigue.

Go home, Jeffcoat, before you drop off your feet.

He squatted to scrape the hawk clean, so tired it took an effort to push himself back up. Yawning, he shrugged into a faded flannel jacket, picked up the bucket of dirty tools, and extinguished the lantern. Indigo shadows fell across the room as he paused a moment to reconsider.

It'll probably be Tarsy Fields you'll share this house with. She's about the best this town has to offer.

Outside, a near-full harvest moon poured milky light over the streets, paling rooftops and promising frost by morning. He glanced at the Big Horns. Already their tips were covered with snow at the higher altitudes, glowing almost purple in the moonlight. Turning his collar up, he headed in the opposite direction, toward Grinnell Street. The town was already bundling up for winter. He passed gardens where housewives had cleared all but an occasional pumpkin or a row of carrots left to sweeten in the first frosts. Foundations were ballasted with straw, whose scent mingled with that of freshly rooted soil spiced by old tomato vines and vestiges of gardeners' fires, which marked the end of the harvest season. He wondered what kind of a gardener Tarsy would make. Out here, where tinned goods came by oxcart and cost a modest fortune, housewives had no choice but putting by foods for the winter. Somehow he couldn't imagine her on her knees, weeding. Canning? The picture seemed ludicrous. Bearing children? Not the satin-and-curls Tarsy.

How about Emily Walcott?

The thought of Emily Walcott rattled him, but she persisted in his thoughts almost daily, probably because Charles talked about her so much. Perhaps she disliked domestics, but he could easily feature her bearing children. A woman who could go through anything as unpleasant as the scene at Jagush's could certainly go through childbirth intrepidly.

So Charles was lucky on that score. So what?

Shake her off, Jeffcoat.

Shake her off? She never was on!

Oh no?

She's engaged to Charles.

Tell that to your heart the next time it quakes when she walks into a room.

So, my heart quakes a little, so what?

You'd like to marry her yourself.

The tomboy?

Why have you been picturing her in your kitchen, and having babies? And don't delude yourself that it's Charles Bliss's babies you picture her having.

He was exhausted, that's why his mind kept wandering off on these improbable tangents. Whatever he thought he felt for Emily Walcott would pass. It had to, because there was no other solution. He ambled along, loose-jointed from weariness, the pail thumping his knee, sending out a muffled chime.

He turned onto Grinnell Street, came abreast of Edwin's livery stable . . . and halted abruptly.

Why was a light burning in Edwin's place at this time of night? Edwin closed up at six o'clock every night—the same as he did—and never came back after dark. And why was the light so faint, as if filtering to the office window from the main body of the barn?

Horse thieves?

Jeffcoat's hair prickled. He slipped alongside the building, flattened his shoulders against the wall, and silently set down his pail. The rolling door stood open no wider than a man's chest. He edged toward it, listening. Silence. Not even a snuffling horse, so no stranger intruded along the stalls. Holding his breath, he peered around the edge of the door into the murky depths of the building. The main barn was black. The light came from the office itself, but so pale it scarcely lit the door rim. If it were Edwin inside, he'd have the wick up. Did Edwin leave his cash here at night, somewhere among the clutter in that ancient desk?

Jeffcoat sucked in his breath and wedged through the door. A sound came from the office—jerky, nasal breathing, followed by the shuffle of paper. He tiptoed along the wall, feeling with his hands, until they touched something smooth and wooden: a pitchfork handle. Silently he slid his hands down to identify the cold, deadly tines. Gripping the fork, warrior fashion, he tiptoed to one side of the office door, tensed to spring.

"Edwin, is that you?" he called.

The breathing and shuffling stopped.

"Who's in there!" he demanded.

Nobody answered.

His chest constricted and his scalp tingled, but he gripped the pitchfork and sprang into the room like a Zambian warrior, roaring, *"Raaaahhh!"*

The only person in the office was Emily Walcott.

She flattened herself against the back of the desk chair, white-faced and terrified, while he landed with the weapon leveled, knees cocked.

"Emily!" he exclaimed, dropping his arm. "What are you doing here?" But he could see what she was doing here: crying . . . in private. Her eyes were swollen and tears continued rolling down her face, even as she gaped in shock.

"What are *you* doing here?"

"I thought you were a horse thief, or somebody rifling the

desk for money. Edwin never comes back after six." He set the pitchfork against the wall and turned back to her, distressed at the tears trailing down her wet cheeks. How dismal she looked, in a pumpkin-colored dress with dark blotches dotting her bodice, giving evidence that she'd been weeping for some time. She swiveled to face the pigeonholes, covertly scraping a knuckle beneath each eye.

"Well, it's just me, so you can go," she informed him through a plugged nose.

"You're crying."

"Not for long. I'm all right. You can go, I said."

Her tears were a surprise. He hadn't taken her for a woman easily unstrung, or himself for the kind who'd be rattled by it. But his heart was quaking.

He kept his tone intentionally humoring. "It's too late now, I already caught you at it. So you might as well talk."

She shook her head stubbornly, but dropped her mouth against a handkerchief while her shoulders shook. He stared at her dress, buttoned up the back, drawn tight across her shoulder blades, at the prim white collar and the disheveled black hairs on her nape. He fought the inclination to spin the chair around and pull her into his arms, hold her fast, and let her cry against him. Instead he asked, "Do you want me to go get Charles?"

She shook her head vehemently but continued sobbing into the hanky, her elbows splayed on the desktop.

He stood, disarmed, wondering what to do while she doubled forward, burying her face in an arm, sobbing so hard her ribs lifted. He felt his own chest tighten and a lump form in his throat. What should he do? Mercy, what should he do? He watched until he felt like bawling himself, then dropped to a squat, swinging her chair to face him. "Hey," he urged gently, "turn around here." Her skirt brushed his knees but she refused to lift her face from the hanky, abashed at breaking down before him. "You can talk to me, you know."

She shook her head fervidly, releasing a series of muffled sobs. "Just g—go away. I don't w—want you to see me like this."

"Emily, what is it? Something with Charles?"

She shook her head till a hairpin fell, bouncing off his knee to the floor.

He picked it up and folded it tightly into his palm while

studying the part in her hair, only inches from his nose. "Me? Did I do something again?"

Another passionate shake.

"Your little brother? Tarsy? Your father? What?"

"It's my mother." The words, distorted by the handkerchief and her plugged nose, sounded like *by buther*. Her devastated eyes appeared above the limp white cotton, which she pressed against her nose. "Oh Tom"—*Tob*, he heard—"it's so hard to watch her die."

A bolt of emotion slammed through him at her pitiful plea and her unconscious and distorted use of his name. It took a superhuman effort to hunker before her and not reach, not touch.

"She's worse?"

Emily nodded, dropping her gaze while gustily blowing her nose. When she finally rested her hands in her lap, her nose was red and raw. "I took care of her today while Fannie went off b—by herself for a wh—while," she explained choppily, the words broken by residual sobs. "Poor F—Fannie, she's with her all day long. I guess I never r—realized before what a terrible task we gave her, seeing after Mother during those last weeks. But today Fannie asked me if I could—could—" Emily paused, battling a fresh onslaught of emotion. "Could find something to help her bedsores, and I—" Trying her utmost to complete her recital without another breakdown, Emily lifted brimming eyes to the top of the doorway. "I saw . . . them." She blinked; her eyes remained shut while she pulled in an immense breath, then opened them once more and struggled on. "Fannie gives Mother her baths and changes her clothes and her bedding. I hadn't realized how b—bad her bedsores were till today. And she's so . . . s—skinny . . . there's n—nothing left of her. She c—can't even turn over by herself. P—Papa has to do it for her. But wherever he touches her it leaves a bl—black-and-blue mark." Her tears built again, in spite of her valiant effort to contain them.

On his knees before her, Tom watched helplessly as she again wept brokenly into her hands, her entire frame shaking. *Damn you, Charles, where are you? She needs you!* His heart swelled while he watched, torn and miserable. *Aw, tomboy, don't cry . . . don't cry.*

But she did, torturously, trying to hold the sound within, only to have it escape her throat as a faint, pitiful mewling. He felt the pressure in his own throat and knew he must either touch her or shatter.

"Emily, hush, now . . . here . . ." Still kneeling, he drew her to him, and she came limply, sliding off the chair without resistance. He folded her tenderly in his arms and held her, kneeling on the bumpy concrete floor of the cluttered little office. She wept on jerkily, limp against him, her arms resting loosely up his back while her sobs beat against his chest.

"Oh, Toooom . . ." she wailed dismally.

He cupped her head and drew her face hard against his throat, while her tears seeped through his shirtfront and wet his skin. She wept to near-exhaustion, then rested weakly against him.

He dropped his cheek against her hair, wishing he were wise and clever with words and could voice the consolation he felt in his heart. Instead he could only cradle her and offer silence.

In time her breathing evened and she managed to offer chokily, "I'm sorry."

"Don't be sorry," he chided gently. "If you didn't love her you wouldn't feel so grieved."

He felt her breasts heave in a great shaky sigh as she dried the last of her tears, still lying with her cheek on his chest, showing little inclination to leave. He fixed his gaze on a yellowed calendar hanging above the desk and lightly stroked the back of her neck.

Minutes passed with each of them dwelling upon private thoughts. At last Emily asked tiredly, "Why can't she just die, Tom?"

He heard both guilt and sincerity in her question and understood how painful it must have been for her to ask it. He rubbed her back and kissed her hair. "I don't know, Emily."

For long moments they abided so, pressed close together, joined by her grief and his distress at being unable to deliver her from it. In a voice soft with understanding he gave her the only ease he knew. "But you mustn't feel guilty for wishing she would," he said.

He knew by her stillness that the words had been what she'd needed: an absolution.

Her weeping had ended minutes ago, but they stole more precious time until—as one—they realized they had remained in each other's arms too long. At some point while she rested against him they had crossed the fine line between desolation and yearning.

He drew back, pressing her away by both arms, letting his hands linger, then dropping them reluctantly to his sides. He watched her cheeks heat and read in her blush the thousand shamefaced wishes she, too, had allowed to flee through her mind. But Charles materialized in spirit, and Emily stared at a button on Tom's flannel jacket while he studied her averted face and sat back on his heels to put more distance between them.

"So . . ." he managed shakily, the word trembling between them like a shot bird waiting to plummet. "Are you feeling better now?"

She nodded and glanced up cautiously. "Yes."

He studied her, shaken and uncertain. If she were to move—the subtlest shift—she would be in his embrace again, and this time he'd give her far more than consolation. For a moment he watched temptation dull her eyes, but he produced a tight laugh and a dubious grin. "Well, at least we got you to stop crying."

She covered her cheeks and gingerly touched her lower eyelids. "I probably look awful."

"Yeah, pretty awful," he offered with a false chuckle, watching her test her upper eyelids, which looked bruised and swollen.

"Oh, my eyes hurt," she admitted, dropping her hands and letting him see.

They were indeed swollen and red, and her hair was rubbed from its knot, her cheeks blotchy, and her lips swollen; but he wanted to kiss them and her poor red-rimmed eyes, and her throat and her breast, and say, forget Charles, forget Tarsy, forget your mother and let me make you happy.

Instead he got a grip on his inclinations and took her hands, drawing her to her feet, then stepping back. "So . . . can I walk you home?"

Her eyes said yes, but her voice said, "No, I came down here to get some lanolin for Mother's bedsores." She gestured toward the muddle of papers and the open book on the desk where both of them knew perfectly well she kept no lanolin. "I . . . I have to look for it, so you go on."

He glanced from the desk to her. "You're sure you'll be all right?"

"Yes, thank you. I'll be fine."

The room seemed combustible with suppressed emotions while neither of them moved.

"Well, good night, then."

"Good night."

I should have kissed you when I had the chance.

As he backed toward the door her words stopped him again. "Tom . . . thank you. I needed somebody very badly tonight."

He nodded, gulped, and stalked out before he could dishonor himself and her and Charles.

Chapter 11

OCTOBER PASSED AND Tom took up residence in his house. It was livable, but bare. The walls were clean and white but begged for wallpaper and pictures, the things a woman was so much more adept at choosing than a man. The windows, with the exception of those in the one bedroom Tom used, remained unadorned. Since he spent most of his time in other places, the livability of his home, for the moment, mattered little. He had an iron bed, a heater stove for the parlor, a cookstove for the kitchen, and one overstuffed chair. Besides these few purchased furnishings he made do with a few empty nail kegs, a crude homemade table, two long benches, and a woodbox. From Loucks he had bought necessities only: bedding, lanterns, wash basin, a water pail, dipper, teakettle, frying pan, and coffeepot. He stored his few groceries—eggs, coffee, and lard—on the kitchen floor in an empty wooden crate from rifle shells.

The first time Tarsy came in, she glanced around and her

face flattened in disappointment. "You mean this is *all* you're going to put in here?"

"For now. I'll get more when the oxcarts start moving again in the spring."

"But this kitchen. It's . . . it's bare and awful."

"It needs a woman's touch, I'll grant you that. But it serves my needs. I'm at the livery barn most of the time anyway."

"But you don't even have dishes! What do you eat on?"

"I eat most of my meals at the hotel. Sometimes I fry an egg here for breakfast, but eggs aren't much good without bread. Do you know anybody I could buy bread from?" Tarsy, he could see, was dismayed by his Spartan furnishings.

On a Saturday night in late November he was sitting in his only chair with his stocking feet resting on a nail keg, feeling somewhat dismayed himself. The place felt dismal. He had closed the parlor and stairwell doors, so the kitchen was warm, but too silent and stark with the curtainless windows black as slates and the ghostly white walls broken only by the stovepipe in one corner. If he were at the stable he'd be polishing tack. If he were at home in Springfield, in his mother's kitchen, he'd be prowling for food. If he were with his friends he'd be at a house party, but he'd begged off again, because Emily would be there with Charles. Tarsy had badgered and begged him to change his mind, then stormed off declaring, "All right, then, stay home! But don't expect me to!" So here he sat, staring at the red toes of his gray socks, listening to the silence and wondering how to fill his evening, thinking about Emily Walcott and how the two of them had been avoiding each other for weeks.

Charles had questioned him about why he never came to the parties anymore and he'd concocted the excuse that Tarsy was becoming too possessive and he wasn't sure what he wanted to do about her, which wasn't far from the truth. She was displaying a sudden, alarming nesting instinct. She'd even started baking him bread (heavy and coarse as horse feed, though he thanked and praised her first attempts at domesticity) and showing up at his door uninvited in the evenings; and dropping hints about how she'd love to live anywhere but with her parents; and asking Tom conversationally if he ever wanted to have a family.

He let his head fall back against the overstuffed chair and closed his eyes, wishing he loved Tarsy. But not once had he felt for her the swell of protectiveness and yearning that had overcome him the day Emily Walcott had cried and confided in him. He wondered how Emily was holding up. He knew from Charles that Mrs. Walcott was worse than ever, clinging to life though Dr. Steele had declared weeks ago there was nothing more he could do for her.

In his silent house Tom rolled his face toward the window, wishing he were with Emily and the others. It was a skating party tonight, the first of the year down on Little Goose Creek, and afterwards the group would move to Mary Ess's house for hot punch and cookies . . . and undoubtedly those damned parlor games. No, best he'd stayed away, after all.

In his pensive state, Tom failed to register the first sounds. He heard only the snap of the fire and his own gloomy monologue. Then it came again, a distant clanging, growing louder, accompanied by shouts and hallooing. He listened closer. What the hell was going on out there? It sounded like a gold prospector's pack mule rolling down a mountainside, only it was coming toward his house. He heard his name being called—"Heyyyy, Jeffcoat!"—and left his chair. "Company coming, Jeffcoat! Yoo-hoo, Tommy boy, open up!" More clanging accompanied by laughter, the commotion now seemingly circling his house. Next came the sound of horses' hooves.

At the front window he cupped an eye and peered out into the winter night. What the Sam Hill? A team and wagon were drawn right up to his front porch steps and people milled everywhere! Footsteps thumped on the hollow porch floor and a face peered back at him with crossed eyes: Tarsy. And beside her Patrick Haberkorn, then Lybee Ryker, then a whole chorus of merrymakers, shouting and rapping on the glass. "Hey, Jeffcoat, open the door!"

He threw it open, stood with his hands on his hips, grinning. They were all supposed to be at a skating party.

"What the hell are you fools up to?"

"Shivareeeeeee!"

Lybee Ryker shook silverware inside a covered pot as if it were corn popping. Mick Stubbs banged a frying pan with a wooden spoon, and Tarsy led the pack playing a pair of kettle covers as if they were cymbals. They were all there, all his friends, making such a clatter it seemed as if it would shake the moon from the sky. They left tracks in the snowy yard, clear around his house. Someone's dog had followed, and its barking joined the din. Tom stood on the front porch, laughing and feeling his heart warm, watching their faces flash past in the light from the open door behind him. She was there, too—Emily—though she hung back in the shadows when they all gathered, breathless and excited at the foot of the porch steps.

Overwhelmed, Tom searched for words. "Well, hell, I don't know what to say."

"Say nothing. Just step aside and let us get this stuff inside!"

They filed past him and deposited pots and pans and cutlery on his plank table. Tarsy wrinkled her nose just beneath his and gave a smug, self-satisfied smile as she carried a white bundle inside. "Look out if you don't want to get your toes stepped on."

"Is this your doing, Miss Fields?" He raised an eyebrow, secretly pleased.

"Might be," she said, twitching her skirttails as she passed. "With a little help from Charles."

Charles was busy on the wagon, sliding things to the rear for unloading.

"Bliss, you underhanded scoundrel, is that you out there?"

"I'm busy, you can call me names later!"

"Jerome, Ardis . . . hello." Tom's head swung as he caught glimpses of housewares and spindle chairs being carried past. Cheery voices, warm smiles, and everywhere motion. And somewhere in the middle of it, a much more subdued "Hello, Emily."

And her equally subdued "Hello, Tom," as she moved past him into his kitchen.

Someone kissed his jaw—Tarsy, going back out.

Someone bumped his arm—Martin Emerson heading back in on the lead end of a beautiful hide trunk with Jerome Berryman at the other end.

"Oh, you people, this is too much," Tom said.

But the parade lasted a good five minutes—in and out—with Charles supervising the unloading, until finally, with the help of all the men present, he unloaded a piece of furniture as wide as three men and taller than their heads.

"Charles, good God, what have you done?"

The piece was too heavy to allow Charles more than a few

grunted words as he lifted it. "Just . . . step aside . . . Jeffcoat . . . or you'll get . . . plowed ov—"

They set it against the south kitchen wall between two long, narrow windows, a beautifully crafted breakfront-server of bird's-eye maple, hand rubbed to the smoothness of an old ax handle. It sported two wide drawers and matching doors below, a wide serving counter at waist level, two more doors and a plate shelf above. Into each of the four doors had been carved shafts of wheat curling up to circle a centered brass handle. Many hours of loving care had gone into the meticulous crafting of the piece.

Tom stood touching it, staggered. "Lord, Charles . . . I don't know what to say."

Someone closed the outside door. Though the kitchen was filled with young people, it had grown silent as Charles brushed a haze of condensation off the top of the piece, then backed off, removing his gloves. "I thought it'd make the place feel more like home."

Gratitude and an undeniable font of love welled up in Tom Jeffcoat as he closed a hand over his friend's shoulder. "It's beautiful, Charles . . . it's . . ." It was more than beautiful. It was a heartful. He embraced Charles hard, with a sincere clap on the back. "Thank you, Charles."

Charles chuckled self-consciously and they backed apart—eyes meeting for an awkward moment—then laughed. And when they laughed, the others followed suit, bringing relief from the emotional moment.

Tom turned to the other offerings. "And, Jerome . . . you made me a trunk?"

"The old man and me."

Jerome Berryman's gift was almost as surprising as Charles's—a beautiful cowhide trunk with wooden hardware and brass hasp, made in his father's leather shop. Tom inspected it minutely and gave Jerome, too, an affectionate thank-you and slap on the back. "Tell your father thank you, too."

"Open it."

Inside was a motley collection: a boot scraper, a cornbread pan, a pair of dented tin kettles, a collection of clean, washed rags tied in a bundle.

"What's this?"

"Rags."

"Rags?" Tom held them aloft by their twine binding.

"Ma says everybody needs rags around a house."

A burst of laughter began a new round of commotion: the women used some of the rags to wipe melted snow off the kitchen floor while others began unpacking an amazing variety of housewares. Curtains, which one contingent hung while another began lining the pantry shelves with butcher paper. The men opened jugs of homemade beer; someone found glasses in the rummage; someone else opened the parlor door and built a fire in the small heater stove; the Fields's gramophone was wound up and a tube put on, filling the house with music; someone unearthed a reflectorized wall lantern and mounted it on the parlor wall; two of the men returned from taking Edwin's rig back to the livery stable and got scolded for stamping snow off their feet; Lybee Ryker produced a braided rag rug for in front of the door; Tarsy untinned sandwiches. And through it all, Tom unpacked his bounty.

What they hadn't made they'd acquired by raiding their homes. The result was a collection of oddments from spoon holders to spigot jars, some useful, some useless. The women found places for everything as he unpacked: four chipped enamel plates in white, edged with blue; some wrinkled metal flatware; a grater; a wooden potato masher; dishtowels; fruit jars of home-canned vegetables and jellies; three scarred spindle chairs of assorted styles; a dented copper cuspidor; a small square parlor table with one cracked leg; a horsehair sieve; antimacassars; pillowcases; a comb pocket for the wall; a cracked mirror; a hair receiver.

"A *hair receiver*?" Tom covered his head as if to hold his hair on. "Lord, I hope not!"

Everyone laughed as Tarsy came over and ruffled his thick black mane. "No danger yet."

He squeezed her waist and gave her a private smirk. "Pretty sneaky, aren't you?" he teased in an undertone, his eyes crinkling at the corners.

"Having fun?"

"Remind me to thank you later."

One of the last things he unwrapped was a beautiful hand-pieced quilt. The women drew closer, oohing. All except Emily.

"It's from Fannie," she announced quietly, keeping the same distance she'd been maintaining all evening.

Tom met her gaze directly for the first time since the party had moved inside. "She made it?"

"Yes, she did."

"It's very nice. Tell her I said thank you, will you?"

Emily nodded.

Looking on, Charles mistook their careful distance for chilliness and—ever eager to promote amity between the two he loved most—moved to take Emily's hand. "Want to see the house?" he asked. "I'll show it to you."

She flashed him a quick, distracted smile. "Of course."

With Charles she walked through Tom's house, the house the two men had built together: up the stairs with a turn at the landing, through three second-story bedrooms, each with its own closet, and with charming gabled windows jutting from the angled ceilings but without so much as a stick of furniture. Charles could not have been prouder were the house his own. He described each feature enthusiastically, holding the lantern aloft, leading Emily by the hand. In the third bedroom they paused, glancing in a full circle at the new floor, freshly milled and fragrant of wood smell, at the attractive ceiling line, the long, slim windows, bare as the day they were installed. The lantern flooded them with a ring of light. Against the black night their reflections shone clearly in the shiny window glass. They both caught sight of their reflection at the same instant; then Charles tightened his hand around Emily's and bent as if to kiss her.

Dipping, she slipped free.

"Is something wrong?" he asked, masking his disappointment.

She turned away. "No."

"You're awfully quiet tonight."

"It's nothing. I'm worried about Mother, that's all."

It wasn't all. It was Tom Jeffcoat; and this house where he expected to live with a wife someday; and his eyes, which had avoided hers all evening; and the memory of the last time she was with him, crying against his collar, wrapped in his arms, feeling secure and comforted.

"That's not all," Charles insisted, moving close behind her, squeezing her arm. "But how can I understand if you won't tell me?"

She groped and came up with a plausible reply. "It's these bare windows, Charles. Anybody could look in and see us."

"So, what if they did? We're engaged to be married. Engaged couples are supposed to kiss now and then."

She had no further justification for avoiding Charles and turned, lifting apologetic eyes. "I'm sorry, Charles."

His expression appeared hurt.

"I am, too."

He had lowered his arm. The lanternlight lit his face from below, making of his eyes great dark shadows. "Do you know what I think is really bothering you?" She stared at him without answer as he continued, "I think it's Tom."

She felt a hot lump burst in her chest and spread tentacles of guilt to her face. "Tom?"

"Whenever you're around him you change. Either you snub him or cut him. Tonight you've hardly spoken to him, yet this party is in his honor. He's my best friend, Emily, and I feel like I'm caught in the middle of a tug-of-war between you two. Can't you try to be his friend for my sake?"

"I'm sorry, Charles," she replied meekly, feeling the color mount her cheeks, dropping her gaze guiltily.

"You haven't even said one nice thing about the house. You know, I spent most of my summer building it, and I'm pretty proud of it myself."

"I know." She stood before him with the crestfallen expression of a chastised child.

"Then act as if you can at least tolerate him." He lifted her chin with a finger and studied her eyes, as shadowed as his own. "All I want is a little harmony between you two."

"I'll try," she whispered.

He kissed her, there before the naked windows, with the lamplight spotlighting them in the center of the vacant room: a light resting of his lips against hers while holding her chin up; then a second, briefer kiss: all is forgiven.

"Now let me show you the rest," he whispered, and led the way from the room, holding her hand. As they moved on, he explained how the rafters were mortised, pointed out double-hung windows, the fit of the doors, the smoothness of the upstairs handrail, the safe, shallow drop of each riser and the extra width of the stairs. At the bottom of them they turned left instead of right and Emily found herself in Tom Jeffcoat's bedroom.

His bed—of white iron with acorn knots where the bars intersected—stood in a corner flanked by a window on either wall. Instead of a spread the blankets were flung up flat over a single pillow, which looked forlorn on the double width. On a nearby nail keg stood an oil lantern and at its base lay a single black hairpin. Catching sight of it, Emily felt her heart take a leap. Her hand flew to her nape as if the pin had only now fallen. *What was it doing beside his bed?* But Charles had eyes only for the house itself, and she lowered her hand unobtrusively. He pointed out the double astragal moldings on the doors while her gaze drifted over the windows, temporarily curtained with flannel sheets nailed to the tops of the sills. With the exception of the hairpin, the room looked as austere as a monk's cell.

"We put a closet in every room," Charles was saying. "I wish I'd thought of it when I built my house." When she turned, he had opened Tom's closet door, revealing a few garments hanging in a largely unused space. She recognized the black dress suit he wore on Sundays and the faded flannel shirt that had absorbed her tears the last time she'd seen him. On a hook at the rear hung one of his tattered blue shirts with the sleeves torn off, and on the floor lay a carpetbag with an underwear leg trailing from it. Braced in one corner was his rifle. The closet smelled like him—of horses and worn clothing and man.

She could not have felt more discomfited had she walked in on Tom Jeffcoat during his bath.

"We put rosettes on all the corners." Charles pointed to the woodwork above their heads. "And extra wide mopboards . . . beaded. This house is built to last."

"It's very nice, Charles," she replied dutifully. And it was. But she wanted to get out of this bedroom . . . fast.

The lower level of the house could be walked in a circle. Parlor into kitchen, kitchen into a walkthrough, which served as a pantry and housed the foot of the stairway, through the pantry into Tom's bedroom, and through a second bedroom door leading back to the parlor again. Entering that room, Emily breathed a sigh of relief. The gramophone crackled out a tinny song and dancing had begun. Tarsy and Tilda Awk were hanging the quilt for display, stretching it across one corner by slamming its corners into the tops of the sliding windows. Tom's kitchen benches had been carried in and a group sat on them, laughing, hanging spoons from their noses. Others were visiting. Tom Jeffcoat stood in the kitchen doorway, drinking a glass of beer, watching Emily and Charles enter from his bedroom. Emily's eyes locked with his as he swigged, then wrist-wiped his mouth. She was first to turn away. She pivoted to join the group on the benches but Charles caught her hand and propelled her straight across the room to another doorway beside Tom, opening it to reveal one last closet. "We even put one in here." It was absolutely empty.

"Ah," Emily said, sticking her head in, aware of Tom standing two feet away, watching.

"Oh, Tom, you have closets!" Mary Ess exclaimed, rushing over to poke her head inside, too. "Lucky you!"

Mary crowded right into the closet while Charles drew Emily out by an elbow. Turning to Tom, aware of the emotional undertow between him and Emily, Charles said, "She likes your house."

Emily gave Jeffcoat a flat glance. "I like your house," she repeated dutifully, then sidled past him into the kitchen to find something to drink.

The party grew livelier. The gramophone got louder and the dancing got faster. Emily consumed three glasses of beer and began genuinely enjoying herself, neither ignoring nor singling out Tom. She danced the varsovienne and grew pleasantly warm. Between dances, she stopped trying to push Charles's arm from around her waist. Once she glanced across the room to find Tom standing with one wrist draped over Tarsy's shoulders, drawing her against his hip. As if he felt her eyes, he looked over and their gazes locked. He raised his glass and took a drink, watching her all the while. Charles's arm rested around her waist; Tom's rested around Tarsy's shoulder. Emily experienced an irrational flash of jealousy, and again proved the first to glance away.

Someone opened a new jug of homemade beer, stronger than the first. Spirits levitated and humor grew infectious. The men dragged the new trunk into the parlor and stuffed Mick Stubbs into it, declaring the only way he could be freed was if a lady would kiss him. Tilda Awk volunteered and raised a chorus of ballyhooing and wolf whistles when she did so in the middle of the room, standing in the trunk with Mick; then the men playfully tried to close the trunk lid over both of them, which, naturally, didn't work. Tilda and Tarsy got giggly and secreted themselves in the corner behind Fannie's quilt, whispering.

Minutes later they flounced out and dragged the rest of the girls behind the quilt, divulging a new game plan.

"We're going to have a toe social!"

"A toe social?" Ardis Corbeil whispered, wide-eyed. "What's a toe social?"

Tilda and Tarsy rolled their eyes and giggled. "My mother told me about it," Tilda said. "And if she could do it, why can't I?"

"But what is it?"

It turned out to be another ridiculous game, and very risqué. The women would strip from the knees down, hike up their skirts, and stand behind the quilt revealing their naked feet and calves while the men would try to guess whom they belonged to.

"And if they guess, what then?"

"A forfeit!"

"What forfeit?"

It was Mary Ess's idea: five minutes in that empty closet . . . with the door closed . . . in pairs.

"I won't do it!" declared Emily. But the girls were giddy with excitement and chastised, "Oh, don't be such a wet blanket, Emily. It's only a game."

"But what if I end up with somebody besides Charles?"

"Sing songs," Mary suggested flippantly.

When the men heard the rules of the game they let out roaring yells of anticipation, stuck their fingers in their teeth and whistled shrilly, began punching each other's arms, then murmuring secretly among themselves and breaking into bursts of conspiratorial laughter. Emily's eyes met Charles's and she could see clearly that *he* wouldn't mind spending five minutes in a closet with her. She found her objections overridden and herself swept along as the game proceeded. The men were sent out of the room while the girls sat down to remove shoes, strip off stockings, and pull up their woolen underwear. All the while Emily sat on the floor she tried frantically to remember if Charles had ever seen her feet bare. When they were children, a long time ago, wading together in the brook while their families picnicked. Would he remember what they looked like? Oh, please Charles, remember! You must remember!

The floor was cold, despite the heater stove in the opposite corner. She stood with the other girls, barefoot, on Tom Jeffcoat's freshly laid hard oak floor and took her place in the lineup behind the quilt like some mindless sheep, afraid to walk out of the party as she wanted to, afraid Charles wouldn't recognize her feet and Tom Jeffcoat would.

Mary Ess called, "All right, you can come in now!" The men filed back in, wordlessly. On the opposite side of the quilt they cleared their throats nervously. Emily stood wedged between Tarsy and Ardis, staring at the quilt, three inches from her nose, staring at Fannie's careful coral stitches binding patches of her old dresses and her father's old shirts, feeling as if her stomach had risen to her throat, wondering what in the devil she was doing here, coerced into a game she had no desire to play. The men's shifting stopped, the room grew silent, ripe with tension.

The girls held up their skirts and felt their faces heat. Some crossed their toes shyly. None of them would look at one another. What would happen if their mothers found out about this?

The forbiddenness held them in thrall.

Emily Walcott prayed Charles would choose first . . . and right.

To her horror, she heard Jerome Berryman suggest, "It's your party, Tom, and it's your house. Even your quilt. You want to go first?"

"All right," Tom agreed.

Emily's fists formed knots in the folds of her hip-high skirts. A cold draft sifted across the floor and seemed to turn her toes to ice. Through her mind raced the picture of Tom Jeffcoat holding her boot and kneeling to help put it back on, the first day she'd ever laid eyes on him. It had been horrible then. It was worse now. Had she been standing before him stripped naked she could not have felt more exposed. Why had she ever let herself get sucked into this stupid game? To prove she wasn't a wet blanket? To prove she wasn't a prude? Well, what was wrong with being a prude? There was a lot to be said for prudery! She found this distasteful and prurient and wished she'd had the courage to say so!

But it was too late.

Tom Jeffcoat moved along the line of bare toes slowly, assessingly, coming to a halt before Emily. She squeezed her eyes shut and felt as if her entire body were puffing with each heartbeat. He moved on to the end of the line and she breathed easier. But he was back in a minute, striking panic into her heart. She glanced down. There were the tips of his black boots an inch away from her bare toes.

"Emily Walcott," he said clearly and covered her distinctive longest second toe with the tip of his boot.

She closed her eyes and thought, no, I cannot do this.

"Is it you, Emily?" he asked, and she dropped her skirts as if they were guillotines. She stood staring at the quilt, unable to move, with her stomach tipping and her cheeks ablaze. Tarsy gave her a nudge. "Get going and don't scratch his eyes out." Then, closer to Emily's ear: "I'm quite partial to his eyes!"

Emily ducked around the side of the curtain with her face glowing like a cranberry aspic. She could not—would not!—look at Tom Jeffcoat.

"I think we have to add a new rule," Patrick Haberkorn jested. "You both have to come out of the closet *alive*."

Everyone laughed except Emily. She sent a silent appeal to Charles, but he called, "Don't hurt him, Em, he's my best friend!" Again her friends laughed while she simply wanted to liquefy and drain away through the cracks between the floorboards.

"Miss Walcott . . ." Jeffcoat invited with a slight bow, gesturing toward the open closet door as if it were nothing more out of the ordinary than a waiting carriage. "After you."

Like a martyr to the stake, Emily walked stiffly into the closet. The door closed behind her and she stood smothered by darkness so absolute it momentarily dizzied her, confined with Tom, close enough to smell him. She swallowed an imprecation, sensing him at her shoulder, unruffled, while she felt as if her breath were driven from her lungs by repeated blows. She reached out, touched the cold, flat plaster, ran her hand to the corner and moved toward it, as far from him as she could get. Turning her shoulders against the right wall, she slid down.

He followed suit against the left.

Silence. Mocking silence.

She hugged her knees, curling her bare toes against the new, smooth floor.

She had never been so scared in her life, not even the time when she was four and believed there was a wolf under her bed after her mother had told her the story about her grandfather being chased by wolves when he was a boy.

She heard Jeffcoat pull in a deep breath.

"Are you mad at me for getting you in here?" he asked, just above a whisper.

"Yes."

"I thought so."

"I don't want to talk."

"All right."

Silence again, thicker than before, while she drew her knees to her chest and felt as if she might explode. It was like being twenty feet underwater and out of air—fright and pressure and her heart banging hard enough to burst her eardrums.

"This is a stupid game!" she hissed.

"I agree."

"Then why did you pick me!"

"I don't know."

Anger sluiced through her, rich and revitalizing, replacing some of her fear. Until he admitted, reluctantly, "Yes, I do."

Her nostrils pinched and her shoulder blades threatened to dent his new plastered wall. "Jeffcoat, I warn you . . ." She put out a fending hand and touched black space.

He let the suggestion hover until the walls seemed to shrink. Then he ordered in a voice low and rife with intent, "Come here, tomboy."

"No!"

His hand closed over her bare left ankle.

She recoiled and cracked her skull against the wall.

"No!"

"Why not?"

"Let go!"

"We've both been wondering. It might be our only chance to find out."

The anger left her voice, replaced by pleading. "Tom, don't! Oh God, please don't." Frantically, she tried to pry his hand off her ankle, but he pulled relentlessly until she felt herself sliding across the closet floor, still bent at the knee and hip.

"If you put up too much of a fight they might guess what's really going on in here."

She stopped struggling . . . with everything except breath. It fought its way up her throat and caught on the lump of foreboding that had risen from her chest.

Outside, someone banged on the door, teasing. Emily jumped but Jeffcoat remained unyielding. His hand slid up her calf and came to rest behind her knee. She sat as still as a monument while his other hand searched the dark, found her cheek, then slipped around her nape, pulling, pulling, while she stiffened against it.

"I'm scared, too, tomboy, but I mean, by God, to find out. Now come here."

His mouth missed hers by an inch. He corrected his course, trailing warm breath while she sat unbending, holding her own breath and keeping her lips stiff as frozen persimmons. His first kiss was cautious, a mere resting of his lips on hers. When she remained rigid he backed up—by the feel of his breath she knew he was still dangerously close—then went at it again, scarcely separating his lips to impart a hint of dampness. "Don't," she pleaded softly, plaintively.

But he went on as if she hadn't spoken, kissing her compellingly, angling his head, lightly swashing her lips with his tongue, thawing them. "Come on, tomboy, take a stab at it," he encouraged, and took her head in both hands, resting his thumbs beside her unwilling mouth and drawing circles as if to reshape it, rubbing his tongue across her lips persuasively.

She swallowed once, with her lips still closed, her heart thundering with an avalanche of forbidden feelings. He was very persistent, very poised, drawing wet figure eights upon her mouth—lightly, lightly—his breath warming her cheek until her own could no longer be contained. It came out in a rush, accompanied by a shudder, and her willpower disappeared like frost from a sun-kissed windowpane. Wilting against him, she lifted her arms and returned his embrace. When she opened her lips his tongue swept inside them at once, hot and inquisitive, inciting hers to do the same. Explorers, they circled, stroked, delved . . . abashed by their mutual, swift excitement.

It grew too intense, too fast.

They broke apart, hearts hammering and breaths pelting while he rested his lips against the bridge of her nose.

"Emily . . ." he whispered, and tipped her head back, found her lips again impatiently, as if unwilling to waste one moment of this stolen time. No darkness was dense enough to disguise her acquiescence; none complete enough to hide her pliancy as she drooped against him like table linen slipping to the floor and opened her soft, willing mouth to his.

This kiss began with full accord, then ripened with eagerness. A swell of impatience rushed up from Emily's toes, finding her unprepared for its impact. It brought heat and deep quivers and the awful need to press her breasts against him. Yet they could not be pressed firmly enough to ease the sudden ache of arousal. He fed it, kissing her full-mouthed, drawing her across his lap, moving his head to seal their fit just right.

And, oh, it was right. Her mouth seemed designed for his. She coiled around his trunk, drawing her knees up to buffet his ribs, crooking one arm over his shoulder, the other around his side.

His wide hand folded around her upraised elbow and rode it tight and smooth down to her armpit and to her breast. She shuddered, then lay motionless, steeping in new sensations. Her bodice fit snugly, enhancing the feeling of his whole hand cupping her, his thumb searching out the warmest, hardest spot. Deep within she felt a glorious spill and drew her knees up tighter while his hand brought a sweet, impelling ache to her breast.

He freed a slim breadth of space between their mouths and whispered, "How much time do you think we have?"

"I don't know."

Their rejoining was greedy: a revelation. She had never kissed so before, not with this abandon, as if to do so were an imperative. She had never given her breasts for fondling, as if to resist were unthinkable. He was more than she had expected, facile, warm-mouthed, her perfect complement.

Reality nagged: the closed door . . . the ticking clock . . . Charles . . . Tarsy . . . the possibility of being discovered.

A little longer . . . only a little . . .

Tom dragged his mouth from Emily's, lightly bit her lips, her chin, and her breast, through her tight bodice, as if to take away as much as possible when leaving this black cubicle. She hadn't a thought of pushing him away; each of his advances felt integral, undeniably necessary. He kissed her mouth again, fondling her breast while a hard knot formed in her belly, woman-low.

She was kissing him heedlessly when he clasped her arms and roughly pushed her back. "Emily, we'd better stop."

She felt flushed and swollen all over. Prudence took an effort. She still saw nothing but unrelieved blackness, but in it she heard his strident breathing.

"He's going to know," she whispered shakily.

"Then sit back where you were." He pressed her against her own wall and slid back to his. She drew her knees up to her clubbing heart while Tom let one leg stretch flat, hoping to appear natural when the door opened. But she realized they were about to be given away.

"I'll be blushing."

"Then tell him I kissed you and I'll apologize to him and say it was the beer."

"I can't tell him that!"

"Then slap me." A swift motion, and suddenly he was on all fours before her, groping for her hand, kissing it fast before putting it on his rough cheek. "Quick! Haul off and give it to me good so it'll leave a mark."

"Oh, Tom, I can't—"

"Quick! Now!"

"But—"

"Now!"

She slapped him so hard he plunked backward and yowled, "Ouch!" just as the door flew open. He looked up into the inquisitive faces of Tarsy, Charles, and the others. Emily's face was buried in her arms, but Tom had the presence of mind to spring immediately from the closet into the light where the stinging shape of her slap glowed on his cheek. Nursing it, he growled, "That's what comes of trying to make friends with your competitors." Clumping away without offering a hand to help Emily up, he groused to Charles, "You can *have* her, Bliss!"

Emily was no good at duplicity; she had to get out of Tom's house immediately or give herself away. She begged off with an early-morning veterinary call and Charles left with her within minutes after the episode in the closet.

Once out in the cold night she could breathe again but her voice sounded strained, even to her own ears.

"Charles, I don't want to go to any more of those parties."

"But they're only innocent fun."

"I hate them!"

"I think it's Tom Jeffcoat you hate."

"Charles, he kissed me in that closet. He kissed me!"

"I know. He apologized to me for it, and said he'd had a couple too many beers."

"Don't you *care*?" she demanded exasperatedly.

"Care?" He took her arm and stopped her in the middle of

the street. "Emily, it was just a game. A silly game. I thought if you two spent five minutes in that dark closet you might come out laughing at yourselves and the way you've been acting ever since he got to town, setting sparks off one another."

Oh, they'd set sparks off one another, all right, but Charles was too trusting to see it. To him it had been just a game, but to Emily it had been much more. It had been a threat and a thrill and a myriad of forbidden feelings so new they left her stunned.

By the time they reached her home she was not only shaken, but angry.

"What kind of a man lets his best friend kiss his fiancée and laughs it off?"

"This kind." Charles grabbed her arm, spun her against himself, and kissed her as forcefully as Tom had. Releasing her, he said throatily, "I love you, Emily, in spite of the fact that you can't treat my best friend civilly."

Minutes later Emily slipped into bed beside Fannie and lay like a fresh-hewn plank, staring up at the ceiling with the quilt edge coiled in both fists beneath her chin. She closed her eyes and saw what she had seen in the closet: nothing. Only blackness, which heightened all her other senses. She had felt him, tasted him, smelled him. Oh, his smell!

She released the quilt and pressed both palms to her nose and sucked in any lingering trace of him that might remain on her skin. Even now on her palms, she recognized it. It was no scent and all scent—clothing, hair, hay, leather, and man in potpourri. Funny, she could not remember what Charles smelled like. But Tom . . .

She rolled to her belly, cupping her breasts in an effort to stop them from aching.

He touched you here and you came alive.

Only because it was dark and forbidden.

It was what you've wanted since that day on the turntable.

No.

And the night he found you crying.

No.

Yes.

I never intended to kiss him. Not even when I walked into that closet. I only wanted to prove I was no prude.

And you did, didn't you?

I never meant to cheat Charles.

You didn't cheat Charles. You only found out what was lacking between the two of you.

The terrifying thought kept Emily awake most of the night.

Chapter 12

THE FOLLOWING MORNING Emily awakened as she had slept—troubled. When she was troubled she wanted to be in only one place: with the animals. She dressed in woolen britches, jacket, and bobcap and slipped from the house before anyone else was up. A new snow had begun falling, brittle and icy. Flat-footed, she skated through it, head hanging, hands buried in her rib pockets.

Inside, the stable was warm, pleasant. Familiarities soothed—the fecund smell, the morning routine, the greetings of the horses, who turned their great heads as she spoke inanities and bumped past their broad bellies while feeding and watering them.

Edwin came at his usual time.

"Up early," he observed.

"Yes," she replied spiritlessly, avoiding his gaze.

"Got the chores done already."

"Yes."

"Anything wrong?"

"Oh, Papa . . ." She went into his arms, closed her eyes, and gulped at the lump of apprehension in her throat. "I love you."

He drew back and held her by both arms. "Do you want to talk to your old papa about it?"

She gazed into his caring eyes, tempted. But maybe she had blown last night out of proportion. Maybe it was nothing more than a kiss in a closet, a silly game already forgotten by Tom Jeffcoat. Though her father's invitation was sincere, in the end she shook her head.

To his credit, Edwin asked no questions. He left Emily to herself and stayed out of the office, where she holed up with her books. But *The People's Home Library* lay between her elbows as she stared unseeingly at the overflowing pigeonholes of the scarred desk, her thumbs pressed against her chin . . . thinking . . . thinking . . . tangled with emotions.

A murky dawn had scarcely grayed the windows when the inset door opened and Tom Jeffcoat marched into the office in lengthy strides, a man with an objective. He spun Emily's chair and pulled her from it straight into his arms.

"Tom, I've—"

He stopped her protest with a kiss. Unapologetically. Blatantly. Without hiding in anyone's closet.

Stunned, she forgot to resist, but stood in his arms letting him kiss her until the feelings of last night rose afresh within her. In time common sense prevailed and she arched away, pushing at the thick sleeves of her sheepskin jacket.

"Tom, my fath—"

"I know." He cut her off again, bending her backward like a strung bow until he felt her remit, then drawing her up with their mouths locked. He kissed her as he had last night—tongue and lips and enough wetness to wash away logic. He caught her unfortified, spreading his taste into her mouth with a straightforward appeal she could not withstand.

By the time they parted to search one another's eyes, her resistance had evaporated.

Out of the gray murk of dawning complications splashed a golden moment of thoughtlessness, while they immersed themselves in one another—young, unchary, and greedy. His tongue came strong against hers, and she opened to him gladly, tasting him as one learning to appreciate a new flavor. The flavor was intrinsically "Tom Jeffcoat," as individual as the flecks of color in his blue eyes. He had shaved, smelled of soap and cold air and old sheepskin—not new smells, only a combination individualized by him.

The kiss changed tone, became a grazing exploration of softness and swimming heads while passing minutes brought a new sortie of heart thrusts within them both. They parted, gazing deep again, introducing a tardy question of willingness before coming together again with more fervid intentions. Her arms took him hard around the neck, crossing upon his thick, standing collar; his doubled around her back, fingers spread like starfish along her ribs.

They imbibed the myriad textures of one another—wet tongues, silky inner lips, smooth teeth—as they had not last night with the threat of discovery but a footstep beyond a closet door.

She thought his name—Tom . . . Thomas—and felt the wondrous upheaval of desire blur the edges of discretion.

He thought of her as he always had—tomboy . . . the one I least suspected would ever light such a fire in me.

His palms rode her back, full width and breadth, over crossed suspenders and her brother's rough shirt and the waistband of woolen britches, then slid up to her shoulder blades in search of a safe place to moor. They hooked her shoulders from behind while he struggled for control.

When the kiss ended they studied each other at close range. Amazed. Quite unprepared for the swift response each had triggered in the other.

"I didn't sleep much," he divulged in a sandpapery voice.

"Neither did I."

"This is going to be complicated."

She drew a shaky breath and fought to be sensible. "You take a lot for granted, Tom Jeffcoat."

"No," he answered simply, admitting what she would not. "I waited a long time for the attraction to die, but it didn't. What was I supposed to do?"

"I don't know. I'm still a little stunned." She laughed disbelievingly.

"Do you think I'm not?"

When he would have kissed her again she retreated. "My father . . ." She glanced toward the door and put distance between herself and Tom, but he breached it, taking her elbow, pursuing as if compelled by some uncontrollable force.

"Last night when you couldn't sleep, what did you think about?" he wanted to know.

She wagged her head in earnest appeal, backing away. "Don't make me say it."

"I will, before we're through. I'll make you say everything you think and feel for me." She backed into something solid and he closed in, bending to her even as his body came flush against hers. She lifted on tiptoe and embraced him. They kissed hard and wide-mouthed, propelled by the incredible attraction from which they both still reeled.

In the middle of the kiss, Edwin entered the office. "Emily, do you know where—" His words died.

Tom swung about, his lips still wet, one hand trailing at the small of Emily's back.

"Well . . ." Edwin cleared his throat, glancing from one to the other. "I hadn't thought about knocking on my own office door."

"Edwin," Tom said gravely, in greeting. The single word held neither excuse nor apology, but outright acknowledgment. He remained as he was, with his arm around Emily while her father's eyes skipped between the two of them.

"So this is what was bothering you this morning, Emily."

"Papa, we . . ." There was little excusable about the scene so she gave up trying.

Tom spoke calmly, filling the void. "Emily and I have some things to discuss. I'd appreciate it if you didn't mention this to anyone, especially to Charles, until we have a little time to sort out a few things. Will you excuse us, Edwin?"

Edwin looked incredulous and distempered by turns; first at being politely excused from his own office; second at leaving his daughter in the arms of someone other than Charles. After ten seconds of silent chafing, he turned and left. Tom glanced at Emily and found her red to the hairline, overtly chagrined.

"You shouldn't have come here," she said. "Now Papa knows."

"I'm sorry, Emily."

"No, you're not. You faced him without the least shame."

"Shame! I'm not ashamed! What did you expect me to do, pretend it wasn't happening? I'm not fifteen anymore and neither are you. Whatever needs facing we'll face."

"I repeat, you take a lot for granted. What about me? What if I don't want people to know?"

He gripped her shoulders firmly. "Emily, we need to talk, but not here where anybody might walk in. Can you meet me tonight?"

"No. Charles is coming to dinner tonight."

"Afterwards?"

"He never leaves until ten."

"So meet me after ten. At my livery barn or the house or anywhere you say. What about down by the creek, right out in the open if you'll feel safer. All we'll do is talk."

She drew free of his touch, for it beckoned as nothing she had ever experienced.

"I can't. Please don't ask me."

"Don't tell me you're going to pretend this never happened! Jesus, Emily, be honest with yourself. We didn't just pop off a couple of kisses in a closet and go away unaffected. Something is happening here, isn't it?"

"I don't know! It's too sudden, too . . . too . . ." Her eyes pleaded for understanding.

"Too what?"

"I don't know. Dishonest. Dangerous. And doesn't it bother you, about Charles?"

"How can you ask such a thing? Of course it bothers me. My stomach is in knots right now, but that doesn't mean I'll turn away from it. I need to know your feelings and to come to grips with some of my own, but we need some time. Meet me, Emily, tonight after ten."

"I don't think so."

"I'll wait for you down by the creek where the boys always fish in the summer, near the big cottonwoods behind Stroth's place. I'll be there till eleven." Moving close, he took her head in both hands, covering her ears and the sides of her red bobcap, resting his thumbs beside her mouth. "And try to stop looking as if you've just broken every one of the Ten Commandments. You really haven't done anything wrong, you know." He landed a light kiss on her lips and left.

She felt as if she'd done plenty wrong—all that day and into the evening, while she made up a lie about the veterinary call that had never existed, when Charles asked how it had gone. While they ate roast beef and vegetables and gravy; and played cribbage with Fannie and Frankie; and while she avoided her father's eyes, and breathed a sigh of relief when he went upstairs to sit with Mother instead of joining in the game; and while Charles kissed her good night and left at quarter to ten. And afterwards, as she told Fannie she'd put away the cards and the coffee cups, and suggested Fannie just go on up to bed.

The house grew still. Emily stood at the window facing the creek and Stroth's place, imagining Tom there kicking at the snow, peering into the shadows, waiting for her. She could walk to the cottonwoods in less than ten minutes, but what then? More illicit kissing? More forbidden caresses? More guilt?

It was undignified. And Charles deserved better. It was the kind of things done by women of questionable reputation.

So she told herself all the while she exchanged button-top shoes for cowboy boots, slipped a hip-length coat over her full-skirted dress, and tugged on her old red bobcap, jamming her hair beneath its ribbing.

This is wrong.

I cannot stop it.

You can, but you won't.

That's right. I can, but I won't.

Papa always did call you willful.

Papa already knows, and he said nothing.

That's rationalizing, Emily, and you know it! He's waiting for you to explain yourself.

How can I explain what I don't understand?

She tiptoed through the parlor and slipped outside soundlessly. The day's sleet had turned to snow—fluffy as eiderdown. It fell yet, in a path straight as a plumb line through the windless night, building up level on every surface it touched. Beneath it, the icy layer crunched with each of Emily's footsteps. Upon it her skirts swept with a sound like an uninterrupted sigh. The moon hid. The sky hugged close, lit from within itself by the thick white dapples it shed. Here and there a window created a gold ingot, but most were dark in a silent, deserted world.

She came to Stroth's place, cut around his house and along his woodpile with its frosting of white, past a forlorn grindstone left out in the weather, beyond his outbuildings to an open meadow where footsteps marked someone's recent passing. She followed them, placing her own within his—long strides, longer than her natural ones—feeling an uncustomary delight in merely walking where he had gone. Ahead, the cottonwoods created shadowless shapes against the white night. They looked warm, blanketed. From beside them a form separated itself—tall, capped in black, standing still as a pedestal, waiting.

Emily stopped, detailing the euphoria brought about by his presence. It was novel and acute in its magnitude. She didn't recall ever feeling it at the appearance of Charles, nor exalting in something so mundane as following the footsteps he had made in the snow. She was a sensible girl who thought it wholly sensible to marry Charles. But sense was a stranger as she approached Tom Jeffcoat.

Behind him the creek ran, open yet, making night music that joined the sigh of her skirts as she continued toward him. With an arm's length to go, she stopped.

"Hello," he said quietly, reaching out two gloved hands.

"Hello," she said, giving him her fat-mittened ones.

"I'm glad you came. I didn't think you would." He wore a black Stetson that had kept the snow off his collar, but the shoulders of his sheepskin jacket were dusted with white.

"Have you been here long?"

"An hour or so." It was only 10:30. She could not help being pleased.

"You must be freezing."

"My toes . . . a little. It doesn't matter. Can I kiss you?"

She chuckled in surprise. "You're asking this time?"

"I promised we'd only talk. But I want to kiss you."

"If you didn't, I'd be disappointed."

They came together easily, no rush, no clutching, only a tipping of his hat brim and a lifting of her chin, their covered hands scarcely crushing the snowflakes on each other's clothing. To Emily it was more devastating than the frantic clutches she'd shared with him before. Three times she'd kissed him since their physical awareness of one another had taken hold, and each had been different. The first time, in the closet, fear had stopped up her throat. This morning in the office surprise had numbed her at his first appearance. But this was different, full agreement, no hurry. When their mouths parted she remained beneath the shelter of his hat brim, where their breaths mingled as ribbons of white in the cold air.

"I thought of you all day," he told her simply.

"I thought of you, too . . . and of Charles, and Tarsy and my father. I had a very bad day."

"So did I. Did your father say anything after I left?"

"No. But he watched me like an eagle all day long. I'm sure he's trying to figure out exactly what's going on between us."

"What is?"

She backed up a step, resting her mittens on his shearling collar, looking into his shadowed face. "I don't know," she admitted. "Do you?"

"No . . . not for sure."

In silence they studied each other, evaluating, doubting and considering by turns, because it was so sudden, so unexpected.

"There are so many things I want to know about you," Tom said. "I feel as if I only met you, since we stopped fighting, I mean. Hell, I'm not making any sense."

"Yes you are. I know what you mean. At the beginning we only antagonized each other."

"Didn't we, though?"

They enjoyed a moment of silence, touching lightly through thick, warm clothes, then Tom asked quietly, "How long have you known Charles?"

"All my life. Since my first memories."

"Do you love him?"

"Yes."

"You say that without a qualm."

"Because it's true. I've always loved him—who wouldn't love Charles? Even you love him, don't you?"

"Yes, I'm afraid I do. I've never had a friend like him." Plagued, he rested his hands on her shoulders and studied a point beyond. After moments he shook his head. "Can you beat him? Building that beautiful piece of furniture for my house? He's done more than anybody else in this town to make me feel welcome."

"Certainly more than I ever did."

"That's what's so unbelievable about this whole thing. You, Emily Walcott, the tomboy—I mean, hell, you hadn't even gotten over resenting me before this . . . this *thing* hit me like an avalanche. I still wanted to throttle you, even when I started thinking about kissing you. It doesn't make any sense. I wasn't even over Julia yet!" He touched her cheek with a gloved finger. "Remember that day on the turntable when we almost kissed?"

"Did we almost kiss that day?"

"You know damned well we did. We were pumping like bellows at a full roar. It was only the thought of Charles that stopped us."

"Charles *and* Tarsy. We can't disregard Tarsy."

"No, unfortunately Tarsy won't let herself be disregarded."

Emily laughed briefly, then sobered. "She does love you, you know. And unless I miss my guess there's probably . . ." She dropped her gaze, discomfited. ". . . well, *more* between you and Tarsy than there is between Charles and me."

"Emily, I'm not going to lie to you. Tarsy and I have been close, in some ways. When I came here I was lonely. I spent a lot of time alone, and between Charles and Tarsy, I've had two good friendships to sustain me. But Tarsy is . . . temporary. She always was, and she understood that. It's Charles who's the permanent fixture between us, and I hate like hell to be sneaking around behind his back."

"I hate it, too."

"So . . ."

"So?"

"We could end it right here and Charles would never be the wiser."

"It would be the honorable thing to do."

But they hadn't the forbearance to stop touching, even as they discussed it.

"Is that what you want to do?"

"I . . ." She swallowed, miserable.

"It isn't, is it?"

Reluctantly, she wagged her head, averting her gaze.

He took her arms and pulled her close to his chest. "Emily, come to the house."

"I'm afraid."

"Nothing will happen, I promise. Just talk. Just for an hour, please?"

"No."

"You might have a little pity on me. My toes really are freezing, after all."

It was a convenient excuse and they both knew it. But neither wanted to part, and nothing had been settled. The frustration had only mounted.

"All right. But only for a half hour or so. Fannie sleeps with me, so she knows I'm gone. I'll tell her I went for a walk in the new snow but a half hour is all I can stay."

They walked back without touching, she along the trail they'd both made, he at her side stamping a new one through Stroth's backyard, along the deserted streets, and into the door through which Charles Bliss had brought his heartwarming housewarming gift little more than twenty-four hours ago.

The kitchen was as black as the inside of a whiskey keg. Stepping in, Emily paused and heard Tom close the door behind them. "There's no fire in the parlor stove, only in here. This way." He nudged her and she followed, touching his sleeve for guidance across the unfamiliar space, around the table to the overstuffed chair pulled up before the kitchen stove, which radiated welcome heat.

"Sit down," he directed. "I'll put some more wood in."

He lifted the stove lid, found the poker, and stirred the embers, lighting the ceiling to a glowing red. He added a log and sparks lifted with subtle pops, then a new flame glowed, and he replaced the stove lid, leaving them in darkness. "You can see through the kitchen curtains and I haven't got shades yet," he explained, adjusting the bottom vent. "Best not light a lamp." He tugged off his gloves, shrugged from his jacket, and tossed it into the darkness, where it hit a bench and slid to the floor. He dropped onto a nail keg and began removing his boots. Two clunks sounded as he set them near the stove, then only silence and a faint hiss threading from the finger-sized airholes at the base of the firebox.

They sat side by side, Tom doubled forward, resting elbows on knees, Emily perched on the edge of her chair. For minutes all was silent. The fire took hold and Tom set a stove lid aside, giving them a glimmering light by which to see each other's faces.

At last he said, "I've been trying to talk myself out of this."

"I know. Me, too."

"I tell myself I really don't even know you, but the hard part is how can I get to if I can't come calling out in the open?"

"What do you want to know?"

"Everything. What were you like as a child? Did you have the whooping cough? Do you like beets? Does wool make your skin itch?" Like a typical smitten man, he felt impatient to catch up with the part of her life that had gone before. "I don't know—everything."

She smiled and accommodated him. "I was inquisitive and willful, I had whooping cough, I can tolerate beets, and the only thing that ever made my skin itch was poison ivy. Mother had to put mittens on my hands in the middle of summer to keep me from scratching it. I was . . . nine years old, I think. There—now you know everything."

They laughed and felt better.

"Is there anything you want to know about me?" he inquired, admiring the pale glow of her face.

"Yes. What was my hairpin doing beside your bed last night?"

Their gazes caught and locked. Silence for several powerful heartbeats before he said, "I think you can figure it out."

"You really ought not leave things like that lying around where your best friend might see them."

"Did he say anything?"

"No. I don't think he noticed. He was too busy pointing out the merits of the house. By the way, I do like your house very much."

"Thank you."

They had exchanged so many double-edged remarks it took some acclimating to get used to the sincere ones. The mood grew heavy and she searched for another question to alleviate the pressure growing in her chest.

"Is your real name Tom or Thomas?"

"Thomas. But the only one who ever called me that was my maternal grandmother."

"Thomas. It has . . . stature. Is she still alive, your grandmother?"

"Very much so. All four of my grandparents are alive."

"You miss them?"

"Yes."

"And your . . . the woman you were supposed to marry, you miss her, too?"

"Julia? Sometimes. I knew her a long time, just like you've known Charles. Naturally you miss someone like that."

"Naturally." She pondered how she would miss Charles if he suddenly were gone, and found to her distress she would miss him considerably.

"I got a letter from Julia though, and she's very happy. She's married and expecting a child."

"Charles wants children. Right away."

"Yes, he's told me."

"I don't."

"He told me that, too."

"He did?" she asked, surprised.

Casting her a sidelong glance, Tom remained silent.

"So you know more about me than you first let on."

He expanded his lungs and shrugged, forcibly relaxing his shoulders. "Would you mind, Emily, if we didn't talk about Charles anymore? Are your toes cold? Do you want to take your boots off?"

"No, I'm fine."

"Your mittens?"

"No, I'm . . . they're . . ." She lifted and dropped her hands, clasping them in her lap as if snug wraps could arm her against incipient feelings.

When Tom continued studying her without comment, she grew uneasy and looked away, staring at the golden circle of light on the stovetop. He sat hunched forward, chin hooked between thumbs and forefingers, watching her silently. After some time he rose from the keg and walked off into the shadows behind her.

He stood at the window, staring out, at odds with his conscience. What did one friend owe another? What did a man owe himself? He turned his head to study the dark bulk of the breakfront at his left. He had touched the smooth top dozens of times in the few hours it had been here, touched it and agonized. He did not touch it now, but kept his hands in his pockets.

He turned to study the dim outline of Emily, her bobcap taking on a halo like a rising orange moon, hair winging out below it on either side, creating a bouquet of lightpricks, her shoulders bowed forward as she perched on the chair like a sparrow ready for flight.

Charles, he thought, his heart hammering wildly, *forgive me.*

He moved around her chair and stood directly before her, gazing down at the top of her head, at her mittened hands pinched between her knees. She refused to look up. Dropping to one knee, he gently drew her hands free and removed her mittens, laying them aside; next her boots, first one, then the other, twisting on his haunches to set them beside his own beneath the reservoir. Pivoting on one knee, he reached for her coat buttons, freed them one by one, then pushed the garment from her shoulders. Last, he dragged the hat from her head, leaving her hair standing out in staticky rays. Only then did she lift her beleaguered eyes to his.

"Stop me if I'm wrong," he whispered and, fitting her to his breast, kissed her. There was no bland hello this time, but instant demand, open mouths and seeking tongues. And hands maintaining a shaky propriety, holding fast to the safest places—shoulders, backs. In time he petted her hair, flattening it with the whole of one hand, shaping that hand to her warm skull. He kissed her throat, her chin, her mouth again, until breath became precious and desire weighted their limbs. He bracketed her breasts, kneaded them with the heels of his hands, then did the same with her hips, cradling them with firm pressure.

"Oh," she might have said, but he imprisoned the word within her throat, and made of it an impassioned murmur. She touched his head all over—temples, skull, neck, jaws, and throat, learning each new texture as if imparting it to memory.

His arms slipped beneath her knees, around her back . . . lifting . . . carrying her across the dimly lit kitchen—a scrape on the floor as he jarred a bench, stepped around it, turned her feet aside to negotiate the doorways of the pantry and his bedroom.

The bedsprings chimed as he lowered her and followed, dropping his full length upon her. Braced on his elbows, he toyed with her hair and breathed on her mouth, letting her adapt to his motionless weight and the advent of imprudence. Dropping his head, he invited her one step further, delivering moist kisses across her lips and chin, along her nose, until she followed like a birdling for its food, drawing him down to halt his sojourn. Their kisses grew rugged and wet. Reactions exploded and temperance fled. They pressed close, lifting knees, rolling, twining in damp skirts and petticoats. He stroked her breast . . . both breasts . . . explored their shape with his fingertips and the heels of his hands, and with his mouth through taut cotton. He buried his face between them and breathed against her, heating her skin and her blood while she cradled his head and gave herself over to sensuality. He slid back up, found her open mouth again, and moved his hips in cadence, a mere rhythmic tipping at first, to the counterpoint of his tongue stroking hers. Prone upon her, he dragged his hands down her ribs and hips, slipped them against the quilt and held her fast from behind, curling his fingers into the folds of her skirt and her flesh. His body flashed against hers with unmitigated desire in each upbeat. She closed her eyes and took the ride with him to the brink of hell.

"Tom . . . stop . . ."

He stilled, dropped his face into the lea of her shoulder, and lay upon her, panting.

"This is a sin," she whispered.

He expelled a ragged breath, rolled to his back, dropped one arm across his eyes and the other across his groin.

She rolled away and sat up, but he grabbed her wrist. "Stay. A minute . . . please." She curled toward him, pressing her knees and forehead against his side. For minutes they lay linked by the three contact points, descending like dandelion seeds on a still day. When his pulse had settled he said, "You don't do these things with Charles, do you?"

"No."

"Then why do you do them with me?"

"I don't know. If you're blaming me—"

"I'm not." Again he held her from leaving. "I'm trying to be honest. I think maybe we're falling in love with each other. What do you think?"

She had known the possibility existed the day she toured his barn, but when faced with the words was afraid to say them; they were so absolute and could bring such tumult into so many lives. "This is not the supreme test, I don't think. This is only lust. I've loved Charles for so long—I know I love him, but it's because of years and years of familiarity. Everybody I know married people they'd known a long, long time—my parents, their parents, even my friends' parents. I never thought love happened this fast."

"I never thought so, either. I was like the other people you know, in love and engaged to a girl I'd known for years. But she had the honesty to break away when she realized she loved someone else. At first I was bitter about it, but now I'm beginning to see what strength it took for her to admit that her feelings had changed."

The longer Tom spoke the more she wished him silent, for she foresaw great hurt ahead for many should this wellspring between them be what he believed.

"Emily?" He found her hand and held it loosely, stroking it with his thumb while lying in thought for a long time. Finally he went on. "It's not just lust. Not for me. It's things I admire about you—your dedication to your work, and to your family, and to Charles, even. I respect you for not wanting to tread on Charles's feelings, and for not wanting me to tread on Tarsy's . . . and your affection for the animals and your sympathy for your mother and the way you do battle to keep me honorable. Those things count as much as any others. And you're . . . different. Every other woman I know dresses in petticoats and aprons." He rolled toward her and laid a hand on her waist. "I like your independence—britches and veterinary medicine and all. It makes you unique. And I like the color of your hair . . ." He touched it. "And your eyes." He kissed one. "And the way you kiss and the way you smell and the way you look . . . and I like this . . ." He found her hand and placed it on his throat where a strong pulse drummed. "What you do to me inside. If it is lust, all right, that's part of it. But I want you . . . I had to say it, just once."

"Hush." She covered his lips. "I'm so frightened and you don't help at all."

"Tell me," he whispered, closing his eyes, kissing her fingertips.

"I can't."

"Why not?"

"Because I'm still promised to him. Because a betrothal is a kind of vow, and I made that vow to him when I accepted his proposal of marriage. And besides . . . what if this is momentary?"

"Does it feel momentary to you?"

"You ask me for answers I can't give."

"Then why did you meet me tonight?"

"I couldn't seem to help myself."

"So what should I do tomorrow, and the day after that and the day after that?"

"Do?"

"I'm the man. Men pursue."

"But to what end?"

Ah, that was the question—to what end? Neither knew the answer. To mention marriage would, after a mere twenty-four-hour liaison, be precipitous. And anything less would be, as she said, iniquitous. No honorable man would expect a woman to settle for that. Yet to go on deceiving Charles was unthinkable.

Emotionally weary, Emily pulled herself to the side of the

bed and sat in a jumble of skirts, holding her head, coiled forward in misery, pressing her elbows against her belly.

Tom sat up, too, equally as heavy-hearted, studying the back of her head, wondering why it had to be she he had tumbled for. In time he lifted a hand and began absently straightening strands of her mussed hair because he could think of nothing else to offer.

"Emily, these feelings aren't going to go away."

She shook her head vehemently, still covering her face.

"They aren't," he repeated.

Abruptly she rose. "I have to go." He stayed behind, staring at the dark floor, listening to her sniffling, donning her outerwear in the kitchen. He felt like hell. He felt like a traitor. With a sigh he rose and went out to her, stood in the dim stovelight watching her button her coat. He followed her silently to the door and stood behind her while she faced it without touching the knob. He touched her shoulder and she spun around, flinging her arms around his neck, gripping him with quiet desperation.

"I'm sorry," he whispered against her bobcap, holding the back of her head as if she were a child he carried through a storm. "I'm sorry, tomboy."

She held her sobs until she was down his porch steps and halfway across his yard, going at a dead run.

Chapter 13

EDWIN AROSE AT six the following morning. Outside, the sky was still black above an unbroken blanket of new snow. Stepping out the back door, he breathed deep, pulling in the fragrance of a fresh world after the cloying odor of Josie's sickroom. There were times when he entered it that the gorge rose in his throat, times when he lay in his cot thinking he would suffocate, times when he stood silently in the doorway, watching her suffer, and thought of the nostrums in his daughter's veterinary case: opium, aconite, tannic acid, lead—if administered in large enough doses, any one of them could bring a merciful end to his wife's suffering.

Edwin moved off the step, dropped his chin, and watched his boots lift snow as he walked to the privy.

Would you do that to your own wife? Could you?

I don't know.

If you did, you'd never be sure whether you did it to put her out of her misery or to end your waiting for Fannie.

Worries, worries. Frankie had become a worry, too. He refused to enter the sickroom or to talk to his mother. She had grown so pitifully emaciated that the boy found himself unable to accept the change in her. Frankie seemed to be denying that his mother was dying.

And now this thing with Emily and Tom Jeffcoat—something else to worry about.

Returning to the kitchen, Edwin found Fannie already up, filling the coffeepot, dressed in a blue plaid housedress and a long white bibbed apron. Most mornings Emily arose at the same time as they and was here in the kitchen creating a welcome buffer over breakfast. Not so today. They were alone in the room, with the stovepipe snapping and the lamplight sealed inside by the long shades, still drawn from the night before.

"Good morning," Fannie greeted.

"Good morning."

Edwin closed the door and stripped off his jacket, revealing black suspenders over the top of his woolen underwear.

"Where's Emily?"

"Still sleeping."

He poured water into the basin, began washing his face and hands while listening to Fannie set the coffeepot on the stove, then get out a frying pan. When he straightened, drawing the towel down his face, he found her standing at the stove watching him, a slab of bacon in one hand, a butcher knife in the other, forgotten. For moments neither of them moved. When they did, it felt as natural as receiving falling snowflakes upon a lifted face; they stepped to one another and kissed—good morning, plain and simple, as if they were man and wife.

They parted and smiled into each other's eyes while his hands continued drying on the towel.

"Have I ever told you how much I love finding you here in my kitchen when I walk in?"

"Have I ever told you how much I love to watch you washing at the sink?"

He hung the towel on a peg and she began slicing the bacon on a board.

He combed his hair and she dropped the meat into the pan, sending up a sizzle.

"How many eggs do you want?"

"Three."

"How many slices of toast?"

"Four." So much like man and wife.

She searched out three eggs and the toasting racks and a plump loaf of bread while he went to find a clean shirt, and brought it back to the kitchen to don. Standing just inside the doorway, he watched her turning the bacon while he flipped down his suspenders, slipped his arms into the starched cotton, and slowly began buttoning it.

"I meant it, Fannie," he said quietly.

"Meant what?"

"That I love having you here, baking my bread, keeping my house, washing my clothes." He stuffed his tails into his pants and snapped the suspenders into place. "Nothing's ever felt so right."

She came to him and ran her fingers beneath one suspender, straightening a twist.

"For me either." Their eyes met, caring and momentarily happy. They kissed again, in a room filled with the scent of toasting bread and boiling coffee. When the kiss ended, they hugged, with her nose pressed against the clean starchy scent of his shirt, which she had happily laundered for him; and with his nose nestled in her hair, which smelled faintly of bacon, which he gladly provided for her.

"God, I love you, Fannie," he whispered, holding her by both arms, gazing into her eyes. "Thank you for being here. I couldn't have made it through these days without you."

"I love you, too, Edwin. It seems fitting that we should go through this together, don't you think?"

"No. I want to spare you, yet I can't bear the thought of sending you away. Fannie, I want to confess something to you, because once I confess it I know I'll never do it."

"Do what, dearest?"

"I've thought of taking something from Emily's bag—laudanum, maybe—and ending Josephine's life for her."

Tears glistened in Fannie's eyes. "And I've watched her shrivel away, fighting for breath . . . and I've thought of putting a pillow over her face and ending her painful struggle."

"You have?"

"Of course. No human being with a dram of compassion could help but consider it."

"Oh, Fannie . . ." He hooked an arm around her neck and

rested his chin on her head, feeling better, less depraved, knowing she'd thought of it, too.

"It's terrible, thinking such things, isn't it?"

"I've felt so guilty. But poor Josie. Nobody should have to suffer like that."

For a moment she absorbed his strength, then patted his back as if punctuating the end of a statement.

"I know. Now sit down, Edwin, and let's not talk of it again."

While they ate, dawn came, paling the shades at the windows to the color of weak tea, bringing the faraway barking of dogs across town. Often Edwin and Fannie gazed at each other. Throughout the meal they felt the false connubial closeness brought about by the sharing of mundane morning routine. Once he reached across the table to touch her hand. Twice she rose to refill his coffee cup. Returning the second time, she kissed the crown of his head.

He caught her hand against his collarbone, brushed his beard along her palm. "Fannie, I have to talk to you about something else. I need your advice."

"What is it, Edwin?"

She sat down at a right angle to him, their hands joined at the table corner.

Holding her gaze, he told her, "I walked into the livery office yesterday and found Emily kissing Tom Jeffcoat."

Fannie's expression remained unsurprised as she sat back and hooked a finger in her coffee cup. "So, now you know."

"Meaning you have?"

"I've suspected."

"For how long?"

"Since the first time I saw the two of them together. I've only been waiting for Emily to admit it to herself."

"But why didn't you tell me?"

"It wasn't my place to voice suspicions."

"They didn't even act jumpy when I walked in. Jeffcoat calmly asked me to excuse them!"

"And what did you do?"

"Why, I left. What else could I do?"

"And so you want to know if you should give her a lecture on the sacredness of betrothal promises, is that it?"

"I . . ." Edwin's mouth hung open while memories gushed back, of being talked out of marrying the woman he loved by his well-meaning parents.

Fannie rose and aimlessly trod the kitchen, sipping coffee. "She went out last night after the rest of us were in bed, and didn't get back till quite late."

"Oh God . . ."

"Why do you say 'oh God,' Edwin, as if it were some calamity?"

"Because it is."

"Now you sound like your own parents."

"Heaven help me, I know." Covering his face with both hands, Edwin pressed his elbows to the tabletop. She gave him time to worry it through. Finally his eyes appeared, troubled. "But Charles is already like a son to me. He has been his whole life."

"And undoubtedly they said the same thing to you about Joey."

Cupping his hands before his mouth, he studied Fannie while she went on. "I cannot speak for Joey, nor can I guess at what you might have felt, but I can tell you what it was like for me. On your wedding day—oh, that day, that dolorous, grief-laden day—I didn't know how to contain my desolation. I wanted to weep, but I couldn't. I wanted to run, but that wasn't allowed. Propriety demanded that I be there . . . to watch the destruction of my happiness. I don't ever remember a sorrow so deep. I felt . . ." She studied her cup, circling its rim with a fingertip, then lifted sad eyes to Edwin. ". . . hapless. I could not function, didn't want to, couldn't project a future without an incentive to live. And you were my incentive. So I went into my father's barn with the intention of hanging myself." She gave a soft, rueful laugh, dropping her gaze to the cup again. "What a ludicrous sight I must have made, Edwin. I . . ." She glanced up sheepishly. "I didn't know how to tie the knot."

"Fannie—"

"No, Edwin." She held up a palm. "Stay there. Let me finish this." She moved to the stove and refilled her cup, stationing herself a goodly distance from him. "I thought about drowning, but it was winter—where could I do it? Poison? I could hardly go to the apothecary and ask for some Paris green, could I? And barring that, I didn't know where to find any. So I lived." She drew a deep breath and set down her cup as if it were too heavy for her. "No, that isn't quite accurate. I existed. Day to day, hour to hour, wondering what to do with my pitiful life." She gazed out the window. "You moved away—I didn't know why."

"Because I wanted you more than I wanted my own wife."

She went on as if he hadn't spoken. "Then Joey's letters began coming. Letters filled with the day-by-day inconsequentialities of married life—the banalities for which I pined. She became pregnant and Emily was born. I wanted Emily to be mine—mine and yours—and I knew that you'd been right to leave, for if you hadn't, I would have borne your child gladly, wed or not.

"Then four years or so after you left I met a man, a married man, the safest kind, I thought . . . the kind who made no promises, presented no expectations. I wrote to you and Joey about him—Ingrahm, was his name, Nathaniel Ingrahm. He was a curator at the museum whose cause I espoused at the time—preservation of the dying art of scrimshanding, or some such vital concern. In those days I was only beginning to take up a long line of vital concerns because I had none of my own." Fannie's thoughts wandered momentarily before she straightened her shoulders and turned toward Edwin. "At any rate, I had a sexual liaison with Nathaniel Ingrahm, chiefly because I wanted to find out what I had missed with you, and I was beginning to see that the chances of my finding a suitable husband were remote. You see, I rejected every prospect when he didn't seem to measure up to you. You were my standard, Edwin . . . you still are."

She drew a staunch breath, coupled her palms, and paced, focusing her attention on the walls, the windows, anything but him. "Within a year I became pregnant with his child. You may recall when I wrote and told you I was recuperating from what my mother referred to as summer muse, some sort of stomach malady that was circulating at the time. That's what I told her I had, but my . . . my *summer muse* was the aborting of the child I wanted by no other man than you. I drank bluing . . . and it . . . it worked."

He sat stunned, pained, wishing futilely that he could change the past, wanting to go to her, embrace her, but held away by her stern posture and evasive eyes.

"Nathaniel Ingrahm never knew." She studied her knit fingers and crossed thumbs. "I gave up my scrimshanding cause and embraced another . . . and another. And there were other men, of course, several—all human beings need love, or whatever substitutes for it—but I was careful. I had learned a trick with a copper coin that prevented conception. You're shocked, Edwin, I can tell. I need not be looking at you to sense your shock."

"Fannie . . ." he breathed, leaving his chair. "My God, I never knew."

"I have done some wicked things in the name of love, Edwin. Unforgivable things."

Reaching her, he gripped her arms. Their sorrowful eyes locked. He drew her to his breast, holding her protectively, cupping her head. "I'm so sorry." He closed his eyes and swallowed, his throat pressed to her hair.

"I didn't tell you to wrest pity from you. I told you so you'd see that you must not chastise Emily. You must let her choose freely, Edwin . . . please." She drew back and appealed with her eyes. "Edwin, I love your children simply because they are yours. I want their happiness because in their happiness they bring the same to you. Edwin, dearest . . ." She took his face in her hands, resting her thumbs at the junction of beard and cheek. "Please don't duplicate your parents' mistake."

When he kissed her his soul felt broken. Tears clogged his throat. He clung to her, aggrieved by the mistakes both of them had made, by the lorn years that had brought them only half-happiness at the best of times, sheer desolation at the worst. Their tongues joined in the testimony—this was meet and fitting, this was how it should have been had they been wiser, more defiant, truer to themselves.

While they embraced they were unaware of the stockinged footsteps of Emily coming down the stairs.

She entered the room and halted in shock. "Papa!"

Edwin and Fannie twisted apart, their hands lagging upon one another.

"Emily . . ."

For tense seconds the room remained silent while the trio stood as if paralyzed. Emily's dismayed eyes flashed from Edwin to Fannie and back again. When she spoke her voice was reedy with accusation.

"Papa, how could you do such a thing!" She glared at Fannie. "And *you*! Our *friend!*"

"Emily, hold your voice down," Edwin ordered.

"And with Mama right upstairs!" Tears sprang to Emily's eyes as she whispered fiercely.

"Emily, I'm sorry you discovered us, but please don't judge what you can't begin to understand." He stepped toward her but she jumped back and pierced him with a look of icy reprehension.

"I understand enough. My mother taught me right from wrong, and I'm not a child, Papa, nor am I stupid!"

"We've done nothing wrong, and furthermore, I don't have to answer to you, girl." He pointed a finger. "I'm your father!"

"Then act like one! Show some respect for the dying and for the rest of your family." Her face flamed with rage. "What if it had been Frankie who came downstairs just now? What would he think? He can scarcely accept Mother's illness as it is!"

"He might have offered us a chance to explain."

"There is no explanation. You're despicable—both of you!" Angry and distressed, Emily ran from the room.

"Emily!"

When Edwin would have followed her, Fannie restrained him with a touch on his arm. "Not now, Edwin. She's too upset. Let her go."

The front door slammed. "But she thinks you and I are carrying on here in this house."

"Aren't we?" Fannie asked sadly.

"No!" he glowered. "We've done nothing to be ashamed of."

"Then why did we jump apart?"

"But she didn't give us a chance to explain."

"And if she had, what would you have said? That you and I are excused because we've loved each other since before you married her mother? The mother who is, as Emily had to remind us, dying upstairs? Would you tell her that, Edwin, and open up a Pandora's box of questions? Or do you think she would calmly accept your explanation and say, 'Very well then, Papa, you may carry on with Cousin Fannie'? Edwin, be realistic." With gentle hands she bracketed his bearded face while his expression remained stubbornly defensive. "She would blame you all the more for not having loved her mother as you pretended. And she would be justified. All her life she's seen you and Joey as paragons of virtue, inviolate in your union. She's had a tremendous shock this morning and we must give her time to adjust to it. We must think very clearly about whether *we* are justified in explaining our past to her. The proper thing for us to do might very well be to let her believe the worst about you and me."

"But, dammit, Fannie, I've honored my vows; I've never so much as touched you in this house before today."

"Yes, Edwin . . . before today." She dropped her hands from his face and stepped away. "Do you remember that day last June when I came here, when we were at the livery stable? I made a vow of my own that day, and I have broken it—whether in the flesh or in my imagination, it is broken just the same. A thousand times I have lain with you since I've been beneath this roof, in my wishes."

"But, Fannie, she doesn't understand that I want to marry you, that I will when it's possible."

"And we may have created an obstruction to that possibility this morning, had you considered that?"

"Emily is eighteen years old, a full-grown woman. And just yesterday I caught her in a similar situation. Did I point fingers?"

"She's not married, Edwin. You are."

He glared at her though his true anger was turned toward himself. She waited patiently for him to realize this, and knew the precise moment at which he did. Releasing a breath and running a hand through his hair, he asked contritely, "So what do we do?"

"For the time being, nothing. She'll let us know when she's ready for either apologies or explanations."

Emily strode through the frigid morning with indignation turning to bitterness. What her father had done to Mother, he'd done to her and Frankie, too. Her father—her shining idol, the one she'd loved unconditionally because he was all good, and honorable. In her entire life she'd never known him to consciously hurt another. Her father had betrayed them all.

It hurt even worse because he had been the gentle one, the understanding one, the one she had always turned to as a buffer against the harshness she often found in Mother. Well, at least Mother was no hypocrite! Mother lived what she taught.

Mother . . . poor, undeserving Mother . . . dying bravely upstairs while downstairs Papa profaned their marriage vows with his live-in harlot!

And that harlot—her friend, the one in whom she'd confided, the one she'd admired and trusted with her deepest secrets. Some friend! A Judas, after all.

Betrayal hurt. No, it stung. It brought a sense of stultifying powerlessness. Emily reached the livery stable with tears stubbornly dammed behind the floodgates she refused to lower.

She saddled Sagebrush and rode, hell-bent, until her legs ached and the horse's hide steamed. West. Toward the foothills, across frozen streams, through thickets of frosty sage, across unbroken snow, past startled rabbits and chipmunks and pines laden with new white, down coulees, up ridges, into a serene morning in which she created the only contradiction: a distraught human pushing a dumb animal who could only obey.

She rode until her eyelids felt frozen open and her exposed skin, afire. Until her lips felt cracked and her legs, hot and cramped. Only when the horse reared and whinnied at the crest of a knoll did Emily realize she was abusing the animal. Sagebrush tossed his head till lather flew and Emily reined in at last, slumping, letting her eyes close, feeling despair overwhelm her. She sat for minutes, listening to the animal pant, then slid from the saddle and stood at his jaw, still fighting her own emotions. Sage's hide was warm and damp and pungent with horse smell, but she needed something familiar right now. She dropped her forehead against his great powerful neck, clamping her jaw, gulping back sobs.

I need somebody. God . . . somebody . . .

Hot from his run, Sagebrush shook his head, forcing Emily to retreat; not even the horse cared, she thought unreasonably.

Flatfooted, she dropped to a squat, arms extended over her knees like a sheepherder rolling a cigarette, stubbornly determined not to cry. Her face burned. Her eyes burned. Her lungs burned. Everything burned—her father's betrayal, Fannie's betrayal, her mother's ceaseless suffering, her own betrayal to Charles. Life was one big burning hell.

She dropped her face between her knees and doubled her arms across the back of her head while she wept.

God, I'm no better than my father.

She returned to the stable for lack of choice. Sagebrush was sheeny, patchy with sweat, like the surface of a pond in an intermittent wind. He was thirsty and tired and hungry and eager for his familiar stall. Where else could she go but to her father's livery stable?

Edwin was there alone, applying a fresh coat of parsley-green paint to a doublebox wagon. The paintbrush paused in midair when Emily led Sagebrush inside and continued toward the stalls without a glance in Edwin's direction.

She watered the horse, removed and wiped down the saddle, brushed his warm chestnut hide until it cooled, caparisoned and stabled him. Passing her father again on her way to mix feed she felt his eyes follow, though he uttered not a word. She stared at the far end of the corridor as if Edwin no longer existed, striding mannishly with a wad of misery in her throat.

God, how she'd loved him.

Returning with a half bucket of grain, she blamed her stinging eyes on the paint fumes, which were thick in the closed building. Again Edwin's gazed followed. Again she stared straight on, sensing his remorse and hurt, unwilling to accept it.

When Sage was fed she headed back toward the office, passing her father a fourth time, maintaining the same silent defiance as before.

"Emily!"

Her feet stopped but her eyes remained riveted on the great rolling door twenty feet away.

"I'm sorry," Edwin offered quietly.

She compressed her lips to keep them from trembling.

"Go to hell," she said, stone-faced, and walked on in a cocoon of pain.

She moved through that day with as much life as a door swung by the whim of the wind. She crossed paths with her father—it was inevitable—and spoke to him when necessary. But her voice was glacial and her eyes relentlessly evasive. When he asked if she wanted to go home for noon dinner first she replied, "I'm not eating." When he returned from his own dinner and set a plate of sausage and fried potatoes at her elbow, she cast it a disparaging glance and returned her attention to her needle and whipcord without offering so much as a thank-you. When he saw her leaving shortly after 2:00 P.M. he called, "Emily, are you going home?" His voice sounded lonely, echoing down the shaft of the long building. With grim satisfaction she answered him with only the roll and thump of the closing door.

Outside, ten feet from the building, she met Tom Jeffcoat, heading in.

"Emily, could I—"

"Leave me alone," she ordered heartlessly and left him staring at her back.

At home there was Fannie to face. Emily gave her the same treatment she'd given her father—gazed through her as if she were of no more substance than a cloud. Minutes later Fannie came to the doorway of their shared bedroom and said, "I'll be washing some bedding in the morning. If you have anything that needs doing up, just leave it in the hall."

For the first time Emily met Fannie's eyes—a fierce glare. "I'll do Mother's bedding!" she spat, shouldering past the older woman without touching her, crossing the hall to her mother's room where she closed Fannie out with a firm click of the latch.

She spent the afternoon at a task she detested: crocheting. She was wholly inept with a hook and thread, but worked on a doily as penance and atonement, staying at her mother's bedside until Papa came home from work and looked in.

"How is she?" he inquired, entering the room.

Emily leaned forward and touched Josephine's hand, ignoring Edwin. "It's nearly suppertime. I'll bring your tray up soon, all right, Mother?"

Josephine opened her eyes and nodded weakly. Emily slipped from the room without waiting to observe her mother's pathetic smile shift to Edwin.

When supper was ready Emily ordered in a tone that would brook no refusal, "Frankie, come. You've scarcely seen mother in over two weeks. Bring your plate up while I feed her. She'll be so happy to see you."

Frankie dutifully followed but sat on Papa's cot, picking at his food, staring at his knees instead of at the skeleton on the master bed. When he asked to be excused, looking pale and guilty, Emily let him go, but ordered him to help with dishes because she was going to stay and read to Mother.

A half hour later Edwin's footsteps sounded on the stairs and Emily quickly shut the book and kissed her mother, escaping to her own room, leaving Edwin standing in the upstairs hall, following her with baleful eyes.

By mid-evening she had reached a major decision, the correct one, she was sure. No matter what Papa and Fannie did to Mama, she would send her to her grave happy about one thing.

Emily donned a clean lavender dress, coiled her hair in a perfect ladylike figure eight, and went to Charles's house to announce that she was ready to set the date for their wedding.

Charles's smile was the full sun after an eclipse. "Oh, Em . . ." With a joyous lunge he picked her up and spun her, giving a whoop of laughter. His ecstatic reaction reaffirmed that Emily was doing the correct thing. Swinging around in his arms, she swallowed the lump in her throat and thought, I won't be like Papa, I won't!

Beaming, Charles set her down. "When?"

She smiled because she'd made him happy at last, and he deserved so much happiness. "Next week?"

"Next week!"

"Or as soon as Reverend Vasseler can perform the service. I want us to be married before Mother dies. It will make her very happy."

Charles's smile faded. "But what about your veterinary certificate?"

"I've decided to give it up. What will I ever do with it anyway? I'll be your wife, taking care of your house and your children. I was crazy to think I could go gallivanting around the country pulling calves anyway. I'll have all I can do to keep the socks white."

Charles frowned. "Emily, what's wrong?"

"Wrong? Why, nothing. I've just come to my senses, that's all."

"No . . ." He backed off, holding her gingerly by the elbows, studying her minutely. "Something's wrong."

"The only thing that's wrong is that time is moving too quickly, and Mother is nearly . . ." She swallowed hard. "I want this very badly, Charles, before Mother dies."

"But it takes time to plan a wedding."

"Not this one. We'll be married in Mother's bedroom so she can hear us exchange vows. Would that be all right with you?"

"You don't want a church wedding?"

"I'm not exactly the lacy kind, am I?" Tom Jeffcoat had never ceased calling her tomboy. "Besides, it would save work and trouble. I . . . I really don't want to ask Fannie to prepare all that food and . . . and . . . well, you know how much fussing weddings can be if you let them."

"And how many guests were you intending to have then, none?"

"Just . . . well, just Tarsy for my attendant."

"And just Tom for mine?"

"Tom . . ." She could not meet Charles's eyes while speaking of Tom Jeffcoat. "Well . . . yes, if that's who you choose."

"Who else would I choose?"

"Nobody. I mean, Tarsy and Tom are . . . are fine. The ceremony will only be a few minutes long anyway."

"Have you talked to Fannie about this?"

"Fannie's got nothing to do with it. It's my decision!"

"Have you talked to your father?"

"Charles!" She bristled. "For somebody who's been lathering at the bit to get a date set you certainly don't act too excited."

"I would if I hadn't known you since you were cutting teeth. You're upset about something and I want to know what it is."

She stood before him with the answer burning deep, compelled to lie to keep from hurting him as she'd been hurt. "If you love me, Charles, please do what I ask. I want this for Mother and I don't think we have much time."

He studied her gravely for a full fifteen seconds before dropping his hands and stepping back. "Very well. If you'll answer me one question."

"Ask it."

"Do you love me, Emily?"

His question seemed to resound in the pit of her stomach. And if her answer revealed only the partial truth, her motives were purely honorable.

"Yes," she answered, and caught the nearly imperceptible relaxing of his shoulders.

She did love him, she did! As she'd said to his best friend, who could help but love Charles?

Her reassurance had brought back his enthusiasm. "Should we go tell them?"

"I already did . . . at supper," Emily lied.

"Oh." The flat word reflected his disappointment and she felt guilty for depriving him of the joy of making the announcement. But if the two of them went now to break the news together her displeasure with Papa and Fannie would be clearly evident, not only to Charles but to Mother. "Things aren't exactly bright and cheerful around our house, Charles, with Mother being so bad. I thought . . . well, I thought it might be easier if I simply told them."

"That's . . . that's fine," Charles said doubtfully. "I just thought maybe . . ." His words trailed off.

She took his hand. "I'm sorry, Charles. The whole thing should have been more festive, shouldn't it?"

He shrugged off his disappointment and forced a grin. "Aw, what the heck—it's our lives together that count, not what kind of wedding ceremony we have. And anyway, your parents have known this was coming for years, haven't they? I made sure they did."

He kissed her happily, his bride-to-be, and lightly caressed her breasts, conveying wordlessly how he would treasure and love her. She felt his tongue in her mouth and answered with her own, putting last night from her mind, assuring herself, *You'll get used to the beard in time. You'll get used to his hands on you.*

But she was the first to break away. "Should we talk to Reverend Vasseler tomorrow?"

"Yes."

"Morning or afternoon?"

"Morning. Then I can talk to Tom and you can talk to Tarsy in the afternoon. Oh, Emily . . ." He clasped her close. "I'm so happy."

"So am I . . . but Charles, I have to go now."

She walked home feeling despondent. Where was the sense of eagerness she had expected after making the commitment? At home the emptiness seemed to expand as she hung up her coat and walked through the silent rooms downstairs. *This is not how it should feel. This moment should be splendid, a sharing of the news, a falling into arms, a rejoicing with those you love and who love you.*

She plodded upstairs and stopped in the light shining into the hall from her parents' bedroom, glanced inside, and paused in distaste. All three of them were there, Mother on the bed, Papa on the cot, and Fannie in a side chair. It twisted Emily's vitals, the hypocrisy of the scene. Not even for Mother's benefit could she smile at the other two as she entered the room.

She sat beside Josephine, turning her back on Edwin and Fannie, and took her mother's hand.

"I thought you'd like to know—Charles and I are going to talk to Reverend Vasseler tomorrow morning. We'll be getting married as soon as he can perform the service . . . right here in your room. Would you like that, Mother?"

"Why, Emily . . ." Josie's voice was a weak whisper, but her eyes showed a faint spark of approval.

"I knew you'd be pleased."

"But . . ."

"No questions now. They only make you cough. It's what I want, and what Charles wants, too. We'll talk more about it tomorrow."

Rising from the bed, Emily caught a furtive exchange of glances between Fannie and her father. When their glances lifted to her, nobody moved. *Papa, Papa, I wanted this moment to be so different. I had always pictured it with smiles and hugs.* But Emily held herself aloof, heart-sore.

Fannie alone recovered and rose quickly to act out the expected felicitations for Joey's benefit. "Congratulations, dearling . . ." When she put her arms around Emily and touched the girl's cheek with her own, Emily stiffened. Fannie stepped back and chided with false blitheness, "Edwin, for heaven's sake, have you nothing to say?"

Emily forced herself to stand in place while he rose from the cot and moved toward her with his contrite eyes asking forgiveness and permission. Waiting, her heart pounded with love and remorse. His lips touched her cheek with enough genuine affection to melt the hardest of hearts. "Congratulations, honey."

She stood like a newel post, resisting his endearment, his touch, the awful love she could not help feeling for him.

"I have to go tell Frankie," she mumbled, and escaped, leaving a roaring silence in the room behind her.

Frankie was fast asleep. She sat on his bed and jostled him. "Hey, brub, wake up, huh?" Somehow tonight she needed to use the childish nickname from her youth.

He burrowed into his pillow and grunted.

"Hey, come on, Frankie, wake up, huh? I've got something to tell you." *Please wake up. I need somebody so badly.*

"Get lost . . ."

She leaned close and whispered, "I'm going to marry Charles, probably before the week is out. Just thought you'd want to know."

He raised his face from the pillow and squinted over one shoulder. "Well, why couldn't you tell me tomorrow! Criminy, did you have to wake me up!" Face first he hit the mattress and pulled the pillow over his tousled head.

Frankie, I needed you, to hug, to get excited with. Don't you understand? Of course, he didn't. He was simply a disgruntled little boy disturbed from his sleep. He knew nothing of the turmoil within his sister. Dejected, she went to her own room to find Fannie already there, preparing for bed.

When the door opened Fannie looked up from her seat at the dressing table where she sat removing hairpins from her hair. It was easier for Emily to remain frigid to Fannie than to Papa: she had not loved her an entire lifetime. Too, Fannie was the intruder, doubtless the one most to blame. In that tense moment while their eyes clashed, she saw the caring in Fannie's, but turned, rebuffing it, closing the door, going about her bedtime routine with insular disregard.

It was unsettling, undressing in the same room with someone for whom you felt such enmity. Neither of them spoke as they donned their nighties, turned back the coverlets, extinguished the lantern, and crawled beneath the covers, back to back, hugging their edges of the bed.

Through Emily's mind glimmered memories of the times she had confided in Fannie, times like this when they'd lain in the dark, friends growing dearer to one another with each passing day. But Fannie no longer felt dear. She had abused the hospitality of this house and had proven herself a two-faced friend to Mama, and for that Emily despised her.

Emily had been lying carefully motionless for a full ten minutes before Fannie spoke quietly into the darkness.

"Emily, you're wrong."

"Shut up! I don't want to hear your excuses any more than I want to share my bed with you!"

Fannie closed her eyes and felt tears burn inside. She crossed her wrists beneath her breasts and pressed hard, cradling the hurt tightly, as a mother might cradle a found child. Emily had misunderstood her meaning; she had not meant, Emily, you're wrong about your father and me, but, you're wrong to jump into marriage this way.

Oh, Emily . . . dearling . . . can't you see you're marrying Charles for all the wrong reasons?

But faced with Emily's cold rejection, Fannie let the earnest warning wither in her throat.

Chapter 14

IT HAD BEEN a frustrating thirty-six hours for Tom Jeffcoat. If he had it to do over again he'd use his head and keep no less than two axe handles between himself and Emily Walcott.

At his anvil he beat a piece of hot metal as if it were his own head, which, he conceded, was about as dense as iron and needed some sense whupped into it.

You had to kiss her, didn't you, Jeffcoat? You had to go groping around in that damned dark closet and putting your hands where they didn't belong. You had to find out. Well, now you did, and what did it get you but miserable? Walking around here feeling like a cat gagging on a hairball. It's that woman who's stuck in your throat, and you can't swallow her and you can't cough her up. So just what in almighty hell are you going to do about it?

He beat the iron until the percussions rippled up his arms and jarred his joints. The iron grew too cool to shape but he kept beating anyway.

Emily Walcott. What was a man supposed to make of her? There were times when he wanted to throttle her. That temper—Christ, where did she get it? She seemed to stride through life in a perpetual state of defiance. Over what? She had nothing to defy!

But he admired her guts and her drive. She had more of both than most men.

He tried to imagine taking her back to Springfield and introducing her as his wife—his wife?—the one in the boy's cap and britches, the one who didn't want babies but would rather treat sick animals for a while. Wouldn't his mother pop her sockets? Especially after Julia, the perfect, proper, pregnant Julia. And his father would pull him aside by one arm and say, Son, are you sure you know what you're doing?

The answer was no. Ever since he'd laid lips on her in that closet he hadn't known what he was doing. Standing here beating a piece of cold iron like a fool. With a throaty curse he flung down his hammer and stood staring, brooding, missing her, wanting her.

She came, she met me, she lay with me and kissed me. And there were feelings between us. Not just heat, but feelings. Then the next time I tried to see her it was "Leave me alone!"

Frustrated, he drove eight fingers through his hair and roamed the confines of his smithy, picking up tools, casting them aside.

So what did you expect her to do, fling her arms around you and kiss you in the middle of Grinnell Street when she's engaged to Charles?

Emily Walcott was no dallier, he knew that. She wasn't toying with him as some women would. If he were to be honest with himself he'd admit that she was just plain scared. Scared of the emotional rush that had caught them both by surprise. Of the intensity. Of the eventualities that hung in the balance and the number of people who could get hurt if they pursued their feelings.

And what about you? You're not?

With a weary gust of breath he dropped to a low stool, shoulders slumped, arms hooking his widespread knees. He pulled her hairpin from his skirt pocket, rubbed it between his fingertips . . . again . . . and again . . . and again, staring, remembering her in a myriad of poses: glancing up across the crowded dance floor . . . cupping her mouth to shout the shrill Basque yell . . . riding toward him on the turntable. He heard again her voice coming to him in a close black closet, pleading, "Tom, don't. Oh God, please don't," because even before they'd kissed she recognized as well as he the fascination that had been smouldering beneath their surface antipathy. The memory of that first kiss brought memories of others—in Edwin's office, in a fresh snow, on his bed.

He covered his face with both hands.

All right, so I'm scared, too. Of hurting Charles. Of being hurt myself. Of making a wrong choice or missing the right one. He lifted his head and stared at the glowing orange forge.

The question is, do you love her?

God help me, yes.

Then hadn't you better tell her without beating around the bush?

And then what?

Do you want to marry her?

He swallowed, but the hairball still stuck.

Then hadn't you better tell her that, too?

While he sat with the thought ripe on his mind, footsteps sounded on the floor of the main corridor. Somebody gave the turntable a nudge in passing and made it rumble softly. Seconds later, Charles appeared in the smithy doorway.

"You won't get much work done that way!" he accused, grinning.

Tom grinned back, struggling with torn loyalties, happy to see Charles while wishing he'd never met the man.

"Yeah, well, neither will you." Pushing off both knees, Tom rose from the squatty stool. "What're you doing hanging around here in the middle of the day? Haven't you got some nails to pound?"

Charles stepped forward, stationed himself just inside the doorway, and smiled broadly. "I came to invite you to my wedding."

"Your w—"

"Friday afternoon at one o'clock."

Tom nearly fell back onto the stool. "Friday? You mean *this* Friday?"

"Yup."

"But that's day after tomorrow!"

"I know." Charles clapped his palms and rubbed them. "The stubborn wench finally said yes."

Tom's hairball seemed to inflate to twice its former size. "But . . . so soon . . ."

Charles respectfully dampened his exuberance and moved farther into the room. "It's because of her mother. Mrs. Walcott's really bad now. Emily thinks she hasn't got long to live, so she wants us to be married right away. Just a small service, right in Mrs. Walcott's bedroom so she can see it." Charles's happiness effervesced again and he beamed at Tom. "Can you believe it, Tom? Emily's actually impatient!"

Or running, thought Tom. "I thought she wanted to get her veterinary certificate first."

"She said she's giving it up." Charles's smile broadened. "Said she'll be too busy raising my babies to have time for anything else."

Night before last she told me she wasn't ready for babies yet.

"Well . . . I'll be damned." Trying to disguise his shock, Tom paced, running a hand through his hair. "That's . . . well, that's . . . congratulations . . ." He flashed a doubtful scowl, as he would have before he'd fallen in love with Emily. "I think."

Charles laughed and slapped Tom's shoulder.

"I think you like her more than you let on."

"She's all right, I guess. Just a little mouthy."

"I'm glad you're finally coming around because I've got a favor to ask you."

"Ask away."

"I want you to stand up for me at the wedding."

The hairball threatened to break loose and pull his stomach up with it. *Stand up for him? And remain silent when Vasseler asked if anyone knew of any reason for this couple not to be married? And pass Charles the ring to slip on her finger? And kiss her on the cheek afterwards and wish her a life of happiness with another man?*

Sweet Savior, he couldn't do it!

Hot seemed to turn to cold on his face. Thank God for the dimness in the room. He blinked, gulped, and offered Charles his hand.

"Of course I will."

Charles covered Tom's knuckles with a rough palm. "Good. And Tarsy will stand up for Em. She's over there asking her right now, at any rate. Can't see why she'd say no any more than you would." Charles squeezed extra hard on Tom's hand. His voice roughened with sincerity. "I'm so damned happy, man, you can't know how happy I am."

Tom didn't know where to hide. Afraid the forge would illuminate the underlying dismay on his face, he crooked an elbow and caught Charles around the neck, hauling him close. "Stay that way, Charles. You stay that way forever 'cause you deserve it."

Charles thumped him on the back.

They stepped apart. "Well . . ." Tom ran a knuckle beneath his nose, sniffed sheepishly, and stuffed his hands into his hip pockets. "This is getting to be a damned sappy conversation."

They laughed together, self-consciously.

"Yeah, and I've got some nails to pound."

"And I've got an angle-iron to make."

"So?"

"So, get the hell out of here."

"All right . . . I'm gone!"

When he was and Tom remained alone in the smithy, the reaction set in, a gut panic, as if a constrictor were preparing him for dinner.

She's going to do it! The damn fool woman thinks that'll solve everything, to hurry and seal those vows so she'll be safe from her own feelings. Don't tell me that's not why she's doing this!

So are you going to stop her or what?

I'm sure as hell going to try.

Some friend you are.

Goddamn it, leave me alone!

He loaded up a wagon with manure from the paddock—the only likely red herring he could dream up on the spur of the moment—and hitched up Liza and Rex to haul it away. He went smack down Main Street to the corner of Burkitt, where he could look up the hill and see her leave Tarsy's house. Whether she crossed the street to head home or came toward town, he'd catch her either way.

"Whoa," he called, reining in with the horses nosing the intersection. As slowly as prudent, he clambered down and circled the team, checking their feet. He lifted Liza's off fore and examined the shoe, the frog, running a thumb over it, glancing surreptitiously up the hill. The shoe fit fine. The frog was clean. He dropped Liza's foot and checked one of Rex's, then dipped between the team's heads and led them forward a step at a time, searching for a nonexistent limp.

Another glance up the hill—not a soul in sight.

He straightened a tug strap, a breech—neither of which needed it—squinted again up Burkitt Street Hill, and there she was, in a brown coat and plaid skirt, crossing Burkitt, heading home. It was a blindingly bright day, the snow almost painful to the eyes beneath an unhampered two o'clock sun. Against the backdrop of white she appeared as stark as an ink spot on a fresh blotter.

He trotted around and boarded, drove up the hill, took a right on Jefferson, and stayed well behind her, watching her skirts flare with each step, feeling his pulse do irrational things at the mere sight of her, with one hand across her chest, chin dropped, pinning the crossed ends of her red scarf to her throat. She walked as she did most things—briskly, with spare efficiency. She'd make some hell of a housewife, whether she knew it or not. She'd run a home and family with the same commitment she gave the stable, the animals. Because that's how she was. He knew it as surely as he knew he wanted the house and family to be his.

When she was a full block from Tarsy's, he came up behind her.

"H'lo, Emily."

She spun as if he'd stuck a gun in her ribs. Her frantic eyes snapped up to his and the arm holding her scarf tightened against her chest.

"You're looking a little pale," he observed somberly.

"I told you to leave me alone." She executed an abrupt about-face and marched on while he followed, off her right shoulder, keeping the team to a sedate walk.

"Yeah, I heard."

"Then, do it."

He considered it . . . for perhaps a quarter of a second.

"Charles just came by with the news." She strode on determinedly, her skirt whipping with each purposeful step.

"You'll pardon me if I don't congratulate you," he added dryly.

"Go away."

"Like hell I will. I'm here to stay, tomboy, so you might as well get used to it. What did Tarsy say?"

"She said yes."

"So you expect the two of us to stand up there in front of the Lord and Reverend Vasseler and give our blessings?"

"That wasn't my idea."

"Oh, that's comforting."

"Would you please find someone else to follow? The whole town can see us."

"Come for a ride with me."

She cut him a withering glance. "On your manure wagon."

"Say the word and I'll be back with a cutter before you can reach home."

She stopped and fixed him with a look of long suffering. "I'm going to marry him, don't you understand that?"

"Yes, I do. But do you? You're running scared, Emily."

"I'm doing the sensible thing." She walked on in less of a rush, as if resigned. He let the horses fall several feet behind, watching her run away from him, from her feelings, from the undeniable truth. When he could see she was determined to outrun him, he reined to a stop and let her get a good fifteen feet away before finally calling, "Hey, Emily, I forgot to tell you something." He waited, but she neither paused nor turned. Though they were flanked by houses on both sides of the street, he stood up on the wagon and shouted, *"I love you!"*

She spun about, her face radiating bald surprise. The town idiot could have detected the magnetism between them as they faced each other across a snow bright afternoon, she fifteen feet up the street, he standing behind a halted team on a manure wagon. More quietly he added, "I suppose you should know that before you marry him."

She gaped at him, stunned, her lips dropped open. "I forgot something else, too. I'd like to marry you." He let the words settle for several heartbeats before sitting down, flicking the reins, and leaving her standing on the edge of Jefferson Street with her breath still trapped in her throat, one mittened hand pressed to her heart and her face pink as a melon.

She spent the day at home, the evening with Charles; Tom knew it and chafed, but could only keep his distance. At his own house that night he paced and worried, wearing a path from window to window in the hope of seeing her coming across his yard. But the yard remained empty, and he became panicky. At midnight he went to bed and lay awake formulating bizarre plans for waylaying her, most of which were too absurd to implement. By two A.M. he'd decided this was a desperate situation, and desperate situations required desperate measures. Judging by the time either she or Edwin opened their livery stable, they roused around six A.M. each morning.

He was waiting in her backyard at 5:30.

It was December, and cold, so cold his nostrils kept freezing shut. He turned up the collar of his heavy sheepskin jacket, covered his bare ears with gloved hands, and propped a shoulder against the back of a shed, peering around its corner, watching the path that led from the kitchen door. His own bootprints appeared enormous and obvious, leading off the compacted path to his hiding spot, but the sky was still inky, the moon low and thin on the western horizon. What's more, anyone coming outside would likely be in too much of a hurry to be inspecting the snow for strange footprints.

Up in the mountains a coyote howled, followed by a chorus of *yip-yip-yaps*. Up at the house a door closed and hasty footsteps squeaked on the hard beaten path with a sound like leather beneath a shifting rider. Tom peeked around the corner. It was Edwin hurrying head-down toward the privy. When the door closed behind him, Tom slipped to the far side of the shed to wait. He watched the moon slip behind the mountains, heard Edwin return to the house, and a minute later someone else come out. When the person got halfway down the path he peered around his corner, making out a short female form and pale hair: Fannie.

Her stay in the privy was brief. When she'd gone back inside the morning felt infinitely colder. God, he'd never shivered so hard. The temperature always dropped before dawn; today it seemed to have plummeted a good twenty degrees. He blew his nose and felt as if his fingers would never thaw after replacing his gloves. His nostrils stuck together again and he skewed his nose to free them. Arms crossed, he stamped his feet and pulled his chin low inside his top button.

Maybe Emily had come out already and he'd missed her. Or maybe she was sleeping late. This was a stupid idea anyway. He should go home and leave her in peace. Maybe she really loved Charles and he'd be doing the right thing.

But he was a man in gut-love, so he stayed.

A full quarter of an hour later Emily appeared. Dawn

hovered in the wings, and by its murky light he watched her all the way from the house: taking careful running steps in footwear that made no sound at all, holding her coat lapped closed over her nightgown. Head down and arms crossed, she hurried, her hair creating a black waterfall over her cheeks and shoulders.

Well before she reached his end of the path Tom had stolen around the far side of the building to wait. But when she opened the privy door and stepped out, he was standing foursquare in the middle of the path, feet planted wide, gloved hands pressed together like a ball and socket.

"Good morning."

She straightened in surprise. "Tom!"

"I need to talk to you."

"Are you crazy! It's six o'clock in the morning!" She gripped her coat tightly against her throat.

"I could hardly do it at six o'clock last night, could I?"

"But it's freezing out here!"

"I know. I've been here awhile waiting for you. I was beginning to think you'd never come out."

"I can't talk to you here. I'm . . ." She glanced at the ground. "My feet . . . I'm in my slippers and nighty. And the sky will be getting light pretty soon. Anyone could see us."

"Emily, goddammit, I don't care! You're going to marry the wrong man tomorrow and I don't have a hell of a lot of time to talk you out of it!" In three enormous steps he reached her and scooped her into his arms.

"Thomas Jeffcoat, you put me down!"

"Quit kicking and listen to me." He hauled her behind the shed, pressed his spine against the cold wall, and slid to a squat, burying himself in snow to his hips. "Put your feet in here. Lord God, girl, haven't you got more sense than to come outside in these flimsy things?" Her slippers were knit of black carpet yarn. Wrapping her nightgown around them he doubled her on his lap and lassoed her with both arms, then looked up into her face, which was higher than his.

"Emily, you don't leave a fellow much spare time. I wouldn't have done this if I'd had any other choice. But I told you, the man pursues, so I'm pursuing in the only way I know how, crazy as it may be."

"Crazy will scarcely cover it. That was a terrible thing you did to me yesterday on the street."

"It made you stop and think though, didn't it?"

"But you just don't . . . don't pull up beside a girl in your manure wagon and ask her to marry you!"

"I know, that's why I came back to ask again."

"Behind the toilet this time!"

"The toilet's over there; this is the shed." He gestured with his head.

"Thomas Jeffcoat, you're a lunatic."

"I'm in love. So I came to ask you again—will you marry me?"

"No."

"Do you love me?"

"How can you ask me such a thing when my wedding is set for tomorrow!" Exasperated, she struggled to free herself but he tightened his hold around her shoulders, pinning both her arms and knees.

"Don't answer my question with a question! Do you love me?"

"That has no bearing on my promise to—"

"Do you?" he demanded roughly, clasping her neck with one thick-gloved hand, forcing her to turn her face to his.

"I desire you. I don't know if it's the same th—"

He slammed her mouth down to his, kissed her hard, infusing the kiss with all the love and desperation and frustration he felt. When he released her his breathing was harsh, his eyes earnest. "I desire you, too—I won't deny it—so much that I'd like to lay you down here in the snow. But it's more than that. I walk around my empty house and imagine you in it with me. I want you at my breakfast table whether you can fry eggs or not. We can eat burned toast for all I care—hell, I'll even do the burning, but I want you there, Emily. And at the livery barn—you're so damned good with horses. Can't you see us walking down there every day and working together? What a pair we'd make at that business!

"And what about your studies? Charles told me you're going to give them up to have babies, right after you told me that you don't want babies yet. That's not right, Emily. And I don't want babies either, not any sooner than you do. For a while I want it to be you and me, running around in that big house in our underwear. I don't know how we'll manage that, seeing as how all this desire will be cropping up all the time, but we can try. Emily . . ." This time he inveighed more tenderly. "I love you. I don't want to lose you."

Folded like an *N* she sat in his arms and allowed herself to be convinced, let his cold nose nuzzle her warm cheek and his welcome lips bias her own. She forgot her imminent wedding. She forgot the cold. She forgot to object. She opened her mouth and kissed him back—an inadvisable, ample kiss leading to nothing but further confusion, yet she partook of him with the relish of one soon to be denied. He tasted as she remembered, smelled and felt alarmingly familiar—a tempting combination of wet and soft, pliable and hard. As his tongue slewed hers, nerve bursts of heat warmed her deepest parts. Her head listed, swayed, but the kiss remained unbroken as she freed a trapped hand and rested it on his face. His cheek was warm, bristled yet with a night's growth; his jaw hard; his collar warm and furry. Tipped back, his head pressed the shed wall, and she slipped her hand there to pillow it from the hard, icy surface.

With tongues dancing, they wooed disaster, letting their feelings build. His hands shifted—one to a slim shoulder, one to a round buttock, where her heavy coat hem gave way to lighter cotton. It slipped between the two garments . . . glove over nightgown . . . thick over thin . . . leather over cotton . . . drawing patterns on her firm flesh while he pretended the hand was bare. When their heartbeats and breathing grew taxed, they ended the kiss out of common frustration.

"Oh, Emily . . ." He whispered, tortured.

"Why didn't you ask me earlier?" she despaired, closing her eyes.

"Because I didn't know until I kissed you."

"Then why didn't you kiss me earlier?"

"You know the reasons—Charles, Tarsy . . . even Julia. I thought I was through with women for a long, long time. I was afraid of being hurt again. Now this hurts even worse. Emily, please . . . you have to marry me." He lifted his face but she avoided further kisses.

"Thomas . . . please, the answer is still no."

"But why?"

Heartsore, she looked into his eyes and decided to tell him the truth, and in telling to remind herself as well. "I'm going to tell you something that I trust you'll never repeat. I'm telling you because it seems the only fair thing to do." She drew a shaky breath and began. "The morning after I went to your house I walked into our kitchen and found my father kissing Fannie. I mean, *really kissing*. You can't guess what it was like, Tom. I felt . . . sick and betrayed . . . and angrier than I ever remember being. For myself, and for my brother, but mostly for Mother, who doesn't deserve all the unhappiness and pain that life is throwing at her right now. It isn't enough that she's in constant pain and dying at such a young age. Her husband is carrying on right under her nose! Right under her own roof!

"It made me take a second look at myself, at what I was doing to Charles."

"But your father is—"

"I won't be like him, Tom, I won't! Charles is a fine and admirable person who doesn't deserve to be deceived by his fiancée and his best friend. Just listen to that—*his fiancée and his best friend*. That's what we are, you know. When we're together we tend to forget that."

"So you're marrying Charles to atone for your father's sins? Is that what you're saying?"

It sounded too much like the truth, and she had no reply.

"What about how we feel?" Tom insisted.

"What I feel might very well be panic, which I think every bride feels at the last minute before getting married. But I can't cope with one more crisis right now. The past three days have been terrible. When I walk into Mother's room, I feel guilty. When I look at Charles, I feel guilty. I see you and I feel confused. Papa and Fannie make me so disgusted I can scarcely tolerate being in the same house with them. What I crave is peace and I think I'll have that with Charles. I'm going to marry him and move into his house and start living my own life. That's what I'm going to do."

"You're going to disregard what you feel for me? What we feel for each other?"

"Emileee?" It was Fannie calling from the house.

Behind the shed, Tom and Emily tensed, holding their breaths.

"Emily, are you all right out there?"

"Don't answer her." Tom gripped Emily's wrists, holding her still while their hearts clamored.

"I have to go in," she whispered, straining to rise.

"Wait!"

"Let me up! She's coming!"

Fannie's voice came again through the crisp morning. *"Emily?"*

Emily raised her voice and called, "I'm fine. I'll be in in a minute!" Struggling to rise, gracelessly disentangling themselves, Emily half fell off Tom's lap. Her ankles and one wrist sank into the icy snow. It fell into her slipper tops in cold, wet clumps. It climbed her cuffs and chilled her wrists. It clung to the bottom of Tom's jacket and burned a frigid ring where it melted on his hindside. Embroiled in emotions, neither of them noticed. He gripped her wrist, straining to hold her while she strained to flee.

"Don't do it, Emily."

"I have to."

"Then don't expect me to stand there and witness it! I'll be *damned* if I will, whether I told Charles I would or not!"

"I have to go in."

"You're so damn blind!"

"Let me go . . . please."

"Emily . . ."

"Goodbye, Thomas."

She ran as if a prairie fire were at her heels.

Josephine Walcott lay at death's door, but she wasn't dead yet. Quite the contrary. During the last twenty-four hours her condition had undergone a peculiar turnabout. She had coughed less, felt stronger, and her perceptions had grown uncommonly keen—as she'd heard was often the case during one's last hours—keen enough to ascertain that something was radically wrong in this house.

Emily had grown icy and brusque with Fannie and Edwin. Edwin walked as if on cinders. And Charles hadn't come to announce his own wedding plans. Most peculiar, yet understandable in light of recent outbursts that had filtered up from below.

Josephine awakened well before dawn on the day preceding Emily's wedding and listened to the sounds of the family coming to life. Doors opening and closing, stove lids chiming, the pump gurgling, bacon frying, muffled voices.

From below came the sound of Fannie, speaking quietly to Edwin.

Then Edwin's deeper reply.

Then Fannie again, outside, calling Emily's name worriedly. Twice. Three times.

What on earth?

The fire roared up the stovepipe as if from too much draft, the back door slammed shut, and Edwin inquired, "Emily, are you all right?"

Emily's voice, brusque and rude, came up clearly from below: "Don't set breakfast for me. I'll eat with Mother," followed by her slippered steps pounding up the stairs at breakneck pace.

Fifteen minutes later she appeared with Josephine's breakfast tray, brought it in, and closed the door that during the day had remained steadfastly open until two days ago when Emily had peremptorily begun closing it.

"Good morning, Mother."

Josephine caught Emily's hand as it deposited the tray on the bed. She gave her daughter a smile and reached up to lay her knuckles against Emily's red cheek.

"Are you ill?" Josephine inquired in a whisper.

"Ill? No, I'm . . . I'm fine."

"I heard Fannie calling you. Your cheek is cold."

"I was outside. It's only ten degrees this morning."

"And so red."

Emily busied herself with the breakfast trappings, avoiding Josephine's eyes. "Oatmeal and bacon and eggs this morning. Here, let me pull your pillow up. I hope you're hungry again. It's so heartening to see you eat like you did yesterday." She rambled on—superfluous chatter clearly amplifying her edginess. Her hands flew nervously from one thing to the next—sugar, cream, salt, pepper—superabundant efficiency further underscoring her jumpiness. "I thought I'd clean your room today and wash your hair. I think we can manage it with some oilcloth over the edge of the mattress while you lie across the bed—would you like that? And press your favorite bed jacket and my own blue dress. And, of course, I've got to wash my hair, too, and pack my things to take to Charles's house, and—"

"Emily, what's wrong?"

"Wrong?" Emily's wide eyes contained a hint of terror.

"You needn't protect me from everything," Josephine whispered. "I'm still very much alive and I want to be part of this family again."

Josephine watched her daughter struggle with some hidden turmoil. For a moment she thought Emily would relent and confide, but in the end Emily shot to her feet, turning away, hiding any secrets her eyes might divulge. "Oh, Mother, you've never stopped being a part of this family, you know that. But please don't worry about me. It's nothing."

Yet Emily scarcely ate any breakfast, and when Edwin stepped in before leaving for the livery barn she coldly snubbed him, turning to the bureau and fussing with things on its top, offering not even her usual good-bye.

Soon after Edwin left Fannie appeared, offering to clean the room, but Emily aloofly informed her that she'd do it herself and that she'd also take care of getting her mother ready for tomorrow. The tension in the room was palpable as Fannie looked across the foot of the bed at Emily, then resignedly turned toward the door.

"Fannie!" Emily snapped.

"Yes?" Fannie turned back.

"It won't be necessary for you to prepare a wedding feast, in case you were thinking about it. When the service is over Charles and I will be going directly to his house."

Emily spent the day as she'd spent the preceding one, lavishing time on her mother, doing all the chores she'd outlined for the day. But as it progressed her busyness came to contain an almost frenetic quality. Distressed, Josephine observed and worried.

It was late in the afternoon before the hair washing began. It turned out to be an awkward process, but by its very awkwardness and the reversal of their roles, it brought mother and daughter closer than they had been in years.

When Josephine was again sitting, with the pillows bolstering her back, Emily combed her hair slowly and said, "It won't take long to dry."

"No, it won't . . ." Josephine said sadly, "not anymore."

The words went straight to Emily's heart. Less than a year ago Mother's hair had been dark, thick, and glossy, her greatest asset, her pride. Now it lay in thin strings, faded to the color of beeswax, with her pink skull showing in spots. Josephine herself had lopped the hair off at collar length to make its care easier during her illness. Her semibaldness seemed a final insult to the deteriorating body of the once-robust woman.

Josephine sensed Emily's sadness and lifted her eyes to find her daughter indeed forlorn.

"Emily, dear, listen to me." She took Emily's hand in both of hers and held it, comb and all, while speaking in a whisper to keep from coughing. "It doesn't matter what my hair looks like now. It doesn't matter that your father sleeps on a spare cot, and that he must see me looking more and more like an old dried apple. None of it matters. What matters is that your father and I have lived together for twenty-two years without ever losing the immense respect we hold for one another."

With downcast eyes Emily stared at her mother's withered hand, the fingers too thin to show a mark where her wedding band had been.

"You've been very troubled the last few days, and I believe I know what's brought it on. I appreciate your loyalty, but perhaps it's been misplaced." Josephine's thumb brushed across Emily's bare ring finger. "I *am* sick, Emily, but I'm not blind or deaf. I've seen your sudden aversion to your father and Fannie, and I've heard things . . . through the floor. Things that my ears were not meant to hear, perhaps." With a sigh Josephine fell silent, studying her daughter's dejected expression.

"We've never been particularly close, have we, Emily? Perhaps that's my fault." She continued holding Emily's hand, a familiarity she had never promoted in eighteen years of mothering. It felt unnatural, even now, but she forced it, admitting her own maternal shortcomings. "But you were always so taken by your father, trailing after him, imitating him. I can see that you're hurting terribly each time you shun him . . . and Fannie, too. You have become very close to Fannie, haven't you?"

Emily swallowed, refusing to lift her eyes. Two spots of color rose in her cheeks.

"I think it's time you were told some things. They may not be pleasant for you to hear, but I trust you to understand. You're a mature young woman, about to embark on marriage yourself. If you're old enough for that you're old enough to understand how it is with your father and me."

Emily's troubled blue eyes lifted. "Mama, I—"

"Shh. I tire so easily, and I must whisper. Please listen." Oddly enough, though Josephine had not spoken this long or this uninterruptedly in months, she neither flagged nor coughed, but went on as if some all-caring benefactor had lent her the strength to speak when she most needed it.

"Your father and I grew up much as you and Charles have, knowing each other from childhood. Our parents told us when we were fourteen years old that they had agreed upon a marriage covenant, which they expected the two of us to honor. It had nothing to do with the joining of lands, or of business, which has often made me wonder why they wanted so badly for Edwin and me to marry. Perhaps only because they were friends and knew what kind of children they had turned out—honest Christian children who would grow up to be honest Christian parents, and into whom the Fourth Commandment had been drilled.

"Our betrothal became official when we were sixteen—the same spring that Fannie came home from two years of studying abroad. Her parents threw a party right after she got back, and I recall the night clearly. It was April and the lilacs were blooming. Fannie wore ivory—she always looked stunning in ivory, with that blazing orange hair of hers—rather like a holiday candle, I always thought. I guess I realized from that first night that your father had eyes for Fannie. They danced a quadrille, and I recall them spinning with their arms linked, studying each other with flushed faces and smiling the way I'd never had Edwin smile at me. I suspect he took her outside and kissed her later in the herb garden because I could smell crushed basil on his clothes when he returned.

"I knew after that that I should free him from his betrothal vow, but I was not the most marriageable girl in Boston, nor the prettiest. I could not flirt like Fannie, or . . . or kiss in the herb garden . . . or carry on idle banter the way young swains like a girl to do. But more importantly, I had been raised to believe I must honor the wishes of my father and mother."

Josephine drew a sigh and fell back, fixing her eyes on the ceiling. "Unfortunately, so had Edwin. I knew that he was falling in love with Fannie, and I saw the strain it put on him. But I suspect his parents put him out of mind of breaking off our betrothal. So when the time came, he dutifully married me.

"I want you to understand, Emily . . ." Josephine still held her daughter's hand loosely on the coverlet. "Our marriage has not been intolerable . . . not even bad, but neither has it been the splendid thing it might have been had we shared the feelings that your father and Fannie did. We understood the limitations of our love. Call it respect, that's a truer word, for I always knew that the one Edwin truly loved was Fannie. Oh, he hid it well, and he never guessed that I suspected. But I knew the reason we left Massachusetts was to put distance between the two of them, to put temptation out of his reach. And though she always addressed her letters to me, I knew they were meant to let Edwin know how she was and where she was, and that she never forgot him.

"Did you know, Emily, that I brought Fannie here against your father's will?"

Emily's startled eyes lifted to her mother's as the older woman continued. "He was very angry when I told him she was coming. He shouted at me, one of the few times ever, and said, no, he absolutely wouldn't have Fannie here, which, of course, only confirmed my suspicions—that the memory of her had not dulled over the years, that he still cared deeply for her. But I had taken the choice out of his hands by withholding the news about Fannie's coming until she was already underway."

Josephine smiled at their linked hands, her own thin and transparent as bone china, Emily's strong and marked from hard work. "You think me a little tetched, perhaps, to throw them together like that?" Her whisper suddenly gained vehemence as she gripped Emily's hand hard. "Oh, Emily, look at Fannie, just look at her. She's as different from me as sea is from earth. She's vivacious and spirited, laughing and gay while I'm helplessly staid and Victorian. I've never been like Fannie, never been the things your father really needed. He should have had her all these years, yet he remained loyal to me and honored the vows we made. He should have had the warmth and affection and the demonstrativeness of a woman like her, but instead he settled for me. And now she's here, and unless I miss my guess you discovered them—what? Kissing? Embracing? Is that it?"

From Emily's downcast eyes Josephine knew she'd guessed right.

"Well, perhaps they've earned the right."

"How can you say that, Mother?" Tears glistened in Emily's eyes as she lifted her head. "He's still your husband!"

Josephine released Emily's hand and studied the ceiling again. "This is very hard for me to say." Moments passed before she went on. "I . . . I cannot say I ever relished the marriage act, and I cannot help but wonder if it wasn't because simple respect for your father wasn't quite enough for me either."

In eighteen years Emily had never heard her mother speak of anything remotely bordering on the carnal. Hearing it now made Emily—as well as Josephine—distinctly uncomfortable. Endless seconds ticked by while they struggled with their private embarrassment, then Josephine added, "I only wanted you to know it wasn't all your father's fault."

Their glances met, then strayed to impersonal objects in the room before Josephine found herself able to continue. "Another thing I want you to remember—in all the time Fannie has been here she has never distressed me, never once hinted that I'd done her a grave wrong by marrying the man she should have had. She has been the soul of benevolence—good, kind, and patient. And honorable to the teeth, I'm sure of it. She has made my dying days more bearable, Emily, just by being here."

The shock of hearing her mother predict her own death brought a denial from Emily. "Mother, you're not dying, don't say that!"

"Yes, I am, dear. And soon. I'm stronger today, but it won't last. And when I'm gone I want you prepared. Oh, you'll mourn me, but please, Emily, not for long. And, please, dear, you must give Edwin and Fannie the right to their happiness. If I can, surely you can. When he marries her, and I'm sure he will—he *must*!—you must be as benevolent to Fannie as she's been to me. And your father—well, surely you can imagine the anguish he's suffered, being married to the wrong woman all his life. Doesn't he deserve *some* happiness?"

"Oh, Mother . . ." Dropping to her knees, Emily fell across her mother's bed with tears streaming from her eyes. Josephine was not a woman often disposed to tears. Had she been, perhaps she could have made her husband happier. Dry-eyed, she studied the ceiling while touching the head of her weeping daughter.

"And what about you?" she inquired. "Are you ready to tell me about you and Charles . . . and this Mr. Jeffcoat?"

Startled, Emily's head shot up, her tearful eyes wide.

"You know?"

"Your father told me."

"He did?"

"Of course he did. What do you think we do up here in this room every evening? He tells me about his day, and you are a very important part of all his days."

Josephine's last disclosure had effectively stopped Emily's tears. Running a knuckle beneath each eye she said, "Papa was very upset when he found Tom and me kissing, wasn't he?"

"Yes. But now you should be able to understand why. He was—is—very concerned about you, just as I am. We love Charles very much. But I don't believe either one of us wants you to make the same mistake we did."

Crestfallen, Emily doubled forward and rested her cheek against the back of Josephine's hand. "Oh, Mother, what should I do?"

Josephine took her time answering, weighing her words. "I can't tell you, and I wouldn't presume to, not anymore. You're a very impulsive young woman, Emily. You close doors with the same vehemence with which you open them, just as you did to your father and Fannie. It's still closed—you see?" She turned to glance at the bedroom door. "The only advice I can give is to open the door—open all your doors. It's the only way you can see where you're going."

"Are you saying I shouldn't marry Charles?"

"Not at all. You seem to be the one who's questioning it."

Leaning across her mother's bed, Emily admitted it was true: she was questioning it, had been since her feelings for Tom had surfaced.

Tom.

Charles.

So great a decision to make in so little time.

Realizing the girl would have to make that decision for herself, Josie sent her on her way to do it. "And now I'm very tired, dear. I think I'd like to rest a while." She sighed and let her eyes close. "Please tell Fannie to wake me when your father comes home for dinner so I can eat with them."

Chapter 15

TIPTOEING FROM HER mother's room, Emily left the door open behind her. She stood in the hall staring at the wallpaper for several minutes. Fannie and Papa . . . since before he'd married Mother? How young had they been? Not much older than she was now. And Mother, resisting Papa's advances much as she, Emily, often resisted Charles's? The admission seemed too incredible to reconstruct. Yet Mother had intimated that carnal urgings should not be disregarded in making a decision about whom to marry.

Dazed, Emily navigated herself to her own room and dropped anchor on the foot of the bed. So many parallels, too many to ignore. She stared at the window ledge behind the lace curtains, imagining a love powerful enough to withstand more than twenty-two years, unrequited; a respect immense enough to withstand the same twenty-two years under a mantle of silent misgivings. How difficult for both Mother and Father. Yet they had persevered, given their children a foundation as secure as any religion or creed, for in all her life Emily had never suspected a rift in their devotion to one another.

And Fannie, the lorn one, how empty her life must have been. Beneath her veneer of gaiety, how much heartbreak must be hidden.

Charles would be like Fannie—lorn and empty and heartbroken—should Emily reverse her decision to marry him. But he would not remain cordial through the years as Fannie had with Mother and Father. He would be hurt and angry and would make it impossible for all three of them, herself and Tom and Charles, to live in a town this small without future bitterness.

The afternoon aged; blue shadows stained the snow-covered window ledge. Downstairs the oven door squeaked as Fannie opened and closed it. Emily checked the time: 4:30. In less than twenty-one hours she was scheduled to stand beside Mother's bed and join her life to Charles's. Irreversibly.

Could she do it?

More to the point, could she *not* do it?

She tried to imagine herself, when Charles came tonight, telling him, I've made a mistake, Charles, it's Tom I love, Tom I want to marry.

She crossed her arms and doubled forward, experiencing a real stab of pain. She had let them go on too long, her daunted feelings about Charles. How could she, at this eleventh hour, make such a decision?

Five o'clock came—full dark now, near winter solstice; five-thirty and Mother woke up across the hall; quarter to six and Papa came home, stamping his boots, washing his hands, asking where everybody was. Frankie banged in, fresh from sliding with Earl and the boys. The smell of roasting chicken drifted upstairs.

Emily rose and smoothed her skirt, moving about her dark bedroom, delaying the inevitable. She could not avoid them forever. In the hall a faint light drifted up from below. She stood at the top of the stairs gathering courage to take the first step. All the way downstairs she imagined facing Papa and Fannie to find them changed somehow, now that they had been redeemed by Mother's words. But when she entered the kitchen she found them looking the same as ever—Papa in his work clothes with underwear showing at the neck and wrists, reading the weekly newspaper, and Fannie in a long apron with her pale peach hair slightly ascatter, working at the stove. They looked much like any ordinary husband and wife, and Frankie—setting silverware on the table—might well have been their son. With a start, Emily realized it could have been true. Frankie might have been their son and she their daughter. The thought brought Emily a sharp feeling of inconstancy on Mother's behalf, yet Josephine was probably right: Fannie and Papa would someday be husband and wife.

Sensing that he was beng studied, Edwin lowered the paper just as Fannie turned, and the two of them caught Emily watching them from the doorway. The room held the same sense of imminence that had predominated since she had discovered them in it kissing.

"Well." Edwin snapped his newspaper flat. "How is your mother? I was just heading up."

"She's better," Emily answered in the kindest tone she'd used with him since that discovery.

"Good . . . good." Silence reeled itself out, uncomfortably lengthy. Finally Edwin spoke again. "I took the liberty of inviting Charles to supper tonight. I thought it might be appropriate since you won't be having a wedding dinner with us tomorrow."

"Oh . . . fine."

Edwin glanced at Fannie while gauging the reason for Emily's sudden docility. "Fannie's made roast chicken—your favorite."

"Yes, I . . . thank you, Fannie. But Mother asked me to tell you she'd like the three of you to eat together in her room."

"If she's feeling strong enough," Edwin suggested, "maybe I could carry her down and we could all eat together just this once."

Frankie had been staring at all three of them and piped up, "What's the matter with you, anyway? You're standing there gawkin' like a bunch of hoot-owls!"

His observation at last jarred the tension. Emily moved into the room, ordering her brother, "Get the glasses and napkins on for Fannie while I help her mash potatoes."

What a meal, what an evening, what a phantasmal set of circumstances. Charles arrived, jovial and excited. Edwin carried his wife downstairs. Fannie served them all a delectable dinner and they ate as if nothing were amiss. But the tension within Emily felt as if it would cut off her air supply.

She tried—oh how she tried—to find within herself the

wherewithal to deal honestly with Charles. But he was so happy, so eager, so amorous when they stepped onto the porch to say good-night.

He kissed her roundly, caressed her as if holding himself on a precipice.

"Tomorrow night at this time," he whispered ardently, "you'll be my wife." He kissed her again and shuddered deeply, breaking the contact to speak throatily at her ear. "Oh, Emily, I love you so."

She opened her lips and began unsteadily, "Charles . . . I . . ."

But he kissed her again, interrupting her confession, and in the end she could not find the means to annihilate him.

When he was gone, she roamed the confines of her room with desperation forming a great knot in her breast and dampening the palms of her hands. Knowing she would be unable to sleep, she went for solace to the animals at the stable, only to discover there another plea from Tom, this one tacked to the outer door where anyone might have found it—a white envelope bearing her name, telling her clearly how desperate he was.

She took it into the office and sat on the creaky, lopsided chair with her heart racing as she withdrew a rich, deeply embossed postcard bearing a swag of roses in shades of mauve and wine and pink, held aloft at the corners by bluebirds from whose beaks bows and ribbons fluttered. In the center of the card more roses and ribbons formed a beautiful floral heart, below which the verse was inscribed in stylized gilt letters pressed deeply into the cardboard:

My hand is lonely for your clasping dear
My ear is tired waiting for your call
I need your help, your laugh to cheer:
Heart, soul, and senses need you, one and all.

Below the verse he had written, *I love you, please marry me.*

Had Charles sent it, Emily would have been less shattered. But coming from a man like Tom—the one who had ceaselessly teased, aggravated, and called her tomboy—the impassioned plea pierced her heart like an arrow from Cupid's own bow.

She pressed her lips to his signature, closed her eyes, and

despaired, loving him, needing him much as the verse on the card had sketched—with heart, soul, and senses. But the clock was ticking off the hours toward her wedding with another, and here she sat, fainthearted and frightened, with tears raining down her face.

There would be times in later life when Emily would study her husband across a lamplit room, feel a surge of love, and be freshly convinced that her mother's last act of mercy was to die that night.

Papa came to break the news, in the predawn hours, sitting on the edge of Emily's bed, shaking her out of a brief and tardy sleep. "Emily, dear, wake up."

"What? . . . mmm . . ."

"Emily, dear . . ."

She sat up with her head pounding from lack of sleep, her eyes gritty and swollen. "Papa? Is something wrong?"

"I'm afraid so, Emily."

He had brought a lantern. She peered through its glare and saw tear tracks gilding Papa's cheeks. She knew the truth even before he spoke the words.

"It's your mother . . . she's gone."

"No!"

He nodded sorrowfully.

"Oh, Papa."

"She's gone," he repeated quietly.

"But she felt so good yesterday."

"I know."

"Oh, Papa," she cried again, rising on her knees on the bed to clasp and cling to him—her first touch since she had condemned him for loving another. She felt his body quake with inheld sobs, though he made not a sound. She spread her hands on his shoulders, inexplicably saddened because he had loved Mama after all. In his own fashion, he had loved her.

"Papa," she whispered brokenly, "don't cry. She's an angel already, I'm sure."

He didn't cry. But when he straightened, Emily saw in his red-rimmed eyes an emotion far more difficult to bear than grief. She saw regret. Wordlessly he squeezed Emily's hands and rose from the bed, waiting while she got up, too, and moved ahead of him to the room across the hall.

There, in the lanternlight, which was already losing intensity as the sun stole up, Fannie sat on the edge of Josephine's bed, tearless, gently smoothing the brittle white hair back from the pale, wrinkled brow of her dead cousin. Across the white sheets and pillowcases, across Josephine's white nightgown and skin and hair a splattered bloodflow had dried and darkened to a rufous brown.

"Ohhh . . ." The mournful syllable escaped Emily as she drifted to the side of the bed opposite Fannie and, kneeling, pressed her hands to the mattress cautiously, as if the form lying upon it could yet be disturbed. "Mother . . ." she whispered as tears slipped quietly down her cheeks.

Having lived with the certainty of her death lent little ease at its coming. It had reached in and snatched her from those who, unsuspecting, took yesterday's turnabout for a healthy sign. They mourned together: Fannie touching Josephine's hand; Emily kneeling opposite, rubbing her mother's sleeve; Edwin standing behind her. While they lamented, Fannie continued smoothing back Josephine's sparse white hair, murmuring, "Rest, dearling . . . rest."

They thought of her in those first despairing moments, not as she was but as she had been, in haler times when her hair was black and her arms plump, her eyes avid and her limbs quick.

"Were you with her, Papa?" Emily asked solemnly.

"No. I found her when I woke up."

"Didn't she cough?"

"Yes, I seem to remember that she did. But I didn't quite wake up."

Again they fell silent, groping to accept the fact that Josephine was truly dead and nothing any of them might have done could have prevented her death.

"Papa, what about Frankie?"

"Yes, we have to wake Frankie."

But neither of them moved. Only Fannie, who knew what must be done to spare a boy only twelve years old. She fetched a basin of water and with a soft cloth tenderly swabbed the mouth and neck of Edwin's dead wife, his children's mother, then found a clean white sheet and spread it over the soiled bedding, hiding the dried brown stains. When the task was done, she straightened, studying Josephine lovingly. Fannie's own nightgown was wrinkled, her feet bare, and her disorderly hair defied all rules of gravity. But she exuded an undeniable air of decorum as she said quietly, "Now go get Frank, Edwin."

Emily went with her father, carrying a lantern and clasping Edwin's hand. Beside Frankie's bed they paused, studying the sleeping boy, reluctant to awaken him with the dread news, bolstering each other during these brimming minutes of heavyheartedness.

At last Edwin sat down and lined Frankie's pretty cheek with his big work-widened hand. "Son?" The word caught in his throat. Emily gripped her father's shoulder and reached beyond it to do her part.

"Frankie?" she entreated softly. "Wake up, Frankie."

When he did, blinking and rubbing his eyes, Emily took the burden from Edwin and said the words herself. "I'm afraid we have some sad news this morning."

Frankie awakened with unusual suddenness, gazing at his father and sister clear-eyed as he rarely was on an ordinary morning. "Mother's dead, isn't she?"

"Yes, son, she is," Edwin intoned.

Frankie was young enough that he remained untrammeled by the stultifying rules of Victorian mourning. He spoke what he felt, without monitoring either the words or his honest reaction. "I'm glad. She didn't like coughing all the time and being so sick and skinny."

He went with them, stood dutifully beside his mother's bed, gulping, staring, then spinning from the room to do his crying in private. The others remained, exchanging uncertain glances, wishing they could run from duty, too. But there were people to inform, a body to be laid out, a wedding to be canceled, a coffin to be built.

The survivors of Josephine Walcott had no precedent to guide them through the hours that lay ahead. They stood momentarily vacuous, wondering what propriety demanded first.

Edwin took the initiative.

"I'll have to go feed the horses, and hang a sign on the livery door until we can get the black wreaths made. Emily, would you see to it that Frankie gets over to Earl's house when he's calmed down? Maybe Mrs. Rausch would let Earl stay home from school today to keep Frankie company. I'll stop by the schoolhouse and let Miss Shaney know, and I'll go by Charles's, too—that is, unless you'd prefer to tell him yourself, Emily."

"No," she replied, already realizing who'd need her most. "I'll stay here with Fannie."

"As for the laying out . . ." Edwin glanced somberly toward the corpse. "Wait until I get back."

But the moment he'd left, Fannie armed herself in a mantle of efficiency. Picking up the basin and heading briskly for the door, she countered, "A husband should be spared this cross. I'll see to it myself."

As Fannie passed Emily, the younger woman reached out as if to touch her shoulder. But she withdrew the hand indecisively and called instead, "Fannie?"

In the doorway, Fannie turned. Their eyes met and both women realized that the last time they had spoken Emily's heart had been filled with enmity. Her expression held none now, only a ravaged, remorseful gratefulness for Fannie's presence. When she spoke, her voice held a plea for forgiveness. "I'll help . . . . it's the daughter's place to help."

"She was your mother and this won't be pleasant. Wouldn't you rather remember her as she was?"

"I will. I'll always remember her with dark hair and heavy arms, but I have to help, don't you see?"

Tears brightened Fannie's eyes and her voice held both understanding and love, as she answered, "Yes, of course, dear. We'll do it together, as soon as Frankie is out of the house."

When Fannie had gone downstairs Emily stood in Frankie's doorway, thrust against her will into a maternal role for which she felt unprepared. Her brother lay facing the wall, as if he'd been thrown onto his bed. She entered and sat behind him, rubbing his back and shoulders. He had calmed somewhat, though an occasional residual sob plucked his breath away.

"Frankie?"

No answer.

"She's happier, just like you said."

Again no answer for long minutes. Then, finally, through a plugged nose, "I know. But now I haven't got no mother."

"You have Papa and me . . . and Fannie."

"But none of you are my mother."

"No, we're not. But we'll help however we can. Now Papa says he wants you to go to Earl's today and spend the day with him. You want me to walk you over there?" He was twelve years old, yet neither of them found the question silly today.

Staring at the corner, Frankie replied colorlessly, "I guess so."

When they were dressed, they walked to Earl's house holding hands. They had not held hands since Frankie had turned seven and given up that sissy stuff, and not since Emily's world had begun revolving around more important matters like her studies and her engagement and growing up. But they walked to Earl's house holding hands.

At the livery stable, Edwin fed the horses and hung a sign on the door: *Closed due to death in the family.* Next, he trudged to Charles's house. When Charles opened the door Edwin told him point-blank: "It's bad news, son. Mrs. Walcott is gone."

Though the unfortunate timing was not mentioned, it was uppermost in both of their minds. Charles masked his disappointment and gripped Edwin's hand hard, drawing him inside. "Oh, Edwin, I'm so sorry." They stood for seconds in silence, still linked by the unbroken handclasp. Finally Charles said, "I'd like to make her coffin if you'd let me, Edwin. I'd like to do that last thing for her."

Their eyes met in mutual affection and regret, and Edwin broke down fully for the first time, clasping the younger man, weeping sorely against his taller shoulder.

"She was a g—good woman but she was never v—very happy. I couldn't make her happy, Charles. I n—never c—could make her happy."

"Aw, Edwin, she was happy, I know she was. She had a good marriage and two fine children. It was just her suffering in the last years, and you did what you could about that. You brought her out here and cared for her. You did all you could."

In spite of Charles's consolation, Edwin's tears continued for minutes. At last he regained composure and stepped back, drying his eyes on a sleeve, hanging his head. To the floor he said, "No sir, when a man lives his whole life with a woman he knows whether or not she's happy, and Josie wasn't. Not very often." Edwin fished a handkerchief from his pocket, cleared his nose, and admitted against the linen, "I didn't do that in front of the women, Charles. Forgive me."

"Aw, Edwin, don't be foolish."

"You're like a son to me, you know that, boy, don't you?"

Charles gulped back emotions of his own. "Yes, sir, I do, and you're like a father to me. I'm sorry . . . awfully sorry."

Edwin sighed, feeling better since his cry. "And I'm damned sorry about your wedding being put off—and not a word of complaint out of you, though you certainly have the right." Edwin squeezed Charles's shoulder affectionately. "You go ahead, you make her coffin and thank you."

"I've got some fine cedar. She'll have the best, Edwin."

Edwin nodded and prepared to leave. When he reached the door Charles inquired, "How is Emily taking it?"

"She's bearing up as well as can be expected, but you know how good Josie felt yesterday—it was a shock to all of us after that."

Charles nodded and reached for his jacket, too. "Well, I'd best get over to see Reverend Vasseler, tell him we won't be needing him today."

But as Edwin left, Charles made up an excuse to stay behind. Alone, he dropped onto a hard kitchen chair and sat lifelessly, his shoulders bowed by disappointment. One thought ran through his mind time and again. *Bless her departed soul, Lord, but when am I ever going to get to marry the woman I love?*

When Emily returned from walking Frankie to Earl's house, Fannie had the kitchen table extended full length, covered with a freshly scrubbed oilcloth. Emily stared at it in horrified fascination while slowly removing her coat. She lifted her gaze to find Fannie with her hair painfully neat, her apron fresh from the bureau drawer, all starchy peaks and pressed planes, her expression grave and respectful.

"I can do it alone, truly I can, but you'd have to help me carry her down."

"No, Fannie. It'll be easier together. All of it."

They carried Josephine downstairs, sharing an unspoken horror at the indignity suffered by the woman who had lived her life with unfailing decorum—being toted downstairs like some ungainly piece of furniture. If only a band of angels might appear and deposit her with stately grace upon the kitchen table.

But the only angels on duty were Fannie and Emily.

They laid Josephine—ignominiously bent—on the table, and Fannie ordered, "Go around. We must straighten her. Press here and here." But Josephine had died as she'd lived the last few months—sitting up, angled at the hip. Hours had passed, cooling and rigidifying her corpse, rendering the women's attempts at flattening her futile.

"Leave!" ordered Fannie abruptly.

"Leave? But what are you going to do?"

"Leave, I said! Outside, where you can't hear!"

"Hear? But I—"

"Dammit, girl, why do you think this is called the laying out?" Fannie's voice slashed. "Now go! And don't come back until I call!"

It struck Emily what Fannie must do and she blanched, gulped, and ran from the room, out into the sweet clean snow, beneath the great bowl of sun-washed sky, into air pure as dew. Nausea threatened and she doubled forward, braced at the knees, gulping drafts of air. Her stomach keeled and reflex tears spurt into her eyes. *She is breaking my mother's bones!*

She covered her ears as if the brittle sound could reach her through the walls, dropped to her knees in the snow and wept, fledging a part of her youth in a single moment of realization as harsh as any life could mete out. *My mother, who gave me life, who nursed and nurtured me and combed my hair and bathed me and walked me to school and made me eat the foods I disliked. My mother is having her bones broken!*

Soon Fannie approached and gently touched Emily's shoulder. "Come, Emily. The rest won't be so hard." Bolstering the younger woman, the older one walked her inside to the table where the form of Josephine now lay supine, a measure of its dignity restored.

What—if anything—Fannie had used to break the bones remained a mystery, for Emily hadn't the fortitude to ask, nor did Fannie volunteer the information.

They worked together, washing the pale body with its withered skin, then clothing it in Josephine's best black silk dress with a white collar of punched organdy. The dress lay slack upon the shrunken form, so Fannie added padding, inside Josephine's undergarments. At her throat she pinned Josephine's favorite cameo brooch.

Meanwhile, Emily washed the blood from her mother's hair and combed it up in an effort to cover the near-bald spot at the back of her head.

"Her hair was always her pride and joy," Emily recollected sadly.

"How I envied Joey her hair," added Fannie. "On her

wedding day she wore it in a pompadour held up by combs trimmed with pearls. My, it was dramatic."

"You were there, then, the day she married Papa?"

"Oh, yes. Oh my, of course, yes, I was there. They made a handsome couple."

"I've seen their daguerreotype."

"Yes, of course. So you know she had an enviable mane of hair. When we were children we would make clover rings to wear as garlands. The flowers always looked so striking on her black hair and so sickly against mine. So one day your mother had the idea to dye mine dark like hers." Fannie chuckled nostalgically. "Heavenly days, the trouble we got into. I said, 'We can't dye my hair, Joey, what will we use?' And she said, 'Why can't we use the same thing Mother uses to dye cotton?' So we sneaked into her mother's pantry and found the recipe for black dye and got what we needed—some of it I believe we stole."

"My mother—stealing?" Emily's eyes widened in amazement.

Again Fannie chuckled. "Yes, your mother, stealing. Potash and lime, as I remember, from one of our fathers' backyard sheds."

"But she was always so . . . so . . ."

"So obedient?"

"Yes."

"She got into her share of mischief, just like all the rest of us."

Emily found herself transfixed by Fannie's tale, which was revealing a new and unexpected side of the rigidly strict mother she had known all her life. "Tell me about the dye," Emily encouraged as she lit a lantern and began heating curling tongs to tend to her mother's hair.

"Well, we stripped sumac bark and boiled it up with potash and something else—what was it again? Copperas, I think. Yes, copperas. Where we got that I don't remember, but what a vile black liquor it made. And when it was brewed it stank so bad I'm not sure how I ever got up the courage to stick my head into it. As I recall, your mother egged me on when I suggested that perhaps red hair wasn't so bad after all. She said, Did I want to spend my whole life looking like a pink rat, and of course I didn't. So we dyed me black as crape, and fixed the color quite indelibly with lime water. Oh, it was a tremendous success!

"And then our mothers saw it," Fannie ended on an ominous note.

"What happened?"

"As I recall, neither one of us sat down for days, and I spent weeks wearing a bandana tied around my head, pulled clear down to my eyebrows, because we'd not only dyed my hair, but my forehead and ears as well, and I looked as if I was coming down with leprosy!" Fannie shook her head fondly. "Heavens, I'd forgotten all about that."

The reminiscence had served its intended purpose: it had made the two women forget their aversion to the task at hand. While Emily curled Josephine's hair and Fannie buffed her fingernails, they did so as lovingly as handmaidens working over a bride.

"She's very pale," Fannie observed almost as if Josephine were alive. "Do you think she would like it if we put a touch of color on her cheeks?"

Emily studied her mother's still face. "Yes, I think she would."

Fannie opened a quart jar of raspberry sauce and painted Josie's cheeks with the juice. When the stain had set she washed them clean again and said to the dead woman, "There, dear, you look much, much better. I know what store you always set by your appearance." To Emily she added, "Not too curly now. She always detested the frizzed look."

"Only enough to sweep it away from her face like she always wore it."

"Yes, exactly."

When they had combed Josie's hair, when her hands lay manicured at her sides, and her shoes were on and tied and her clothing plump, they stood on either side of the kitchen table, looking down at her with a measure of ease restored to their hearts.

"There, Mother," Emily said quietly. "You look fine."

"Edwin will be pleased, I think."

At the winsome tone of Fannie's voice Emily looked up. She had never taken time to consider how difficult the last half year must have been for Fannie, loving both Mother and Papa as she did. And she *had* loved Mama; this morning had made that indelibly clear. Studying Fannie, she saw not a woman who had loved another's husband, but one who had selflessly eased a family's burdens during the last six months. Fannie was all the things she'd always been: understanding, strong, cheerful, good. She had come into a home weighted with cares and lightened those cares daily, not only by her good deeds, but by her indefatigable spirit. And who had there been to lighten Fannie's spirit when she needed it? Only Papa. And now, Emily herself.

"Mother told me about you and Papa," Emily admitted gently. "She wanted me to know before she died."

Fannie studied Josephine's berry-stained cheeks for a long moment before speaking. "If I could have loved him less, I would have. It was a great cross for her to bear all her life."

"Fannie . . ." Emily swallowed. "Forgive me?"

Fannie looked up. In her eyes was a sadness that ran as deep as her lifelong love for Edwin.

"There is nothing to forgive, dearling. You are their daughter. What were you to think?"

Emily's eyes stung. "I want you to know, Mother's last wish was that you marry Papa and that I give you both my blessing. I intend to."

Fannie made no reply. She studied Emily a long time, and finally reached down to collect the buffer, washcloth, and towel from the tabletop. "We must make a satin pillow for the casket, and prepare the front parlor and make black wreaths and armbands and press our black dresses and . . ."

"Fannie . . ." Emily came around the table and touched Fannie's arm. The two women stared at each other through a blur of tears, then pitched together and clung.

"I don't know what I'd have done without you this morning," Emily whispered. "What any of us would have done without you."

Fannie lifted her eyes to the ceiling as her tears spilled. "Yes, you do. You would have persevered, because you're very much like me."

Edwin came home with Reverend Vasseler to find Fannie and Emily sitting side by side in the kitchen beside Josie, forming roses of black crape: cutting circlets, stretching them over their thumbs, then stitching the tiny petals together to shape the flowers.

Reverend Vasseler stood beside the table, said a prayer for

the departed and another for the living, resting his hands on Emily's and Fannie's heads, offering special condolences to the younger woman, whose wedding was to have been today. Edwin stood transfixed by the sight of his wife all laid out, grateful he had been spared the agony of having to perform undertaking duties. *Fannie, bless you, dear Fannie.* His eyes remained dry and unblinking and he forgot about Reverend Vasseler's presence until the minister spoke softly and touched his arm consolingly. "She's in the Lord's hands now, Edwin, and He is all good."

The day evolved into a series of vignettes: good Christian women coming to help sew black crape roses, to carry away the soiled bedding, to bring custard pies and chocolate cakes and hamburg casseroles; Edwin carrying the copper hip-tub upstairs and emerging after his bath wearing his black Sunday suit on a Thursday; Frankie returning from Earl's to take his turn in the bath; then the women doing the same, Tarsy, arriving owl-eyed and uncharacteristically silent, volunteering to press Emily's black dress, then remaining at her side throughout the afternoon; the family standing motionless while Fannie stitched mourning bands onto their sleeves; the sound of the church bell announcing the death hourly; and late in the day, Charles arriving with a buckboard, bringing a pungent-smelling cedar coffin, as lovingly and meticulously joined as the cupboard he'd made for Tom Jeffcoat.

He entered the kitchen, hat in hand, encountering the ladies still sitting in a circle, within a dozen roses of completing the second impressive black crape wreath, which lay on their laps. Emily glanced up at Charles's long face and laid aside her needle. The ladies murmured, lifting the wreath from Emily's knees so that she might rise and go to him. One of them reached back to squeeze Charles's wrist, offering a low word of consolation. But Charles's eyes remained fixed upon Emily as she rose and left the group with slow-moving dignity.

"Hello, Charles," she said, a subdued stranger in a black tight-necked dress and skinned-back hair parted down the center.

"Emily, I'm so sorry," he offered sincerely.

"Come," she whispered and, without touching him, led the way into the dining room, around the corner from the black-garbed women whose needles continued flashing. In the empty room she faced him.

Sadness lined her face but she stood before him with all other emotion hidden. Reaching down, he scooped her gently against him. A sound came from her throat as her cheek met his jacket—a sob, swallowed; gratitude, unspoken. He felt solid and comforting, and smelled of wood and winter.

"I've brought the coffin," he said against her hair.

She drew back and reached into his eyes with her own. "Thank you for making it, Charles. Papa appreciates it so. So do I."

"It's cedar. It'll last a hundred years."

She wiped her eyes, smiled dolefully, and rested her hands on his arms. "I'm sorry about the wedding, Charles," she told him.

"The wedding—awk, what does that matter?" For her benefit he assumed a note of false bravado. "We can do that any old time."

She experienced a sharp sting of guilt for feeling reprieved when it took such an obvious effort for Charles to mask his deep disappointment. Unable to hide it from her, he dropped his gaze and fiddled with the crease in his black Stetson. He was dressed in proper mourning garb—a black suit and stringtie over a starched white shirt. She stared at his chest while her mind absorbed the fact that the customary period of mourning measured one full year—surely he was aware of that, too.

"Charles," she whispered, covering his wrist, stilling his hands. "I am sorry."

He swallowed thickly, still staring at his hat, then made a visible effort to put secondary concerns aside until a more appropriate time.

"You doing all right, Em?" he asked throatily, as always more concerned for her than for himself.

"Yes. Are you?"

"I was glad to have the coffin to work on, to keep my hands busy today."

With both of her hands she squeezed one of his, then drew a deep breath and squared her shoulders. "And I was glad to have the wreaths."

"Well." Charles lifted his bereaved eyes, fingering the hat crease unnecessarily. "I'd better go find Edwin to help me carry it in. You go sit down, Emily. It's going to be a long night."

And so it was Charles who helped Edwin lay Josepine in the aromatic cedar box, who moved her broken bones for the last time and arranged them on white muslin, and centered her head on the white satin pillow, and handed Edwin her prayer book and waited nearby as Edwin placed it in Josephine's crossed hands. Then, together they carried the coffin to the parlor, placed it in the bay window upon two wooden chairs, and propped the lid on the floor before it.

In the kitchen the ladies formed the last black rose and affixed it to the wreath. Emily respectfully placed it against the coffin lid, then stood in a circle of loved ones, gripping Tarsy's hand on her left and Charles's on her right.

"It's a beautiful coffin, Charles."

It was. And by his making it, and helping Papa lay Mother in it, and standing beside all of them through this difficult ordeal, Charles had endeared himself to the family more than ever.

Chapter 16

THE HARD KITCHEN chairs were arranged in an arc facing the coffin. Sitting on one, Emily experienced some wholly profane thoughts about wakes. What possible good could they do either the loved one or those who kept their all-night vigils over the corpse? Comfort for the living and prayers for the dead, she supposed, though she found herself praying little and comforted less. The townsfolk were kind to come and pay their last respects, but it put a tremendous strain on the family. How many times could one repeat the same trite phrase? Yes, Mother was better off now; yes, she'd lived a good Christian life; yes, she'd been a good woman. But Emily found Fannie's story about the hair dye a more proper elegy than the doleful study of those who came to gaze down into the casket and shed tears.

Guiltily she put such thoughts from her mind, but as she glanced at her brother, the irreverence persisted.

Poor Frankie. He sat dutifully between Papa and Fannie,

squirming on his chair, being touched on the knee and reminded of propriety if he slouched or slipped too far forward or perched on the edge of his seat. Frankie was too young to be here. Why burden him with this depressing memory? Tomorrow's funeral would be enough. He slouched, toyed with a button on his suit for two full minutes, and sighed, slumping back. Fannie touched his knee again and he straightened obediently. Emily caught his eye, mimed a kiss, and felt better.

Her gaze moved on to Papa. Each time she'd looked at him today a knot of tears had formed in her throat and she'd wanted to lunge into his arms and pour out her apologies and tell him about her last talk with Mother. Why was it that the one to whom she most needed to offer an olive branch was the one to whom she had scarcely spoken? There had been people around them all day, lending no chance to speak privately. But that was only an excuse, Emily admitted. It was hardest to go to Papa because she loved him most.

She closed her eyes and prayed for strength and made a silent promise to put things right between herself and her father.

She opened her eyes again and watched Tarsy quietly open the door to admit another friend of the family. What a surprise Tarsy was turning out to be, loyal to a fault, quietly greeting mourners and taking their coats, thanking them for coming. And Charles was equally as helpful, greeting neighbors as if he were already one of the family, drawing up chairs for the older women who wanted to pause longer and pray, making sure the stoves were kept stoked with coal.

Reverend Vasseler began another mournful incantation. Emily attempted devoutness but when she closed her eyes the oak seemed harder, the smell of the black dye in her dress seemed poisonous, and she kept wishing she had a watch.

Dear Lord, make me properly mournful about my mother's death. Make me consider it the loss it truly is instead of the fortuity that saved me from marrying Charles today.

At the end of the prayer she opened her eyes to find Tom Jeffcoat standing just inside the parlor door dressed in his sheepskin jacket, doffing his Stetson, gazing at her. Within Emily, alarm and glory set up opposing forces. The emotion she'd been unable to dredge up for lamentation swelled abundantly at the sight of him.

You came.

I wanted to come as soon as I heard.
You mustn't look at me that way.
Your wedding is canceled.
My wedding is canceled.

Tarsy came forward to greet Tom, whispering a thank-you on behalf of the family, taking his jacket and hat. They spoke together, low, and Tarsy touched his hand before slipping away. Charles formally escorted him through the candlelit room to the front tier of chairs, where Papa was the only one to rise.

"Edwin, I'm so sorry," Tom offered, squeezing Papa's hand protractedly.

"Thank you, Tom. We all are."

"I feel like an outsider here. I didn't know her well."

"Nonsense, Tom, we're all happy you came. Mrs. Walcott was fond of you."

"Don't worry about your horses tomorrow. I'll see to them if you like."

"Why, thank you, Tom. I appreciate that."

"And my rigs are yours for anyone who needs a ride to the graveyard. I'll have them ready to go."

Edwin squeezed Tom's arm.

Tom moved on to Frankie, extending a hand as he would to an adult. "Frankie, I'm awfully sorry about your ma."

"Me too . . . sorta."

"If she's in heaven, you know what they say about heaven." Tom leaned near Frankie, daring a brief note of lightness for the boy's benefit. "You got to keep on behaving or she'll know about it."

"Yessir," Frankie replied respectfully.

Tom's eyes softened as he moved on. "Fannie." He took her hand in both of his and kissed her cheek. "My condolences, Fannie. If there's anything I can do—anything—all you have to do is say so."

"Thank you, Tom."

He straightened and moved to the last family member, standing above her for some seconds before speaking. "And Emily," he said somberly, extending his two hands. She placed hers in them and felt the contact warm a path straight to her heart. His eyes, dark with concern and love, fixed upon hers, bringing a momentary suspension of grief, a delight in the memory of kissing him only a short time ago. Her heart swelled, and she felt healed. *I needed this so badly, just to see your face, to touch you.* The pressure on her knuckles threatened to change their shape. Her mother's admonition came back, granting sanction to the intense feelings she had for him, but Charles and Tarsy looked on so she repressed all outward displays and sat gazing up at him formally.

"Tom," she said quietly, the mere pronunciation of his name easing a deep need to rise into his arms.

"I'm sorry," he whispered fervently, and she understood that he spoke not merely of her mother's death, but of the fact that he could not embrace her as he wished, and that in the days ahead he would force a painful break between herself and Charles, that even her friendship with Tarsy would be threatened. There would be difficult confrontations for both of them. But in that moment as they held hands before Josephine Walcott's coffin, the decision was sealed. As if Josephine's death had been a sign for them, they realized nobody but they could correct the course of their lives, and they would. It was only a matter of waiting for the proper time.

Throughout the night neighbors stayed in shifts, sitting beside whichever family members remained in the parlor while others broke to rest. But little sleep came to Emily during the one- or two-hour respites. When she closed her eyes she saw Papa, hurt and mournful; or Charles, true and trusting; or Tarsy, noble and supportive; or Tom, offering with his eyes what he dared not speak aloud.

By dawn everyone looked haggard and drawn. The last of the neighbors went home, leaving the family members to tiptoe about the silent rooms and dress for the funeral.

At the funeral itself Emily and Tom remained decorous when they met. They encountered one another at the graveyard, across a snowswept knoll separated by most of the residents of Sheridan. He gave her a slight, formal bow, which she returned, but he remained carefully expressionless when, during the dropping of the symbolic spadeful of dirt, she gave way to weeping and Charles bolstered her with a supportive arm.

Back at the house, where mourners gathered for a repast, they bumped into each other in the dining room archway, he with a plate in his hand, she with a guest's coat in hers.

"Tom," she said simply.

His gaze took in the purple shadows beneath her eyes, but he remained properly formal. "Emily."

"Thank you for lending your carriages for the funeral."

"No thanks are necessary, you know that."

"And for taking care of Papa's stock today."

With a finlike motion of his palm he made the help seem of little consequence.

"How are you?" he asked.

"Terrible. Relieved and feeling guilty about it."

"I know the feeling."

"Tom, I have to go, greet people at the door."

"Sure, I understand. Is that someone's coat? I'll take it if you like."

"Oh, thank you. You can put it upstairs on any of the beds."

He took it from her and headed away, but she called, "Tom?"

He turned back to find the doleful expression softened in her eyes. "I love you," she said quietly.

His decorum suffered a near-collapse. His Adam's apple bobbed and his lips dropped open. His eyes widened with a smitten expression as unmistakable as the tinge of pink that painted his cheeks. But he only nodded formally and turned away with the feelings still churning his blood. As he mounted the stairs with a stranger's coat, he pondered 365 days of mourning and damned every one of them.

The house had emptied of all but the family. Dusk had fallen and a pale paring of a moon hovered above the southeast horizon. The parlor was back in order, the dining room neat, the lanterns lit. Footsteps sounded unnaturally loud in the empty house, so nobody moved much. Speaking felt disrespectful so nobody said much. Eating seemed decadent so nobody ate much. The four who had laid their loved one to rest clustered in the kitchen, experiencing a disquieting reluctance to be alone.

Fannie sat in a hard chair, silently reading a book of poems. Frankie sprawled in the rocker, chin to chest, thoughtlessly enlarging a hole in the knee of his everyday pants. Emily spiritlessly shifted a salt shaker back and forth across the tabletop. Edwin stood at the window, staring out with melancholy listlessness. He sighed—a deep, burdened sigh—and reached toward the coat peg for his jacket.

"I think I'll go down to the stable, look in on the horses," he told the others. "I won't be gone long." The door opened and closed, sending a cold puff of winter air into the room.

Emily stared after him.

Fannie raised her eyes from the page. "Why don't you go with him?" she suggested.

The salt shaker tipped over as Emily thrust herself from her chair, grabbed a jacket, and ran into the crisp dusk, calling, "Papa, wait!"

Edwin turned, surprised, and watched her jog down the snowy path toward him. Reaching him, she came up short, closing her throat button, then stuffing her hands into her pockets. "I'll walk with you," she offered quietly. The moment lengthened while they studied each other uncertainly.

"All right," he answered, turning toward town as she joined him. They walked without touching, Edwin studying the horizon, Emily watching her feet. They had mourned together, had hugged and held and consoled one another. But the subject of Fannie remained unsettled between them. How difficult it was to unravel a lifetime's snarls.

At last Emily took Edwin's arm and pressed close against it. Silently, he glanced down at her while they continued walking. Edwin drew a deep, ragged sigh. "Should have a nice clear day tomorrow," he predicted in a conspicuously gruff voice.

"Yes . . ." She looked up, too. "Cold but clear."

Tomorrow's weather was the last thing on their minds. They walked on with arms linked as it used to be.

In time she took the plunge. "Papa?"

"Yes?"

"I think I've grown up a fair bit through all this."

"Yes, I imagine you have. Sometimes growing up can hurt a lot, can't it?"

"Yes, it can."

Any tears that slipped from Edwin's and Emily's eyes did so without the other seeing. They moved on in silence for some time before Edwin remarked as if in summation, "I did love your mother, you know. And I suppose she loved me, too, in her own way. But we had trouble feeling close to one another."

"I know. She told me."

"I assumed she had, that day you came downstairs and offered to help Fannie get supper on the table."

"Yes, that was the day."

"What else did your mother tell you?"

"Everything. About you and Fannie, and how you loved her before you married Mother. And how angry you got when Mother wanted to bring Fannie here." Emily paused before finishing more quietly, "And that I must accept Fannie when you marry her."

Edwin covered Emily's hand on his elbow, and squeezed it with his wide, gloved hand. He fixed his attention on the street ahead while asking, "Would you mind?"

Their gazes met. They stopped walking. "Not at all. I love her, too."

"And would you mind if an old man gives you a hug right here in the middle of Loucks Street?"

"Oh, Papa . . ." They moved as one against each other, Emily seizing his sturdy neck and pressing her cheek against his graying beard. "I love you so much."

Smiling, he crushed her in a powerful hug and kissed her temple. "I love you, too, honey." They rocked from side to side until the brunt of their emotions had passed, then Edwin suggested, "Now what do you say we go poke around that livery barn? There's nothing that makes us feel better than the smell of horses and the feel of hay under our feet."

Renewed, they walked on, arm in arm, through the gathering night.

During the days that followed, the Walcott home took on a sense of disburdening so quick and facile it sometimes left the family members feeling guilty for not missing Josephine more. They wore black armbands but felt less aggrieved than during the months of her suffering. They hung the black crape wreath on the door, but within the house contentment settled. Emily and Fannie penned appreciation notes to all who had sat vigil or brought foods, but the delivery of the notes seemed to signal the end of repining.

The house became tranquil as it had never been during its two years as a hospice. Daytime, it thrived under a routine relieved of the strains imposed by one ailing. At night it was blessedly silent without her coughing, allowing everyone the bliss of uninterrupted sleep. Mealtimes became especially pleasant, with the entire household gathered around the kitchen table, sharing tidbits about their days and exchanging bits of town gossip. Evenings held a sense of leisure with all of them clustered in the kitchen for popcorn, or in the parlor for Parcheesi. Sometimes Fannie would play the piano, and Frankie would lie on the floor, leaning on one elbow, and Emily would hum, and Edwin would doze with his head dropped back against his chair.

Charles was conspicuously absent during this time, for, after the funeral, the first time he had suggested coming over in the evening Emily had used as an excuse the responses she and Fannie had to write. The second time he suggested it she told him she needed some time alone with her family, and that when she was ready to spend more time with him she'd let him know.

Charles looked hurt, but complied.

Two weeks went by, and he stayed his distance. Three weeks passed while she felt underhanded and small for not making a clean break with him. But it seemed untimely to do so before she and Tom had the opportunity to cement their own plans. That opportunity had not arisen because he was keeping his formal distance—that distance dictated by the strict rules of Victorian mourning. The situation was stultifying and—in Emily's mind—silly, but shunning those rules was unheard of.

One night, a month after the funeral, the Walcotts were all gathered in the kitchen when Emily glanced up to find Edwin watching Fannie over the top of his newspaper. Fannie was writing a letter, unaware of Edwin's intense regard. She signed her name, laid down the pen, and glanced up. Heat lightning seemed to flash between the two while Emily observed, feeling like a voyeur. Papa's eyes appeared dark with leashed ardor, while Fannie's became polarized in return. For a full ten seconds their feelings were as readable as the signature Fannie had just penned upon the paper.

Fannie recovered first, dropped her flushed gaze, and slipped the letter into an envelope. Giving her attention to waxing it, she inquired, "Would you like me to see after Joey's personal things, Edwin?"

Edwin cleared his throat and raised the newspaper between them once more. "What had you intended to do with them?"

"Whatever you like. I'm sure there will be keepsakes Emily will want, but the rest we could give to the church. There are always needy people."

"Fine. Give them to the church."

When Fannie turned to discuss the sorting of the clothes with Emily, the younger woman found herself absorbed by the impact of what she'd just witnessed. Why, it was no easier for Papa and Fannie to pretend indifference to one another than it would have been for herself and Tom, had he, too, been sitting across the table. Apparently Mama had been right: Papa and Fannie smoldered with an intense attraction for one another, and the only thing that kept it dampered was the awesome stringency of propriety.

But as long as they observed the rules of mourning, how could Emily herself hope to forgo them?

Emily was one hundred percent correct about her father. Edwin walked around feeling like a volcano ready to erupt, remaining aloof from Fannie by the sheer dint of will. But he gave himself one consolation—since Josephine's death, he had developed the habit of running home for coffee and a sweet at mid-morning, simply to get a glimpse of Fannie. He never stayed more than ten minutes, and he never touched her. But he thought about it. And so did she. In the clean, quiet privacy of the house they shared, where she performed all the duties of a wife, save one, they both thought about it.

On the day following their exchange of glances over the newspaper Edwin indulged himself his ten A.M. Fannie-break.

He entered the kitchen to find it empty. On the sideboard a cake cooled—his favorite: brownstone front. He crossed the room and plucked a raisin from it, marring its smooth top, something he wouldn't have dreamed of doing to one of Josie's cakes. He smiled and filched another one, plus a walnut, warm and flavored of cinnamon and cloves from the cake.

Above, he heard sounds from his bedroom and went upstairs to find Fannie kneeling on the floor before the open chifforobe, folding one of Josie's shirtwaists on her lap. He hadn't made any secret of his arrival, clunking up the stairs as noisily as Frankie might. But when he came to a halt in the bedroom doorway, Fannie refrained from acknowledging his presence. She placed the garment aside and began folding another as he circled the foot of the bed and shuffled to a halt behind her, gazing down at her head.

"There's coffee on the back of the stove," she told him, forbidding herself even a backward glance. "And a brownstone front cake."

"I know. I already sampled it. Thank you."

They had never been alone in this room before. Always, Josie had been in it with them. But Josie was gone now.

Edwin dropped a hand to Fannie's pale hair and idly caressed it. For the space of two heartbeats her hands stopped their task, then sensibly continued.

"Am I expected to wait a whole year before making you my wife?"

"I believe so."

"I'll never make it, Fannie."

She drew an unsteady breath and said what had been on her mind for four weeks. "Which is why I feel it would be best if I leave soon."

He answered by closing his hand around her neck possessively, kneading it, sending shivers down her spine.

"It doesn't look good, Edwin, my staying on."

"Since when have you been concerned about how things look, you who ride bicycles and wear knickerbockers?"

"If it were only for myself I wouldn't be concerned, but you have two children. We must consider them."

"You think they'd be happier if you leave?"

She spun on her knees, knocking his hand aside, and lifted her face in appeal. "You're intentionally distorting my meaning."

"If you think I'm going to let you go, you're crazy, Fannie," he warned vehemently.

"And if you think I'm going to allow any improprieties between us as long as I'm single and living in your house with your children, you're crazy, too!"

"I already have Emily's approval to marry you, and I'm sure Frankie won't mind a bit. You've been as good a mother to him as his own was. Maybe better."

"This is not the time or the place, Edwin."

"I only want to know how long I have to wait."

"A year is customary."

"A year!" He snorted. "Christ."

She considered him with gentle reproof in her gaze. "Edwin, I'm only now packing up Joey's clothes. And I didn't want to repeat the graceless old saying about not letting the body cool, but perhaps you need to hear it today."

He stared at her for five tense seconds, then spun about and clumped from the room with frustration in every footstep.

Fannie was right, of course, but her clinging to gentilities did little to relieve the overburdening sexual suppression Edwin practiced in the days that followed. He gave up the habit of going home for coffee, making sure he was there only when one of the children was also present. He carefully guarded his watchfulness, and kept a proper distance, and to his immense relief Fannie mentioned no more about leaving.

Meanwhile, Emily, too, suppressed her need to see Tom Jeffcoat until the proper time could come for her to make the break with Charles. She had chosen not to tell her family until after the deed was done, so when they asked what had happened to Charles lately, she said he was busy in the evenings building furniture on speculation, stockpiling it for sale to the preempters who'd begin rolling through again in the spring.

During the first two weeks following the funeral she saw Tom only from a distance, across the length of the block dividing their livery stables. The first time they stood and stared. The second time he raised a hand in silent hello and she raised hers back, then they stared again, lovelorn, bound by the same strict rules that held Fannie and Edwin apart.

Not until a full month after the funeral did they bump into each other accidentally. It happened as Emily left Loucks's store with a basket of drygoods she'd picked up for Fanny. Tom was coming in just as she was going out, and they nearly ran each other down on the boardwalk.

He steadied her by both arms—a lingering excuse to touch—while their blood rushed and they stared into one another's eyes with thwarted longing seeming to flush their entire bodies.

Finally releasing her arms, Tom touched his hat brim. "Miss Walcott."

How obvious. He had not called her Miss Walcott since the first week he'd come to town.

"Hello, Tom."

"How are you?"

"Better. Everyone's adjusting at home."

His Adam's apple bobbed like a fishing cork and his voice dropped to a whisper. "Emily . . . oh, God . . . I wish I were." He sounded miserable.

"Is something wrong?"

"Wrong!" He glanced furtively up and down the boardwalk. Though it was empty, he made fists to keep from touching her. "That was a hell of a thing you said to me the day of the funeral. You can't just say a thing like that and walk away."

She felt suddenly buoyed and optimistic, realizing he'd felt as lonely and denied as she. "You did the same thing to me one day on the street. Remember?"

They both remembered, and smiled and basked in each other while they could.

"Charles tells me you haven't been seeing him much."

"I asked him for some time to myself. I've been trying to ease away from him."

"I want to see you. How long do I have to wait?"

"It's only been a month."

"I'm losing my mind."

"So am I."

"Emily, if I—"

"Howdy!" Old Abner Winstad came out of the store just then, stepping between the two without bothering to apologize for interrupting.

"Hello, Mr. Winstad," Emily said.

"Well, give your family my best," Tom improvised, tipping his hat to her before adding, "How're you, Mr. Winstad?"

"Well, to tell the truth, sonny, my lumbago's been acting up lately and I went to see Doc Steele, but I swear that man's got no more compassion than a—"

Abner found himself talking to thin air as Tom headed down the boardwalk, forgetting whatever it was he'd been heading into Loucks's Store for.

Abner scowled after him and groused, "Young whippersnappers . . . got no respect for their elders anymore."

Another two weeks went by during which Emily saw little more than a glimpse of Tom down the street. It was late February and dreary outside, and the snow had turned dirty, and she missed Tom so much she could scarcely bear it. She had decided she'd give herself two more days, and if she hadn't run into him she was going to make a clandestine late-night trip to his house, and the devil pay the consequences!

Who made up these damned rules of mourning anyway?

She applied more oil to her rag and began working it into another piece of harness while Edwin crouched beneath Pinky. He let the forefoot clack to the floor and straightened, announcing, "Pinky's thrown a shoe. Will you take her across the street?"

Emily's heart suddenly burst into quick-time, and she stared at her father's back. Did he know? Or didn't he? Was he intentionally giving them time alone or didn't he realize he'd just answered her prayers? She stared at his crossed suspenders and squelched the urge to press her cheek to his back, slip her arms around his trunk, and cry, "Oh, thank you, Papa, thank you."

Instead, she dropped her oiling rag, wiped her palms on her thighs and replied tepidly, "I suppose."

Turn around, Papa, so I can see your face. But he left Pinky tied in the aisle and moved off toward the next stall without giving his daughter a clue about his suspicions or lack of them.

With her heart racing, Emily plucked an ancient, misshapen wool jacket off a peg and gratefully led Pinky away. Out on the street, walking toward Tom's stable, she became flustered by an uncharacteristic rash of feminine concerns.

I-forgot-to-check-my-hair-I-wish-I-were-wearing-a-dress-I-probably-smell-like-harness-oil!

But she'd run from their own barn thinking of only one thing: getting to Tom Jeffcoat without wasting a solitary second, relieving this immense, insoluble lump of longing that she had carried in her chest day and night since the last time she'd been in his arms.

She led Pinky into Tom's livery stable through the "weather door," a smaller hinged access set within the great rolling door. Inside, she heard his voice and stood listening, entranced by each inflection and tone merely because it came from him. Little matter that he spoke in the distance, to a stranger, about fire insurance. The voice with its own distinctive lilt and lyricism was his, unlike any other, to be savored just as she savored each glimpse of him, each precious stolen touch.

She closed the weather door and waited with anticipation pushing against her throat. He appeared in the office doorway and she experienced the giddy joy of watching pleasant surprise flatten his face and color his cheeks.

"Emily . . . hello!"

"Pinky needs a reshoe. Papa sent me." She saw him bank his urge to come to her, saw him tense with impatience over the unconcluded business still waiting in his office. "Take her down to the other end. I'll be there in a minute."

She felt as if she had stepped into someone else's body, for the sensations aroused by him were foreign to her. There was impatience, welling high, counteracted by as great a sense of unrush now that she was here in this realm, where everything around her was his, had been built and touched and tended by him. *Take your time coming back to me. Let me bask in the knowledge that you will. Let me steep in this place that is yours, where you have slept and labored and thought of me.*

She walked Pinky to the smithy at the far end of the barn, tethered her outside the door, then wandered inside where it was warm and smelled of hot metal and charcoal and—was she only imagining it?—the sweat of Tom Jeffcoat. She unbuttoned her heavy jacket and stuffed her gloves into the pockets, wandered past his tool table, touched the worn, smooth handles of hammers that had collected the oils from his hands and maybe those from his father's and grandfather's hands as well. Wood . . . only wood . . . but precious and coveted for having been closer to him than she. She stroked the anvil, scarred at the blunt end and worn brilliant as a silver bullet at its point; beside it he had stood as a boy, watching his grandfather at work. Upon it he had learned as a man. Steel . . . only steel . . . but the anvil seemed as much a part of him as his own muscle and bone.

Pinky nickered at being left on a short line and Emily sauntered back to her, glancing down the corridor to where Tom and the salesman now stood near the weather door, exchanging final comments.

"Maybe in the spring then, Mr. Barstow, after the first cattle drive comes through and the homesteaders start showing up again."

"Very good, Mr. Jeffcoat, I'll pay you a call then. In the meantime, if you want to reach me you can write to the address I gave you in Cheyenne." The two men shook hands. "You've got a mighty nice setup here. Well, I'd better let you get back to your customer."

"Appreciate your stopping, Mr. Barstow." Tom opened the door and saw the man out.

When the door closed he turned to find Emily watching him from the opposite end of the corridor. For moments neither of them moved, but stood transfixed by one another, marking time to the beat of their own leaping hearts, experiencing the same ebb and rush of protracted yearning that she had felt earlier. He started moving toward her, slowly at first . . . and disciplined. But he hadn't taken four steps before she was moving, too, with much less discipline than he, striding long and purposeful.

Then they were running.

Then kissing, wrapped together openmouthed and urgent after weeks of deprivation, feeling one agony end while another began. They kissed as if starved—deep, engulfing, whole-mouthed kisses that knew no limit of possession.

Tearing his mouth from hers Tom demanded breathlessly, "Tell me now . . . tell me again."

"I love you."

He held her head, smattered her with hard, impatient, celebratory kisses. "You really do. Oh, Emily, you really do!" He clutched her possessively, swiveling them both in a circle, dropping his head over her shoulder. "I missed you. I love you . . ." And realizing his tardiness in saying so, chastised himself, "Oh, damn me, I should have said that first. *I love you*. It's been the longest six weeks of my life." Again they kissed, futilely trying to make up for lost time—wet, wide kisses during which they caressed each other's backs, ribs, waists, shoulders.

"Just stand still for a minute," he breathed, clasping her near, ". . . and let me feel you . . . just feel you."

They pressed together like leaves of a book left out in the rain, with Tom's aroused body pocketed against her stomach, both of them shaken and wanting so much more than allowed.

"You feel so good," she whispered. "I think about you all the time. I imagine being close to you like this."

"I think about you, too. Sometimes during the day I stand and stare out the window at your dad's livery stable, at the office window, and I know you're in there studying, and it's all I can do to keep from marching up there and hauling you back here."

"I know. I do the same thing. I stand in the window and read the sign above your door and tell myself it won't be long. It won't be long. But it is. The days never seem to end. When I bumped into you in front of Loucks's store it was terrible. I wanted to follow you back here so badly."

"You should have."

"Afterwards I went home and curled up on my bed and stared at the wall."

He chuckled—a sound rife with suppressed desires. "I'm glad."

"It scares me sometimes. I never used to be this way but

lately I grow listless and I can't seem to concentrate on anything and I miss you so much I actually feel sick."

"Me, too. Sometimes I find myself banging away on a piece of iron that's too cool to shape."

They laughed tightly, falling silent at the same moment, overwhelmed to learn that they'd suffered the same agonies. They hugged again, straining together, rocking from side to side while his hands stroked her ribs, narrowly avoiding her breasts. With her upraised arms overlapped upon his shoulders she waited breathlessly for the touch she had no intention of fighting.

Please, she thought, *touch me just once. Give me something to survive on.*

And as if he heard, he found her breasts, but finding them, realized they stood in the main corridor where anyone might enter and discover them.

"Come here . . ." he whispered, and hastily drew her through the smithy door into the warm, shadowed room where he backed her against a rough wood beam. Slipping his hands inside her coat, he captured her breasts straightaway, cupping and caressing them, pushing her suspenders aside, dropping his open mouth over her uplifted one. From her throat came a muffled sound of accession as she rested her arms upon his shoulders.

"Em . . ." he breathed against her face as the kiss ended.

She'd brook no endings, but picked up where he left off, keeping his mouth, and curling her hands over his upon her breasts when they would have slipped away. He emitted a muffled groan and dipped at the knees, matching their hips, marking her with a controlled ascent that drove her against her leaning post. His caresses became reckless, splendid, rhythmic.

When the effort of breathing seemed to crush his chest, he reluctantly dropped his hands to her waist and his forehead against the post. Resting lightly against each other, they regrouped. For moments their minds emptied of all but the welcome truth—they loved with equal passion; it had not been imagined or embroidered during their weeks apart into something it wasn't. What they had felt then, they felt now, mutually and intensely.

"Em?" The name came out muffled against her shoulder.

"What, Thomas?"

"Please marry me."

She closed her eyes and whispered simply, "Yes."

He reared back. Even in the dimness she saw the grand shock possess his face. "Really? You mean it?"

"Of course I mean it. I really have no choice in the matter." She hugged him rapturously, taking a moment to envision herself as his wife, in his bed, at his table, in this livery barn with a half dozen black-haired stairsteps fighting over who was going to hand Daddy the next horseshoe nail. It surprised her not in the least to be imagining herself with his children after purporting to be in no hurry to have them. She savored the image, breathing the scent of his neck while her breasts lifted against him. "Oh, Thomas, this is how it should be, isn't it? It's what my mother meant."

He leaned back to search her face. In the meager light from the forge her eyes appeared as black jets.

"I have so much to tell you," she said. "Could we sit down? Close, where we can hold hands, but not this close. I can't think too clearly when you're touching me this way."

They sat side by side on a pair of short nail kegs, their fingers linked on his left knee. When they were settled Emily began in an evenly modulated voice.

"The day before my mother died she enjoyed a remarkable spurt of vigor. She felt strong and could breathe well, so she talked a lot. We all took it as a good sign, and we were so happy. Papa even carried Mother down to the supper table, and she hadn't been strong enough to sit through a meal for months. I've thought about it often since, how we all thought it meant a real turnaround, but it ended up being quite the opposite. It seems almost as if she was fortified for a very good reason—to tell me the truth about herself and Papa and Fannie."

Staring at their joined hands, Emily told Tom the entire story. He sat quietly, moving only his thumb across the creases in her palm. Minutes later she finished, ". . . and so I'm reasonably certain Papa and Fannie intend to get married as soon as it's decent. But Mama wouldn't have had to tell me, would she? She could have let me go on believing that her marriage to Papa was all a bed of roses. When she died it seemed—this is hard to say because sometimes it sounds absurd even to me—but it seemed as if her death was deliberately timed to prevent my marrying the wrong man."

They stared at their hands, thinking of Charles. When their eyes met their gazes held underlying regret for having to hurt him.

"If I could only be taking you away from somebody beside Charles. Why does it have to be him?"

"I don't know." She pictured Charles and added, "If he were unscrupulous or unlikable this would be so much easier, wouldn't it?"

"Emily?" Their gazes remained rapt. "We have to tell him. Now . . . today. We can't sneak around behind his back anymore."

"I know. I knew it at the wake when you came and took my hands."

"Would you like me to tell him?" Tom asked.

"I feel like I should."

"Funny . . . I feel the same way." They thought about it for a moment before he suggested, "We could tell him together."

"Either way, it won't be any easier . . . for him or for us."

Abruptly Tom dropped her hand and covered his face, heaving a deep sigh into his palms. For minutes he sat thus, knees cemented to elbows, the picture of gloom. She felt dejected for him, wishing she could ease his sense of traitorousness, yet it was no greater than her own. Her eyes stung and she touched his forearm, fanning a thumb over the coarse black hair that reached well past his wrist onto the back of his hand.

"I didn't think love was supposed to hurt this much," she ventured at length.

He laughed once, mirthlessly, scrubbed both hands down his cheeks, then flattened his lower lip with two fists, staring at his anvil. Minutes passed, bringing no solution to the anguish both felt.

"You want to know something ironic," he mused at length. "While you've been keeping him away, he's been spending more time with me. Every night I've been listening to him wail about how much he loves you and how he's losing you, but he doesn't understand why. Christ, it's been torture. I was on the verge of telling him so many times."

She searched her mind for consolation and found only one. "But Thomas," she told him honestly, "I've never loved him the way I love you. It would have been wrong to marry him."

"Yeah," he mumbled, only half-convinced, and they sat silently until their backsides began feeling the raised rims of the nail kegs.

Finally Emily sighed and pushed to her feet. "I should go so you can shoe Pinky. Papa is probably wondering where I am."

Tom withdrew from his moroseness and stretched to his feet. "I'm sorry I got so moody. It's just hard, that's all."

"If you took it lightly, I wouldn't love you as much, would I?"

He wrapped both arms loosely around her shoulders and rocked her from side to side. "This might very well be one of the hardest things we'll ever do, but afterwards we'll feel better." He stopped rocking and asked, "Together then? Tonight?"

She nodded against his chin.

"Emily?"

"What?"

"Could I pick you up at your house?"

Her stillness warned him that she'd guarded their secret well. Again he drew back to search her face. "There's been enough cat and mouse. If we're going to do this, let's do it right. Your father was honest with you, isn't it time you're honest with him?"

"You're right. Seven o'clock?"

"I'll be there."

Chapter 17

HOW DOES A woman dress for the breaking of her engagement? In her bedroom that evening, with the lamp at her elbow, Emily studied her reflection in the mirror. She saw a worried face framed by coal-black hair, troubled sapphire eyes, a frowning mouth, and a scoop of bare throat above a white shift. She had little choice of dress—not for a full year—yet mourning garb seemed appropriate for tonight's mission.

The dress was plain, trim above, full below, constructed of unadorned black muslin. As she buttoned it up the front she saw her body shape it, rounded here, concave there, until the high cleric collar drew the last inch tight and she studied herself as a woman. She had rarely thought of herself in the feminine sense, but since she'd fallen in love with Tom she saw herself through his eyes—thin, trim, not unpleasantly curved. She touched her hips, her breasts, closing her eyes, recalling the swell of feelings aroused by Tom. A year . . . dear Lord, a year . . .

Guiltily she opened her eyes, plucked up a brush, and began punishing her hair, currying it mercilessly before winding it up in a severe figure eight and ramming the celluloid pins against her scalp.

There. I look like a woman filled with remorse for what I have to do.

But minutes later she felt more like an anxious schoolgirl as she waited in the dark at the top of the stairs for the sound of Tom Jeffcoat's knock. From the parlor below, beyond her range of vision, she heard Fannie playing the piano while Papa, she knew, read his newspaper. Earl had come over tonight; he and Frankie more than likely lay on their bellies on the floor, building card houses.

When a knock sounded Frankie exclaimed, "I'll get it! Maybe it's Charles!" He shot across Emily's range of view while she clattered downstairs in an effort to cut him off.

"I'll get it!"

"But it might be Charles!"

"I *said* . . ." She skidded to a halt in the entry and forced his hand off the knob. ". . . *I'll get it, Frank!*"

He backed off, looking maligned. "Well, get it then. What're you standin' there for?"

"I will," she whispered through clamped teeth. "Go back to your cards." Instead, he sat down on the second step to be a thorn in her side. Peering through the lace curtains she saw the outline of Tom's shoulders and felt a twinge of desperation. Fannie stopped playing the piano. Papa's paper rustled as he lowered it to his knee, waiting to see who appeared around the stub wall. Earl was probably gawking, too, and he'd certainly spread the news as soon as he got home.

"Well, for pity's sake," Edwin called exasperatedly, "will one of you open the door!"

"Open the door, Emileeee," her little brother repeated in a sing-song.

She drew a fortifying breath and did the honors.

"Hello, Emily."

He looked incredible! Ruggedly attractive in his sheepskin jacket, with cheeks freshly shaved and ruddy from the cold, hat in hand, and hair flopping attractively over his forehead. Emily stared, tongue-tied.

"Emily, who is it?" Papa called from the parlor.

He stepped inside, closing the door. "It's Tom, sir."

"Tom!" Dropping his paper, Edwin hustled to the foyer, followed by Fannie. "Well, this is a surprise." He reached for Tom's hand, inviting enthusiastically, "Come in! Come in!"

"Thank you, Edwin, but I've come to take Emily out."

Nonplussed, Edwin glanced between the two. "Emily?" he repeated disbelievingly. Fannie smiled vacuously. Frankie thumped from one step to the next on his butt. Five full seconds passed in utter silence, then from the parlor Earl complained, "Aw shucks, the wind knocked my cards down!"

Fannie recovered first. "Well . . . that's nice. Are you going for a walk?"

"Yes, to Charles's," Emily replied hastily.

"Oh, to Charles's." Edwin looked relieved. "We haven't seen him around for a couple weeks. Tell him hello."

"Can I come along?" Frankie asked, popping off the step.

"Not tonight," Emily answered.

"Why not? There's no school tomorrow and Charles says—"

"Frank Allen!" Emily demanded. "Enough!"

"Tom doesn't care, do you Tom?" The boy appropriated Tom's wrist and suspended himself from it. "Tell her I can go, pleeeease?"

"Afraid not, Frankie. Maybe some other time."

"Aw, jeez," he mumbled and clunked to the parlor to fling himself down petulantly.

Fannie advised, "It's a chilly night, Emily, be sure to wear a scarf."

Emily caught her coat from the hall tree and began stuffing her arms into it, unaided, but Tom stepped behind and held it while the others watched and assessed his gallantry with undisguised fascination.

"We shouldn't be gone more than an hour or so," Tom remarked, opening the door for Emily.

She flashed Edwin and Fannie a tight smile. "Good night, everyone."

"Good night," Fannie responded.

Edwin said nothing.

The porch steps might have led down from a gallows as Tom and Emily descended them with their gazes trained straight ahead. Not until they reached the street did Tom release the tension from his shoulders.

"Whew!"

"Fannie knows."

"You mean you've told her?"

"No, she's guessed, I can tell. She guessed that I had a yen for you from the first week you came to town."

"Oh, really?" His voice held a teasing note. He glanced back over his shoulder, gauging their distance from the house, and took her hand. "This is news."

She turned a spare grin his way to find a similar one aimed at her. They walked in silence, fingers linked, enjoying the momentary lift of spirits.

Eventually he asked, "What about your father?"

"I think he's putting off admitting what's right before his eyes."

"I thought it would be best to get this thing over with, with Charles first, before we told him."

"I agree. Charles deserves to be the first one who knows, and until he does, I can't draw an easy breath."

On Charles's porch they no longer held hands. They no longer teased. They avoided glancing at each other. "Everything's dark. It doesn't look like he's home." Tom knocked, then backed off to stand a proper distance from Emily.

They waited. And waited.

Tom glanced briefly at Emily, then knocked again, but still no answer came. The windows remained dark.

"Where could he be?" Emily raised distraught eyes to Tom.

"I don't know. What should we do, try to find him?"

"What do you want to do?"

"I want this over with. Let's go see if we can dig him up." He tugged her hand and they set off toward town. Loucks was closed up for the night. The saloons were open so Tom went into the first alone—women wearing mourning bands wouldn't dream of entering a saloon—leaving Emily to wait on the boardwalk. Inside the Mint he drew a drunken slur from Walter Pinnick, an invitation to a poker game from a trio of Circle T ranch hands, and a suggestive glance from a powdered whore named Nadine. He ignored them all and questioned the bartender, came out a minute later, reporting to Emily, "He's been here but he left and said he was going to my place."

"But we passed your place and he wasn't there."

"Do you suppose he went to the livery after he found out I wasn't home?"

"I don't know. We can try."

They ran Charles to ground midway between Walcott's and Jeffcoat's Livery Stables, where he'd obviously been searching for Tom. From twenty yards away he spied them and waved, hurrying toward them.

"Hello, Emily! Hey, Tom, where have you been? I've been looking all over for you!"

Tom called, "We've been looking for you, too."

They met in the middle of Grinnell Street, shifting their feet for warmth, sending puffs of white breath into the air as they spoke.

"Oh yeah? Something up for tonight? Lord, I hope so. This town dies after six o'clock. I went down to the Mint and had a beer, but there's only so much of that a man can stand, so I came looking for you." He appropriated Emily's arm. "I didn't expect to find you, too, what with the mourning and all." He dropped his eyes to her coat sleeve, still with its broad black band sewed in place, while she averted her gaze to the rutted street.

"We'd like to talk to you, Charles," Tom said.

"Talk? Well, talk away."

"Not here. Inside. Why don't we go down to my stable?"

For the first time Charles grew wary, flashing assessing glances from Tom to Emily, who carefully avoided all eye contact. "About what?" He fixed a questioning gaze on Emily but she dropped her eyes guiltily.

"Come on, let's get out of the cold," Tom suggested sensibly.

Charles spent another worried glance on his two best friends, then forcibly lightened his attitude. "Sure . . . let's go."

They walked the frozen street three abreast, with Emily between the two men and not an elbow touching. Tom opened the weather door and led the way into the dark barn. Inside, they stood in dense blackness surrounded by the smell of horses until Tom found and struck a match, and reached overhead for a coal-oil lantern. Squatting, he set it on the concrete floor. Watched by the other two, he opened its door with a metallic *tink*, lit the wick, rose, and replaced the lantern on the nail overhead. During the process the tension in the barn multiplied tenfold.

The lantern shed an eerie light on Tom's unsmiling face as he dropped his arm and confronted Charles. The sheer somberness of his expression lent additional gravity to the scene. For moments he remained silent, as if searching for the proper words.

"So what is it?" Charles demanded, glancing from Tom to Emily and back again.

"It's not good," Tom replied honestly.

"And it's not easy," Emily added.

Charles snapped his regard to her, suddenly angry, as if he already knew. "Well, whatever it is, say it!"

A spur of dread gripped her, shutting her throat. Dry-eyed, she stared at him and began, "Charles, we've been friends for so long that I don't know how to begin or how to—"

Tom interrupted. "This is the hardest thing I've ever had to say in my life, Charles. You're a true friend and you deserve better."

"Better than what?" Charles remained silent, stiff-faced, waiting.

"Neither one of us wanted to hurt you, Charles, but we can't put off telling you the truth any longer. Emily and I have fallen in love."

"Son-of-a-*bitch*!" Charles' reaction was immediate and forceful. His fists bunched. "I knew that was it! One look at your faces and a blind man could see you're both guilty as hell!"

"Charles." Emily reached for his arm. "We tried not to—"

"Don't touch me!" He twisted sharply, elbowing free. "Don't, by God, touch me!"

"But I want to explain how—"

"Explain to somebody else! I don't want to hear it!"

Tom tried to reach out. "Give her a chance to—"

"You!" Charles lunged and slammed Tom in the chest, sending him quickstepping backward. "You sonofabitch!" The attack was so unexpected it temporarily stunned Tom. "You underhanded, sneaking sonofabitch!"

Recovering, Tom cajoled, "Come on, Charles, we don't want to make this any hard-*ergh!"* A second shove ended the word on a grunt and set Tom back another step.

"My *friend*!" Charles sneered, pushing Tom again, just hard enough to force him backward. "My two-timing, back-stabbing, double-crossing sonofabitch friend!"

Tom went lax, letting himself be manhandled. "All right, get it off your chest."

"Y' goddamn right I will, you sneaky bastard! And you're gonna be mighty sorry when it's over!"

Tom let himself be thumped again, and again, arms hanging loose, until his shoulders struck a buckboard on the turntable and his hat tipped askew. He reached up slowly to right it, then took a spraddled stance and raised his palms. "I don't want to fight you, Charles."

"Well, you're going to, and it's not gonna be pretty! If you think I'm going to let you steal my woman and walk away untouched, you're wrong, Jeffcoat! Not after I had a claim on her since I was thirteen years old!"

Horrified, Emily came out of her stupor. "Stop this, Charles!" She grabbed Charles's arm. "I won't let you fight!"

"Back off!" With a thrust of his elbow he tossed her aside, then glared at her. "You wanted to play Jezebel and pit one friend against another, well, fine, now you can just stand there and watch the results! You're going to see some blood before this is over so you better take a last look at his pretty face before I mess it up!"

Pivoting unexpectedly, Charles threw his full weight into a violent punch that snapped Tom's head back and cracked his shoulders against the buckboard. His hat flew. He grunted and doubled over, holding his belly.

Emily screamed and came at Charles with both hands. She dragged him back no more than two feet before he swung and pinned her arms at her sides, slamming her against a stall door with enough force to clack her teeth together. "Keep off or by God, I'll lay one on you, too, woman or not! And believe me it wouldn't take much right now, the way I feel!"

Incensed, Tom came at Charles from behind. He spun him, gripping his coat front, raising him to tiptoe. "You try it and it'll be the last move you ever make, Bliss! All right, you want to fight . . . you think it'll settle anything . . ." He backed off, crouched, beckoning with eight fingers. "Come on . . . let's get it over with!"

This time when Charles lunged, Tom was prepared. He took a shoulder in the chest, but dug in and braced, throwing Charles upright and catching him beneath the chin with both forearms, following with an immediate left to Charles's jaw. The crack sounded like a rake handle breaking. Charles landed on his ass on the concrete and sat for a moment, stunned.

"Come on," Tom challenged again, his face pinched with intensity, "You want a fight, you've got it!"

Charles rose slowly, grinning, wiping his bloody lip with a knuckle. "Hoo-ey!" he goaded, centering his weight in a crouch. "So he's in love." His face turned hard. His voice became threatening. "Come on, bastard, I'll show you what I think of your—"

A solid right shut Charles up and bounced him off the buckboard. Rebounding, he threw his momentum into a volley that dented Tom three times below the waist. Before Tom could straighten, Charles caught him by the throat, forcing him backward across the corridor until they crashed into a stall door. Inside a bay gelding whinnied and danced, rolling his eyes. Emily leapt to life, screamed, and attacked from the rear, pulling at Charles's jacket collar while he gripped Tom's windpipe. She hung on until the neck opening wedged above Charles's Adam's apple and cut off his own air supply.

"How long, Jeffcoat?" Charles demanded in a raspy, constricted voice. "How long have you been after my woman? I'll make you pay for every goddamned day!"

"Charles, stop it! You're choking him!" Emily drew rein on Charles's collar but a button popped off, dropping her to her rump. Shooting up, she collared Charles again, this time with an arm, leaping like a monkey onto his back.

"Get off me and let us fight!" With a flying elbow Charles knocked her off and she stumbled backward, cradling one breast, wincing with pain.

"You sonofabitch, you hurt Emily!" Tom roared, enraged. The rage felt wonderful! Hot and healing and revitalizing! His knee came up and thrust Charles off, sent him pedaling backward, followed by Tom, who propelled himself through the air with an intensity outdistancing any he'd ever known. Two well-aimed clouts knocked Charles to his back, but he was up in a split second, and Tom took as good as he gave. Both men were powerful, with chests like drafthorses, forearms thick as battering rams—a blacksmith and a carpenter, conditioned by years of swinging weighty hammers. Augmented by sudden enmity, their strength became immense. When they set out to punish, they did.

Flatfooted, they bare-knuckled one another—faces, stomachs, shoulders—exchanging a flurry of punishing blows and grunts that carried them from one side of the stable aisle to the other. Against a stall door, onto the floor, then up, riding the splintery wood with their shoulderblades, accidentally opening the latch, further adding to the confusion as the horse inside whinnied and pawed in terror. Neither man heard. When Tom upended Charles with a punishing uppercut, Charles picked himself up and returned the favor.

In minutes their faces bled. The skin on their knuckles split. Still they fought, growing weaker with each punch.

A dying blow caught Charles and sent him stumbling backward, tripping over a buckboard trace. He plopped onto the turntable, setting it in motion, carrying him several feet away from Tom, who followed unsteadily, weaving on his feet. Panting, the two rested for ten seconds before obliging one another again, this time on the floor, rolling, too close for effective swings.

Still they tried, cursing, clouting each other with ineffectual close-range shots until they struck the far wall, where they lay in a tangle of arms and legs. Nose to nose, they panted, gripping each other's jacket fronts.

Charles scarcely had the breath to speak. Still, he taunted brokenly, "How far . . . did you . . . go with her, huh, f—friend?"

Tom was in no better shape. "You got a d—dirty mind, B—Bliss!"

Dizzy and stumbling, Tom struggled to his feet, hauling Charles with him. He pulled back for another swing but inertia nearly tumbled him backwards. Charles was equally as sapped. He reeled onto his heels with his fists clenched weakly. "Come on . . . you bastard . . . I'm not through!"

Tom faced off, quarter-bent, swaying, his arms hanging like bell clappers. "Yes you are . . . I'm m—marrying her," he managed between strident breaths. Talking hurt nearly as much as slugging. Still they hung before one another, close to exhaustion.

"You wanna . . . call it quits?" Tom got out, wobbling on his feet.

"Not by a . . . damn sight."

"Awright then . . ." He hadn't the strength to throw a punch, but came at Charles with his entire body. Backwards they went, stumbling into the opened stall, against the withers of the frightened bay gelding, smashing him against the stable wall as they fell in a loose tangle of diminished force.

On her knees near the turntable Emily wept, covering her mouth with both hands, afraid to interfere again.

"Please . . . please . . ." she prayed behind cold fingers, hunkered forward over her knees.

The men crashed out of the stall, falling apart, swaying on their feet, sidestepping like drunks, trying to focus through swollen eyes. Their jackets looked as though they'd been worn in a slaughterhouse.

"You . . . had . . . enough?" Tom managed through battered lips.

"So . . . help . . . me . . . God . . ." Charles never finished. He collapsed to his knees, buckling at the waist.

Tom followed suit, falling forward onto all fours, his head dangling as if connected to his body by a mere string. For seconds the stable was filled with the sound of their harsh breathing. Then came Tom's voice, pitiful with emotion, very near tears.

"G—Goddamn you . . . why'd you hafta . . . b—bring her to my h—house for that shivaree?"

Charles wobbled on his knees, barely upright. He tried to point a bloody finger at his foe but his arm kept falling. "You k—kissed her in that g—goddamn cl—closet . . . didn't you!"

Winded, Tom nodded, unable to lift his head.

Charles fell off his knees with a loose-jointed thump, dropping to his side and catching himself on an elbow.

"What a s—sucker I was, b—building you furniture . . ."

"Yeah . . . stupid sonofabitch . . . I'm gonna . . . take an axe . . . and b—bust that thing . . . to smithereens . . ."

"Do it! . . . g'wan . . . do it . . ." Charles let his head flop back against his shoulder. "I don't give a d—damn."

Emily stared at them, dumbfounded, crying, with her hands clapped to her mouth.

Still on all fours with his head hanging, Tom spoke as if to the floor. "I didn't mean . . . to fall in . . . love with 'er, man . . ."

The two men breathed like engines running out of steam, their enmity gone as suddenly as it had appeared, both of them pitiable now as truth came to take its place between them. After a full thirty seconds Charles collapsed onto his back, eyes closed. He groaned. "Christ, I hurt . . ." His right knee, upraised, undulated from side to side.

"I think . . . my ribs're broke." Tom remained on all fours, his forehead hanging inches above the floor, as if unable to rise.

"Good. So's my . . . goddamn heart."

On hands and knees, Tom crawled painfully across the aisle until he knelt above Charles and peered down blearily into his friend's face. There he hung, with the breath catching in his throat, until he finally whispered gutturally, "I'm sorry, man."

Charles closed his fingers over a puny lump of hay and flung it at Tom's face, missing. His hand dropped to the concrete, palm-up.

"Yeah, well, go to hell, you bastard." He lay exhausted, eyes closed.

Emily watched their breakdown through a blur of tears. In her many years of friendship with Charles, Emily had never heard him curse so much, nor had she ever seen him strike a soul. Neither had she suspected Tom would engage in violence. She had witnessed the past five minutes with horror and fear and a heart that broke for both of them. It was obvious their real pain was not that inflicted by fists. Those wounds would heal.

But now that it was over her stomach trembled and reason rushed in, bringing with it justifiable anger. How horrible that two human beings would hurt each other so.

"You're both crazy," she whispered, wide-eyed. "What good did this do?"

"Tell 'er, Jeffcoat."

"I would, but I dunno. I feel like a chunk of beef that's been put through the meat grinder . . . both ways." Tom sucked in his belly and tested it tenderly with one limp hand.

"Good."

"I think I have to puke."

"Good."

Still staring at the floor, Tom spit out a mouthful of blood and the nausea passed. "Ohhh, gawwwwwd!" he groaned, settling back gingerly onto his heels. "Oh, holy . . . jumpin' . . . Judas." He closed his eyes and cradled his ribs with an arm.

Charles opened his eyes and rolled his head. "They broke?"

The pain became so intense that Tom could only shake his head and mouth the words, *I don't know.*

"Emily?" Charles said thickly, the word distorted by his bruised lips as he blearily searched for her.

She sat above and behind him. "What?"

He skewed his head and peered at her backwards. "Maybe you better go get the doc. I think I busted his ribs."

Instead, she sat where she was, appalled by what they'd done to one another. "Oh, look at your faces, you fools, just look at them," she cried plaintively.

They did. Surprised by her vehemence, Tom and Charles took a good look at the carnage they had reaped and it mellowed them further. Emily's outburst seemed to snap belated common sense back into both men's heads and make them realize they'd fought first without discussing anything—just slammed each other with fists, as if that would fix everything. But it wouldn't. They'd have to talk, and as they rested on the bricks, emotionally as well as physically exhausted, the realization came slowly, bringing with it a pathos magnified by Charles's first question.

"All right . . . so how did it happen?"

Tom shook his head, studying his soiled knees despondently. "Hell, I don't know. How did it happen, Emily? Working with the horses together, playing those stupid damn parlor games, I don't know. How does it ever happen? It just does, that's all."

"Emily, is he telling it straight? Did you tell him you'd marry him already?"

"Yes, Charles," she replied, studying the top of Charles's head as he remained on his back on the floor.

"He's an asshole, you know." Charles's voice held a trembling note of affection. "You want to marry an asshole who'd steal his best friend's fiancée?"

She swallowed and felt tears forming afresh, watching the two men stare at one another.

Tom's voice softened and became as emotional as his friend's. "I wish it could've been another woman. I tried Tarsy. I wish to hell it could have been Tarsy. But she was like . . . like too much divinity . . . you know what I mean?" His voice dropped to a near-whisper. "I tried, Charles, but it just didn't work." After a long pause he touched Charles on the hand. "I'm sorry," he whispered.

Charles shook him off and flung an arm over his eyes. "Aw, get out of here. Go on, get out of here and take her with you!" Horrified, Emily watched Charles's Adam's apple bob and realized that beneath his bloody jacket sleeve he was battling tears.

She struggled to her feet, her skirt wrinkled and strewn with straw.

"Come on, Tom . . ." She took his arm. "See if you can get up."

He drew his sad eyes away from Charles and straightened like an arthritic old man, accepting her aid. He hobbled as far as the open stall door and clung to it for support. When he'd caught his breath he remembered.

"You all right, Em?"

"Yes."

"But you caught an elbow, I saw it."

"I'm not hurt. Come on," she whispered. "I think Charles is right. I think we ought to find Doc Steele and have him take a look at you."

"Doc Steele is a quack, and cranky to boot. Everybody says so."

"But he's the only doctor we have."

"I don't need any doctor." Walking half the length of the barn proved too much for Tom, however.

"Stop," he pleaded, slamming his eyes shut. "Maybe you're right. Maybe you'd better go get Doc and bring him back here. That way he can check both of us."

She lowered Tom where he stood, and left him sitting propped against a wooden half door on the cold brick floor.

Three minutes later, when she beat on the front door of Doc Steele's house, Hilda Steele answered, wrapped in a robe with her hair in a frowsy braid.

"Yes?"

"It's Emily Walcott, Mrs. Steele. Is the doctor here?"

"No, he's not. He's out on circuit till the end of the week."

"Till the end of the week?"

"What is it? Is it something serious?"

"Would you . . . I . . . no . . . I'm not sure . . . I'll get my father."

She ran home instinctively, her mind empty of all but worry for Tom and Charles. When she burst in the front door Edwin and Fannie were seated side by side on a sofa. Earl had gone home and Frankie was nowhere in sight.

"Papa, I need your help!" Emily announced, wild-eyed and breathless from running.

"What's wrong?" He met her halfway across the parlor, taking her icy bare hands.

"It's Tom and Charles. They've had a fight and I think Tom has some broken ribs. I'm not sure about Charles. He's lying flat on his back at Tom's livery stable."

"Unconscious?"

"No. But his face is a mess and I can't move either one of them. I left them there and ran to get Doc Steele but he's gone somewhere and Tom can't walk and . . . oh, please, help me, Papa. I don't know what to do." Her face crumpled. "I'm so scared."

"Fannie, get my jacket!" Edwin sat down and began pulling on his boots. Fannie—a bundle of efficiency in any emergency—came running with his jacket, already thinking ahead. "What do you have in your medicine case for setting bones, Emily?"

"Adhesive plasters."

"A styptic?"

"Yes, crowfoot salve."

"We'll need some sheets for binding. Edwin, go along while I get them. I'll follow as soon as I can."

Hurrying down the snowy streets, Edwin asked, "What were they fighting over?"

"Me."

"I thought as much. Fannie and I spent the evening speculating about what was going on. You want to fill me in?"

"Papa, I know you're not going to like it, but I'm going to marry Tom. I love him, Papa. That's what we went to tell Charles tonight."

Jogging, Edwin spoke breathlessly. "That's a hell of a thing to do to friends."

"I know." Tears leaked from Emily's eyes as she added, "But you should know how it is, Papa."

He jogged on. "Yes, d—damned if I don't."

"Are you angry?"

"I might be tomorrow, but right now I'm chiefly concerned about those two you left bleeding down there."

On their way past Walcott's Livery Emily tore inside, snatched her bag, and joined her father on the run. They entered Tom's place like a train of two, bumping nose to shoulder blade. The scene inside was ironically peaceful. The single coal-oil lantern cast murky light over the near end of the corridor where Tom sat propped against the right wall; farther down, Charles sat against the left. Beside the turntable one stall door gaped open. The bay gelding had roamed out and stood peering inquisitively into the dark smithy at the far end of the building.

Edwin hurried to Tom first and dropped to a knee beside him. "So you've got a messed up rib or two," the older man observed.

"I think so . . . hurts like hell."

"Fannie's bringing something to bind them up with."

Emily explained, "Doc Steele wasn't home. I had to get Papa."

Edwin moved on to Charles. "I'm glad to see you propped up. She said she left you laying flat on your back and not moving. Scared the daylights out of us."

Through swollen lips Charles said, "Unfortunately, Edwin, I'm not dead or even close to it."

"That face is a mess though. Anything else hurt?"

Staring morosely beyond the turntable at Emily and Tom, Charles wondered aloud, "Does pride count, Edwin?" Then he glanced away.

On her knees beside Tom, Emily wailed, "Oh, Thomas, just look what you've done to yourself. Who asked you to fight over me?"

"I guess you're not too pleased."

"I should put another lump on your head, that's what I should do." She touched his cheek tenderly, whispering, "Don't you know I love this face? How dare you mutilate it?" They spent a moment delving into each other's eyes—hers troubled, his bloodshot and swollen—then she rose from her knees. "I'll get some water to clean you up." She found a chipped enamel pail in one of the stalls and returned with it full of water, knelt and retrieved gauze from her veterinary bag. When she dabbed at the first cut, Tom winced.

"Good enough for you," she declared unsympathetically.

"You're a hard woman, tomboy, I can see that. I'm gonna have to work on softening—*ow!*"

"Be still. This will stop the bleeding."

"What is it?"

"Crowfoot weed—old Indian cure—modernized some."

"Humph."

Fannie bustled in, hatless, toting a striped canvas bag with handles. "Whom should I see to first?"

Emily answered. "Get Tom's shirt off while I see after Charles's cuts."

While Edwin and Fannie stood Tom on his feet, Emily slipped across the aisle and knelt uncertainly beside Charles. How awkward, looking into his bruised face, meeting his hurt, reproachful eyes.

"I should get rid of some of that blood so we can see how bad the cuts are."

His reproof continued as he silently stared at her. Finally he demanded in a grieved whisper, "Why, Emily?"

"Oh, Charles . . ." She swung her gaze high, trying not to cry again.

"Why?" he entreated earnestly. "What did I do wrong? Or what didn't I do right?"

"You did everything right," she replied, abashed, "it's just that I've known you too long."

"Then you should know how good I'd be to you." His eyes, already bruised, looked even sadder as he spoke.

"I do . . . I know . . . but something was . . . was missing. Something . . ." Searching for graceful words, Emily studied her thumbs, which were needlessly flattening a wad of wet gauze.

"Something what?" he insisted.

She lifted dismayed eyes and whispered simply, "I've known you too long, Charles. When I kissed you it felt like kissing a brother."

Above his beard a pink tinge appeared between the bruises on his cheeks. He sat in silence, digesting her words for moments before replying with hard-won approbation, "Well, that's a damned hard one to argue with."

"Please, could we talk about it some other time?"

Again he fell silent, his mood deteriorating before he agreed dully, "Yeah, some other time . . ."

When she washed his face and knuckles he remained stoic, studying a wheel hub on the wagon. She swabbed his bruises with damp gauze, then applied the styptic salve, touching his face, his eyebrows, his beard, his lips for the last time. She discovered in a hidden corner of her heart an undeniable ache because it *was* the last time, and because she had hurt him so terribly, and because he loved her so much. She wrapped his bruised knuckles, tied the last knot, and sat back dropping her hands primly into her lap.

"Is there anything else?" she asked.

"No." He stared at the wheel, stubbornly refusing to look at her. Oddly, she needed him to look at her just then.

"Nothing feels broken?"

"No. Go on. Go bandage him up," he ordered gruffly.

She remained on her knees, studying him, waiting for some sign of exoneration, but none came. No glance, no touch, no word. Just before rising, she gently touched his wrist while whispering, "I'm so sorry, Charles."

A muscle contracted in his jaw but he remained taciturn, distant.

She crossed the corridor to tend Thomas, aware all the time that she had at last attracted Charles's attention. His hard eyes followed every move she made, like ice picks in her back.

Edwin and Fannie had rolled down the top of Tom's underwear and had implemented an uneducated fingertip examination.

"Fannie and I think something's broken."

Having touched Tom so few times before and never this intimately, Emily was naturally reluctant to do so now before three pairs of watchful eyes. She swallowed her misgivings and traced his ribs, submerging personal feelings and watching his face for reactions. His wince came on the fourth rib she tested.

"Probably fractured."

"Probably?" Tom asked.

"Probably," she repeated. "A green-stick fracture, I'd guess."

"What's a green-stick fracture?"

"It breaks like a green stick—curled on the ends, you know? Sometimes they're harder to mend than a clean break. I can plaster it or you can wait till the end of the week until Doc Steele gets back," Emily told him.

He glanced from Edwin to Fannie to Emily before inquiring dubiously, "Do you know what you're doing?"

"I would if you were a horse or a cow . . . or even a dog. Being a man, you'll just have to take your chances on me."

Sighing, he decided. "All right, go ahead."

"When I plaster an animal I shave the area so it doesn't hurt when the plaster comes off. We'll bind you first in sheeting, but sometimes the plaster soaks through."

Tom dropped a baleful glance at the wedge of black hair on his chest. Emily averted her eyes out of self-consciousness, feeling Charles's watchful stare as well as Fannie and Papa's closer regard.

"Oh, hell . . . all right. But don't take off any more than you have to."

She shaved the point of his hirsute arrow from waist to midway up his pectoral arch—an unnervingly personal area made the more distracting by the fact that he kept jumping and flinching from the cold soap and blade, and because it was, after all, the naked stomach of the man she was going to marry.

Once he twitched and complained, irritably, "Hurry up, I'm freezing." She bit back a smile: so he would have his grouchy moments, as a husband. Maybe, as a wife, she could find ways to sweeten him at those times.

While Fannie wrapped his ribs with cotton, Emily measured, cut, and wet the adhesive plaster strips. She ordered Tom to drop his hands to his sides and expel his breath, and while he stood so, she wrapped him from back to breastbone with overlapped pieces until his trunk resembled the armor on a gila monster.

"There. It's not fancy, but it'll help."

He glanced down, cursed softly in self-disgust, and asked, "How long do you think I'll have to keep this on?"

"Four weeks, I'd guess, wouldn't you, Papa?"

"Don't ask me! I don't even know what you came to get me for. I haven't done a thing but watch."

It was true. Under stress, Emily had performed with proficiency and calm, as she had that day at Jagush's. Though Tom admired the fact, she made light of it, telling Edwin, "You were my moral support. Besides, I wasn't sure if I'd have to lift them. Thank you for coming, Papa. You too, Fannie."

"Well," Edwin announced, "I guess I'd better hitch up a rig and haul these two home." First he moved back to Charles. "Charles, how're you doing, son?"

Edwin had called Charles *son* for so long, doing so seemed second nature to him. But the word caused an uncomfortable lull as he helped Charles to his feet. Until now there'd been distractions to override much of the tension between the two suitors. But as they faced each other across the dim corridor, polarity surfaced between them, at once repellent and attractive. Broken engagements and broken bones and broken hearts. All were present in their silent exchange of glances.

Then Charles shuffled toward the door. "I'll walk home," he said glumly. "I feel like I need the fresh air."

"Nonsense, Charles—" Edwin began, but Charles pushed past him and left the livery stable without a backward glance.

In his wake Edwin exhaled a heavy breath. "I guess you can't expect him to be overjoyed, can you?"

Tom spoke up. "I know Charles means a lot to you, sir. I meant to plan a better time to tell you about Emily and me. I meant to ask you for her hand properly. I'm sorry you had to find out this way."

"Yes, well . . ." Edwin blustered, searching for words to hide his own dismay at losing Charles as a son-in-law. While playing the part of humanitarian Edwin had set aside his own consternation at the turn of events, but it surfaced now in an unexpected and tactless outburst. "Now I know about it, and she tells me she loves you, but young man, let me warn you . . ." Edwin shook a finger at Tom. "The period of mourning is a year long, so if you have any other ideas you'd better put them out of your head!"

Chapter 18

Emily rode behind her father, smoldering with mortification while they took Tom home in a four-seater buggy. She could not believe Edwin's crassness!

Edwin drove—mulling events silently, feeling ambivalent, even a little sheepish after reconsidering his outburst. At Tom's house he cast a reproving eye upon Emily as she anxiously watched her injured swain alight. Tom moved by increments, guarding his ribs as he stepped onto the foot bracket and over the side. When he reached the ground Emily stood as if to follow, but Edwin ordered, "Stay where you are. You're coming home with us."

"But, Papa, Tom needs—"

"He'll make out just fine."

Anger flared and Emily retorted acidly, "I can make my own decision, Papa, thank you!" She propped her fists on her hips and glared at her father.

Tom looked up and advised diplomatically, "He's right,

Emily. You go home. I'll be all right. Thank you for your help, Edwin . . . Fannie."

"Yeah," Edwin replied ungraciously to cover his own growing discomposure over his lack of discretion. "Giddap!" He slapped the reins so suddenly Emily sat down with a plop.

"Papa!" she railed, outraged, gripping the edge of the seat.

He drove on without turning around. "Don't Papa me! I know what's best for you!"

"You're being unspeakably rude! And I never thought I'd live to see the day when you became domineering!"

"You're in mourning," Edwin declared with stubborn finality.

"Oh, *I'm* in mourning, so that means I'll have to put up with *your* surliness for a year?"

"Emily, I'm your father! And I'm not surly!"

"You're surly! Is he surly, Fannie? Tell him!"

Fannie had opinions but decided it best to withhold them until she and Edwin were alone. She had no intention of playing devil's advocate with Edwin's daughter as witness. A flourish of her hands ordered clearly, *Leave me out of this.*

"Not only is he surly but he's rude to my fiancé!"

"Your fiancé—hmph!" Edwin scowled at the rumps of the trotting horses.

"You found him totally likable when he knocked on the door earlier tonight. Why, your face lit up like a rainbow when you saw him coming in."

"You have damn near a full year of courtship ahead of you, young lady, and I won't have you tucking him into bed!"

"Tucking him into . . . oh, Papa!" Abashed, Emily fought the sting of tears.

"Edwin," Fannie upbraided, abandoning her vow to remain silent. "That was uncalled for."

"Well, dammit, Fannie," he blustered, "Charles is like a son to me!"

"We know that, Edwin, so perhaps you need not reiterate the fact quite so often. There is a new fiancé to be considered, and he has feelings, too."

In strained silence they rode the remainder of the way home. Pulling up, Edwin stared straight ahead while Emily leapt from the wagon and stormed into the house in a state of dudgeon. Fannie silently squeezed Edwin's hand before following.

Inside Emily paced turbulently, spinning to Fannie the moment she entered. "How could he say such a thing!"

Fannie calmly lit a lamp and drew off her coat. "Give him a day or two to get used to the idea of you and Tom. He'll come around."

"But to point his finger at Tom and give him orders as if he were . . . as if he were anything less than a gentleman! I was absolutely mortified! And his remark about my tucking Tom into bed was absolutely inexcusable! I wanted to die on the spot!" Indignant tears spurted into Emily's eyes. "We've done nothing to be ashamed of, Fannie, nothing!"

"I know, dearling, I know." Fannie hooked Emily in her arms and tucked her close. "But you have to remember it hasn't been an easy time for your father. His whole world is in a state of flux. He's lost your mother, now he feels like he's losing Charles. You're making plans to marry and move away from the nest. It's natural that he's upset, and if he displays it in ways that could sometimes be more tactful, we must be patient with him."

"But I don't understand, Fannie." Emily pulled back, too agitated to be held immobile. "He's always been on my side, and he always said that the most important thing in life is to be happy. Now I am . . . I . . . I'm going to be, when Tom and I are married. You'd think Papa would think about that, would want that for me, instead of wanting me to marry somebody I don't love. The remarks he made tonight were totally unlike him. I'd expect Mother to say something like that, but not Papa. Never Papa."

Fannie studied the younger woman, smiling benignly. For seconds she pondered whether or not it was prudent to speak what was on her mind. Would it be fair to Edwin to speculate on the underlying reason for his outburst? Perhaps not, but it might at least help Emily understand some of the stresses that had come to bear on her father. "Come here. Sit down." Fannie took Emily by the hands and drew her down onto a kitchen chair, taking another herself, clasping Emily's hands across the corner of the kitchen table. She chose her words carefully. "You're nineteen years old, Emily, a full-grown woman." She spoke placidly, in a voice eloquent with understanding and wisdom. "Certainly you're old enough to have been exposed to the temptations that come along with falling in love. They're natural, those temptations. We fall in love and we want that love consummated. Well, it's no different for your father . . . and me. Perhaps now you can understand that the warning Edwin inadvisedly issued to Tom was really directed at himself."

The anger fell from Emily like a stripped garment, replaced by a wide-eyed stare of incredulity.

"Oh, you mean . . ." she stammered to a halt, her face still and open. And again, quieter, she breathed, "Oh."

"Have I shocked you, dear? I didn't mean to." Still smiling, Fannie dropped Emily's hands. "But we're both women, both in love, both trapped in this execrably *stupid* convention they call mourning. Perhaps we just handle it better than the men do. Perhaps that's our strength, after all."

Emily stared at Fannie, too amazed for words.

"Now, dearling, it's late," Fannie observed, ending the intimate revelation with her usual grace. "Hadn't you better get ready for bed?"

Two hours later Emily lay in bed wide awake, still pondering the unexpected and startling disclosure made by Fannie in the kitchen. Even at their age, Papa and Fannie still experienced carnality! The realization relaxed much of Emily's rancor for Edwin.

How often she had wondered, but it wasn't a subject about which one inquired, certainly not of a parent. Certainly not of *her* parents! Lying beside the sleeping Fannie, listening to her measured breathing, Emily absorbed the truth that the other woman had so honestly revealed, truth that Fannie undoubtedly understood every bride-to-be would be wondering about: these feelings that she and Tom felt for one another could and very likely *would* persevere through much more of their lives than she had ever guessed.

In recent days, since Tom's first kisses and caresses, Emily had devoted many long insomniac hours to speculation about that very subject. Carnality. It was awesome and overpowering and intimidating. And, before marriage, a woman's responsibility seemed to be to combat it for both herself and the man.

Contemplating it, Emily conjured up the image of Tom, his lazy blue eyes, his smile, his lips, kisses, hands. She lay with the quilts caught tightly beneath her arms, her own hands flattened over her pelvis where a restive throb beat, deep inside. Warmth came with it, and nubilous images spawned by memories of the few times Tom had held and petted her.

It brought speculation on the marriage act. There were words for it—copulation, conjugation, consummation, coupling, intercourse, sowing oats (Emily smiled) . . . making love (she sobered).

Yes, making love. She liked that phrase best.

What would it be like? How would it begin? Would it be dark? Light? Between sheets or on top of quilts like that one night at Tom's house? Would it be halting or spontaneous? What would he say? Do? And herself, how was she expected to react? Or *act?* And afterwards, would they feel awkward and self-conscious? Or would the marriage act create a magical lingering intimacy?

The marriage act. Another phrase, though sometimes untrue. Sometimes it happened outside the marriage—Tarsy had educated Emily on that point. Perhaps Tom had done it with someone already, someone he knew before, someone experienced in the proper ways. His former fiancé? Tarsy, even?

Emily opened her eyes and stared at a streak of moonlight bending around the corner of the room. She gulped at the stone lying in her throat. Suppose he had done it with Tarsy after all. Emily had tried to believe otherwise, but sometimes she wondered.

Tarsy, who had admitted how close they'd come.

Tarsy, who had also admitted that she sometimes thought of "trapping" Tom into marriage.

Tarsy, who had changed so much in the past several months because she loved Thomas Jeffcoat.

Tomorrow I must tell Tarsy. Tomorrow, before word reaches her from any other source.

At 5:30 the following morning Emily left a note on the kitchen table: *Going to feed Tom's horses. Back in an hour. Emily.*

She went first to his house. All was dark, so she circled around and knocked on his bedroom window, backed off and waited, but no response came. She banged again, harder, and pictured him rolling from bed, groaning, wrapped in plaster. It took a full minute before the shade flicked aside and his face appeared as a white blur in the shadows beyond the distorting window glass.

"Tom?" On tiptoe, she put her mouth closer to the window. "It's Emily."

"Em?" His voice came faintly through the wall. "What's wrong?"

"Nothing. Stay in bed. I'm going to take care of your stock today. You just rest."

"No, you . . . to . . . up . . ."

Emily lost most of his reply to the buffering wall.

"Go back to bed!"

"No, Emily, wait!" He flattened a palm on the window. "Come to the door!"

The shade dropped and she stared at it, hearing again her father's admonition about tucking him into bed. Before she gathered the intelligence to walk away the shade turned golden as he lit a lamp, then faded as he carried it out of the room toward the front of the house.

5:30 A.M. The very hour created intimacy, the very fact that he'd been asleep. Emily paused, staring at the shade, fully intending to leave without putting a foot on his porch.

From around the house she heard him calling. "Em?" Faintly, in a half whisper.

Firming her resolve, she rounded the front corner and mounted two porch steps, then stopped dead in her tracks.

His head and one naked shoulder poked through the door. "Come on in here, it's cold!" His breath made a white cloud in the chill predawn air.

"I'd better not."

"Dammit, Emily, get in here! It's freezing!"

She thumped up the steps and inside, keeping her hands in her pockets and her eyes on the floor. He closed the door and rubbed his arms to warm them. She knew without looking, that his feet and chest were bare, and he wore only trousers and the white bindings around his ribs. Again, Emily wondered what her father would say.

"I'm sorry I woke you up."

"It's all right."

"I didn't want you to get out of bed. I thought if I just knocked on the window I could tell you and leave." Her glance flickered up to his shoulders, then quickly down.

"What time is it?"

"Five-thirty."

"Is that all?" He groaned and flexed gingerly. "Lordy, I couldn't get to sleep last night. My ribs hurt."

"How do you feel this morning?"

"Like I've been pulled through a keyhole." He spread a hand over the bandages, then reached up and tested his incisors, adding, "I think some of my teeth are loose."

"To say nothing of your bones. You've got no business throwing hay with cracked ribs. I'll take care of your livery stable today."

"I want to say no, but the way I feel I think I'd be wiser to say thank you. I really appreciate it, Emily."

She shrugged. "I don't mind, and I know your horses by name."

His eyes drifted fondly over her face and her boyish attire. "Besides," he said softly, "someday they'll be yours, too."

She swallowed, feeling herself blushing, realizing once again that they were in his home, in total privacy, and he was far from decently dressed. To remind him of the same thing, she broached the subject that could not be avoided forever. "I'm sorry about what my father said last night."

She felt his eyes probing and studied his bare toes, imagining them beneath her own as the two of them curled together like spoons beneath the quilts.

"Is that why you're scared to look at me, Emily, because of what he said?"

She felt herself color, and gulped. "Yes."

"I'd sure like it if you would."

"I'm dressed in my barn clothes."

"And I'm not complaining."

She lifted her head slowly and her lips dropped open, her eyes grew dismayed. "Oh, Thomas . . ." His face was swollen and discolored. His hair stood in tufts like that of an old buffalo after a hard winter. His left eye was opened less than a quarter inch and the right one squinted without his intending it to. Beneath it a pillow of skin had turned magenta, tinged with blue. His beautiful mouth and jawline were those of a mutilated stranger. "Look at you."

"I suppose I'm a mess."

"You must hurt terribly."

"Bad enough to keep from kissing you the way I'd like to," he admitted, taking her elbows anyway, and drawing her off-balance.

She resisted discreetly and said, "Tom, I need to talk to you." There were things that needed airing and they were best said with a minimum of intimacy involved.

"So serious," he chided gently.

"Yes, it is."

He dropped his playful mood. "Very well . . . talk."

She drew a deep breath and told him, "I hated it, your fighting over me. I felt helpless and . . . angry."

His eyes probed hers with a hint of rebelliousness in the brows. But after a moment's silence he offered, "I'm sorry."

"I hate seeing you disfigured this way."

"I know."

"I would never have taken you for a fighter."

"I never was . . . before."

"I wouldn't like it very much if you did it after we were married."

They both recognized the moment for what it was; not a squaring-off but a structuring for their future. His answer—the one she'd hoped for—spoke of the deference with which he would hold her wishes when she became his wife.

"I won't. That's a promise. I didn't *want* to fight him, you know."

"Yes, I know."

She stood with her gaze pinned on his black-and-blue eyes, wrapped in a queer combination of emotions—regret for having had to take him to task; pity for his poor, abused body; desire for that same body, no matter how unsightly it looked. She wanted badly to reach, soothe, press her face to his naked neck and touch his warm shoulders. A startling thought surfaced: *I love him so much that Papa is right. I have no business here in his house, not even in barn clothes.*

Instinctively she moved to leave, but reaching the door she turned. "I'm going to tell Tarsy about us this morning. As soon as I feed your horses I'm going over to her house and get it over with. I just wanted you to know."

"Do you want me with you?"

"No, I think it's best if I go alone. She's probably not going to be any more understanding than Charles was. The two of you will want to talk privately once she knows. I'll understand that and I promise I won't be jealous."

"Emily . . ." He moved toward her.

"I've got to go." She opened the door quickly.

"Wait."

"You know what Papa said."

"Yes, I know what Papa said but Papa isn't here now."

Advancing, he thumped the door closed and positioned himself between it and her. He hooked an elbow around her neck and drew her lightly against him, resting one bruised cheek against her floppy wool cap. In a husky voice he said, "I think it's a damn good thing I'm so bruised up or we'd be in a peck of trouble here."

Oh, his smell. A little musky, a little mussed, a little male, the natural scent of skin and hair aged by one night. Thank God for gloves, she thought, with her own resting against his hard white bindings, inches from his bare chest. She wanted nothing more than to touch all of him that was naked, to learn his texture with her bare fingertips. While she steadfastly refrained, he slipped his hand up inside the back of her jacket and pulled her lightly against him, lazily rubbing her spinal column through a rough flannel shirt. He explored her slowly, his hand moving up, as if counting each vertebra, gently urging her closer. A warm hard hand, a warm hard man—how easy it would be to succumb to both.

Her heartbeat hearkened and her breasts felt heavy.

"Thomas . . ." she whispered in warning.

"Don't go," he begged softly. "It's the first time without Charles between us. Don't go."

She felt it, too, the easing of constraint upon their consciences since her engagement was formally broken. But constraints took other forms, and she drew back reluctantly. "I can't come here anymore, not to your house. We have almost ten months to wait, and that's too long. I have to go," she repeated, backing away from him.

He watched her walk backward till her shoulders bumped the door. They gazed at each other with frustrated desire drawing long lines upon their faces.

He moved toward her slowly, and her heartbeats seemed to fill her throat. But he only reached behind her for the doorknob. Opening the door for her he said softly, "Let me know how it goes with Tarsy."

"I will."

At ten o'clock that morning Tarsy answered the door herself, wearing a trim-bodiced dress of candy-pink stripes with flattering shoulder-to-naval tucks that minimized her dainty waist, and a generous gathered skirt that exaggerated her rounded hips.

Emily wore the same clothes in which she'd fed Tom's horses and cleaned his stalls—a wool jacket, trousers, and soiled leather boots.

Tarsy's hair was freshly curled and caught up on the back of her head with a matching pink ribbon.

Emily's was jammed up inside her brother's floppy wool cap.

Tarsy smelled of lavender soap.

Emily smelled of horse dung.

Tarsy turned up her pretty nose. "Phew!"

Apologetically, Emily left her boots outside the door and stepped into the front entry stocking-footed. Mrs. Fields arrived from the kitchen, her hands coated with flour. "Well, Emily, for goodness sake, this is a surprise. We hardly ever see you this early in the day." She was a buxom woman with wavy blond hair done up in a French twist, the only woman Emily had ever known who wore cheek paint in her kitchen and scented herself at this hour of the day. The smell of honeysuckle toilet water wafted in with her, covering that of yeast from the dough on her fingers.

"Hello, Mrs. Fields."

"How is your father?"

"Fine."

"And Miss Cooper?"

"Fine."

"Will she be leaving soon, going back East?"

Emily detected a bit of nosiness and took pleasure in replying, "No, ma'am. She's staying."

"Oh." Mrs. Fields's left eyebrow elevated.

"She has no family back there. Why should she?"

Mrs. Fields allowed her eyebrow to settle to its normal level and blinked twice, as if taken aback by Emily's quick defense of Fannie.

"Well . . . I thought that since your mother is gone—may she rest in peace—Miss Cooper's services would no longer be needed."

"On the contrary, we all need her very badly and begged her to stay. You see, I've decided to continue my veterinary studies after all, and to work at . . . at the stables indefinitely, so I'm abandoning most of the domestic duties to Fannie. I just don't know what we'd do without her anymore."

Mrs. Fields's mouth drew up as if she were attempting to

pick up a coin with her lips. "I see." She flashed a glance at Tarsy, then added, "Well, give your family my best," and returned to the kitchen.

When she was gone, Tarsy took Emily's arm and turned her toward the steps. "Come upstairs and see the new piece of organdy that Mama's going to make into a spring gown for me. It's called pistachio—whatever that means!—and we've decided on the most absolutely smashing design from the latest issue of *Graham's*. Mama has agreed to let me have a soiree here—don't you just *love* the word?—soiree . . ." Reaching the top of the steps, Tarsy lifted her skirt in two fingers and performed a dipping swirl toward her bedroom door. Whisking through it, she caught up a piece of green fabric from the tufted stool before her vanity. Petting it, she swung back to Emily. "Isn't it de-*lus*cious?"

Emily dutifully touched the organdy with a knuckle that hadn't been washed since she'd been handling a pitchfork, gazing down absently in a way that Tarsy took for longing.

"Oh, poor Emily, I just don't know *how* you'll tolerate wearing black for a *whole year*. I would simply wither away and die if it were me. Maybe someday you can sneak up here and try on my pistachio gown after it's made up!"

Emily remained stone sober. "It's very nice, Tarsy, but I have to talk to you about something important."

"Important?" Tarsy's brow wrinkled delicately: what could be more important than a new gown of pistachio organdy for a soiree?

"Yes."

"Very well." Tarsy obediently laid the cloth aside and plunked onto the foot of the bed in a billow of pink skirts, her folded hands lost in her lap.

Emily dropped onto the tufted stool facing her friend, wondering how to begin.

"Well?" Tarsy's hands flashed, then disappeared once more into the folds of her skirt.

"I've decided not to marry Charles."

"Not to . . ." Tarsy's jaw dropped. Her eyes widened. "But, Emily, you and Charles are . . . are . . . well, heavens! You two simply go together . . . ham and eggs! Peaches and cream!"

"Not really."

"He's absolutely going to *die* when you tell him."

"He already knows."

"He does?"

"Yes."

"Well, what did he say?"

"He was very angry . . . and hurt."

"Well, I imagine so." Tarsy plucked fussily at the peaks of her skirt. "My goodness, you two have known each other forever. What reason did you give?"

"The true one, that I love him more as a brother than as a husband."

Tarsy considered, then lowered her voice to a conspiratorial whisper. "But how do you know, Emily, when you've never . . . I mean . . ." Tarsy shrugged and gave Emily an ingenuous gaze. "You never have . . ." Her head jutted forward. ". . . have you?"

Emily colored, but answered, "No."

"Well then, maybe you'd feel different." Hurriedly she added, "After you're married, I mean."

"No, I won't. I'm sure of it."

"But how do you know?"

"Because . . ." Emily clamped her palms between her knees and forged on. "I know now what it feels like when you really love somebody."

Tarsy's face lit like a gas jet. Her eyebrows shot up and her expression turned avid as she bent forward. "Oh, Emily . . . who?"

How ironic it felt to be confronting a woman of Tarsy's pulchritude: the ugly duckling telling the swan she had won the drake. Ironic and frightening. Emily's heart felt as if it would flop clear out of her body as she answered steadily, "Tom."

"Tom?" Tarsy repeated in a faint, colorless voice. Her face flattened and she straightened cautiously, reluctant to assimilate the truth.

"Yes, Tom."

"Tom Jeffcoat?" Tarsy's pretty mouth distorted.

"Yes."

"But he's—" She stopped herself just short of adding, *mine*. Nevertheless it reverberated in the air between the two women. Tension suddenly buzzed as Emily watched Tarsy struggle to understand. A gamut of reactions fleeted across her face—disbelief, doubt, and finally amusement. Flinging her arms high, Tarsy fell back onto the bed, throwing her breasts into prominence—a woman who believed she had no competition from this unfeminine, board-chested veterinarian who didn't know diddly-squat about charm, enticement, or flirting. What man would prefer a woman who boldly admitted hating housework and disdaining babies? Not that Tarsy herself was any too anxious to embrace either, but Tom would never guess the truth until she was comfortably sleeping in his bed nights.

"You? Oh, Emily . . ." Supine, Tarsy laughed at the ceiling till the mattress bounced. Then she braced up on an elbow, catching a jaw on one shoulder. Her blond hair cascaded over one arm and her bewitching eyes took on a gleam of confidence. "Emily, if you want a man like Tom Jeffcoat to notice you you'll have to trade your smelly boots for button-top shoes and learn to curl your hair and wear dresses instead of those wretched pants." Tarsy fell back onto both elbows, once again throwing her breasts into relief. She set her legs swinging and decided to be generous with her advice. "And it wouldn't hurt you to wear a corset that . . . well, you know . . . sort of helps you out a little up here. And as for admitting that you don't like housework and you don't want b—"

"I'm going to marry him, Tarsy."

Tarsy's legs stopped swinging. Her lips clamped shut and her face blanched. The room held a knotty silence before Emily continued as kindly as possible.

"I wanted to be the one to tell you before you found out from someone else, and chances are you would have the minute you left the house."

"You . . . marry Tom!" Tarsy snapped erect, her face pale. "Don't be absurd! Why the two of you couldn't recite the Pledge of Allegiance without fighting over it!"

"He asked me and I said yes. We told Charles together last night and the two of them had a terrible fistfight, which you're also bound to find out. I'm really sorry, Tarsy. We didn't mean to—"

"Why you two-faced, conniving bitch!" Tarsy shrieked, leaping off the bed. "How dare you!" She swung full-force, slapping Emily's face so hard it knocked her sideways, teetering the vanity stool.

Emily's heart contracted with shock and fright. Stunned, she righted herself on the seat and stared while Tarsy's face turned unattractively rubicund. "I wanted him and you knew it! You knew I planned to marry him and you plotted to get him from me all the while, didn't you! You *milked* me for *personal, privileged* information!" Enraged, Tarsy threw herself around the bedroom while Emily, who'd never witnessed female anger of such magnitude, sat too stupefied to move. Gripping her temples, Tarsy raved, "*Urrrr!* You low . . . cunning . . ." She swung about abruptly, nosing Emily backward on the bench. "You let me tell you things I *never* would have told anyone else. *Never!*" Suddenly she backed off with a malevolent sneer, dropping her hands onto her hips. "Well, how's this for privileged information, Miss Judas Walcott! What I convinced you of a few months ago was nothing but a convenient lie. *You* may be a virgin, but I'm not! *I did it!* With your precious Tom Jeffcoat, who wouldn't take no for an answer! Take *that* to your wedding bed and sleep with it!" Reveling in her malevolence, Tarsy tossed her head and gave a spiteful laugh. "Go on, marry him and see if I care! If Tom Jeffcoat wants a freak who dresses like a man and smells like horse apples, he can have you! You're exactly what he deserves! Huh! You probably haven't got the right equipment to make him babies anyway!" Tarsy's expression turned hateful. "Now get out! . . . *Get out!*" She grabbed Emily's jacket and jerked her roughly to her feet, then thrust her through the doorway.

"Girls, girls, girls!" Mrs. Fields arrived, puffing, at the top of the stairs. "What's all this shouting about?"

"Out!" Tarsy screeched, shoving Emily past her mother, bumping her against the handrail and down two steps.

Emily grasped the rail to keep from tumbling to the bottom. "Tarsy, you're not being fair. I wanted us to talk about it and—"

"Don't you ever speak to me again! And you can tell that toad-sucking swine Tom Jeffcoat that I wouldn't cast him so much as a moldy crumb if he was starving to death at your kitchen table, which he'll be soon enough, since you don't know the first pathetic thing about cooking! But he'll learn that, too, won't he, along with the fact that all you care about is stupid animals! Well, go! What are you waiting for, standing there like a moron with your mouth hanging open. Get out of my house!"

Demoralized, Emily fled. Racing from Tarsy's yard, she gulped back tears and bit back tardy rejoinders, holding her hurt inside until she could find privacy to do her crying alone. But where? Fannie was at home. Papa was at their own livery.

She went to Tom's livery barn, inside the building with the sign on the door saying, "Closed for the day," into the familiar scent of hay and horses and liniment and leather, where she mounted the stairs to his loft and sank down into the hay. At first she sat as stoically as an Indian before a council fire, doubling her knees up tightly against her chest and hugging them hard in an effort to relieve the tight band of misery that seemed as if it would crack her ribs. She rocked in slight short thrusts, staring dry-eyed while the hurt pinched her vocal cords and stung her nose and throat. Deep within, minute trembles shook her belly and tensed her thighs. She pulled them tighter to her chest and, as the avalanche of misery descended, dropped her forehead to her knees.

She wept bitterly—hurt, degraded, demoralized.

I thought you were my friend, Tarsy. But friends don't hurt each other this way, not on purpose.

While racking sobs filled the hayloft and shook Emily's shoulders, she heard again and again Tarsy's abasing evaluation. A flat-chested freak who dresses like a man and smells like horse apples and probably hasn't got the right equipment to make babies anyway. A moron.

Hurt piled upon hurt as Emily realized Tarsy's friendship had been false all along. Today she had revealed her true feelings, but how many times had Tarsy secretly laughed behind her back, ridiculed, derided, probably even among their crowd of mutual friends?

But as if the vindictive assessment were not enough, Tarsy had exacted her revenge by imparting one last pernicious arrow, and this one aimed straight at Emily's heart.

She and Tom had been lovers after all.

Emily wept till her entire body hurt, until she fell to one side, clutched her belly, and curled into a tight, wretched ball. *Tarsy and Tom, together.* Why should it hurt so much to know? But it did. It did! Knowing was different from speculating. Oh, Tarsy, why did you tell me?

She wept until her entire frame ached from recoiling, until her face was swollen, her cheek raw from rubbing against the scratchy hay, and her stomach muscles hurt to be touched. When the worst was over she lay listless, shaken by leftover sobs, staring at her own limp hand lying knuckles-down in the hay. She closed her eyes, opened them again because, closed, they stung. How long had she been here? Long enough to be missed. But she remained, weighted by an apathy more immense than any she had experienced before, studying her hand, dully opening and closing her fingers for no reason that came to mind.

In time her thoughts clarified.

Perhaps the men's way was more civilized after all. A swift, clean fistfight would have been preferable to this insidious, long-term venom inflicted by Tarsy's words. Emily understood now why the men had fought. If it were possible she would do it herself, go back to Tarsy's and take ten smacks on the chin and crack a couple ribs, then go home and lick her wounds as the men were doing today. Instead, she would live for years festering with the knowledge of her own shortcomings as a woman, and of Tom's sexual predilection for another. Emily sighed, closed her eyes, and rolled to her back, hands lax near her ears.

Tarsy and Tom had been lovers.

Forget it.

How?

I don't know, but you must, or Tarsy will have won.

She has won and both of us will know it on my wedding night.

She took her heartache to Fannie, whom she found in the kitchen, making chicken noodle soup.

"F—Fannie, can I talk to you?"

Fannie turned from the stove where she was dropping noodles into a pot of boiling broth.

Try though she might, Emily could not hold her tears back. They began falling as her face crumpled.

"Dearling, what is it?" Dusting off her hands, Fannie hurried toward Emily.

"Oh, Fannie . . ." Emily went gratefully into the older woman's arms. "It's Tarsy." Some moments passed before Emily could continue. "I just came from her house. I told her I'm going to marry Tom and she . . . she turned so hateful. Oh, Fannie, she sl—slapped me and c—called me thc most awful names. I thought she was my f—friend."

"She was. She is."

Emily shook her head. "Not anymore. She said t—terrible things to me, things to deliberately hurt me."

Fannie's own heart ached for Emily. Holding her, she loved her with a maternal intensity, simply because she was Edwin's flesh and blood. She felt privileged to be able to share Edwin's children, even through such a painful ordeal as this.

"What did she say?"

Emily poured out her hurt, eliminating nothing. By the time she ended, her face and eyes were freshly swollen from weeping. "I just don't understand how she could have t—turned on me so. I know she loves Tom. I *know* that, and I was sorry to have to . . . to hurt her, but the things she said to me were malicious, meant to inflict as much pain as they could."

"Ah, dearling, growing up is hard, isn't it?" Fannie cradled and rocked the young woman who, given other circumstances, might have been her own daughter. "So you've paid a price already for your love and you're asking yourself if he's worth it." She gently pushed Emily back to look into her streaming eyes. "Is he?" she inquired softly.

"I thought so . . . before today."

"What you must do, dearling, is weigh the gain of him against the loss of Tarsy. You knew she would be hurt, didn't you, even before you told her?"

"Yes, but she had changed so much. I thought she'd grown up and become . . . become . . ." Emily found it hard to delineate the recent changes in Tarsy. "The way she helped at the funeral, the way she'd stopped dramatizing everything. I liked the new Tarsy. I thought I had a friend for life."

Fannie found a handkerchief and dried Emily's cheeks. "She's a woman spurned. Spurned women are dangerous creatures. And oddly enough, though you thought she had changed, I find her reaction quite in character. So she has unleashed her wrath on you, and called you names and hurt you with insinuations about herself and the man you love. The question is, what are you going to do about it?"

"Do?"

"You can believe her and let it eat inside you like a bad worm in a good apple. Or you can reason it through and come to grips with the fact that though Tom may have liked, even loved, Tarsy at one time, if he truly loves you now, it takes nothing away from that love. Nothing."

As the eyes of the two women locked, Fannie's words

resounded in Emily's heart. Who should know better than Fannie about a man who had genuinely loved two women?

"I want you to do something for me," Fannie said, taking Emily's hand. "I want you to promise that the next time you're with Tom you won't confront him with this, that you'll give yourself at least a full day, maybe two, to decide if you even should. Will you do that for me?"

In a near-whisper Emily agreed, "Yes."

"And I want you to do one other thing."

"What?"

"Saddle a horse and go for a ride. You need it far more than you need chicken noodle soup right now."

Wishing to avoid her father and the questions her red eyes were sure to raise, Emily went back to Jeffcoat's Livery Stable and saddled Tom's buckskin, Buck. She led him outside into a noonish day that couldn't decide between sun and cloud. She buttoned her jacket high, stuffed her hair into Frankie's cap, drew on her soiled leather gloves, and mounted. Heading in the opposite direction of Edwin's livery stable, she circled through town and headed upland, walking Buck, which suited her mood.

Think of other things. Look around you—life goes on.

Ravens wheeled and cawed overhead, scolding the horse and rider while accompanying them up-mountain. A pair of unwary ermine came swiveling out of a deadfall, then scampered back beneath. Upon a frozen cactus paddle two black-capped chickadees whistled, perkily tilting their heads. The sound of Buck's hooves breaking the crust of snow cracked like pistol shots in the still cold day. The winter air felt cool upon Emily's hot face while the sun on her shoulders felt warm. The greasewood trees hunkered close to the earth, tangles of black lace against the white, white snow. Beneath them deer had pawed away the snow, leaving great patches of exposed grass. Spires of brown grasstips speared up, connected by a network of mice tracks that looked like hieroglyphics on the snow. The ravens grew brazen and flapped nearer, their wings as black as Tom Jeffcoat's hair.

Undoubtedly Tarsy had run her fingers through it more than once.

Remember her rubbing against his pant leg while they played Poor Pussy? Remember them kissing during a forfeit and how his hands caressed her back? How long were they lovers? How often? If I'm not as good as she—and how can I be?—will he be disappointed and seek her out again?

Emily rode with her head hanging until her abstraction was interrupted by the sound of wind chimes.

Wind chimes?

She lifted her head at the same moment Buck stopped moving, and found herself at the edge of an upcountry meadow, and there before her grazed the straggling remnants of a buffalo herd. Few of the great beasts remained, and those that did were considered precious relics of the past. She'd never seen any this close and sat motionless, afraid of scaring them off. Pawing the snow, foraging beneath it, they presented their rumps until one old bull raised his head and assessed her with a wary black eye, warning the others. As one, they poised to run, ugly beasts, humped and hairy, their faces unlovable, their coats matted and tangled. But suddenly they moved in concert, trotting away, setting into motion hundreds of sparkling icicles that hung from their shaggy undersides and tinkled like an orchestra of wind chimes. The sun glanced off them, creating prisms while the sound drifted across the snowy meadow in a sweet glissando.

Emily heard it and her cares seemed momentarily lifted by finding the unexpected beauty in such an unlikely place.

She sat watching the buffalo until the chiming grew distant, then faded into silence.

Sighing heavily, unsure of what she faced the next time she saw Tom, Emily touched her heels to the warm flank beneath her and said, "Come on, Buck, let's go home."

Chapter 19

TOM WAITED ALL that day to hear from Emily, but he heard nothing. At three in the afternoon he rolled from his bed with all the speed and agility of an iceberg. Ohhh, sweet Savior, did it hurt. He sat on the edge of the mattress, eyes closed, breathing shallowly, trying to work up the courage to rise to his feet.

Next time you fight a man, make it someone punier than Charles Bliss.

Cautiously he creaked to his feet, standing with knees crooked, clutching the footrail of the bed while waiting for the meatgrinder to stop tenderizing his pectorals.

Damn you, Bliss, I hope you hurt as much as I do.

A shirt. Reach slow . . . one arm . . . second arm—Lord Almighty, something's tearing apart in there!

Eventually he got the shirt over his shoulders to find that, buttoning it, his hands ached. He glanced down: what pitiful knuckles—black and blue and swollen as dumplings. Donning his trousers and boots, he swore off fighting forever, but by the time he was halfway to his livery stable he'd begun to move easier.

Emily's note hung on the door: *Closed for the day.* He glanced back at Edwin's to find Charles standing out front, motionless, staring at him. Yesterday Tom would have raised a hand in greeting; today he forcibly tempered the urge. Seconds ticked past while the two men assessed one another, then Tom turned and went inside.

"Emily?" he called.

Only silence answered.

Was she at Edwin's stable? Had Charles been there with her only minutes ago? So what if he was? It was bound to happen if they all expected to live in this town together.

He glanced at the turntable, the stall whose door had been knocked open during the fight, the spot where Charles had sat, propped against the wall. A wave of regret struck Tom. Friends were precious commodities; it hurt like hell to lose one.

He did what paltry work he could, passing time until evening, but Emily remained strangely absent. He fed the horses their supper—slow as he was, it took twice as long as usual—and puttered around until well after nightfall, but still she hadn't shown her face. He considered going to the hotel for supper, but decided against answering the inevitable questions that would be raised by his bruised, swollen face. Finally, he went home, ate some bread and sausage, and went to bed.

He expected her to show up all the next day, but once again he was disappointed. In the evening on his way home from work he detoured by her house, stared at the lighted windows, and cursed under his breath for no reason he could name. Upon second thought, the reasons became very clear: he'd lost his best friend; the girl he loved was showing signs of withdrawal; and her father was openly displeased about their announced plans to marry.

Well, Edwin, you'd better get used to it, Tom thought defiantly, mounting the porch steps and knocking on the door.

Frankie answered, his mouth smeared with grease.

"Is Emily here?"

"She's eatin' supper."

"Would you call her, please?"

"Emileeeeee! Tom's here!" the boy bellowed, then inquired, "Are you really gonna marry her instead of Charles?"

"That's right."

"Then who's Charles gonna marry?"

Tom forced back a smile at the boy's simplistic imquiry: as if that were the full depth of the problem.

"I don't know, Frankie. I hope he finds somebody just as nice as your sister."

"You think she's *nice*?" The boy turned up his nose.

"Give yourself about three or four years and you'll discover she's not the only nice girl around here. You'll probably discover a dozen that'll turn your head."

"Hello, Tom," Emily greeted quietly, appearing silently and standing with her hands crossed upon her spine. She wore a simple, high-necked dress of unadorned black that emphasized the wan color of her face and the contrasting blackness of her lashes and eyebrows. Her hair was prettier than he ever recalled seeing it, caught back with combs—like curled midnight falling to her simple round collar. She appeared the quintessential woman in mourning, for she neither smiled nor fidgeted, but stood studying Tom with polite reticence.

"Hello, Emily." They stared at each other, Tom with the gut feeling that something terrible was amiss, not knowing what. "Sorry to interrupt your supper."

"That's all right." She glanced down at her brother. "Frankie, tell Papa and Fannie I won't be a minute."

"You really gonna marry him instead of Charles?"

"Frankie, you're excused!"

The boy disappeared and Emily invited, "Come in," but her voice and eyes held cordiality in reserve.

Tom stepped inside and closed the door more carefully than necessary, taking the extra seconds to gather his own emotional equilibrium. He'd realized the moment she'd come around the corner that her displeasure with him was real. When he turned to face her again he knew that whatever was wrong went deep and strong in her. He felt a flash of apprehension that heated quickly into outright foreboding as she stood prim and withdrawn and somber, with her hands folded demurely behind her back.

"How are you?" she inquired politely.

"Why didn't you come over after you talked to Tarsy?"

"I've been busy."

"All day yesterday and all day today?"

"I've been studying. I have to take a test on diseases of the nervous system in horses and it's hard to remember all the terms."

His troubled eyes sought and held hers. "Emily, what's wrong?"

"Nothing's wrong." But her glance fell and her lips drooped.

"What did Tarsy say?"

Emily brushed the top of the wainscot on the stub wall beside the door, studying her fingertips as she spoke. "What you'd expect. She was angry."

Tom reached out and took Emily's hand. "What did she say?"

"She showed me the door."

"I'm sorry."

Emily retrieved her hand, still with eyes averted. "I guess I should have expected it. She's not exactly the most tactful girl in the world, or the most mannerly."

"Emily, you haven't answered me. I want to know what she *said*. When you left me yesterday morning you were reasonably happy, and you said I'd see you after you talked to her. Now, two days later, I come to your door and you ask me 'how are you,' as politely as you'd ask Reverend Vasseler. And you won't look at me or let me hold your hand. Tarsy said something, I know she did. Now what was it?"

Emily's eyes, when they lifted to Tom, were filled with grave disappointment. "What would you think she'd say, Tom?"

He stared at her, frowning and puzzling for several seconds until he realized that whatever had passed between the two women would not be divulged by Emily. He straightened and announced stubbornly; "All right, I'll ask her myself."

"As you wish," Emily replied coolly.

Dread seized him. What had he done? What could have changed Emily so drastically in less than forty-eight hours? Relenting, he took her hand and stepped close, but she refused to raise her eyes. "Emily, don't be this way. Talk to me, tell me what's bothering you."

"I'd better get back to supper." Again she freed her hand and put distance between them.

"Will I see you tomorrow?"

"Probably."

"When? Where?"

"Well, I don't know, I—"

"Can I come here after supper? We could maybe go for a walk, or a ride."

"Fine," she agreed unenthusiastically.

"Emily . . ." But he was lost, forlorn, without a clue as to his wrongdoing. He approached her once more and took her shoulders as if to lean down and kiss her, but at that moment Edwin spoke from the far end of the parlor. "Your supper is getting cold, Emily."

Tom sighed, put-upon, and dropped his hands from Emily. He set the edges of his teeth together and studied his fiancée with growing dissatisfaction, then stepped forward where Edwin could see him.

"Good evening, sir," he said, formally.

"Tom."

"I just stopped by to say hello to Emily."

"Yes—well, it's suppertime." Edwin flapped a white napkin toward the dining room behind him and admonished his daughter, "Emily, don't be long."

When he had returned to his meal Emily whispered, "You'd better go, Tom."

His patience suddenly snapped and he made little effort to hide the fact. Stepping back, he gave his hat brim an irritated jerk and said, "All right, goddammit, I'm going!" The porch door opened with enough force to suck dustballs outside, then slammed behind him with equal force. His footsteps pounded across the porch floor as he clunked away, unkissed, unwelcomed, royally pissed off and scared to boot.

What had happened? What the hell had happened? Stalking down the snow-packed path Tom felt his irritation mount. Women! Emily was the last one he'd expect to act like a sulky brat without explaining why. Two days ago he'd fought for her and he thought he'd won her, but she had grown as tepid as second-round bathwater. Something had happened to change her, and if not Tarsy, what else?

Goddamn that Tarsy! Tom took a decisive right-face at the street. She'd said *something* and he aimed to find out what!

Several minutes later, when he knocked on Tarsy's door, the reverberations shook the entire wall. Tarsy herself answered, but she hadn't opened the door two feet before she saw who stood on the porch and tried to slam it again. Tom wedged his foot inside and grabbed Tarsy's wrist.

"I want to talk to you," he informed her in a voice harsh and flat with warning. "Get your coat and get out here."

"You can go straight to hell on a saw blade!"

"Get your coat, I said!"

"Let go of my wrist, you're hurting me!"

"So help me God, I'll break it if you don't get out here!"

"Let go!"

He yanked her so hard her head snapped. "All right, you can freeze!" Effortlessly he whirled her out onto the dark porch and slammed the door, planting himself before it.

"Now, talk," he ordered threateningly.

"You bastard!" She slapped him so hard his head hit the doorframe and his ears rang. "You scum-sucking, two-timing peckerwood!" She kicked his shin.

Recovering from surprise he caught her by both forearms and crossed them on her chest as he threw her against the cold wall. "You're some lady, you know that, Tarsy?" he sneered, nose to nose with her.

"You don't want a lady, and you know it, Jeffcoat. You want something that dresses like a muleskinner and smells like horse shit! Well, you've got her and you can have her! She's the saddest excuse for a female this town's ever seen and I hope the two of you dry up and wither away together!"

"Watch it, Tarsy, 'cause I'm just one step away from giving you a sample of what I gave Charles the other night. Now, what did you say to Emily?"

Tarsy bared her lips in a parody of a smile. She lifted her chin and her eyes glittered with vindictiveness. "What's the matter, lover boy, isn't she so eager to let you paw her anymore? Won't she unbutton her pantaloons, or does she wear a union suit like the boys?"

He thrust her arms so tightly against her that stitches popped in her sleeves. "You're talking about the woman I'm going to marry, and you'd do well to remember that men don't marry the ones who let men paw them."

Tarsy's nostrils flared. "And maybe you'll find out women don't marry men who sample others."

"You told her that!"

"Why not? It might as well be true. There were plenty of times you wanted to."

"Why, you lying little bitch," he ground out through clenched teeth.

"You wanted to, Jeffcoat," she goaded with malicious satisfaction. "A dozen times you touched me like I never let any other man touch me, and you loved it. You got so hot I could see steam rising from your pants—so what's the difference? You know my body better than you'll ever know hers, and I'm not about to let her forget it, not after she stabbed me in the back. I wanted to marry you, you philanderer! Marry you, you hear!" Tarsy shouted, her eyes fiery with rage. "Well, if I can't have you nobody else can either. Just wait and see what you get out of her on your wedding night!"

Tom had never hated any living being with such pagan intensity. It built within him like lava heating, boiling toward the surface, bringing the overwhelming wish to punish. But she was dirt—not worth bruising his knuckles upon. He dropped his hands, unable to bear touching her a moment longer.

"You know," he remarked quietly, "I pity the poor sap who gets snagged by you. That won't be a marriage, it'll be a life sentence."

"Ha!" she barked. "At least he'll know he's in bed with a woman!"

"Quiet!" Tom's mood changed abruptly from belligerent to wary as he cocked an ear toward town, listening.

"Can't you take—"

"Quiet, I said!" His fight with Tarsy ended as swiftly as it had begun. "Listen!" He turned toward the porch steps and peered into the darkness. "Did you hear that?"

"Hear what?"

"There it is again . . . bells. And shouting."

The sounds drifted up from the town below, a churchbell, ringing clamorously, and the faint faraway accompaniment of distraught shouting. Tom moved to the top of the porch steps and waited, tense, staring out into the sky over the town below.

"Oh, my God," he whispered. "Fire."

"Fire?"

He launched himself into thin air, sailed above five porch steps, and hit the yard running. "Tell your father! Hurry!"

He neither waited nor cared if Tarsy followed. Instincts took over and he hurtled pell-mell across the yard toward the street, and on toward the business section of town where already a telltale orange glow had begun lighting the sky. *Whose place? Whose place?* If it wasn't on Grinnell Street, it was damned close. Propelled by adrenaline, he raced, ignoring the pain that jarred his ribs with each thud of his heels on the frozen roads. His heart hammered. His throat hurt. He plummeted downhill, feeling the street drop beneath him until the houses cut off his view of the horizon and he lost sight of the pale golden dome blooming in the nighttime sky.

Ahead, panicked voices shrilled. *"Fire! Fire!"* The frantic ringing of a second bell joined the first. Around Tom, house doors opened and people spilled into yards and began running almost as if mesmerized, without stopping for coats. "Whose is it?" everyone asked, their voices jarred by the impact of barreling downhill.

I don't know. Tom didn't know if he answered aloud or only in his thoughts. His legs churned like steel drivers. His eyeballs dried. His lungs burned.

The man behind him fell off to begin throwing open doors along Burkitt Street, shouting into houses. Somewhere the faint *ting* of a dinner triangle joined the *clong* of the churchbells, but Tom scarcely heard. Nearing the foot of Burkitt Street, he joined a mass of others who had been galvanized into motion with the same abruptness as himself. Footsteps thundered louder, growing in number as the crowd approached Main Street, where runners funneled together and bumped one another like a stampeding herd.

Whose place? Whose place?

The throng sailed past the Windsor Hotel, joined by a quintet of men running out the door with their arms full of blankets, and a contingent of women carrying buckets. "Looks like one of the liveries."

Some ran too hard to voice speculation. Others puffed along, trailing the word that seemed to taint the very air Tom sucked in as he raced.

Liveries!

Through a haze of fear and the roaring of his own pulse he caught other scraps of words . . . she's a big one . . . it's got to be hay . . .

From three blocks away he smelled it. From two blocks away he knew it wasn't Edwin's place. From the corner of Grinnell Street he saw the flames already eating the sides of his own livery stable.

Oh Jesus, no!

"Get the horses!" he screamed from a hundred yards away,

racing wildly. *"I got a pregnant mare in there!"* Ahead, figures appeared like charred stick-men as they scurried before the burning building, filling buckets, forming a brigade, pumping at the cistern out front. The red fire wagon, with its trio of bells clanging, bounced along the frozen ruts ahead of Tom, pulled by running men because it would have taken more time to hitch the horses than to tow it manually the two blocks from its storage shed. He passed it and arrived in the tumult just as someone led Buck out. The stallion reared in fright while the man fought to calm him and lead him to safety.

Tom screamed frantically, "My mare! Did anybody get my mare out!"

"No! No mares! Only this stallion so far!"

Another voice yelled, "Man the pumps! Stretch that hose out!" A dozen volunteers gripped the handles of the old Union fire rig, but she was an ancient side-stroke pumper, built in 1853, and scarcely up to the day's standards. As the paltry jet of water fell from her hose Tom shouted at the fire crew, "Aim the water to the right. The mare is in the third stall!"

Another voice bellowed, "Pump, boys, pump!"

On either side of the fire wagon men worked furiously on the wooden handles. Horses whinnied in terror. Men shouted orders. Dogs barked. Women formed a bucket brigade to refill the tank on the old Union pump while others held their children back to watch from a distance.

"Who's getting my horses! Is anybody getting my horses!"

"Easy, boy . . . it's gotten too—"

"Get your hands off me!" Tom tore a blanket from one of the hotel contingent and ran toward the hose men, yelling, "Wet me down! I'm going in!"

The pump had gathered enough force to set him back a step as the stream of water hit him in the chest. A man grabbed his arm, momentarily blocking the spray. It was Charles.

"Tom, you can't!"

For a split second Tom's eyes flashed hatred. "Goddamn you, Charles, you didn't need to do this! Goddamn you to hell!" Tom shouldered past him, roughly bumping him aside. "Get out of my way!"

"Tom, wait!"

Emily and Edwin appeared in the confusion, grasping Tom's elbows, pleading and warning, but he knocked all hands aside and dashed into the flaming barn.

Behind him, Charles ordered, "Give me one of those blankets!"

"Don't be foolish, boy—"

"Edwin, you do what you want, but I can't let those animals die without trying to help them! Gimme some water, Murphy!"

"Papa, let me go!" Emily screamed, fighting Edwin's hands as she, too, struggled to get a blanket.

"Get to the pump!" he ordered her. "You'll be no help to him dead! Get to the pump and help the women!"

"But Buck is in there and—"

"They got Buck out!"

"—and Patty. Papa, she's in foal!"

"Emily, use some sense! Go get your medicine bag. If they get any more horses out, they'll need it. Then get to the pump with Fannie and keep that water running! Wet down more blankets! I'm going in, too!"

"Papa!" She caught his hand. In the midst of the chaos they exchanged frightened glances. "Be careful."

He squeezed her hand and ran.

Inside, Tom hunkered beneath the wet blanket, running through a sea of smoke. Immediately his eyes smarted and teared, blinding him further. Water splattered around him, sizzling as it struck flaming wood. Sweet Jesus, the beams were already burning and spreading along the loft floor. The stench of scorched leather, wood, and dung stung his nose. He swabbed his eyes with a corner of the sopped blanket, then plastered it over his face. Squinting, he made out the outline of his pride and joy, a new Studebaker carriage standing on the turntable as he'd left it. A chunk of flaming debris fell from above onto its leather bonnet. Surrounded by the terrified shrieks of horses and the thumps of their hooves he forgot about everything that was not flesh and blood. Down one bank of stalls he ran, throwing doors open, yelling. "Git! Git! Hyah! Hyah!" Back up the other side, forgetting about singling out any particular animal. Behind him some of the terrified horses balked at leaving their stalls or milled about, afraid of moving toward the fire surrounding the exits. He threw open the last stall door and charged inside only to be flattened against the wall by a muddled, wild-eyed mare named Bess who tried to turn around in the narrow space. He flung the blanket over Bess's head and, clutching it in a clump beneath her jaw, dragged the animal forward. Terrified, Bess braced her forelegs and whinnied.

"Goddamn it, Bess, you're comin' if I have to drag you!"

An immense roar rose—hay igniting somewhere, filling his ears like a hurricane. He stretched out a leg and kicked Bess hard in the groin. She fishtailed violently, then reared high, swinging Tom clear off his feet as he gripped the blanket. His ankles slammed against the wall. But when he landed, still clutching the wet wool, Bess followed at a frenzied trot.

He burst from the burning building already tearing the blanket off the horse. "Water!" he shouted. "More water here!" As the spray fanned over him he removed his leather hat and doused his hair, then slammed the hat back on and lowered his hands to fill his gloves. Turning, shrouded again by the blanket, he headed back into the barn with the jet pelting his back, running in an icy river down his plaster cast.

Ten feet inside the barn, he collided with Charles coming out. "I got Hank!" Charles shouted above the roar, leading a dun saddlehorse. "You've got time to get one more but that's all!"

Tom plunged into the wall of heat and light. Running, he sucked hard against the blanket, but even through it he breathed and tasted acrid smoke and singed wool. It burned all the way to his lungs until they felt as if they would explode. Through stinging, watering eyes, he searched and found a frantic Rex who, thankfully, followed him without resisting. But by the time he got Rex outside he turned back to watch a rafter at the far end of the building collapse in a roaring golden rain of sparks that changed swiftly to a white sheet of flame. Emily rushed forward to take Rex.

"Don't go back in, Tom, please!"

"Patty!"

"Leave her! You won't make it!"

"One more trip!"

"No!" She grabbed his arm but he lurched free, heading back inside.

"Water!" she shrieked maniacally, watching him go. "Give him water!"

Sucking in his last clear air Tom flung the blanket over his head and bent low, heading inside. Five feet from the door someone tackled him from behind. He rolled through the dirt and came up kneeling, incensed, facing Charles, who was picking himself up from the ground.

"Sonofabitch, Bliss, what're you doing!"

"You're not going back in!"

"The hell I'm not."

"You do and she'll be a widow before she's a bride!"

"Then take good care of her for me!" Tom shouted, bolting into the conflagration before Charles could stop him. Emily witnessed the exchange biting back tears. She watched helplessly as Tom disappeared into the flames; then to her horror, Charles turned and yelled back at the hose men, "Train 'er right on my back!"

His call jolted Emily out of her stupor. "Charles! No!" she called, straining forward only to be dragged back by Andrew Dehart, who'd appeared with his waterwagon to help fight the fire.

"Don't be foolish, girl!"

"Oh God, not Charles, too," Emily despaired, flattening her mouth with the palms of both dirty hands. But Charles ran into the inferno trailed by a puny jet of water.

"You got a horse who could use a little attention," Dehart reminded her, and she grimly forced herself to turn back to Rex, who had a gash on his withers and a raw burned patch on his rump. Someone called from nearby, "Got one over here that needs your help, too, Emily!" Suddenly it seemed that everyone needed her at once. With fear gripping her throat, she immersed herself in duty, substituting efficiency for tears, dusting burns with boric acid, applying pineoleum to others, even slapping a quick bandage on a burned arm in between animals. The pregnant mare showed up, led by Patrick Haberkorn, but she was burned badly, demented with pain, wild-eyed and sidestepping in terror.

"Get Tom!" Emily ordered, grabbing Patty's bridle, already realizing she'd have to be put down.

"I don't know where he is."

"But he went in after her!"

"She ran out on her own."

Patty shrieked in pain, rearing back and yanking Emily off-balance. She stared at Patrick's soot-streaked face, feeling hysteria threaten. The fire leapt and licked the sky fifty feet above the barn. It lit the night to a blinding brilliance. It burned the skin and dried the eyes and turned faces into orange caricatures of gaping awe. The mare whinnied again, reminding Emily of her responsibility.

"Get me a gun," she ordered dully.

Fannie cane running up just then, frantic. "Your father—have you seen him?"

Emily turned to Fannie, feeling as if a winch had tightened about her throat. "Papa?"

"Didn't he come back out?"

"I don't know."

Patrick was handing her a pistol and she could only handle one emergency at a time. Emily took the gun, put it to the mare's head, and pulled the trigger. She closed her eyes even before the dull thud sounded, and turned away from the sickening sound of the mare's last reedy breath. Opening her eyes, she saw Fannie facing the inferno and moved to take her hand and watch it, too. Flames erupted through the roof, sending a section of it dropping into the hayloft. An explosion of sound lifted into the night as another section of hay ignited. In a shocked, disbelieving voice, she said, "Oh God, Fannie, Tom's in there, too."

Watching tragedy occur before their very eyes, the two women stood helplessly, gripping one another's hands. The heat scorched their faces. Tears and heat waves distorted their view of the awesome, shimmering spectacle, which danced and wavered against the night sky.

Men formed a cordon, pressing the crowd a safe distance away. "Get back . . . get back!" Emily and Fannie stumbled backward dumbly. At some time during their vigil Frankie appeared, his eyes immense with fright. "Where's Pa?" he asked dubiously, slipping his small hand into his sister's, staring at the inferno.

"Oh, Frankie," she despaired, dropping to her knees and wrapping both arms around him. She pressed her cheek to his and held him hard, their faces lit by the blaze. She felt him swallow, felt his jaw slacken as he stared at the awesome spectacle before them.

"Pa?" the boy appealed quietly, his body absolutely still.

Emily's throat filled, her eyes smarted, and she hugged Frank harder. Hot tears rolled from her eyes, evaporated by the intense heat before they reached her chin. Beside her, Fannie stared dully at the flames, crying without moving a muscle.

In the chaos around them none of the three heard Edwin until he called breathlessly behind them.

"Fannie? Emily?"

As one, they spun.

"Pa!"

"Papa!"

"Edwin!"

Frankie catapulted into his father's arms, bawling. Emily flung a stranglehold about his neck while Fannie took two halting steps toward him, covered her mouth, and began sobbing as she had not when she'd thought Edwin lost.

"Pa! Pa! We thought you was in there," Frankie cried while he and his sister clutched Edwin's filthy neck.

He gave a choked, emotional laugh. "I led two horses out the rear door and took them down to our own paddock."

"Oh, Papa!" Emily couldn't quit saying the word.

Still holding Frankie on one arm, he circled her with the other.

"I'm all right," he whispered thickly. "I'm all right." He looked beyond his clinging children to find Fannie still standing with eyes streaming, mouth covered tightly.

"You thought so, too?" he asked, fading out of his children's embraces. He opened his arms and Fannie came into them.

"Thank God," she whispered, closing her eyes against his soot-covered cheek. "Oh, Edwin, I thought I had lost you."

His hand covered her hair and he held her fast against him, little caring that a circle of curious gazes were directed their way as dozens of townspeople witnessed their unguarded embrace. Fannie was the first to pull back, with concern furrowing her brow. "Edwin, did you see Tom or Charles come out the other side?"

Edwin's attention swerved to the structure, which by now had begun to crumble in upon itself. Even the pump men had stopped their helpless firefighting. Those manning the hose held it lifelessly while mere drips of water fell from its nozzle. At the cistern the women's hands rested inertly upon the steel pumphandle, which had turned lukewarm from the intense heat. At their feet pails sat, filled but unused.

Edwin gulped and murmured, "Dear God."

Emily and Frank stood motionlessly at his side, holding hands tenaciously, staring at the fire.

At that instant someone called, "Emily, come quick!" It was the hotel owner, Helstrom, gesturing frantically, then taking Emily's arm and dragging her with him. "Around back. Those two men o' yours are out there in a pile!"

Everybody ran—Emily, Edwin, Fannie, and Frank, trailed by a string of others, following Helstrom through the pole gate, around the paddock, to the rear of the building where a knot of men knelt over a sodden heap containing the inert bodies of Tom and Charles. Tangled in wet blankets, the pair lay sprawled on the ground, their eyes closed, their faces streaked and filthy. Doc Steele was already there kneeling beside Tom, opening his bag. Emily skidded to her knees beside him.

"Are they alive?"

Steele pulled up one of Tom's eyelids, popped a stethoscope in his ears, and listened intently. "Jeffcoat is. His breathing is bad though. Must've taken in a lot of smoke. Bring snow!" he called, already beginning a cursory inspection—from Tom's tangled wet hair, which had been protected by a wide leather Stetson; to his midsection, wrapped in wet plaster as effective as asbestos; down his trunk and thighs, which had been covered by heavy sheepskin whose natural fur lining had absorbed a protective barrier of water. Even the narrow space between it and his calf-high leather boots had come through unscathed. Steele assessed it all, then pulled off Tom's gloves, inspected his hands, and pronounced, "I'll be damned. Not a burn on him, nothing but singed eyebrows."

While Steele shifted his attention to Charles, Emily knelt over Tom, still overtly concerned about his breathing. Even without the benefit of a stethoscope she heard the strident hiss accompanying each breath, and saw with what effort his lungs labored.

Don't die . . . don't die . . . keep breathing . . . I'm sorry . . . I love you . . .

Behind her, Doc Steele's voice announced, "Bliss is in no grave danger. His hands got burned, though. Where's that snow?"

Charles! How could Emily have forgotten Charles? She turned to find him lying on his back, staring at the stars with his hands being submerged in two overturned pails of snow. When she leaned above his face he smiled weakly.

"Hiya, Em," he whispered.

"Hiya, Charles," she returned chokily, gulping back a knot of emotion. "How're you doing?"

"I'm not too sure." He lifted one limp hand to test his face, dropping clumps of snow onto it. "Think I'm still alive."

She gently pushed his arm down. "Your hands are burned. You'd best keep them in the snow until Dr. Steele can dress them." She tenderly brushed the snow from his cheek and, in a voice that trembled on the brink of tears, scolded affectionately, "You dear, foolish man—where were your gloves?"

"I didn't stop to think."

"You two are getting to be a lot of trouble, you know, always needing patching up in the middle of the night."

He smiled wanly and let his eyes drift closed. "Yeah, I know. How is he?"

"He's still breathing, no burns, but he's unconscious. Who brought who out?"

He opened his eyes again, wearily. "Does it matter?"

So she knew it was Charles who had carried Tom out. She struggled with a heartful of gratitude and lost the battle to contain her tears. "Thank you, Charles," she whispered, bending low, kissing his forehead.

As she straightened he said in a cracky voice, "Em?"

She couldn't speak through the lump in her throat, could only gaze at him through the tears that distorted his beloved, sooty face with its singed beard and red-rimmed eyes.

"He thinks I set the fire. Tell him I didn't. Will you tell him—"

"Shh." She touched his lips.

"But you've got to tell him."

"I will as soon as he wakes up."

"He's going to, isn't he, Em? He isn't going to die." Tears leaked from the corners of Charles's eyes, washing a pair of white paths as they fell down his temples. Suddenly Charles rolled to one side and grabbed Tom's thick jacket sleeve, dragging himself closer to the unconscious man. "Tom, I didn't do it, you hear me? Don't you die without listening to me! Jeffcoat, damn you, d—don't you dare d—die!"

As Charles's strength gave out he fell back, sobbing, with an arm thrown over his eyes. His chest heaved pitifully. Snow dripped from his fingertips.

Fresh tears stung Emily's eyes as she leaned over, shielding him from the curious stares of others.

Oh, Charles, my dear, dear Charles. I don't think I've ever loved you more than I do at this moment.

Doc's voice intruded. "Let me at that man's hands and somebody get Jeffcoat inside under some warm blankets."

Within minutes Charles's hands were dressed—the worst burns on their backs—and the two men were loaded on wagons. Watching the rig take Charles away, Emily felt heartsick, but Tom lay stretched on the second wagon bed, unconscious, and his fate still hung in the balance.

As the wagon rolled through the night, its riders remained respectfully silent. The stench of smoke hung over the town and children were being slowly herded home by their mothers.

At Tom's house a group of somber volunteers carried him inside, laid him on his bed, and nodded to Emily as they filed out. Her father came last.

"I'll be staying," she told him quietly, "to see after him until he's better."

Edwin's sad, loving eyes rested on Emily's.

"Yes, I know," he said, accepting her decision without dissent.

"And I'll be marrying him as soon as he's strong enough to stand on two feet."

"Yes, I know."

"Papa—"

"Sweetheart—" She was in his arms before the endearment had cleared his lips. More tears—hot, and healing—wrinkled the world she saw beyond Edwin's shoulder.

"I'm so damned sorry," he managed in a broken voice.

"Oh, Papa, I love him so much. He's just got to live."

"He will."

She sniffled and clung to his familiar bulk. His arms—oh, his wonderful reassuring father's arms—how substantial they felt and how badly she needed them at this moment. She may have defied him, but she had never stopped needing his comfort, friendship, and approval. Without them she had been miserable. "I thought I was going to have to choose between you and I didn't know what I was g—going to do without you."

"You won't have to worry about it anymore. I'm a stubborn old fool—Fannie made me see that. But you won't hear another word out of me. You're getting a good man. I knew it all the time, but I was just too ornery to say so. I'm sorry I said those things the other night."

She squeezed him harder, feeling as if she had just emerged from shadow into sun.

"You're the best father there ever was."

He crushed her against him, then drew back, clearing his throat self-consciously while she wiped her eyes with a sleeve.

"Well . . ." Edwin said.

"Yes . . . well . . ."

Neither of them knew how to end the delicate moment.

Finally Emily asked, "Will you send Frankie back with some clean things for me?"

"I'll do better than that. I'll bring them myself as soon as I make sure Charles is settled. They took him to our place, you know. Fannie insisted."

"Good. He deserves the best."

Edwin caught one of her dirty hands and raised it to his lips. "I'm afraid the best has been taken by someone else, though."

"Oh, Papa."

"You'd better go see after your young man," Edwin said, dangerously close to getting emotional again.

She pecked him on the cheek in a fond farewell. "And you'd better take a bath. You stink."

Chapter 20

CLOSING THE DOOR behind Edwin, Emily stared at it exhaustedly. The bedroom seemed miles away. Her shoulders ached, her eyes burned, her throat felt parched and raw, but she forced her feet to move. In Tom's bedroom doorway she paused, studying his still form on the bed, holding her breath and listening to his. It sounded grainy and labored, no better than before. When he inhaled, an invisible wind whistle seemed to play in his throat. When he exhaled, his breath was accompanied by a rattling wheeze.

She stood at his bedside and studied him despondently, tempted to cry, realizing that to do so would serve no purpose. If only there were some way she could help. But Doc Steele had said, "There's nothing we can do for his lungs—either they'll make it or they won't. Clean him up some. Keep him warm. Keep the windows closed because the town is full of smoke. If he wakes up, feed him lightly. A resting body doesn't need much nourishment, it lives off its own fat."

Clean him up some, keep him warm. It seemed too little to do when you loved someone this much and had rebuffed him the last time the two of you had spoken.

She knelt and touched her lips to his dirty right hand. *Don't you die, Tom Jeffcoat, do you hear me? If you die, I'll never forgive you.*

When she'd spent another bout of useless emotionalism, she pushed herself heavily to her feet and went to the kitchen, built up the fire, and drew warm water from the reservoir. Carrying a basin, she returned to the bedroom to bathe Tom.

She did so lovingly, with no burdening sense of impropriety. Instead, she felt entitled, for she loved him wholly and would—if he lived—see after his welfare for the remainder of their lives. She washed his face, with its motionless eyelids and its poor bruised features, cataloging each, praying that she might see that face on the adjacent pillow each morning for the rest of her life, that she might watch it take on years and creases and character as the two of them aged together.

She washed his long-fingered, calloused, limp hands, which would know all of her in all ways, would stroke her skin in passion and rub her tired back when she grew weary, would hold their children someday, and, with his forefathers' anvil and eight surviving horses, would provide for them all through years to come.

She washed his arms and chest—broad chest, sturdy arms—above a fringe of dirty white plaster, and paused with her hand upon his slow and regular heartbeat, then kissed him there for the first time ever.

She washed his long legs and feet, which would carry him down an aisle with her, and over a threshold, and into this room one fine, wondrous wedding day soon.

They would, oh, they would.

And when he was clean, she covered him to the neck, then dragged his oversized kitchen rocker into the room, dropped heavily upon it, and slumped forward across the bed near his hip.

Edwin found her that way when he returned with her clean clothes—exhausted and haggard and dirty, but he hadn't the heart to awaken her. Leaving her clothes nearby, he tiptoed from the house with a heavy heart and a prayer for Tom Jeffcoat's safe delivery back to consciousness.

Emily awakened later at the sound of Tom stirring. She leapt to her feet and leaned above him, gazing into his unfocused eyes. "You're going to be all right, Tom," she whispered, taking his hand.

"Em'ly?" he croaked. His heels shifted restlessly against the sheets and he seemed to be searching for the source of her voice.

"Yes, Tom, I'm here."

His bleary eyes found her. His left index finger crooked against his soiled white plaster wrap as if trying to coax the rest of the unwilling hand to lift. He managed only two words in the same pathetic croak as before: "She lied."

"Tom?" Emily called anxiously, bending even closer. "Tom?"

But he had already slipped back into oblivion, leaving her with no opportunity to apologize or reassure. Disappointed and worried, she perched on the chair, holding his unresponsive hand. He had been through such hell. He had fought a fire that he believed was set by his best friend. He had lost his barn, some of his stock, and his livelihood. He had suffered shock and physical damage enough to put him in a state of unconsciousness. Yet through it all his chief worry was that he might lose her because of Tarsy's lies.

Emily's unwanted tears started again, stinging like a douse of kerosene in her poor maltreated eyes.

I'm sorry I believed her, Tom. I should have known Tarsy would use any means available to get satisfaction—honest or dishonest. Please get well so I can marry you and we can put all this strife behind us.

In Edwin Walcott's home the baths were done, the invalid bedded down, the boy long asleep, and the place blissfully quiet. Dressed in a nightshirt, Edwin stepped from his bedroom and crossed the hall to rap quietly on his daughter's bedroom door.

"Come in," Fannie called softly.

He opened the door and stood framed within it, motionless. Fannie sat at a vanity table glancing back over her shoulder. She wore a dressing gown of pale blue scattered with violets, belted at the waist. Her hair—wet—trailed down her back; her hand—poised—held a tortoiseshell comb.

"Come in, Edwin," she repeated, swiveling to face him, dropping the hand to her lap.

"I just came to say good night and to thank you for having the bath water all hot. It felt wonderful."

"Yes, it did, didn't it? But there's no need to thank me." She smiled serenely, her eyes lingering on his wet hair, rilled with fresh comb tracks, his shiny forehead and the brushed beard, whose attractiveness still took her by surprise each time she saw it. It created the perfect frame for his lips, making him appear the more highly colored when contrasted against the dark facial hair, more soft for the beard's crisp outline. It complemented, too, his dark, dear eyes.

"You must be very tired."

"I am." He smiled softly. "You?"

"No. Just thinking."

"About what?"

"About the children—Tom and Emily. You gave Emily your consent to stay there, didn't you?"

Leaving the door discreetly open, Edwin wandered in and, while he spoke, touched things—incidental things—a picture on the wall, the back of a chair, the knob on a bureau. "It seemed ridiculous not to. She would have stayed in any case."

"She's very much in love with him, Edwin."

"Yes, I know. She says she'll marry him as soon as he can stand on two legs."

"And you gave her your consent for that, too?"

"She didn't ask for it. She's a grown woman. I guess it's time I treated her like one."

"Yes, of course you're right. And after what they've been through who in Sheridan would dare point a finger?"

Edwin gave up his distractions to study Fannie across the room, hoping the same thing was true regarding the two of them. In the lamplight her wet hair gleamed like liquid copper. Edwin thought he could smell it clear across the room, it and the lilac soap with which she'd bathed. The bodice of her dressing gown revealed a narrow wedge of bare throat, and as she dragged a fallen tress behind her ear her sleeve fell back, baring one fine white arm, lightly peppered with freckles. She was lovely and warm and all the things he had ever desired. But Edwin repressed the urge to cross to her, though he could not resist talking, staying—just a while longer.

"You were thinking about us, too, weren't you?"

"Yes."

"What about us?"

She considered momentarily, dropping her gaze as she placed the comb on the vanity behind her, then returning her uplifted eyes to him and tucking her hands between her knees. "About what I'd have done if I'd lost you."

"But you didn't. I'm still very much alive and unharmed."

"Yes," she replied in the most dulcet of tones, letting the word drift winsomely before adding, "I see."

She studied him unwaveringly, this man she loved: scrubbed, shiny, masculine, and decidedly less than decent in only a nightshirt and bare feet. If he had come here to test her he was succeeding with little effort. She could no more turn him away than she could have stopped tonight's fire. "Is that what you always sleep in?"

"No. Not always." The striped garment reached Edwin's mid-calf. "My underwear got sooty and wet. I left it in the tub downstairs."

"I didn't think I remembered ever washing that before." She let her eyes trail down to his naked toes and back up. From across the room she thought she saw his cheeks take on color above the crisp, dark border of his beard.

When she spoke again, her tranquil voice held no coquetry, only an abiding certainty that what she was suggesting was right and deserved. "Why don't you close the door, Edwin?"

She saw him carefully bank his surprise. Their gazes locked and the universe seemed devoid of all creatures save them. Then he closed the door—without haste, without sound—and turned, lifting his gaze to her as he crossed the room. She followed with her eyes, lifting her face as he neared and paused before her. For moments he stood motionless, his eyes delving into hers. At length he reached out to stroke her damp hair back from her face, which he tipped to a sharp angle.

"It'll be tonight then?" he asked simply.

"Yes, darling, tonight."

Leaning low, he kissed her dear mouth, a tender, fleeting touch; likewise, her left eyelid, her right, and each cheek. His heart repeated a cadence it had known only years ago, when they were both young and raring but had banked their urges as all properly raised children were taught to do. So many years ago. So many mistakes ago. He drew back to question softly, "Because you almost lost me?"

"Because I almost lost you. And because life is precious and we've squandered too much of ours."

Again he covered her mouth with his own and drew her up by the jaws, the kiss a gentle thing of rediscovery. In time he urged her lips apart and tasted her fully, still holding her jaws, for to touch her anywhere else would be to rush this sweet reunion for which they had waited so long. Scarcely lifting his head, he murmured, "We have a houseguest."

"He's asleep."

"And Frankie."

"He's asleep, too, though I believe I should not care if either of them opened the door this moment and walked in. Oh, Edwin, my heart has been yours too long without making it official."

"I love you, Fannie Cooper. I've loved you longer than I've loved any other human being on this earth."

"And I love you, Edwin Walcott . . . as much as I might have loved any husband, any father of my children, which in my heart you always were. I love you unconditionally . . . shamelessly."

"Oh, Fannie, Fannie." His voice grew ardent with passion and he strewed fevered kisses across her face and throat. "We should have done this years ago."

"I know."

He bracketed her breasts; their swells filled his hands as he kissed her again with a lifetime's restraints at last abandoned. As their tongues joined, he found the twist of her belt and freed it straightaway, slipping both hands inside and caressing her through a thin muslin nightgown—breasts, buttocks, spine—then settling her against his hips to discover that their bodies blended as he remembered. Abruptly he drew back. "Let me take this off." As his hands rose, so did hers, and he removed her garments in one clean sweep, relegating them to a puddle at her ankles. "Ohh . . . Fannie." His eyes dropped from her pleased smile to the sight of his own great hands lifting her breasts, his thumbs sweeping up lightly to brush their crests. He flattened a palm upon her soft abdomen, examined with his fingertips the nest of feminine curls the color of sunset. "I knew you'd look this way. Small . . . pale . . . freckled . . . I love your freckles."

"Oh, Edwin, nobody loves freckles."

"I do, because they're yours." He kissed some that tinted

her most intimate places while she watched his head from above, loving the sight of him bowed low to her. In time she urged him upright.

"I'm impatient . . . let me see you, too, Edwin." He stood and lifted his arms, and she took his nightshirt the route hers had gone, up and away until it landed with as much forethought as a seed borne upon wind. "Oh, my . . ." she praised, spreading a hand upon his hirsute chest, riding it down his belly and lower, touching him first with the backs of her knuckles. "Aren't you magnificent," she breathed, watching her fingers skim over his hot flesh.

He chuckled once, deeply and affectionately. "You *are* shameless, Fannie, aren't you?"

"Absolutely." She smiled, lifting her face for his kiss as she took him in hand without a trace of diffidence.

A shock rippled through him at her first stroke.

"Fannie—" he whispered, the word throaty and broken.

He touched her likewise, without compunction, inside her warmth and wetness, bringing a shudder to her frame as she hunched slightly and sucked in a swift breath. He stirred her until she arched, whispering, "Oh, Edwin . . . at last . . . and so good . . ."

Within seconds impatience bore down upon them and weighted their limbs. He swept her up and onto the bed, dropping down beside her, kissing her breasts and belly, murmuring praises against her skin while her hands threaded his hair.

She was wholly unencumbered by false modesty, giving access where he would seek, touch, explore. She had always been a woman who knew her own mind, and when that mind was decided, as it was now, she flew free.

"My turn," she whispered, rolling him to his back, taking the same liberties she had allowed. Where he'd touched her, she, too, touched him. Where he'd kissed, she, too, kissed, until both had learned the long-denied flavors and textures of the other. Only when she had taken her fill did she allow him dominance again.

Once more upon her back, Fannie stretched, catlike, smiling first for herself and secondly for him as he stroked her and watched her arch in unrestrained satisfaction. There, stretched supine, with her arms upthrown, she experienced a grand, racking climax, lifting and shuddering with unexpected swiftness beneath Edwin's hands. Upon its dying ebbs he kissed her beaded breast and said against her skin, "I knew you'd be like this, too. I just knew it. Fannie, you're wonderful."

"Mmm . . ." she murmured, eyes closed, lips tipped up in plain delight. "Come . . ." And with her small hands she steered him, stirred him, settled him where he should have been since they were seventeen, full upon her waiting, welcoming body.

When he entered her Fannie's eyes remained open, feet flat on the bed, hips raised in welcome. He settled himself deep—the first time, deep.

"Ahh . . ." he breathed as they took their due.

She smiled, watching the meshing of his black locks with hers of apricot hue. "We're beautiful together, aren't we?"

"Beautiful," he agreed.

When he moved, she moved in counterpoint, spellbound by the wonder of their bodies expressing what they had felt for so long. In time she threw her head back, chin high, rocking against him. When he shuddered, she watched, thinking how beautiful his face, gone lax in the throes of fulfillment. She watched to the end, savoring the sight of his closed eyes, his trembling arms as he waited out the last ripple of feeling.

With its passing, his eyes opened.

They smiled with newfound tenderness. Having believed for so many years that they could not love more, they found themselves awed by the force of their feelings now that they had shared each other physically.

"Edwin . . ." She cupped and stroked his silken jaw. "My beloved Edwin. Come closer. Let me hold you the way I've always dreamed of holding you . . . afterwards."

He rested upon her, warming her collarbone with his breath, wetting it with a faint, suckling kiss. A very weary kiss.

"I'm so tired," he admitted, the words nearly indistinguishable against her flesh.

"And so beautiful."

He smiled, near exhaustion. "You will marry me, Fannie . . ." he murmured as he drifted off to sleep. ". . . soon, won't you?"

She smiled at the ceiling, combing his clean, damp hair with her fingers. "Absolutely, Edwin," she replied serenely. "Soon."

* * *

Dawn came, and crossed their bed, and another across town.

Tom Jeffcoat flexed his legs and winced behind closed eyes. He opened them and saw sunstreaks on the ceiling, angled, oblique—the heavy gold of earliest morning. Outside a dog barked, faraway. Sparrows chirped in the eaves. His bare shoulders were cold, and in the room he caught a scent reminiscent of charcoal. He swallowed with a dry, parched throat and remembered: the fire . . . the stable . . . the horses . . . Emily . . . Charles . . .

Disconsolate, he let his eyes fall closed.

Oh God, nothing's left.

The mattress jiggled—barely a flutter. He rolled his head and there sat Emily—dirty, drooping, asleep on his kitchen rocker, with her feet—in soiled stockings—sprawled on the mattress.

Emily, you poor bedraggled girl, how long have you been there?

He studied her without moving, feeling the weight of depression descend, wondering how he was going to support her, how many horses he'd lost, if they'd gotten the mare out, who else was in the house, if they'd apprehended Charles yet, how he was going to repay his grandmother, how long he'd have to wait now to get married.

He let his eyes drift closed and gave way to despair. I'm so thirsty . . . and tired . . . and broke . . . and burned out. Charles, damn you—why did you have to do a thing like this? And you, too, Tarsy. I thought you were both my friends.

He opened his eyes and willed them to remain dry. But it hurt, dammit, it hurt to think they'd turn on him this way! His throat felt as if he'd swallowed a piece of his own burning building. While he was still trying to gulp it down, Emily sighed in her sleep, rolled her head, and opened her eyes. He watched awareness dawn across her face, then a quick succession of emotions—fear, relief, pity—before she lunged to her knees beside the bed, capturing his hand and pressing it to her mouth.

"I love you," she said immediately, lifting brimming eyes. "And I'm sorry I believed Tarsy."

His thumb moved forgivingly across her knuckles. Their gazes lingered while his thoughts became laced with a jumble of emotions too profound to voice. He rolled slightly and drew her close by the back of her uncombed head and put his face against it. He held her thus, breathing the scent of smoke from her hair, feeling tears gather in his throat, segregating matters of superficial importance from those of real consequence. Life. Happiness. Loving. These were what really mattered. As he sorted and logged these realizations, Emily spoke, her voice muffled against the bedding.

"I was so afraid you wouldn't wake up so I could tell you. I thought you might die." At the hollow of her breast she clutched his hand, gripping it so hard her nails dug into his flesh. "Oh, Tom, I was so scared."

"I'm all right," he managed in a scraping whisper. "And it doesn't matter about Tarsy."

"Yes it does. I should have trusted you. I should have believed you."

"Shh."

"But—"

"Let's forget about Tarsy."

"I love you." She lifted her face, revealing streaming eyes. "I love you," she repeated, as if afraid he would not believe her.

"I love you, too, Emily." He touched her dirty face with a cluster of bruised knuckles and dredged up a weak smile. "But do you think I could have some water? My throat feels like my barn must look."

"Oh, Tom, I'm sorry . . ." She popped up and ran out to the kitchen, returning with a big glass of wonderful-looking water. "Here."

He struggled up, with her ineffectually trying to help, and, propped on one hand, downed the entire glassful while she watched.

"Another, please."

He drank a second in the same fashion, then leaned back as she adjusted the pillows behind him.

"How do you feel? Does it hurt to breathe?"

Rather than reply he asked a question of his own. "The mare—did she get out?"

Emily's sorrowful expression answered, even before her words. "I'm sorry, Tom."

"How many did I lose?"

"Only two—Patty and Liza."

"Liza, too," he repeated—one of the pair who'd brought him here from Rock Springs, his first pair. "Is anything left?"

"No," she answered in a near-whisper, "it burned to the ground."

He closed his eyes, let his head fall back, and swallowed.

The sunny room suddenly seemed gloomy as Emily watched him battle despair, willing herself to keep dry-eyed while she searched for words of consolation. But there were none, so she simply sat down and took his hand.

"What about Charles?" he asked, still with his eyes closed.

"Charles is at my house. He's got burns on the backs of his hands, but otherwise he's all right."

Tom lay motionless, giving no clue to his reaction, but she knew what he was thinking.

"Charles didn't set fire to your barn, Tom."

He lifted his head and fixed her with judgmental eyes. "Oh, didn't he?"

"No."

"Then who did?"

"I don't know. Maybe it was lightning."

"In February?"

Of course, he was right, and they both knew it. Though she hated to suggest it, she ventured, "Maybe it was Tarsy."

"No. I was standing on her porch steps exchanging insults when we heard the firebells start."

"Then who's to say it was *started* at all? It could have been an accident."

But he was a careful man who put out lanterns before he closed up for the night. And a forge, contrary to popular belief, was one of the most fire-safe structures built, by virtue of its being a constant threat if improperly constructed and insulated.

He heaved a deep sigh. "God, I don't know." His head fell back and she sat uselessly, feeling so sorry for him. He looked defeated and weary and worried.

"Are you hungry?" she asked, a paltry offering, but the only one at her disposal.

"No."

"Your lips are dry. Would you like me to put some petroleum jelly on them?"

He lifted his head and studied her for a long, silent moment, then answered softly, "Yes."

She produced a squatty jar of the ointment and sat down on

the edge of the mattress to apply it. Her touch upon his mouth healed more than his chapped lips. It began easing the infinite ache in his heart.

"You stayed here all night." He spoke quietly.

"Yes." She capped the jar and dejectedly studied it in her lap.

"Your father will come in here and have the rest of my hide," he speculated gently.

"No, he won't. Father and I have come to an understanding."

"About what?"

She set the jar aside and said to the sunny wall. "I told him I intended to stay here and take care of you until you're back on your feet again." Glancing over her shoulder she met his gaze foursquare. "I also told him that the moment you are I intend to become your wife."

He remained expressionless, watching her for a long time before she saw hopelessness overtake him again. He drew a shallow sigh and puffed it out as if holding his pessimism to himself.

"What's wrong?" she asked.

"Everything."

"What?"

"Listen to me, Emily." He took her hand and rubbed his thumb over her knuckles, concentrating on it as he detailed his disastrous situation. "I've got two cracked ribs. Who knows how long it'll be before I can work again? My livery stable is burned to the ground and I have no money to pay for the one that's lying in ashes, much less to rebuild. You've just told me my carriages are gone, and two of my horses died, and you want to marry me?"

"You'll heal and we'll rebuild," she announced stubbornly, leaving the bed and lugging the rocker to the corner of the room, where she clunked it down with a note of finality.

"With what?" he said to her back. "I've got no fire insurance, no hay, nothing."

"Nothing?" She turned and accosted him with common sense. "Why, of course you've got something. You've got this house, and a great big lot in a prime location in a town that's growing every year, and an anvil that belonged to your grandfather, and eight healthy horses in my father's paddock." She joined her hands stubbornly over her stomach. "And you've got me—the best veterinarian and stablehand in Johnson County. How can you call that nothing?"

He hated playing devil's advocate, but believed he had little choice. "Emily, be sensible."

She approached the bed and fixed him with a look of determination. "I am being sensible. I did all my being stupid last night while I sat in that chair and worried and bawled and acted like a perfect ninny. Then I made up my mind that worrying is idiotic. Nobody ever succeeded by worrying. It's a waste of energy. Hard work is what succeeds, and I'm willing to do plenty of it if you are, but I think the first step is to get ourselves legally married so we'll have that hurdle out of the way."

"And what about the period of mourning?"

"The period of mourning be damned," she decreed, dropping to the bed and taking his hand again while her voice softened with sincerity. "If you had died in that fire I would never have forgiven myself for mourning away the few happy weeks I might have had with you. I love you, Thomas Jeffcoat, and I want to be your wife. Conventions and burned barns don't matter as much as our happiness."

He sat studying her, comparing her to Tarsy and Julia and the other women he'd known. None had her spirit, drive, or optimism. None would have stood beside him staunchly in the face of the defeats he'd just suffered. Emily was ready to plow ahead, undaunted, and take him and his dismal financial prospects and a future whose only certainty seemed to be a lot of hard work and worry. And he had no doubt that if anyone raised an eyebrow over her nursing him overnight in the privacy of his own home *before* they were married, she'd take them on over that issue, too.

"Come here," he ordered quietly.

She came, and lay in the crook of his arm with her head tucked in the hollow of his shoulder. The golden sun poured across the bed, gilding their faces. They listened to the sparrows in the eaves. They listened to their own breathing and the sounds of the town awakening on a Saturday morning. They linked fingers atop his bandaged ribs and watched the sun streaks slant down the walls.

Emily fit the pad of her thumb against Tom's and said thoughtfully, "Thomas?"

"Hm?"

"Charles didn't set fire to the barn. He wouldn't do such a thing. He's the one who pulled you out of it and saved your life. I was there, so I know. When he thought you might die . . ." Emily paused before admitting, ". . . he cried. Please believe me, Tom."

He pressed his lips to her hair and closed his eyes for a long moment, telling himself to believe it. Wanting to believe it.

"You still love him, don't you?" he asked against her hair.

She sat up and studied Tom, unruffled. "Of course I do," she admitted. "But not the way I love you. If I felt that way about him I'd have married him when I had the chance. If I can believe you about Tarsy, you must believe me about Charles. Please, Tom. He would never destroy what was yours, because in hurting you he'd hurt me, too, don't you see?"

He considered the three of them and their incredible triangular love. "Do you honestly think we can survive in this town—all three of us?" Tom asked.

"I don't know," Emily answered honestly.

They sat thinking, troubled, for long minutes before he asked, "Would you go back East with me?"

She felt the grip of loneliness at the thought of leaving her father, Fannie, and Frankie, but there was only one answer she could give.

"Yes, if that was your choice."

His respect and love for her increased tenfold as he recognized the emotional strife that had accompanied her answer. They were still sitting, holding hands, with tens of questions unanswered, when someone knocked on the front door. Emily stirred and went to answer.

At the sight of the two familiar faces on Tom's porch, her spirits lifted. "Hello, Papa. And Fannie . . . I didn't expect to see you both here."

"How is he?" Fannie asked, stepping into the house.

"Awake, tired, feeling like a piece of oversmoked jerky, but quite alive, and he's going to stay that way. Oh, Fannie, I'm so relieved."

They exchanged hugs and Edwin said, "We want to talk to both of you."

"Papa, I'm not sure he should talk a lot. His voice is raspy and his throat hurts."

"This won't take long." Edwin brushed past his daughter

and led the parade into the bedroom, observing jovially as he entered, "So you made it, Jeffcoat!"

"Seems that way."

"Looking a little the worse for wear."

Tom chuckled and boosted himself up higher against the pillows. "I'm sure I do."

Edwin, in an unusually expansive mood, laughed and took Fannie's hand, drawing her along with him to the bed. He ordered his daughter, "Here, Emily, sit down. We have some news you'll both want to hear."

Emily and Tom exchanged curious glances while she perched at his shoulder with Fannie at his knee and Edwin standing beside the bed.

"First of all, they've arrested Pinnick for setting fire to your barn. He tied on a good one down at the Mint Bar last night and when they found him this morning, curled up on the boardwalk, still half-pickled, he was holding on to a bottle of whiskey and blubbering about how sorry he was, he didn't mean to burn the whole thing down, he only meant to set you back a spell so he'd get back the business he lost when you moved into town."

"Pinnick?" Tom repeated, flabbergasted.

"Pinnick!" Emily rejoiced, clapping her hands, then reaching for one of Tom's.

Edwin continued: "And I was barely into my britches this morning when Charles comes stomping downstairs and through the kitchen buttoning his jacket and cussing a blue streak about that damned Jeffcoat and what a nuisance he was. The way I remember it, he said, *How many buildings does a man have to put up for him, anyway?* Then he bellers that he's heading off to see Vasseler about a barn-raising and that it's by God the last one he's going to do for Tom Jeffcoat. So they're out there right now, Vasseler and Charles, rounding up a work crew to get started the minute the ashes cool. And on top of that, Fannie and I—"

"I get to tell this part," Fannie interrupted, hushing Edwin with a squeeze on his arm.

Edwin paused in mid-word, glanced at his future wife, clapped his jaws shut, and gave her the floor with a wave of a hand.

Fannie looked bright and happy as she continued, "It seems I was quite indiscreet last night when I threw my arms around your father and kissed him in the middle of all that hubbub with almost everyone in town watching. Since they all know the truth by now, Edwin and I have decided it would be most expedient if we got married posthaste. We were wondering if the two of you would like to plan a double wedding, perhaps at the end of next week?"

Before Tom and Emily could wipe the shock from their faces, Fannie added, "Unless, of course, you'd prefer separate ones, in which case we'll certainly understand."

In the resulting outburst everyone talked and hugged and shook hands at once, and laughter filled the room. Felicitations rebounded from the walls and the sense of goodwill multiplied among all four. Like conspirators in an innocent prank, they agreed with Fannie, who said, "What's good enough for a father is certainly good enough for a daughter! Just let anyone wag a tongue now!"

When Fannie and Edwin had gone, Emily and Tom stared at each other in renewed amazement, then burst out laughing.

"Can you believe it! In two weeks!"

"Come here," he ordered as he had earlier, this time with a much brighter outlook.

She slipped beside him, doubled her knees up against his hip, and hugged him voraciously around the neck. They kissed in celebration and he said against her ear, "Now, I won't take any back talk from you. You're picking up your bundle of clothes and going home where you belong."

"But—" She pulled back.

"No buts. I can take care of myself, and one night in my house is all the tarnish I want to put on your halo. The next time you come into this room it'll be as my wife. Now, git, so I can get up. There's a carpenter I've got to see."

"But, Tom!"

"Out, I said! But if it would make you feel any better, you can pump me some water and put it on to heat before you leave. Then I'd suggest you go home and do the same for yourself. You smell like a chimney sweep." She laughed and shimmied off the bed while he pulled himself to the edge of the mattress and sat with the sheet across his lap. Happy, and hopeful, and suddenly gay, she swung back to him and looped her arms around his neck.

"Know what?" she inquired teasingly.

"What?" he repeated, nose to nose with her.

"I gave you a bath last night."

"You did!"

"And you've got ugly knees."

He laughed and spread his hands near the sides of her breasts. "Miss Walcott, if you don't get out of here I'm going to be on them and I'll probably overwork my poor scorched lungs and die in the process, and how would you feel then?"

"Thomas Jeffcoat, for shame!" she scolded.

"Good-bye, Emily," he returned with a note of warning.

"Good-bye, Thomas," she whispered, kissing the end of his nose. "You're going to miss me when I'm gone."

"Yes I will, if you give me half a chance."

"I love you, knees and all."

"I love you, smoke and all. Now will you get out of here?"

"What are you going to say to Charles?"

"None of your business."

"After we're married, I might invite him to supper sometime."

"I'll tell him you said so."

"Fine."

"Fine."

"And I might invite Tarsy, too."

He scowled menacingly.

"All right, all right, I'm going. Are you coming courting tonight?" she asked blithely from the doorway.

He rose from the bed, giving her a flash of ugly knees and bare calves as he said, "Always keep 'em guessin', that's my motto," and closed the bedroom door in her face.

Thirty minutes later Tom found Charles down at Edwin's livery stable. When he stepped inside, there was the man he sought, hitching up a pair of Tom's own horses to a buckboard, with bandaged hands.

Tom closed the door and the two stood staring at each other, then Charles returned to his task, bending to connect a tug strap to the doubletree. Tom approached slowly, his bootsteps sounding clearly through the cavernous barn. Near Charles, he stopped.

"Hello," Tom said, looking down at Charles's worn Stetson.

"Hello."

"Where are you taking my horses?"

"Out to the mill for a load of wood to put up the last goddamned stable I'm ever gonna build for you."

"Need some help?"

Charles peered up past his hat brim with a sarcastic gleam in his eye. "Not from any broken-down cripple with two cracked ribs."

"Yeah, well, look who cracked 'em."

Charles walked around to the other side of the team and continued buckling harness parts.

"I hear your hands got burned."

"Just the backs. The palms're still working. What do you want?"

"I came to thank you for hauling my carcass out of that building last night."

"You're one hell of a lot of trouble, you know that, Jeffcoat? This morning I'm wishing I would've left you in it."

"Bullshit," Tom replied affectionately.

From the far side of the horses came a rueful chuckle, then, like an echo, "Yeah, bullshit."

Charles squatted and Tom stared at his boots, visible beneath the team's bellies. "I'm marrying her at the end of next week."

"What day?"

"I don't know."

"Saturday?"

"I don't know."

"You marry her Saturday, I'll have the damn barn done by Friday. You marry her Friday and I'll have it done by Thursday."

"What does that mean?" Tom stepped around the horses just as Charles stretched to his feet. Their eyes met directly.

"You didn't expect me to hang around and be your best man, did you?" Charles nudged past Tom and kept a shoulder intruding as he threaded the reins through the guides. "I'll be cracking a whip over that building crew, then I'm gone."

"You're leaving?"

"Yup." Charles folded his lips tightly to his teeth as he moved to the other side of the team.

"Where to?"

"Montana, I think. Yeah, Montana. There's a lot of open land up there, and the big drives are winding up there. Plenty of rich ranchers settling in Montana and all of them needing barns and houses . . . buildings'll be going up all over hell. I'll be rich in no time."

"Have you told Emily?"

"You tell her."

"I think you should."

Charles laughed mirthlessly and threw the other man a cutting glance. "Take a leap, Jeffcoat!"

"You don't have to go, you know."

"Like hell, I don't. I'd hang around here and I'd have her one day, come hell or high water, but it might not be till after both of us were old married folks raising a batch of kids. Wouldn't that be just fine and dandy?"

"Charles, I'm sorry."

"Don't make me laugh."

"For what I said last night at the fire."

"Yeah, well, don't be. Pinnick just thought a little faster than me, that's all. Damned old drunk . . . if I'd've lit the fire myself I'd be on my way to Montana already instead of wasting another week puttin' up your goddamned barn." The horses were hitched. Charles clambered onto the wagon and took the reins. "Now open the door so I can roll, you two-bit iron twanger."

Tom slid back the great rolling doors, then stood outside with his hands in the pockets of his jacket, his hat pulled low over his eyes as he watched Charles pass him with the rig.

To his back Tom shouted, "You take care of my horses, Bliss! You can't put 'em away dry like a damned old piece of oak, you know!"

"And you take care of my woman, 'cause if I hear you didn't I'll come back and kick your ass clear to the other end of the Bozeman Trail!"

"Shee-it," Tom muttered, watching the wagon roll away. But when it was gone, he remained beside the open doors, feeling bereft and heavyhearted, and missing Charles even before he was gone.

Chapter 21

THE MARRIAGES TOOK place on a day in early March when the chinook winds descended the eastern slope of the Rockies, fanning the earth with a breath warm as summer. A real snow-eater, the townsfolk observed, stepping out their doors at midmorning, recognizing the warm, dry current that came each year unannounced. It brought the smell of the sea, from which it originated, and of the earth, which it bared along its way, and of spruce and sprouts and spring. Billowing down from the Big Horns across the wide Sheridan Valley, the chinooks flattened an entire winter's snow in a single day, sipped half of it up and sent the other half glistening in runnels that caught chips of sun and scattered them back toward the cobalt sky. They breathed on brooks and streams, which chimed with a tinkle of breaking ice to the unending background sigh of rushing water. They brought an unmistakable message—rejoice, winter's over!

By high noon the transformation was well underway, and when the bells of the Sheridan Episcopalian Church pealed, they drew a congregation whose winter spirits had been magically lifted.

They came in open carriages, breathing deep of the warm air and turning their faces to the sun. They came smiling, happy, dressed in lighter clothes and lingering outside to soak up the miraculous day until the last possible moment.

That's where they all were, outside in the chinook and the sun, when Edwin Walcott's finest Studebaker landau came briskly down the street with its twin tops down, making no excuses for shunning Victorian mourning in honor of this glorious occasion. The landau itself gleamed in yellow paint with black trim, and Edwin had chosen his blackest black gelding, Jet, to do the wedding day honors. Along Jet's shiny black flanks the harness was studded with cockades of white ribbon trailing streamers that undulated gracefully as the gelding, enlivened, too, by the chinooks, pranced smartly. In his mane more ribbon was braided and on each of his blinders and between his ears perched a crepe-paper rosette. The wagon traces looked like maypoles, twined with ribbons and rosettes and wands of pussy willows. The landau itself was nothing short of a bower. Cockades, streamers, and more pussy willows circled its seats, nestled in bunting of pale green net that had been fixed in the downturned bonnet.

In the front seat sat Fannie Cooper, in ivory, holding an enormous net-swathed hat on her head while beside her Edwin Walcott perched proud-chested and beaming, wearing a dapper beaver top hat and cutaway coat of cinnamon brown, holding a buggy whip trimmed with yet another paper rose and streamers.

Behind them rode Emily Walcott, wearing her mother's elegant silver-gray wedding dress, with a sprig of dried baby's breath in her hair, beside Thomas Jeffcoat, dashing in dove gray—top hat, gloves, Prince Albert coat, and striped trousers. Squashed between their knees on the edge of the seat rode Frank Allen Walcott, sporting a new brown suit with his first winged collar and ascot, beaming fit to kill, standing up well before his father drew rein, waving and hollering at the top of his lungs, "Hi, Earl, look at this! Ain't this something!"

So the wedding guests were laughing when Edwin drew Jet to a halt before the Sheridan Episcopal. Frankie clambered excitedly over Tom's legs and leapt down to show Earl his new duds and to exclaim over the decorated landau. Edwin slipped the buggy whip into its bracket and vaulted from the wagon like a man of twenty, unable to dim his smile as he swung Fannie down. Tom alighted less agilely, hiding a clumsy plaster cast beneath his wedding finery, but when he reached up a helping hand to his bride-to-be the eagerness on his face was unmistakable. With his gray-gloved hand he took her bare one, squeezing it much harder than necessary, sending her a silent message of joy.

"They're smiling," he whispered, with his back to the church.

"I know," she replied secretly while stepping down. "Isn't it wonderful?"

They were smiling—the entire waiting crowd—infected by the obvious happiness that shone from the faces of the nuptial couples as they alighted from the carriage with not a garment of black in sight.

Emily and Tom faced the crowd, watching Edwin and Fannie move before them up a pair of wooden planks that Reverend Vasseler had provided as a moat across the streaming ditch, Edwin keeping a possessive grip on Fannie's elbow. Tom claimed Emily's elbow, too, as they followed the older couple, who were receiving felicitations, left and right, even before the vows were spoken.

Reverend Vasseler waited on the church steps, with Bible in hand, smiling down on the new arrivals, shaking hands with each of them as they stopped on the step below him.

"Good morning, Edwin, Fannie, Thomas, Emily . . . and Master Frank."

"It's a beautiful day, isn't it?" Edwin spoke for all of them.

"Yes, it is." Reverend Vasseler scanned the flawless sky as a wayward chinook breeze lifted his thinning hair from his forehead and set it back down. "One would think the Lord was sending a message, wouldn't one?"

Upon the heels of the minister's benign postulation they entered the church in procession, with Vasseler himself in the lead, followed by the resplendent couples and Frankie, then the entire fold.

The organ played and the wind came in the open windows. The church was trimmed with more pussy willows and white cockades on every pew. Frankie sat up front between Earl and his parents, and when the sound of settling bodies silenced,

Reverend Vasseler lifted his chin and let his voice ring out clear and loud.

"Dearly beloved . . . we are gathered here today, in the sight of God, to join this man and woman . . ." The minister paused and shifted his gaze from one couple to the next. ". . . and this man and woman . . . in the state of holy matrimony." Smiles broke out everywhere, even a small one on the face of the man officiating.

The smiles disappeared, however, at the speaking of the vows, for when Edwin took Fannie's hands and gazed into her eyes, the love that radiated between them shone as unmistakably as the silver in their hair.

"I, Edwin, take thee, Fannie . . ."

"I, Fannie, take thee, Edwin . . ."

There was a special radiance in the older couple that sparked tears in the eyes of many looking on and held them in thrall as Edwin, upon the last words, placed Fannie's right hand over his heart and covered it with his own for all to see.

Then Tom and Emily faced each other and once again hearts went out to them as they clasped hands and exchanged vows with their eyes even before doing so with their lips. They emanated a serenity surpassing their years as they stood before God and man, conscious only of each other, and spoke their vows in voices that could be heard clearly in the rearmost pew.

"I, Thomas, take thee, Emily . . ."

"I, Emily, take thee, Thomas . . ."

When their last words were spoken and a blessing called down, Reverend Vasseler opened his arms wide as if in a blessing of his own, and said, "Now you may kiss your brides."

As the two couples exchanged their first married kisses, the women looking on drew handkerchiefs from their sleeves while the men stiffened their spines and stared straight-on to keep from divulging the fact that their eyes, too, held a conspicuous glint of moisture. Emotions billowed even more as, upon the heels of the first kisses, the newlywed couples broke apart and exchanged partners. Edwin kissed his daughter, and Tom his new mother-in-law, followed by a heartfelt embrace between the two women and a congenial handshake between the two men. The organ burst forth with recessional tidings, and four smiling faces turned toward the open rear doors, poising for a moment with arms linked, four-abreast, as if to tell the world that love, honor, and respect went four ways among them.

Arm in arm, Emily and Tom led the exit, followed by Edwin and Fannie, who, while passing the first pew, collected a smiling Frankie and left the church holding his hands between them.

Outside, rice flew, and the brides ran across the bouncing wooden moat and boarded the ribbon-bedecked landau and drew their skirts aside while two happy husbands stepped up behind them. Frankie scrambled into the front seat and begged to take the reins, beaming like a full moon when Edwin said yes and handed him the supple buggy whip with the streamers trailing from its handle.

They rode through town with the brides crooked in their husband's arms, nestled in a bower of pussy willows and white roses, followed by the splash of shoes and kettles trailing through the swimming streets behind the Studebaker.

At Coffeen Hall they were feted with a wedding feast provided by their friends, customers, and fellow church members. The celebration lasted into the late afternoon and by the time it ended the chinooks had stolen the last of the snow and left behind a naked valley waiting for its spring raiments.

An hour before sunset, two brides and grooms boarded the landau once more. Frankie stayed behind, waving them good-bye in his bedraggled, food-stained wedding suit. He would spend the night at Earl's, and tomorrow, he promised his father, he and Earl would wash down the landau as a wedding gift of their own.

But now, it wheeled through the March mud as spattered and bedraggled as the two boys had looked, its streamers soiled and its rosettes crushed. No matter. Soiling it had been joyous and memorable.

The evening was mellow, the sound of the wheels a susurrus. Edwin drove while Fannie pressed her cheek against his sleeve. In the backseat Emily sat holding hands with Tom in the folds of her pearl-gray skirt. Her cheek lay not against his sleeve, however, but straight toward the wind, for it was warm with expectation while Tom squeezed her hand fiercely and their thumbs played games of pursuit and capture.

At Tom's house Edwin brought Jet to a halt. He turned, resting one arm along the top of his seat, looking back at his daughter and her new husband.

"Well . . ." His smile passed affectionately between both of them. "Happy wedding day," he said with soft sincerity. "I know it's been for us." On the seat he took Fannie's hand and momentarily shifted his smile to her.

"For us, too," Emily returned. "Thank you, Papa." Over the back of the seat she kissed him, then Fannie. "Thank you both. It was a wonderful day, and the landau was a grand surprise."

"We thought so," Fannie agreed. "And it was certainly fun picking those pussy willows, wasn't it, Edwin?"

They laughed, momentarily relieving the heart-tug that accompanied the moment of good-bye as a daughter left her father's abode forever. Tom alighted and helped Emily down, then stood beside the carriage looking up at the couple above him. He reached and took two hands—one of Edwin's, one of Fannie's, squeezing them earnestly. "Don't worry about her. I'll make sure she's as happy as the two of you are going to be, for the rest of her life."

Edwin nodded, uncertain of his voice, should he try to speak. Tom released his hand and leaned forward to kiss Fannie. "Be happy," she whispered, holding his cheeks. "Happiness is everything."

"We are," he replied, and stepped back.

"Fannie . . ." Emily, too, accepted a kiss while fresh emotions welled up.

As usual, Fannie knew how to end the delicate moment with the proper mixture of affection and finality. "We'll see you tomorrow. Congratulations, dearling."

"You, too, Fannie."

"Good-bye, Papa. See you tomorrow."

"Good-bye, honey."

The landau pulled away, trailing bedraggled streamers. A bride and groom watched it go, but even before it reached a corner they had turned their regard to one another.

He smiled.

She smiled.

He took her hand.

She gave hers gladly.

They walked to his house together. At the porch steps he said, "I'm sorry I can't carry you in, Mrs. Jeffcoat."

"You can do it on our silver wedding anniversary," she told him while they mounted the steps shoulder to shoulder. He opened the door and the two of them entered his kitchen, where all was silent and serene and bathed in sunwash. They locked palms, standing close, toe to toe, projecting ahead not twenty-five years, but a single night.

"It was a wonderful wedding day, wasn't it?" he said.

"Yes, it was. It is."

"Are you tired?"

"No, but my feet are wet."

"Your feet?"

"From crossing the yard."

"You're home now. You can take your shoes off anytime." His grin, unformed, remained a mere suggestion in his eyes.

"All right, I will, but will you kiss me first? It takes a long time to take shoes off."

He smiled wide, overjoyed at her lack of guile. "Oh, Emily . . . there's nobody like you. I'm going to love being your husband." They stood so close he had only to bend his arms to tip her against him. He kissed her obligingly, averting his face to meet her upraised one, gathering her into the curve of his shoulder while they stood almost stock-still against one another, twisted slightly at the waist. It was a sweet beginning, tasting each other with unhurried ease, letting their mouths form and fit and feast while remaining still everywhere else. When their mouths parted—a hairsbreadth only—she seemed to have forgotten how to move.

"Your shoes," he whispered, his breath brushing her lips.

"Oh . . . my shoes," she said dreamily. "What shoes?"

He smiled and delicately kissed her upper lip . . . then her lower one . . . then the corner of her mouth where he probed inquisitively with the tip of his tongue before riding it, as if crossing a rainbow, to the opposite corner. "You were going to take your shoes off," he reminded her in a velvet voice.

"Oh, yes . . . where are they?"

"They're down there someplace."

"Down where?"

"Someplace on your damp feet."

"Mmmm . . ."

"Should I take them off for you?"

"Mmmm . . ."

He tipped his head farther and fit his mouth upon hers with incredible perfection. As their tongues dipped deep for second tastes his hand played idly over the small of her back. They took third tastes, and fourth, still resting against each other with only the faintest contact, his fingers drawing circular patterns along her waistline, where fasteners and ties and boning formed lumps within her silver dress. In time she freed her lips reluctantly and whispered against his chin, "Thomas?"

"Hm?"

"My shoes."

"Oh yes." He cleared his throat and drew her by the hand to one of his kitchen benches, where she sat gazing up at him, her cheeks colored by a becoming blush. He went down on one knee before her and searched beneath her skirts to find one delicate ankle, which he drew forth and studied silently. Her shoes were high and buttoned, made of pearl-gray leather and silk vesting, which encased her foot tightly well past the ankle.

"I see this won't be as easy as the time I pulled your boot off. Did you bring a buttonhook?"

"It's in the bedroom with my things."

He looked up and neither of them spoke while his thumb stroked her anklebone through the silk vesting, heating a spot that shimmied straight up her leg. At length he said quietly, "I guess I'll have to go get it. Would you like to come with me?"

Sitting in his gold-streaked kitchen with an hour yet to go before sunset, she nodded with virginal uncertainty.

He dropped her foot and rose. Her eyes lifted to him and he read that uncertainty, drew her up by the hand, and ended her misgivings by leading her through the long spears of light slicing across his kitchen floor, past the foot of his staircase and into the bedroom where now the windows were trimmed with curtains and shades and her own bureau stood against one plastered wall.

"Get it," he ordered quietly, with all traces of teasing gone, "and take them off."

He removed his top hat and put it in the closet, where her clothing now hung beside his. She found the buttonhook and sat on the edge of his bed, which was spread with Fannie's homemade quilt, the quilt she'd been standing behind the night he'd chosen her bare feet from among all the others. She bent forward, concentrating on her shoe buttons, while he removed his gloves from his pocket and lay them on her bureau, then shrugged from his jacket and hung it neatly in the closet. He went to the north window and pulled it up but left the shade at half-mast, letting the remnants of the chinooks drift into the room from the uninterrupted grassland beyond. He went to the east window—the one facing the street—opened it, too, but drew that shade to the sill.

She slipped off one shoe and began unhooking the buttons on the other while he took off his boots, standing first on one leg, then on the other, and set them in the closet.

When her second shoe was removed, Emily crossed her toes and looked up uncertainly. Tom stood watching her, drawing the tails of his shirt from his trousers while his suspenders trailed down beside his knees.

"You can put them in the closet beside mine," he invited.

She crossed before him, feeling doubtful and ignorant and taken unawares because it seemed that what she thought would not happen until well after sundown would happen well before. She bent to set her shoes beside her husband's and as she straightened his arms came around her from behind. His warm, soft lips kissed her neck.

"Are you scared, Emily?" His breath made dew upon her skin and fluttered the flossy hair upon her nape.

"A little."

"Don't be scared . . . don't be." He kissed her hair, her ear, the ruching of her high collar while she covered his arms with her own and tipped her head aside acquiescingly.

"Thomas?"

"Hm?"

"It's just that I don't know what to do."

"Just lean your head back and let me show you."

She dropped her head back onto his shoulder and his hands skimmed up her ribs . . . up, up. She closed her eyes and leaned against him, breathing with increasing difficulty as he taught her the myriad shapes of pleasure; moving his hands in synchronization over her firm breasts, lifting, molding, flattening; then lifting once again. He kneaded circles upon them with the flat of his hand before the pressure disappeared and only his fingertips explored the hardened cores, as if picking up stacked coins. She grew heavy and drugged by arousal, warm within her clothing, and confined by it. Her breath became hard-beating. His right hand slid down and covered the back of hers, his fingers closing tightly in her palm, which he lifted to his mouth and kissed hard before releasing her completely and stepping back to search through her hair for pins.

One by one he plucked them out and dropped them to the floor at their feet. They fell like ticks of a clock marking off the last minutes of waiting. When all were heedlessly strewn, he combed her hair with his calloused fingers, spilling it in a black waterfall down her back. He plunged his face into its waves and breathed deep. He kissed it, gripping her arms from behind, working them almost as he'd worked her breasts, in hard, compact circles. He made of her hair a sheaf, and drew it over her left shoulder,then stood away, touching her only with his fingertip while opening the long line of pearl buttons down her back, to her hips. He found, within, the string-ties at the base of her spine, and tugged them free, loosening them to her shoulder blades. He unbuttoned the petticoat at her waist, then skimmed it all down—dress, corset, garters, petticoat, and stockings—in one grand sweep, leaving her clothed in only two white brief undergarments. Caressing her arms, he dropped his head and kissed her shoulder, then her nape, then turned her—still standing in a billow of abandoned clothing—to face him.

"Could you do that to me?" he asked in a soft, throaty voice. "Mine is much simpler."

Feeling herself blushing, she dropped her eyes from his face to his throat, from his throat to his wrinkled shirt.

"If you want to," he added in a whisper.

"I want to," she whispered back, and caught up one of his hands to free first a cuff button, then its mate, while he held his wrists at an obliging angle. She had just turned her attention to his collar button when he reached out and, with the backs of four knuckles, brushed the peak of her left breast through its white cotton covering.

"I love you, Mrs. Jeffcoat," he whispered, bringing an added glow to her cheeks while continuing his seemingly idle caress, watching as she shyly avoided his eyes. With each successive button she moved slower, until, reaching the bottom one, she gave up her task and closed her eyes while his knuckles went on fluttering over her nipple.

"I . . ." she began, but her whisper faded as she leaned both forearms against his hard plaster cast. For seconds she stood thus, balancing against him, absorbing the grand rush of sensation created by so faint a touch it might have been only the warm chinook fluttering her chemise against her skin. The fluttering stopped and his hands brushed upward between her elbows to free four tiny buttons between her breasts.

"You . . . ?" he whispered, studying her closed eyes, reminding her of her unfinished thought.

"I . . ."

He spread her chemise wide and slipped both hands inside, laying them flat upon her naked breasts for the first time.

She lifted languorous eyes to his and let her body be rocked gently by his caresses, drowning in the deep blue of his eyes, then closing her own as his open mouth descended to hers. With warm tongue and warm hands he stroked her, teaching her open mouth and naked breasts how rapture begins and builds. When she was taut and ruched he removed her chemise and pantaloons, slipped his hands to her back, and caressed it with widespread fingers. He drew her firmly against him, against cold, hard plaster above, and warm, hard man below. Barefoot, she lifted on tiptoe and wrapped her arms about his sturdy neck, lavishing in the play of his hands over her naked skin.

Still caressing her back, he leaned away, and, searching her eyes, freed his last shirt button with one hand. Following his lead, she divested him of the garment, reaching up to push it from his shoulders with polite decorum that oddly suited the moment—one of her last as an innocent. When she had laid his shirt with great care atop her own fallen dress he captured her wrists, gripping them firmly and skewering a thumb into each of her palms. He kissed the butt of the left . . . and the right . . . then laid them on his chest, above the white plaster, teaching her the ways a man likes first.

"We're married now . . . you can do what you like . . . here . . ." He played her palms across his firm pectoral muscles. "Or here . . ." He took them to his waist. "Or here . . ." He left them at his trouser buttons.

These, too, she freed, slipping her fingers between his waistband and the worn edge of plaster. She did it all, all he bid, self-conscious but willing until both of them were naked, and they walked that way to the side of their bed where he threw back the covers, piled the pillows one atop the other, and lay down first, then reached a hand to her in invitation.

She lay down beside him and suddenly everything was natural—to twine her arms around him and be taken flush against his body, to feel the sole of his foot ride up the back of her calf and follow his lead with her own, to make a place for his knee, which cradled high against her, to feel his hand on her hip, then on her stomach, and his tongue in her mouth while he touched her within for the first time and groaned into her mouth. To feel her own hand guided to his distended flesh and taught a love lesson which she was more than eager to learn. To feel the rivers of her body flood their banks as if the chinooks had melted a winter's snowfall there inside her as it had outside their open window.

He touched her in all ways—wondrous, deep strokes, and tender surface petting. He wet her breasts with kisses, and suckled them, and fired her body with befitting want, along with his own. He made her quiver and seek and damn the wrappings around his ribs that robbed her of the flesh that was rightfully hers.

"I love you," he told her.

"Do," she said when desire had bent her to his every whim but one.

"I'm sorry about this damn cast," he said in a gruff, breathless voice.

But the cast created no barrier whatsoever as he arched above her and entered her in a long, slow stroke. She closed her eyes and received him, becoming his for life—wife and consort, inseparable. She opened her eyes and looked up into his face as he poised above her, still for the moment, waiting.

She whispered three words. "Heart, soul, and senses."

And as he began moving they sealed the vow forever.

It was a splendid thing, of thrumming hearts, and souls in one accord. And senses—ah, the senses, how they reveled. She closed her eyes and loved the feel of him filling her body, and the sound of his harsh breathing matching her own, and the smell of his hair and skin when he closed the space between them, and as the beat accelerated, his soft throaty grunts and sheer, swift thrusts. Then at her own unexpected spill, a rasping cry—hers—followed in short succession by his deeper, throatier one as he shuddered upon her.

Then silence, broken only by their own tired breathing and the caressing scrape of his thumb against her skull going on . . . and on . . . and on.

She lay upon her side with her mouth at his throat and his heavy hand on her head, the thumb still in motion. She felt beneath her ear his relaxed arm, and upon her knee his heavy enervated leg. She experienced her first total repletion—a wholly unexpected gift—lying there surrounded by his tired limbs.

"Mmmmm . . ." She felt the sleepy syllable vibrate against her lips and pictured his cheek against the pillow above her, his eyes closed, his hair disheveled.

She stroked his naked hip—only once; she hadn't the further energy. Her hand fell still and they lay on, drifting in the realm of the blessed. She had not expected the satisfaction. It was a gift as precious and unforeseen as the arrival of the spring winds.

When she'd thought him asleep, he spoke in a soft rumble, the words resounding through his arm to her ear. "Heart, soul, and senses."

"Yes." She kissed his Adam's apple.

He pulled himself from his lethargy to tip his face on the pillow and look down into her eyes.

"How are your heart, soul, and senses now?"

"Happy."

"Mine, too." He touched her nose lovingly and they basked awhile, appreciating each other silently, recounting the last half hour. "Did I bang you up with my cast?"

"Only a little."

"I'm sorry, tomboy."

"Say that again."

"Tomboy." He grinned.

"The first name you ever called me, and the last before you kissed me."

"Did I?"

"In the closet. 'Come here, tomboy,' you said."

"You remember it very well."

"Very well."

"Come here, tomboy." He grinned and drew her close to renew old memories.

Sunset had come and gone, and he had taught her a few ways to avoid being bruised by his cast. She slipped from bed and found in her bureau drawer the postcard with the floral heart and verse and propped it up against the base of the lamp where they could both see it first thing upon waking in the morning.

The town was still and the wind had died. At the sill the curtains hung motionless. Emily stood looking through the lace, feeling the air cool toward nighttime. Tom came up behind her and doubled his forearms across her chest. They rocked peacefully.

She hooked her hands over his arm and spoke for the first time of those who'd been absent from their wedding ceremony.

"I missed them," she said.

"So did I," he replied against her hair.

"Even Tarsy. I didn't think I had any feelings left for her, but I do."

"I don't think she'll come around too quickly, probably never."

They ruminated for minutes, staring out the window toward the north, rocking still, before she asked, "Do you think Charles is in Montana by now?"

"No, not yet."

"Do you think he'll ever come back?"

Tom sighed and closed the window, then put an arm around her shoulders and walked her toward the bed. "The world's not perfect, tomboy. Sometimes we have fires and fistfights and lose friends."

"I know."

They got beneath the covers and snuggled, back to belly, facing her valentine.

She found his hand and cupped it upon her breast. She felt his warm breath on the back of her head and asked winsomely, "Is it all right if I keep loving him, just a little?"

He kissed the crown of her head and said, "He'll come back someday. With both of us here waiting, he'll come back."